Streets of Night

Streets of Night

John Dos Passos

Edited by
Michael Clark

Selinsgrove: Susquehanna University Press
London and Toronto: Associated University Presses

Associated University Presses
440 Forsgate Drive
Cranbury, NJ 08512

Associated University Presses
25 Sicilian Avenue
London WC1A 2QH, England

Associated University Presses
P.O. Box 488, Port Credit
Mississauga, Ontario
Canada L5G 4M2

The paper used in this publication meets the requirements
of the American National Standard for Permanence of Paper
for Printed Library Materials Z39.48-1984.

Library of Congress Cataloging-in-Publication Data

Dos Passos, John, 1896–1970.
   Streets of night / John Dos Passos ; edited by Michael Clark.
   p.   cm.
   Includes bibliographical references.
   ISBN 0-945636-02-4 (alk. paper)
   I. Clark, Michael, 1946 Jan. 16–   II. Title.
PS3507.0743S77   1990
813'.52—dc20   88-43406
                                                     CIP

PRINTED IN THE UNITED STATES OF AMERICA

Contents

Acknowledgments

I would like to thank Widener University for the sabbatical that allowed me to complete this project. In addition, many people at Widener University helped me along the way: Robert Bruce, Lawrence P. Buck, William Fairweather, Ernest Hilbert, Patricia Lenkowski, Ilene Lieberman, Robert Melzi, Barbara Norton, Philip O'Neill, Ken Pobo, Kym Rummel, Julian Skaggs, Charles B. Smith, Betty Twarog, Eva Tremoglie, and Suzanne Williams.

Many others also assisted me: Stephen Godsall-Myers of West Chester, Pennsylvania; Rebecca Knight of the University of Delaware Library; Mickey Dygert, director of the Revere Public Library; Edna Cardillo of the Boston Public Library; the staff of Houghton Library, Harvard University; and Edmund Berekely and his staff at Alderman Library, University of Virginia Library.

Finally, special thanks go to my good friend Martin Bock, who contributed many constructive suggestions; Townsend Ludington, who helped in deciphering Dos Passos's handwriting; and Mrs. Elizabeth Dos Passos, who granted permission for my use of Dos Passos's autograph corrections to the manuscript of the novel; she was always generous with her encouragement and made this project possible.

Introduction

Sometime in 1916, when he was a senior at Harvard University, John Dos Passos began to make notes for *le grand roman,* which was to become *Streets of Night.* He probably worked sporadically on the novel during the next seven years. The typescript of one draft, which is currently housed at the Houghton Library at Harvard, is dated 1922. Finally published in 1923 (in both New York and London), the novel sold approximately thirty-four hundred copies[1] and was reprinted in English only once, a 1962 paperback edition. Consequently, it is not generally available, the most accessible copies being those in rare book collections and research libraries. Because the study of John Dos Passos's fiction is currently enjoying a small renaissance, the republication of this novel is an opportunity for the reader to become acquainted with a still infrequently read and little-known work. And because *Streets of Night* deals with many issues that are central to Dos Passos's later and, I believe, better novels, this reprinting of the book can only help to give us a fuller and clearer picture of Dos Passos's career.

When *Streets of Night* was first published, the reviewers either ignored it or condemned it roundly, an evaluation that has been echoed by the judgment of literary history. The reviewer for *The New York Times Book Review* (18 November 1923) takes a dismissive attitude, often resorting to sarcasm. The tone is established in the first sentence: "The disastrous results of inordinate tea drinking are set forth at considerable length and with much detail in Mr. John Dos Passos' new novel, 'Streets of Night.'" The reviewer goes on to describe the major characters as "jellyfish" (i.e., lacking backbone). Of Nancibel's rejection of Wenny "at about 7:30" in the morning, the reviewer notes that she is not to be blamed, for "many people are not at their best in the early morning." The reviewer then states that the "book is quite without plot, form or reality," and that the characters "never become genuine human beings." He laments the novel's preoccupation with the sordid aspects of reality and states that "the odor of insufficiently washed human bodies is wafted through its pages, along with a generally fetid atmosphere of degeneracy and decay." The reader feels "gratitude," he says, when Wenny leaves the novel early through suicide.[2] The reviewer ends the critique, however, by noting that Dos Passos's descriptions of places and crowds are often good.

Another review—this one in H. L. Mencken's *American Mercury*—is equally sardonic. The reviewer complains that the major characters fail to be "logically credible." Furthermore, the "natural mooniness of youth is permitted to pass into something indistinguishable from lunacy." He then complains of the formlessness of the novel, asserting that it is "simply a series of puerile and often improbable episodes in the lives of two silly boys and an even sillier girl." Interestingly, he sees *Streets of Night* as continuing the "ineptitudes" of Dos Passos's previous novel,[3] *Three Soldiers*, a book that was generally well received by the critics, including H. L. Mencken.

A third contemporary notice of *Streets of Night* appeared in Joseph Collins's survey of literature, *Taking the Literary Pulse*. Under the rubric of "Unpleasant Novels," Collins objects to the modern tendency to focus on "disease or degeneracy." Concerning Dos Passos in particular, he is offended by the author's "useless, profane and vulgar words." He notes that the night watchman in the cemetery needs to be "muzzle[d]."[4] (Collins probably didn't realize that the publisher had already provided a large muzzle by censoring the cemetery scene.) Like the two previous critics, Collins finds little of value in this novel.

The objections these reviewers make—some of which are valid enough—should not blind us to the novel's virtues: it evokes a sense of place and time and in its own way is an effective novel of ideas. Even the reader who knows little about Dos Passos's life at Harvard will suspect that *Streets of Night* is in some measure autobiographical, drawing on the sights, sounds, and people familiar to the author. Although it might be misleading to suggest that *Streets of Night* is a *roman à clef*, this novel is Dos Passos's attempt to give order to his college experience. The characters of Fanshaw and Wenny are first and foremost expressions of personal values with which the author was struggling. The lives of the "weak boy" and the "strong boy" illustrate two different ways of dealing with reality. Neither character can be said to be "successful" in coping with the world, but Fanshaw's effete aestheticism, a pale reminder of a lost romanticism, is less admirable than Wenny's advocacy of empirical detail, which strongly aligns him with the modern temper.

The third of the major characters, Nancibel, is in many ways the strongest, as has been noted by Linda Wagner.[5] After Wenny's suicide and Fanshaw's gradual sinking into dormancy, Nan is the lone active person, although her resorting to the Ouija board at the end of the novel suggests that she too has compromised with reality. At any rate, she is presented as having the potential for full growth and development. For example, she responds to Wenny both intellectually and physically: "There was a warmth about her body as if his vehemence had communicated itself to her." But like Wenny and Fanshaw, Nan is stalked by New England repressiveness, in her case, a "little demon"[6] that repeatedly whispers "careful" to her. In this Boston of the prewar years, no traditional heroes or heroines exist, and the lives of the novel's characters replicate Dos Passos's feelings about his own time at Harvard: "four years under the ethercone."[7]

In some measure, the reader can see how the novel was shaped by Dos Passos's academic career at Harvard. The occasional references to Greek and Roman culture reflect the courses Dos Passos took: "Greek Literature," "Latin Literature," "Homer and Herodotus," "History of Ancient Philosophy," "Philosophy and Religion in the Greek Poets," and "Philosophy of the Hellenistic Period." Likewise Fanshaw's interest in art history devolves from Dos Passos's having enrolled in "Art and Culture of Italy in the Middle Ages and the Renaissance," and Wenny's interest in anthropology reflects Dos Passos's own experience in Anthropology I.

Another influence on the novel was William James's philosophy, pragmatism. Although Dos Passos never had the occasion to take a course from the Harvard philosopher (who died in 1910), he eventually came to read James's *Varieties of Religious Experience, Shorter Psychology*, and *Essays in Radical Empiricism*, and he found James's pragmatism congenial with his own outlook on life. The strength with which he adhered to a pragmatic epistemology can be seen in his staunch rejection of the idealistic school of thought: Plato, he writes in 1920, is "an utter windbag."[8] Consequently, the values that one might expect to find in *Streets of Night* are empirical and manifest themselves even in such details as Wenny's savoring of an Italian meal.[9] Clearly, in this novel as well as in his later works, Dos Passos's sympathies lie not in theory and ideals, but in the commonplace and even the coarse details of life.

A more obvious influence is the American poet Walt Whitman. Dos Passos maintained a lifelong admiration for Whitman, and at one point even asserted that "I read him a great deal as a kid and I rather imagine that a great deal of the original slant of my work comes from that vein in the American tradition."[10] Because Dos Passos's diary entries, letters, and essays frequently mention this American poet, the reader should not be surprised to find many allusions to Whitman's poetry in *Streets of Night*. Generally, the purpose of such references is to suggest the revivifying power of nature. When humans are at their best, nature and human nature are in harmony, which seems to be the case with Wenny. Fanshaw, conversely, is unharmoniously divorced from both his natural self and his natural environment.

The numerous allusions to art and art objects throughout *Streets of Night* suggest that Dos Passos was thoroughly imbued with the sentiments of the 1890s and the "art for art's sake" movement, whose dying embers were still occasionally glowing. Clearly, Fanshaw is an aesthete, devoted to appreciating Botticelli and Brueghel. He appreciates fact less than artifact. When he looks at the seashore at Marblehead and observes the landscape, he interprets it according to a preconceived idea, the English seascape in art, with which he is so familiar: "Look down the coast now. . . . With the dark clouds and the rays from the sun and the sailboat and everything, isn't it exactly like one of those funny old English engravings? Seascapes they used to call them. Even to the musty color."[11] The frequent interpretation of natural surroundings in terms of art objects suggests that Fanshaw is alienated from his environment and can see life only through art. But "art for art's sake"—which suggests a separation of aesthetic issues from all others, including the moral—is not a doctrine with which Dos Passos could rest easy. In some ways, *Streets of Night* doggedly works out Dos Passos's argument with pure aestheticism, largely by using Wenny and Fanshaw as foils, much to the disadvantage of the latter.

Fanshaw's exquisite consciousness is much in the manner of the Harvard aesthetes, whom Robert Rosen has called the "elite devotees of Walter Pater and Renaissance painting, sensitive young men . . . who felt trapped in a hopelessly vulgar and hostile world."[12] The mention of Pater is appropriate here, for his devotion to the aesthetic dimension made him the idol of the art-for-art's-sake crowd. But for Dos Passos, Pater does not represent simply pure aestheticism. In many ways, Pater's work served as a catalyst for Dos Passos, representing on the one hand the aesthete's values, but on the other an earnest moral sensibility that was vital to life and art. Thus, in his own way, Wenny is as Pateresque as Fanshaw.

For Wenny, art is not an end in itself, and in this respect he is different from Fanshaw, who seeks through the art of the Renaissance what he should be experiencing firsthand. Wenny's attitude can be clarified by examining Pater's philosophy. For Pater, life was best, not when it was dominated by art, but when it shared with art the subliminal power of the universal, when the everyday occurrence gave an insight into the absolute. In many ways, Wenny illustrates Pater's prescriptions. The following quotation from Pater's work can be seen as a gloss on Wenny's aspirations:

Not to discriminate every moment some passionate attitude in those about us, and in the very brilliancy of their gifts some tragic dividing of forces on their ways, is, on this short day of frost and sun, to sleep before evening. With this sense of the splendour of our experience and of its awful brevity, gathering all we are into one desperate effort to see and touch, we shall hardly have time to make theories about the things we see and touch.[13]

Unlike Fanshaw, both Pater and Wenny renounce "theory" in favor of seeing and touching. The numerous references to Pater throughout *Streets of Night* suggest that he was an important influence on Dos Passos. A more detailed look at his work will clarify Dos Passos's views in this novel.

Behind Pater's call for an immediate appreciation of experience is an assumption that the modern world inhibits an enjoyment of the truly beautiful. Pater advocates a reawakening of the whole person, even the elemental and primitive aspects of one's being. Thus, many of Walter Pater's essays return to the Renaissance or to the ancient Greeks, not to escape the present, but to recapture the quality of consciousness that Pater believes modern people must possess in order to truly live. In particular, the figure of Dionysus seems to have embodied the qualities that Pater thought were necessary. For the ancients, he says in *Greek Studies*, "the thought of Dionysus and his circle . . . covered the whole of life, and was a complete religion, a sacred representation or interpretation of the whole human experience. . . ."[14] The modern world, by way of contrast, has lost this holism. Pater also examines Dionysus in his essay "Denys L'Auxerrois," in which he symbolically portrays a medieval reappearance of Dionysus. The implication of this seems to be that for Pater the Dionysian spirit is not only desirable but also possible in every age.

In 1917, John Dos Passos showed that he had very similar concerns. In his essay "Against American Literature," Dos Passos laments the fact that modern people have lost touch with the elemental facts of existence. The American writer, he says, is "floundering" because people have no "ghosts," no "nymphs," "no tradition of countless generations tilling" the soil. We have nothing to tie us "to the soil, to the eternal powers of corn and wine and resurgent earth." Art in older, European countries, conversely, has always been "based on primitive folklore," and the artist has been provoked by the "primitive savageries," and "old cults of earth and harvest."[15]

Dos Passos's solution to this problem was to create a modern-day Dionysus. Clearly, Wenny—whose name is evocative of Pater's Dionysus, Denys—suggests a return to the soil. He asserts that "the only genuine thing I ever did in my life was get drunk,"[16] which associates him with Dionysus, the god of the vine. Wenny's "vitality,"[17] as well as his association with the "animal" world,[18] connects him with a primitive and elemental nature. Remembering that Wenny dies on the first day of spring—and just as the weather turns—the reader might also recall that Dionysus was a god of vegetation and resurrection. Wenny, as avatar of Dionysus, is Dos Passos's answer to America's lack of ghosts.

Finally, the question of Dos Passos's style is significant. However, the word does not sufficiently describe the issue at hand. Many critics have failed to notice that for Dos Passos this complicated matter involves not only aesthetic issues but moral ones as well. In a letter to Edmund Wilson, Dos Passos describes his style, which achieves its greatest expression in *The U.S.A. Trilogy*, as "the behavioristic method" of writing. This, he explains, is the "method of generating the insides of the characters by external description."[19] Aesthetics here is inextricably linked with what must ultimately be termed a moral stance (showing the "insides" of characters). Both aesthetics and morality have a close relationship in his fiction, and this dual concern is evident even as early as *Streets of Night*.

When speaking of the sources of a writer's aesthetics or his "style," one must be careful. Is style the result of a writer's environment—or perhaps of his heredity? To what extent does formal education or informal acquaintance affect a writer's beliefs and actions in writing? No simple answers to these questions exist, as Dos Passos realized. Writing on this subject in a letter to Rumsey Marvin, he asserts "I think that reading people in order to get 'style' from them is rather soft-headed. Your style is like the color of your hair or the cut of your pants—half accident, half act of God—to take thought to change or improve it results usually in rank affectation." He says further that "Reading Pater 'for his style' is like going to a restaurant and ordering a dinner in order to admire the crockery it is served up on."[20] Dos Passos intuitively mentions Pater in this context not only because Pater's style is distinctive but also because it has affinities with Dos Passos's own writing. For Pater, too, the style is inextricable from subject matter.

As Ruth Child noted long ago, the distinctive feature of Pater's aesthetics is that "form and content must be so completely fused as to be one indivisible unit."[21] This result is accomplished by the imaginative synthesis of writer's mind, objective world, and language. Although this goal may be described simply as an example of "organic form," no other writer brings this aesthetic prescription to the reader's attention as forcefully as Pater. In his essay "Style," Pater argues that "All the laws of good writing aim at a similar unity or

identity of the mind in all the processes by which the word is associated to its import. The term is right, and has its essential beauty,
when it becomes, in a manner, what it signifies, as with the names of
simple sensations." Pater then states that the writer must "give the
phrase, the sentence, the structural member, the entire composition,
song, or essay, a similar unity with its subject and with itself." The
final effect of the finished composition, he says, is gained by the
author's giving "some strong and leading sense of the world, the tight
hold of which secures true *composition* and not mere loose accretion."
This is accomplished by "setting joint to joint."[22]

In broad outline, Pater makes three major points here. First, a
work of art is made by a joining of discrete elements, in workmanlike
manner, like constructing a "house," though more like an organic
"body."[23] Second, the composition must be a unified whole. Third,
the entire process depends on an identity of three elements: subjec-
tive idea, objective reality, and language. When this synthesis occurs
and when it presents some "new or old truth about ourselves and our
relation to the world," it is "great" art.[24]

Dos Passos's beliefs—and often his language—mirror Pater's. Dos
Passos gives a poetic evocation of his aesthetic principles in the
"Camera Eye" sections of *The U.S.A. Trilogy*. In "Camera Eye 47," he
too emphasizes the close relationship of author's mind and objective
reality in describing the creative process. It is in "words" that the
fusion occurs: "from the upsidedown image on the retina painstak-
ingly out of color shape words remembered light and dark straining."[25] In "Camera Eye 49," he continues his prescription, like Pater,
in a metaphor of the building trade: "pencil scrawls in my notebook
the scraps of recollection the broken halfphrases the effort to intersect
word with word to dovetail clause with clause to rebuild out of
mangled memories unshakably (Oh Pontius Pilate) the truth."[26] It is
notable that for both Pater and Dos Passos, the ethical and the
aesthetic elements are indistinguishable. To examine this similarity
from a slightly different angle, it is worth noting that both authors
shared a fascination with ancient Greek culture. Here, the reader
might look for an understanding of the dynamics of Dos Passos's
beliefs.

When John Dos Passos was sixteen years old, he was touring
Europe with his tutor. On 19 February 1912, he visited the Temple at
Eleusis, and in a playful letter to his father he recounts the experience. He had dinner, he said, and afterward slept in the cave in the
Acropolis of Eleusis. There he dreamt of a "great altar" with a white
bird—who identifies itself with "Truth" and who is covered with a
thick veil—hovering over it. A procession of people who represent the

course of civilization follows: a savage, a Mycenaean warrior, Solon, Pericles, Aristotle, Plato, Cicero, Virgil, and, finally, "a great wave of Barbarism." Then Dos Passos analyzes this experience: "I had seen the results of the Eleusian Mysteries; though the Mysteries themselves are lost in the depths of time they had brought the scholars, philosophers and poets and all the initiated in Greece and Rome nearer the snow-white Bird and had lightened ever so slightly the veil that hung about it."[27]

Notably the whole range of human character types here—savage, warrior, lawgiver, philosopher, poet—all have a single aim: truth. Although it is difficult to attain, it is—and has been throughout history—the object of the human quest. Dos Passos's subsequent career would take him into literature, but the reader should not think that art for Dos Passos—even as early as *Streets of Night*—was strictly for art's sake. Art, morality, aesthetics, and truth are all intertwined.

Dos Passos's interpretation of Greek literature is very similar to the attitudes expressed by G. Lowes Dickinson, whose book *The Greek View of Life* (along with Pater's *Greek Studies*) Dos Passos recommended in 1919 to a friend studying Greek literature.[28] (It should be noted that Dickinson's book was a lifelong possession: it was part of Dos Passos's personal collection given to the University of Virginia Library.) According to Dickinson, ancient Greek culture fostered a holistic sense of life that the modern-day person lacks. Spiritual entities were inseparable from material realities. "Religion" and "Nature" were one, notes Dickinson.[29]

Dickinson's comparison of Greek religion to American Puritanism might be especially helpful in understanding *Streets of Night*, for in some degree Nan, Fanshaw, and Wenny are all defined by America's Puritan heritage, especially as it manifests itself in the "genteel paralysis" of Boston culture. Wenny's case is most pertinent, because his father is a Congregationalist minister. As Dickinson notes, "To the Puritan, the inward relation of the soul to God is everything; to the average Greek, one may say broadly, it was nothing."[30] One way to read *Streets of Night*, then, is to see that Wenny must escape from his Puritan heritage in order to discover his Grecian, Dionysian self. Dickinson's commentary in Dionysus might well be a description of Wenny's situation:

He, the god of wine, was also the god of inspiration; and the ritual with which he was worshipped was a kind of apotheosis of intoxication. To suppress for a time the ordinary work-a-day consciousness, with its tedium, its checks, its balancing of pros and cons, to escape into the directness and simplicity of mere animal life, and yet to feel in this no degradation, but rather a submission to the divine power, an actual identification with the deity—such, it would seem, was the intention of those extraordinary revels. . . . All this points to an attempt to escape from the bounds of ordinary consciousness, and pass into some condition conceived, however confusedly, as one of union with the divine power.[31]

Significantly, the Greek "alternative" to ordinary life does not represent an escape from morality. This paganism, in fact, represents a holistic fusion of diverse elements: body and soul, spirit and matter, temporal and eternal. This holism finds its highest expression in the art of the Greeks, in which, as Dickinson notes, the ethical and the aesthetic viewpoints fuse. Morality and art are one.[32] Such an attitude must have appealed to both Pater and Dos Passos.

In *Streets of Night,* the double concern of aesthetics and morality can best be seen in the generalizations that Wenny and Nan make about art and life. According to Wenny, the average person leads an unsatisfactory life, because humanity's concern with surface realities hides their authentic selves, their "joy and agony."[33] The solution that Wenny sees to this problem is very much like the solution that the writer must find to the puzzle of art: words. But this aesthetic solution is not an art-for-art's-sake answer. As I have noted, aesthetics for Dos Passos means an expression not just of pleasure or beauty but of morality as well. Wenny is "in search of words,"[34] words that "explain all the joy and agony he felt."[35] At one point, he imagines finding these words on a "yellow, half-obliterated parchment" that would "resolve the festering chaos of the world into radiant Elysian order."[36] Such a goal points to moral insight as attained by the ancient Greeks—not simply to the pleasure principle of the nineteenth-century art-for-art's-sake advocates.

Nan has a similar aesthetic concern. She is searching for "sentences," for language that speaks to the universal. She wants to utter words that "will make that moment permanent": "Epigram, that was the word. There had been Greeks who had cut the flame of an instant deep on stone in broad letters for centuries to read."[37] For both Wenny and Nan, Greek literature serves as a worthy model, just as the Greek Eleusian mysteries—symbolized by the white bird of truth—captured the imagination of the sixteen-year-old John Dos Passos. Like Wenny and Nan, Dos Passos wanted to capture for posterity the present moment—the "insides of characters"—in the solid external form (in the characters' actions and in the "words" that captured those actions). If the reader considers the larger cultural and mythological elements in this novel, perhaps it can be said that Dos Passos succeeded to an extent greater than his first critics thought.

Although *Streets of Night* does have serious shortcomings—ineffective characterization, purple passages, failure to express the author's ideas adequately—the novel certainly does not lack interest, especially in light of Dos Passos's growing reputation as one of the twentieth century's foremost writers. If the reader is to understand Dos Passos's mature style, the "behavioristic method," and how that method is more than a stylistic trick, how it has a serious intent, and how it incorporates an essentially moral view of the world, he must look back to Dos Passos's appreciation of Greek literature and to his fascination with Pater's writing. The continuity between these influences and Dos Passos's behavioristic method shows how that method finds its tentative expression in this novel about Harvard and Boston. An understanding of Dos Passos's later career rightfully begins with an examination of *Streets of Night*.

NOTES

1. Jack Potter, *A Bibliography of John Dos Passos* (Chicago: Normandie House, 1950), p. 25.

2. "Latest Works of Fiction," review of *Streets of Night*, *New York Times*, 18 November 1923, sec. 3, pp. 8–9.

3. "Rambles in Fiction," *The American Mercury* 2 (July 1924): 380–81.

4. Joseph Collins, *Taking the Literary Pulse: Psychological Studies of Life and Letters* (New York: George H. Doran Company, 1924), p. 156.

5. Linda W. Wagner, *Dos Passos: Artist as American* (Austin: University of Texas Press, 1979), p. 24.

6. *Streets of Night*, p. 41.

7. John Dos Passos, *U.S.A.: The 42nd Parallel, Nineteen Nineteen, and The Big Money* (New York: The Modern Library, 1938), p. 301.

8. John Dos Passos, *The Fourteenth Chronicle: Letters and Diaries of John Dos Passos*, ed. Townsend Ludington (Boston: Gambit, 1973), p. 306.

9. *Streets of Night*, p. 116.

10. Dos Passos, Fourteenth Chronicle, p. 516.

11. *Streets of Night*, p. 133.

12. Robert C. Rosen, *John Dos Passos: Politics and the Writer* (Lincoln: University of Nebraska Press, 1981), p. 4.

13. Walter Pater, *Walter Pater: Three Major Texts (The Renaissance, Appreciations, and Imaginary Portraits)* ed. William E. Buckler (New York: New York University Press, 1986), p. 219.

14. *Greek Studies: A Series of Essays* (New York: Macmillan and Co., 1895), p. 2.

15. John Dos Passos, "Against American Literature," *The New Republic*, 8 (14 October 1916), p. 270.

16. *Streets of Night*, p. 117.

17. Ibid., p. 53.

18. Ibid., p. 42.

19. Dos Passos, *Fourteenth Chronicle*, p. 522.

20. Ibid., p. 181.

21. Ruth Child, *The Aesthetic of Walter Pater* (New York: Macmillan, 1940), p. 55.

22. Pater, *Three Major Texts*, p. 403–4.

23. Ibid., p. 404.

24. Ibid., p. 413.

25. Dos Passos, *The Big Money*, p. 196.

26. Ibid., p. 436.

27. Dos Passos, *Fourteenth Chronicle*, pp. 16–18.

28. Ibid., p. 253.

29. G. Lowes Dickinson, *The Greek View of Life* (Ann Arbor: University of Michigan Press, 1958), p. 3.

30. Ibid., p. 17.

31. Ibid., pp. 30–31.

32. Ibid., pp. 146–55.

33. *Streets of Night*, p. 112.

34. Ibid., p. 89.

35. Ibid., p. 112.

36. Ibid., p. 88.

37. Ibid., p. 54.

A Note on the Text

Dos Passos's final draft of *Streets of Night*—the copy from which the first American edition was prepared—is apparently no longer extant. The two existing typescripts of *Streets of Night* are at the Houghton Library, Harvard University, and at the Alderman Library, University of Virginia. Both of these typescripts (exact copies, though the Virginia copy lacks some chapters) were revised by Dos Passos independently, and both contain significant emendations, additions, and deletions in Dos Passos's hand. The Harvard typescript as corrected by Dos Passos was used to set the type for the first British edition. The revisions made on the Virginia typescript were not incorporated into the American or the British first editions, nor into the 1962 paperback reprinting of the novel.

The text of the novel printed here largely follows the first American edition but includes the changes that Dos Passos made in the Harvard and Virginia typescripts. In some cases, certain passages in the first edition differ from the typescript in places where Dos Passos made parallel but different revisions in one or both of the typescripts. In those instances, the original first American edition reading is retained, and the competing readings in the typescripts are reproduced in the lists of substantive variants and changes.

Streets of Night

Et si per talen
Pert tot mi joven,
Pauc mi valdran chan d'auzel.

—PEIRE VIDAL

I

"*B*UT I don't think I want to, Cham."

"Come along, Fanshaw, you've got to."

"But I wouldn't know what to say to them."

"They'll do the talking. . . . Look, you've got to come, date's all made an' everything."

Cham Mason stood in his drawers in the middle of the floor, eagerly waving a shirt into which he was fitting cuff-links. He was a pudgy-faced boy with pink cheeks and wiry light hair like an Irish terrier's. He leaned forward with pouting lips towards Fanshaw, who sat, tall and skinny, by the window, with one finger scratching his neck under   10 the high stiff collar from which dangled a narrow necktie, blue, the faded color of his eyes.

"But jeeze, man," Cham whined.

"Well, what did you go and make it for?"

"Hell, Fanshaw, I couldn't know that Al Winslow was going to get scarlet fever. . . . Most fellers'ld be glad of the chance. It isn't every-body Phoebe Sweeting'll go out with."

"But why don't you go alone?"

"What could I do with two girls in a canoe? And she's got to have her friend along. You don't realize how respectable chorus girls are."   20

"I never thought they were respectable at all."

"That shows how little you know about it."

Cham put on his shirt with peevish jerks and went into the next room. Fanshaw looked down at Bryce's *American Commonwealth* that lay spread out on his knees and tried to go on reading: This decision of the Supreme Court, however . . . But why shouldn't he? Fanshaw stretched himself, yawning. The sunlight seeped through the brownish stencilled curtains and laid a heavy, warm hand on his left shoulder. This decision of the Supreme . . . He looked down into Mount Auburn Street. It was June and dusty. From the room below   30 came the singsong of somebody playing "Sweet and Low" on the mandolin.—And Mother needn't know, and I'm in college . . . see life. A man with white pants on ran across the street waving a tennis racket. Stoddard, on the *Lampoon,* knows all the chorines.

Cham, fully dressed in a tweed suit, stood before him with set lips, blinking his eyes to keep from crying.

"Fanshaw, I don't think you're any kind of a . . ."

"All right, I'll go, Cham, but I won't know what to say to them."

"Gee, that's great." Cham's face became cherubic with smiles. "Just act natural."

"Like when you have your photograph taken," said Fanshaw, laughing shrilly.

"Gee, you're a prince to do it. . . . I think Phoebe likes me. . . . It's just that I've never had a chance to get her alone."

Their eyes met suddenly. They both blushed and were silent. Fanshaw got to his feet and walked stiffly to the bookcase to put away his book.

"But Cham." He was hoarse; he cleared his throat. "I don't want to carry on with those girls. I don't . . . I don't do that sort of thing."

"Don't worry, they won't eat you. I tell you they are very respectable girls. They don't want to carry on with anybody. They like to have a good time, that's all."

"But all day seems so long."

"We won't start till eleven or so. Phoebe won't be up. Just time to get acquainted."

From far away dustily came the bored strokes of the college bell.

"Ah, there's my three-thirty," said Fanshaw.

It was hot in the room. There was a smell of stale sweat from some soiled clothes that made a heap in the center of the floor. The strokes of the bell beat on Fanshaw's ears with dreary, accustomed weight.

"How about walking into town instead?"

Fanshaw picked up a notebook out of a patch of sun on the desk. The book was warm. The beam of sunlight was full of bright, lazy motes. Fanshaw put the book up to his mouth and yawned. Still yawning, he said:

"Gee, I'd like to, but I can't."

"I don't see why you took a course that came at such a damn-fool time."

"Can't argue now," said Fanshaw, going out the door and tramping down the scarred wooden stairs.

*   *   *

"You ask the clerk to call up and see if they're ready," said Cham. They stood outside the revolving door of the hotel, the way people linger shivering at the edge of a pool before diving in. Cham wore a straw hat and white flannel pants and carried a corded luncheon basket in one hand.

"But Cham, that's your business. You ought to do that." Fanshaw felt a stiff tremor in his voice. His hands were cold.

"Go ahead, Fanshaw; for crissake, we can't wait here all day," Cham whispered hoarsely.

Fanshaw found himself engaged in the revolving door with Cham pushing him from behind. From rocking chairs in the lobby he could see the moonfaces of two drummers, out of which eyes like oysters stared at him. He was blushing; he felt his forehead tingle under his new tweed cap. The clock over the desk said fifteen of eleven. He walked firmly over to the desk and stood leaning over the registry book full of blotted signatures and dates. He cleared his throat. He could feel the eyes of the drummers, of the green bellboy, of people passing along the street boring into his back. At last the clerk came to him, a greyfaced man with a triangular mouth and eyeglasses, and said in a squeaky voice:

"Yessir?"

"Are Miss . . . Is Miss . . .? Say, Cham, what are their names, Cham?" Guilty perspiration was trickling down Fanshaw's temples and behind his ears. He felt furiously angry at Cham for having got him into this, at Cham's back and straw hat tipped in the contemplation of the Selkirk Glacier over the fireplace. "Cham!"

"Miss Montmorency and Miss Sweeting," said Cham coolly in a businesslike voice.

The clerk had tipped up one corner of his mouth. Leaving Cham to talk to him, Fanshaw walked over to a rocker by the fireplace and hunched up in it sulkily. With relief he heard the clerk say:

"The young ladies will be down in a few minutes; would you please wait?"

Fanshaw stared straight ahead of him. He'd never speak to Cham again after this. When the bellboy leaned over the desk to say something to the clerk, the eight brass buttons on his coattails flashed in the light. The clerk laughed creakily. Fanshaw clenched his fists. Damn them, what had he let himself be inveigled into this for? He looked at the floor; balanced on the edge of a spittoon a cigar stub still gave off a little wisp of smoke. The temptations of college life. As he sat with his neatly polished oxfords side by side, making the chair rock by a slight movement of the muscles of his thin calves, he thought of the heart-to-heart talk Mr. Crownsterne had given the sixth form this time last year about the temptations of college life. The soapy flow of Mr. Crownsterne's voice booming in his ears: You are now engaged, fellows, in that perilous defile through which all of us have to pass to reach the serene uplands of adult life. You have put behind you the pleasant valleys and problems of boyhood, and before you can assume

the duties and responsibilities of men you have to undergo—we all of
us have had to undergo—the supreme test. You all know, fellows, the
beautiful story of the Holy Grail . . . Galahad . . . purity and con-
tinence . . . safest often the best course . . . shun not the society of
the lovely girls of our own class . . . honest and healthy entertainment . . . dances and the beautiful flow of freshness and youth . . .
but remember to beware, in whatever circle of life the duties and
responsibilities of your careers may call you to move, of those unfortunate women who have rendered themselves unworthy of the society of
10   our mothers and sisters . . . of those miserable and disinherited
creatures who, although they do not rebuff and disgust us immediately with their loathsomeness as would common prostitutes, yet
. . . Remember that even Jesus Christ, our Savior, prayed not to be
led into temptation. O, fellows, when you go out from these walls I
want you to keep the ideals you have learned and that you have taught
by your example as sixth formers . . . the spotless armor of Sir
Galahad . . .

The rocking chair creaked. The clock above the desk had ticked its
way to eleven fifteen.—Old Crowny's phrases certainly stayed in your
20   mind. Suppose we met Mother on the trolley? No, she'd be at
church. Nonsense, and these were respectable girls anyway; they
wouldn't lead into temptation. A heap lot more respectable than lots
of the girls you met at dances. Why don't they come?

"Gee, I bet they weren't up yet," said Cham, giggling.

"What, at eleven o'clock?"

"They don't usually get up till one or two."

"I suppose being up so late every night." Fanshaw could not get his
voice above a mysterious whisper. The bellboy was looking at him.
What's he thinking? Fanshaw was wondering as he sat in the rocking
30   chair without moving and stared at the clock. Eleven thirty-six. The
bellboy stood in front of the desk, his eyes fixed on vacancy. The
bellboy grinned and drew a red hand across his slick black hair.

"Did ye think we'd passed out up there?" came a gruff girl's voice
behind him, interrupted by a giggle. He smelt perfume. Then he was
on his feet, blushing.

They were shaking hands with Cham. One had curly brown hair
and a doll's pink organdy dress and showed teeth, even as the grains
on an ear of white corn, in a continual smile. The other had a thin face
and tow hair and wore the same dress in blue.

40   "I was coming up to help," shouted Cham.

"Ou, what's that?"

"It's a present." The blue dress hovered over the lunch basket.

"A case of Scotch!" They all shrieked with laughter.

"That's our eats," said Cham solemnly.

"And this is Mr.———?"

"Beg pardon, this is my friend, Mr. Macdougan . . . answers to the name of Fanshaw."

Fanshaw shook their hands that they held up very high.

"This is Miss Phoebe Sweeting, and this is Miss Elise Montmorency."

"We'll never be able to eat all that," said the blue girl tittering.

"We'll drink some of it," said Cham. "There's some champagny water."

"My Gawd!"

"You carry it now, Fanshaw," said Cham in a hurried undertone and pushed the pink girl out in front of him through the revolving door.

Fanshaw picked up the basket. It was heavy and rattled.

"O, I just do love canoeing," said the blue girl as they followed. "Don't you?"

*   *   *

They stood on the landing at Norumbega. A man in a seedy red sweater torn at the elbows was bringing a canoe out of the boathouse. A cool, weedy smell teasing to the nostrils came up out of the river.

"Ou, isn't it deep?" said Elise, pressing her fluffy dress against Fanshaw's leg.

"Stop it, I tell you . . . You'll push me in the water . . . Ow!" Cham was brandishing a bullrush at the pink girl, tickling her with it. She was protesting in a gruff baby lisp full of titters. "If you spoil my dress . . ."

"I'm sure you paddle beautifully. . . . D'you mind if I call you Fanshaw? . . . It's a funny name like a stage name. Look at them!"

Phoebe had snatched the bullrush and was beating Cham over the head. The brown fluff fell about them bright in the streaming sunlight. Fanshaw found himself picking up Cham's straw hat, palping a dent in the rim with his finger. Cham's hair shone yellow; he grabbed the pink girl's hand. The bullrush broke off and the head fell into the river, where brown shiny rings spread from it.

"Ow, damn it, you hurt," she cried shrilly. "There now, you made me say damn."

"Momma kiss it an' make it well."

Fanshaw found the blue girl's grey glance wriggling into his eyes.

"Silly, ain't they? Kids, are they not?"

The ain't stung in Fanshaw's ears. The girl was common. The thought made him blush.

"Come along, let's get started. Man the boats," cried Cham.

"I'm scared o' canoes. You can paddle all right, can't you, Fan-shaw?" The blue girl pressed his hand tight as they stood irresolute a moment looking down into the canoe. The other canoe was off, upstream into the noon dazzle.

"Come along," shouted Cham. The sun flashed on his paddle. He began singing off key:

> I know a place where the sun is like gold
> And the cherryblooms burst with snow
> And down underneath . . .

10   "All right, missy, step in," said the man in the red sweater who was holding the canoe to the landing with a paddle. "Easy now."

"Let m-m-me get in first," said Fanshaw, stuttering a little. "I hope this isn't a tippy one."

"I'll help you in, missy," said the man in the red sweater. Fanshaw, from the stern seat he had plunked down in, saw the man's big, red hand, like a bunch of sausages against the blue dress, clasp her arm, press against the slight curve of her breast as he let her down among the cushions. "Thanks," she said, as she tucked her dress in around her legs, giving the man a long look from under the brim of her hat.

20   "Ou, I'm scared to death," she said, leaning back gingerly. "If you tip me over . . ."

Fanshaw had pushed the canoe out from the landing. Over his shoulder he caught a glimpse of a grin on the face of the man with the red sweater. He paddled desperately. The other canoe was far ahead, black in the broad shimmering reach of the river. He was sweating. He splashed some water into the canoe.

"Ou, you naughty . . . Don't. You've gotten me all wet."

"I think I'll take my coat off, if you don't mind."

"Don't mind me, go as far as you like," giggled Elise.

30   Fanshaw took off his coat and rolled up his sleeves. He was trying not to look at the pink legs in stockings of thin black silk with clocks on them that stretched towards him in the canoe, ending in crossed ankles and bronze high heel slippers.

"Warm, isn't it?"

"Hot, I call it. I hope they don't go awfully far. I don't want to get all sunburned. . . . A boy swiped my parasol." Her grey eyes flashed in his. She was giggling with her lips apart.

"How was that?"—How solemn I sound, thought Fanshaw.

"I dunno, one o' them souvenir hunters out at the Roadside Inn."
40   She pulled down her babyish-looking hat that had blue and pink roses on it so that it shaded her eyes.

"Whew, smell that!" she cried.

"Must be a sewer, or marshgas."

"Clothespins! Clothespins!" Elise was holding her nose and wriggling in the bottom of the canoe. Then she burst into giggles again and cried: "Gee, this little girl loves the country, nit!"

"Now it's better, isn't it?"

"I want to eat. Cham's crazy to go so far."

"They've got the picnic basket, so I don't see what we can do but follow."

"Follow on, follow on," sang Elise derisively.

Upstream, Cham's canoe had drawn up to the bank under a fringe of trees grey in the noon glare. Behind it a figure in white and a figure in pink, close together, were disappearing into the shadow.

"They'll have every single thing eaten up," wailed Elise.

"I'm afraid I'm not a very good paddler," said Fanshaw through clenched teeth.

"There you go again."

"Well, I didn't mean to. I'm sorry."

"You'll have to get me a new dress, that's all."

The canoe ran into the bank with a sliding thump.

Phoebe was looking at them from behind a clump of maples. She cooed at them in her most dollish voice.

"What have you kids been doing all by yourselves out in the river?"

"We saw you, don't you worry dearest," said Elise, balancing to step out of the canoe. "O murder, I got my foot in it!"

"Bring the cushions, Fanshaw," shouted Cham, who was kneeling beside the open picnic basket with a bottle in his hand.

*   *   *

Fanshaw's hands were sticky. The warm champagne had made him feel a little sick. He sat with his back against a tree, his knees drawn up to his chin, looking across the gutted lunch basket at Cham and Phoebe, who lay on their backs and shrieked with laughter. Beside him he was conscious of the blue girl sitting stiff on a cushion, bored, afraid of spoiling her dress. Overhead, the afternoon sun beat heavily on the broad maple leaves; patches of sunlight littered the ground like bright, torn paper. Through the trees came the mud smell and the restless sheen of the river. Fanshaw was trying to think of something to say to the girl beside him; he daren't turn towards her until he had thought of something to say.

"Doggone it, I've got an ant down my back," cried Cham, sitting up suddenly, his face pink.

"Momma catch it," spluttered Phoebe in the middle of a gust of laughter.

Cham was scratching himself all over, under his arm, round his neck, making an anxious monkey face till at last he ran his hand down the back of his shirt.

"Yea, I got him."

"He's a case, he is," tittered Elise.

Cham was on his hands and knees whispering something in Phoebe's ear, his nose pressed into her frizzy chestnut hair.

"Stop blowin' in my ear," said the pink girl, pushing him away. "Wouldn't that jar you?"

"What we need is juss a lil' more champagny water." Cham picked
10 the two bottles out of the basket and tipped them up to the light. "There's juss a lil' drop for everybody."

"Not for me . . . I think you're trying to get us silly," said the blue girl.

"God did that."

"Well, I never."

"Ou, somethin's ticklin' me. . . . Did you put that ant on me?" The pink girl scrambled to her feet and made for Cham.

"Honest, I didn't . . ." cried Cham, jumping out of her way and doubling up with glee: "Honest, I didn't. Cross my heart, hope I may
20 die, I didn't."

"Cham, you're lyin' like a fish. I got an ant down my dress. Ou, it tickles!"

"I'll catch it, Phoebe."

"Boys, don't look now. I'm goin' fishin'. . . . Ou . . . I got him. O, it's just a leaf. . . . O, he looked. He's a cool one. I'm goin' to smack your face."

"Catch me first, Phoebe deary," cried Cham, running off up a path. She lit out after him. "Look out for your dress on them bushes," cried Elise.
30 "I should worry."

Fanshaw watched the pink dress disappear down the path, going bright and dull in the patches of sun and shadow among the maple trees. Their laughing rose to a shriek and stopped suddenly. Fanshaw and Elise looked at each other.

"Children must play," said Fanshaw stiffly.

"What time are we goin' home, d'you know?" said Elise, yawning.

"You don't like—er—picnicking?"

There was a silence. From down river came the splash of paddles and the sound of a phonograph playing "O Waltz Me Around Again
40 Willie." Fanshaw sat still in the same position with his knees drawn up to his chin, as if paralyzed. With tightening throat he managed to say:

"What can they be doing? . . . They don't seem to be coming back."

"Ask me something hard," said the blue girl jeeringly.

Fanshaw felt himself blushing. He clasped his hands tighter round his knees. He felt the sweat making little beads on his forehead. Ought he to kiss her? He didn't want to kiss her with her rouged lips and her blonde hair all fuzzy like that, peroxide probably.—A fool to come along, anyway. What on earth shall I say to her?

She got to her feet.

"I'm goin' to walk around a bit. . . . Ou, my foot's gone to sleep."

Fanshaw jumped up as if a spring had been released inside him.

"Which way shall we go?"

"I guess we'd better go the other way," said Elise, tittering and smoothing out the back of her fluffy dress.

They walked beside the water; along the path were mashed cracker boxes, orange peel, banana skins. The river was full of canoes now. Above the sound of paddles occasionally splashing and the grinding undertone of phonographs came now and then a giggle or a man's voice shouting. Elise was humming "School Days," walking ahead of him with mincing steps. He saw a woodpecker run down the trunk of an oak.

"Look! There's a woodpecker." Elise walked ahead, still humming, now and then taking a little dance step. "It's a red-headed woodpecker." As she still paid no attention, he walked behind her without saying anything, listening to the tapping of the woodpecker in the distance, watching her narrow hips sway under the pleats of her dress as she walked. A rank, heavy smell came from the muddy banks. He looked at his watch. Only four o'clock. She caught sight of the watch and turned round.

"What time is it, please?"

"It's only four o'clock. . . . We have lots of time yet."

"Don't I realize it? Say, what's the name of this old, damn-fool park?"

"Norumbega."

"It's never again for me," she cried, giggling. Then all at once she dropped down on the ground at the foot of a tree and began to sob, with her dress all puffed up about her.

"But what's the matter?"

"Nothing. . . . My God, shut up and go away!" she whined through her sobs.

"All right, I'll go and see nobody swipes the canoe."

Biting his lips, Fanshaw started slowly back along the path.

*   *   *

The air of the examination room was heavy and smelt of chalk. Through the open windows from the yard drifted the whir of lawn-

mowers and the fragrance of cut grass. Fanshaw had just finished
three hundred words on "The Classical Subject in Racine." He found
himself listening to the lawnmowers and breathing in the rifts of warm
sweetness that came from the mashed grass. It almost made him cry.
The spring of freshman year, the end of freshman year. The fragrance
of years mown down by the whirring, singsong blades. He stared at
the printed paper: "Comparative Literature I. Devote one hour to
one of the following subjects. . . ."—And the girl in the blue dress
had plunked herself down under a tree and cried. What a fool I was to
walk away like that. "What's that perfume?" "Mary Garden," she had
said, and her grey glance had wriggled into his eyes, and his hands
had moved softly across the fluffy dress, feeling the whalebone corsets
under the blue fluff. No, that's when I helped her back into the canoe.
Elise Montmorency, the girl in the blue dress, had plunked herself
down under a tree and cried because he hadn't kissed her. But he had
kissed her; he had come back and lain on the grass beside her and
kissed her till she wriggled in his arms under the blue fluff and the
sunshine had lain a hot tingling coverlet over his back.

He sat stiff in his chair staring in front of him, his hands clasped
tight under the desk. All his flesh was hot and tingling. He breathed
deep of the smell of cut grass that drifted in through the window,
under the mashed grass and cloverblossoms, sweetness, heaviness,
Mary Garden perfume.—Gee, am I going to faint?

> There on Beds of Violets blue,
> And fresh-blown Roses washt in dew,
> Fill'd her with thee a daughter fair,
> So buxom, blithe, and debonair.

Fanshaw felt the blood suddenly rush to his face.—If the proctor
sees me blushing, he'll think I've been cribbing. He hung his head
over his paper again.

Devote one hour . . . She was common and said ain't. That was not
the sort of girl. He was glad he hadn't kissed her. . . . The spotless
armor of Sir Galahad. Maybe that was temptation. Maybe he'd re-
sisted temptation. And lastly, Mr. Crownsterne's voice was booming
in his ears: "And lastly, fellows, let me wish each one of you the best
and loveliest and most flower-like girl in the world for your wife." A lot
old Crowny knew about it. Marriage was for ordinary people, but for
him, love, two souls pressed each to each, consumed with a single
fire.

> And neither the angels in heaven above,
> Nor the demons down under the sea,

Can ever dissever my soul from the soul
Of the beautiful Annabel Lee.

The moth's kiss, dearest. He was in a boat with red sails, in the stern of a boat with red lateen sails, and she was in his arms, and her hair was fluffy against his cheek, and the boat leapt on the waves, and they were drenched in droning fragrance off the island to windward, wet rose gardens, clover fields, fresh-cut hay, tarry streets, Mary Garden perfume. That perfume was common like saying ain't.

Gosh, only thirty-five minutes for those two questions! Sudden panic seized him. The clock was at twenty-five past. The nib of his fountain pen was dry. He shook a drop out on the floor before he began to write.

II

"AND did I tell you he said you played as if you had a soul?"

They were standing beside the coatrack. Miss Fitzhugh was buttoning up her gloves with little, jerky movements of a hairpin, talking all the while breathlessly. From the parlor at the end of the narrow green-papered hall came a whiff of tea and the sound of cups clinked against saucers.

"What he said was . . . You won't mind if I tell you all, will you, dear? . . . Anyway, I've always admired your way of playing Chabrier. He said your technique was rotten, but that you had a soul. And he
10 turned down Mrs. Glendinning to come here this afternoon, honest he did. Will you turn on the light a sec? My hat's crooked. . . . There! . . ."

Miss Fitzhugh put back the hairpin and made a few jabs at the yellow hair under her hat.

"If you want my plain opinion . . . O, I do look a sight. . . . I think you've made a conquest, Nancibel. O, you are a lucky girl! And that Wendell boy's dreadfully good-looking too. . . . Well, I must go." Miss Fitzhugh drew the taller girl down on her firm, plump bosom and kissed her moistly—"Just think of being loved by Salinski!" She
20 kissed Nancibel on the mouth again and fled with a little giggle out the door.

"Poor fool!" muttered Nancibel. With her lips tightly compressed, she walked back towards her guests. While still in the dark of the hall, she closed her eyes and let her mouth drop for a second—O, I hope they go soon. Then with a smile she went back to her place by the teathings.

"Was Fitzie telling you all the Boston Theater gossip?" asked a little girl with light fuzzy hair and a green dress.

"No, it was only about Mr. Salinski."
30 "She's jealous because he played here, I bet you."

"She doesn't want him to play with that dreadful ladies' orchestra, does she?" put in a tall girl with large teeth and a picture hat.

"You shouldn't laugh at people's misfortunes, Susan," said the fuzzy-haired girl and let out a shrill titter.

"What are Miss Fitzhugh's misfortunes?" asked Fanshaw, who

stood tall and blonde in a light grey suit, with his back to the fireplace.

"She's cellist on the famous ladies' orchestra."

"How delicious. The Fadettes!"

"Fitzie's an awful fool, but I like her," said Nancibel gruffly.

"Susan, we must go," said the fuzzy-haired girl.

"Must you, dear?" said Nan automatically.

Their dresses swished, and kisses were exchanged in the hall beside the coatrack. When the door had closed behind the two women, Nancibel hurried back to the parlor.

"O, what a relief!" she cried. "I was so afraid there would be somebody left I'd overlooked."

"I'm about dead," said Wendell. "Nan, you ought to warn people when you have tea fights and celebrities. I tried to escape once I'd got in, but Fanshaw held on to my coat." He got up from where he had sat crouched in the corner by the window and walked over to the tea-table. "Any food left?"

"Here, you poor child," said Nan, bouncing a section of sticky chocolate cake on to a plate. "I'll make some fresh tea in a minute. Do you realize that this afternoon is the first triumph in a career of fashionable music? O, it's too silly. . . ." She burst out laughing, letting herself drop limply into a chair.

"I thought it was going a little far when the stout, red-haired lady sailed in with those two poor little men like a liner being tugged up to the wharf," said Fanshaw, who still stood with his back to the unlit gaslogs.

"That's the famous Mrs. Hammond Tweed, who writes animal stories," burst out Nan, carried off on a fresh gust of hysterical laughter. "The way she said 'Ah' when Salinski wriggled out of a cadenza, like people watching skyrockets."

Nan rolled about on her chair. What fun it was to be giggling like this with Wenny and Fanshaw, like children who've done something naughty. Through the tears in her eyes, she could see, beyond the big brass-topped teatable stacked with used teacups and crumb-covered plates where here and there a cigarette butt blackened with its ash a few drops of tea left in a spoon, Wenny's brown face convulsed with laughter and greediness as he stuffed hunks of chocolate cake into his mouth.—And Fitzie thinks I'm angling after old Salinski. The thought came to make her laugh the harder. Her foot knocked against the leg of the teatable, and all the cups rattled.

"Look out, Nan, you'll have it over," said Fanshaw.

"Wouldn't care if I did. I'd like to smash something."

"You shan't smash Confucius there, young lady. I'll not let you."

Fanshaw put the big blue teapot in a place of safety on the mantelpiece.

Nan got to her feet and wiped her eyes with her handkerchief.

"O, dear! . . . But I must give you children some fresh tea to make up for all you've suffered."

She ran out to the kitchenette to put fresh tea in the pot. From there she called: "Wenny, bring the debris; I'll leave it for the maid to clean up." The glasses in a row along a shelf whined with the vibration of her voice. She felt all at once curiously constrained. Absurd. She'd known Wenny when he was in knickerbockers. Why should it embarrass her to be alone with him in the kitchenette? The tea sizzled faintly, and the steam came up scalding in her face as she poured the boiling water into the pot. She did not turn around, she was flushing so when she heard Wenny's step and the rattle of china behind her.

"After the battle mother," sang Wenny as he put the tray of tea things down beside the sink.

"Here, you cut this lemon and bring it in, Wenny, if you don't mind," she said and fled with the pot and a couple of clean cups into the other room. Fanshaw's voice was always so soothing when one was excited.

"There's still a bit of the afterglow," said Fanshaw from near the window. "It's wonderful how long it lingers these fall evenings."

Wenny had come back with the lemon and dropped a piece into each of the three cups. Then he sniffed at his hands.

"That's a splendid lemon. It's wonderful how good it makes your fingers smell."

She watched his lips form the words. Semitic lips, like in the Assyrians in the museum, she thought.

"Gertrude said," Fanshaw was taking little sips of tea as he spoke, "you'd be taken up with the spirits."

"Not gin, I hope." She tossed her head up suddenly, lips pressed together. "Fine gesture that," whispered some mocking demon in her.

Fanshaw smiled indulgently with thin lips.

"No, I mean spooks," he said. "Gertrude said you did extraordinary things with a Ouija board. She's very silly, you know."

"Made me out a regular witch of Endor, did she?" Her voice was tense in spite of herself.

"O, I hate the longfaced way people talk about that guff . . . as if people dead could be more important than people alive," Wenny blurted out angrily.

Nan found herself looking in his eyes; the black pupils widened as she looked in them. There was a warmth about her body as if his vehemence had communicated itself to her. Then the eyes flashed away.

"What nonsense, Wendell," she said. "Don't be so silly. I just played with a Ouija board to see what people would say. We talked to Robinson Crusoe."

Fanshaw waved a long, thin hand in the air.

"For heaven's sake, don't squabble. After all those young women, I feel weak. There must have been a thousand of them. . . . I say, Nan, did you invite the whole conservatory?"

"No, but as they were all dying to say they'd been in the same room with Salinski, I went the limit."

"You certainly did."

"Gosh! The size of that star," came Wenny's voice from the window. In his black silhouette, Nan was imagining the molding of the muscles of the arms, the hollow between the shoulders, the hard bulge of calves. She got to her feet. The grey jade beads hung down from her neck as she lifted the teatable out of the way. The little demon in her head was hissing "Careful Nancibel, careful Nancibel," as she walked over to the window. Her arm hanging limp at her side touched his arm; writhing, hump-backed flares danced an insane ballet through her body. Down the street a grindorgan was playing "The Wearing of the Green."—What wonderful lashes he has, she caught herself thinking, so much nicer than mine. Warm shudders came from his cheek to her cheek, from his moving lips.

"It looks as big as a chrysanthemum," he was saying.

She had forgotten the star. She saw it then bristling with green horns of light.

Wenny wore a woolly suit that had been wet, as it had been raining; the smell of it mixed with a tang of tobacco filled her nostrils. She was looking at the star that seemed to palpitate with slow, sucking rhythm, afloat in the evening like a jellyfish in shallow bay water. For an instant all her life palpitated hideously with the star. She turned. Her lips almost brushed Wenny's cheek.

"L'étoile du berger," said Fanshaw. His voice rasped through Nan's head.

Her hands were icecold. The little demon in her head with a voice like Aunt M.'s was whispering: "You must meet my niece Nancibel Taylor; she's such a clever violinist." She pulled the shade down sharply in Wenny's face.

"You'ld be there all night mooning at that star," she said and tried to laugh.

They sat down in their chairs again.

"Well, Wenny, how have you been wasting your time?" Her voice rang false in her ears.

Wenny's brown eyes looked at her timidly for a moment. He spread his square hands on his knees and glanced down at their large knuckles. In Nan a cold voice exulted: "He has the hands of a ditchdigger."

"I wish I knew," he said.

She looked at Fanshaw. His bluish-green crepe necktie was the
10 color his eyes were behind the round tortoiseshell spectacles. His arched nose and high forehead were what had made one of the girls say: "There's a clever-looking man." She was glad he was here. She always felt sane where Fanshaw was.

"It's time, Wenny," Fanshaw was saying as he got to his feet.

"What's the matter?"

"Don't go," said Nan in a sudden panic at the idea of being left alone.

"But, Nan, I promised the Perkinses I'd bring Wenny to dinner, and we are late already."
20 "O hell," muttered Wenny.

"I promised you'd come, and I'm going to drag you along even if your shirt is dirty."

"It looked clean this morning," said Wenny, flushing.

"Well, it's filthy now."

"That seems to me a darn good reason for not going."

The jade beads clinked as she followed them down the hall towards the door. For some reason she held out her hand to them formally. After the limpness of Fanshaw's hand, Wenny's seemed hard and hot. Again the phrase came to her mind: ditchdigger's hands.
30 "I don't want to go a bit, Nan. . . ."

"Well, good evening," interrupted Fanshaw, pushing Wenny towards the door with a gesture of proprietorship. As they turned towards the elevator, her eyes followed the fuzziness of Wenny's hair down the nape of his neck under the soft collar. The collar had a line of grime round it.—Dirty little animal, said the voice in her. She closed the door, her nostrils full of the greasy smell of the elevator. The smile went out of her face.

The beads clinked as she walked back to the parlor. What was the matter with her today anyhow?—An old maid, that's what you are,
40 like Aunt M. Nonsense, I'm too alive for all that rubbish. She stood with compressed lips looking about the room. How beastly small it was. There was a design in reddish orange on the bright blue curtains that was echoed by the orange shade on the tall lamp that stood on the

floor beside the piano. She'd thought herself clever to think up the colorscheme, with the warm buff walls as a background. It seemed hideous to her at that moment, like the decoration of a room in the window of a department store. There were still soiled teacups on the tables and along the mantel and little plates with bits of sandwich and cake on them. She picked up the fat, blue teapot Fanshaw had named Confucius. The smooth bulge of it in her hands was reassuring for a while. Then solitude poured in upon her again. The Jacobean table with knobby legs opposite the fireplace and the books crammed into the bookcase and the battered Buhl cabinet in the corner all seemed 10 squared and tiptoe with hostility. There was a faint, bitter smell of tealeaves and burnt-out cigarette butts about everything.

She put down the teapot and flung herself on the pianostool. She would play madly. She would compose. A momentary thrill of huge chords, rising cadences to carry her with immense wingbeats out of the pit of sick yearning. She struck the keys with all ten fingers. The sound jangled loud through the room. She winced. "Idiot," she said aloud, and went to the window. She raised the shade part way and let it fall behind her. The green star trembled in the west just above the dark mass of a building the other side of the Fenway. She watched it, 20 breathless, while it sank out of sight.

*   *   *

Nan climbed painfully out of slumber as one climbs a ladder. Sparrows were twittering outside. Her white bedroom was full of sunlight that poured through the wide window opposite her bed, smouldered hotly on the red and blue of the carpet, glinted on the tall mahogany bedpost and finally struck a warm, tingling coverlet over her feet and legs. She snuggled into the bedclothes and lay staring at the ceiling wrapped in a blank haze of sleepiness. A motortruck rasped by outside, grating on her drowsy quiet, and rattled off into silence. Through the window she could see a lacework of treetops and 30 the expressionless cubes of some further apartment houses and, beyond, a blue, vaguely clouded sky. Two little sparrows, fat, fuzzy, with bright eyes, fluttered down past the window. She closed her eyes. In her ears something formed the words: "So wonderfully secure."

She woke with a start from her doze. What was she trying to remember? She was suddenly wide-awake, her heart pounding. The warm bulge of his arm against her arm, hard, male, and the bright jelly of his eyes between black lashes, last evening looking at the star. She tried to brush the memory off; it clung about her the way the sticky spiderwebs used to cling to her face and hair walking through 40 the woods last summer. She didn't want to think of Wenny that way, she told herself. It would spoil everything, she must have more self-control. "No, no," she said aloud as she put her toes into her slippers. She went about her dressing with compressed lips.

She threw herself into a flurry of things to be done. Sunday and late and the maid not coming. There was the percolator to put on, the water to run for her bath, the milk to take in, and the paper, and the caps to take off the milkbottle and the creambottle, and the flame under the percolator mustn't be too high and the bath mustn't be too hot. The familiar morning smells, gasflame, soap, bathwater, cof-
10   feesteam, were vaguely distasteful to her this morning, gave her a feeling of days succeeding days and years, years, as alike and meaningless as milkbottles. As she was cleaning her teeth, she stopped with her mouth full of lather and the toothbrush in her hand. It was two years and eight months she'd been living in this apartment.—O, something must happen soon. When she had rinsed her mouth, she looked at herself a long while in the tilted mirror over the washbasin. On one side the nickel fixture of the shower over the bathtub, on the other a glimpse through the open door into the hall and a patch of blue and green curtain; in the middle her face, chestnut hair caught
20   loosely away from the narrow forehead, straight eyebrows, darker than her hair, fine lashes. She stared for a moment intensely into her own grey eyes, then closed them with a shudder. "I have the thin New England lips," she said to herself. She pulled the nightgown off impatiently and stood with her hands on her scarcely-formed breasts looking down into the pale green of the bathtub. Somewhere at the end of a long corridor of her mind she ran through the dappled shadow of woods, naked, swift, chased by someone brown, flushed, goatfooted. She could feel in her nostrils the roughness of the smell of Wenny's damp homespun suit. *Après-midi d'un Faune*, the words
30   formed in her mind, Music by Claude Debussy, Choreography by M. Nijinski; the big program in her hands with its smell of glazed printer's ink and the rustling of dresses about her at the Opera. "What are you dawdling about?" she muttered, and stepped into the water and began briskly soaping the facecloth.

Half an hour later, Nancibel Taylor sat at the table beside the window in the livingroom, sipping coffee and putting dabs of butter on the broken pieces of a sugared bun left over from tea. The sky had clouded over. Through the black tangle of twigs of the low trees in the Fenway here and there, a slaty gleam of water flashed out. From a
40   long way off came the unresonant tolling of a churchbell broken into occasionally by the shrill grind of a streetcar round a corner. Still chewing the last mouthful, Nan picked up the cup and plate, absent-mindedly brushing a few crumbs off the blue tablecover with one

hand, and carried them into the kitchenette; putting them in the sink, she let the hot water run on them, and with her hand still on the tap, paused to think what she must do next.—O, the garbage. She picked up the zinc pail a little gingerly, holding her face away from it, and put it on the dumbwaiter, then pulled on the grimy cord that made the dumbwaiter descend past the kitchenettes of the apartments below into the lowest region of all where the janitor was and a smell of coalgas from the furnace. After that, with a feeling of relief, Nan washed her hands and put her hat on in front of the pierglass in her bedroom, a hat of fine black straw without trimming that seemed to her to go very well with her light grey tailored suit. Pulling on her gloves, with a faint glow in her of anticipation of streets and movement and faces, she walked down the stairs.

Outside, the air was raw with a faint underlying rottenness of autumn. Nan walked briskly, rejoicing in the tap of her little heels on the even pavement, down a long street of brick apartments that merged into older brownstone houses with dusty steps and several bells beside the front door. The pianos were quieter than usual because it was Sunday, but occasionally the high voice of a girl doing her scales jerked out through a pair of muslin windowcurtains or there came the shriek of a violin being tuned. Down Commonwealth Avenue, the elms were losing their leaves. In the windows bloated chrysanthemum flowers stood up stiffly out of jardinieres. In the Public Garden, where there was still a bit of flame in the leaves of the trees, in front of a bench where sat an old man with his chin on a silverhandled cane beside a tiny grey woman in a porkpie hat, Nan found herself all of a sudden looking into the eager black eyes of Miss Fitzhugh.

"O, Nancibel, I'm so glad to see you."

Nan felt her fingers squeezed with sudden violence.

"Why, what's wrong?"

"Just let me tell you . . . O, I'm so upset. I haven't been able to practice a minute all day. I haven't been so upset since I broke off my engagement and sent Billy back his ring. . . . It's about Mabel Worthington."

"But Fitzie, who's Mabel Worthington?"

"I must have told you about her. She was such a lovely girl, one of our second violins. . . . Nancibel, you never pay any attention when I tell you things; I think it's mean of you. . . . O, it's too dreadful, and I'm just miserable about it. . . . Look, dear, won't you walk a little up Huntington Avenue? I was just going to get a soda . . . so soothing, you know, dear, and I know the nicest candy store just a block up."

As they followed the path towards the Unitarian Church between grass patches dappled with russet of leaves, Nan could feel the eyes of the men on the benches, eyes indolent after a bloating Sunday breakfast, dazzled by following the smudgy, sharpscented columns of Sunday newspapers, eyes blurred by Saturday night parties; their glances seemed to weave a warm shameful net to catch her wellpoised ankles and the erect slenderness of her figure closely tailored in grey tweed. Their glances were like sticky cobwebs in the woods. Fitzie was still talking.

"But you must have seen her, dear, the last time you went to hear us play. . . . You did go, didn't you, that time I sent you the ticket? You said you'd been. . . . She was to the left, beside the stage, just beside the first violin, a lovely girl with black, curly hair."

At the corner they threaded their way among groups of heavy-jowled people coming out of the church, men bristling with decorous stiffness, white points of starched collars, prickly scarfpins in satin of neckties, black curves of hats and gleaming shoetips, women fuzzy with boas and bits of fur and spotted veils.

"I had always thought," went on Fitzie's voice in a whine of dismay, "that she had a great future, and she seemed so much the best educated and . . . you know . . . most refined person there."

"But what's happened to her?"

"I must begin at the beginning. . . . You see, dear, it was this way. . . . O, this is it. What will you have, dear?"

A smell of sodawater and chocolate and polished nickel encompassed them about. They sat at a little white table on which was a lace doily covered by a round piece of plate glass.

A waitress in black with tight, starched bands at the wrists and waist hung over them.

"What are you having, dear?" said Fitzie again. "I'm goin' to have a banana split. I just love banana splits. Isn't it greedy of me? And before lunch, too."

"D'you know, if you don't mind, Fitzie, I won't take anything. I'm going to dine with Aunt M., and she always feeds one a dreadful lot of stuffing on Sundays. She has such old-fashioned ideas about food."

"Well, as I was telling you, Nancibel, the first time I guessed anything was wrong was about a month ago, when I noticed a young Italian waiting outside the stage door. I was in a hurry and didn't notice him until I'd brushed against him. He was very poorly dressed and smelt dreadfully of garlic, but I had to admit to myself that he was good looking, like a young Greek god!"

"Young Greek gods probably smelt of garlic too," said Nan, laughing.

The banana split had arrived in a boatshaped plate. Miss Fitzhugh took up a dab of whipped cream on her spoon.

"Won't you have just a taste, Nancibel? . . . No? O, you are a Puritan, dear. . . . Well, to make a long story short, one day last week I met them on Washington Street, Mabel Worthington and that dreadful Italian. I was brushing by, pretending not to see them. . . . I thought it would be less embarrassing for them, you understand, dear. . . . But not a bit of it, she stopped me and chatted for a minute, calm as a cucumber, and then she introduced me to him. . . . 'This is Giovanni,' she said, and that's all she said, though they both flushed crimson. He bobbed his head awkwardly at me and smiled, showing the most beautiful teeth. And that was all."

Fitzie was quiet for a minute and took three or four spoonfuls of yellow icecream in succession. She was talking in a rapid whisper, leaning far over the table towards Nan's unsmiling face.

"And yesterday morning she didn't turn up at rehearsal. And now it appears that she has gone off with him. Isn't it frightful? Because she was a lovely girl, really, a lovely girl. She reminded me of you."

"Well," said Nan, "she was probably in love with him."

"But I'm coming to the most dreadful part. . . . The wretched man had a wife and two squalling, filthy little babies. They came round to the theater and made a dreadful scene, a horrid, coarse woman just like an immigrant. . . . And he is nothing but a common laborer, just think of it. O, how can people do such things? It just makes me sick to think of that lovely girl in the power of that horrible, garlic-smelling ruffian. . . . It just makes me sick to think of it."

Miss Fitzhugh caught up the last yellow liquid on her plate with several swift, scraping little strokes of her spoon. She started delving with two fingers in the back compartment of her alligatorskin purse.

"Just think of it, Nancibel, a common laborer. If he'd been a musician or a composer or something, it would have been different, even if he was an Italian, but . . . O, Nancibel, won't you please let me have your hanky a sec, I declare I've lost mine."

Nan handed over her handkerchief.

"I suppose she's in love with him," she said. "It's a good thing she makes her own living."

"But don't you think it's dreadful?"

"How can we tell? But, anyway, I must run along. Aunt M. always expects me at twelve every Sunday, and she thinks I have come to some dreadful end if I don't get there on the dot."

Nan was out in the street again. A dusty wind had come up and was making dead leaves and scraps of newspapers dance in the gutters and tearing ragged holes in the clouds.—O, how poor Fitzie gets on my nerves, Nan was saying to herself, and a picture flashed through her mind of how Fitzie, her eyes wide, rapt, had said, pausing with her mouth open a little between the words, "Like a young Greek god."

She walked over to Beacon Street and down the row of houses that faces the Public Garden, looking now and then into front windows massed with ferns and autumn flowers. On small, wellcleaned windowpanes a reflection of sky and clouds, shadows of sombredressed people passing, fleeting glint of limousines, then, in a bay window beside a bunch of yellow, curlypetalled chrysanthemums the face of Aunt M. Nan thought how ashy and wrinkled it looked beside the yellow flowers. The face smiled and bobbed, showing a straight part and hair steelgrey slicked against the head on either side. Nan pulled
10   at the shining brass knob of the bell. Immediately the door opened.
"Yer late, Miss Nancibel; the missus was agettin' anxious an' alookin' outa the winder," said the old woman in flounced cap and apron metallic with starch who let her in.
"I'm not so awfully late, am I, Mary Ann?"
Pulling off her gloves, Nan brushed through portieres of salmoncolored brocade into the parlor.
"O, my dear Nancibel, how glad I am to see you," said Aunt M., throwing stubby arms round her niece's neck. Nan's lips touched the wrinkled, lifeless skin.
20   "I'm sorry to be late, Auntie."
"Well, one can't expect a budding virtuoso . . . I suppose one should say virtuosa . . . to be very punctual. And punctuality is fallen into disrepute among young people nowadays. . . . Now run up and take your things off like a good girl and come back quickly and talk to me so that we can have a good chat before the Turnstables come."
"Are they coming, Auntie?"
"Yes, Cousin Jane Turnstable and her boy and girl are coming to dinner at half after one. It's quite thrilling to have so many young people in the house."
30   Running up the thickcarpeted stairs, Nan caught herself remembering running up those same stairs when she was still in short skirts, a Scotch plaid it was, accordionpleated, that day, and Mary Ann was polishing the brass rails that kept the carpet down, and her Aunt M., a tall omnipotent person then, had told her not to sing "O My Darling Clementine," because it was a low, vulgar song, and somehow she hadn't been able to keep it in and had shouted out without meaning to:

Herring boxes without topses,
Sandals were for Clementine.

40   And Aunt M. had come out on the landing suddenly, very cold and sharptoned, and had made her stay in her room all afternoon and

learn "The Slave's Dream." As Nan went into the little room with
Dutch blue wallpaper, which Aunt M. always called Nancibel's room,
to throw her hat on the bed and give a hasty pat to her hair in front of
the mirror,

> Beside the ungathered rice he lay,
> His sickle in his hand,

bubbled up from somewhere deep in her mind. She smiled, thinking
how as the years had passed her relation to Aunt M. had changed,
until now it was she who seemed the tall, omnipotent person, skilled
in all the world outside the house, and her aunt the timid one the   10
housewalls protected from the shaggy world.

"Well, dear, what have you been up to all the week?" said Aunt M.
when Nan had run down the stairs and back into the parlor. "I hope
you haven't been gadding about a lot, like last week."

"Not a gad," said Nan, laughing. They sat side by side on the
curvebacked sofa in front of the window. Nan was looking down at
Aunt M.'s old hands swollen at the knuckles that lay halfclenched on
the full, mauve satin of her dress. In her nostrils was a tang from the
chrysanthemums.

"And how's your practicing?"   20

"Pretty good this week."

"You know how I feel about your music, Nancibel." There was a
flame of blue in Aunt M.'s hazel eyes.

"You mustn't put too much faith in it," said Nan roughly. She went
on hastily in a high, nervous voice like her voice when she had people
to tea: "Practiced every day but Thursday. Worked to a frazzle, really.
How the neighbors must hate me. And there's somebody two floors
down who plays the cornet all the morning, so we do a sort of distant
duet with the effect quite . . . modern."

"Why didn't you practice Thursday, dear?"   30

"I went out to Nahant with Fanshaw and Wendell to see the surf.
There was a wonderful nor'easter blowing."

"You see a lot of those two young men."

"Of course I do. . . . But, Auntie, what have you been doing?
When did you get the chrysanthemums? They're lovely."

"You can't get me off the track that way," said Aunt M. with a sly
smile. "Which of them is it, Nancibel?"

"No, it's different from that. . . . O, I can't explain it." Nan saw
herself and Wenny and Fanshaw running arm in arm on the turf at the
cliffedge, leaning against the wind, the taste of spray on their lips.   40

"It's so difficult to classify feelings. That's what Wenny says. . . . O,
you wouldn't understand, Auntie."

Nan felt the old woman beside her wince.

"O, I didn't mean that; Aunt M., why am I so dreadfully inconsiderate?"

"I wonder why Cousin Jane Turnstable doesn't come. I hope they
won't be late. It upsets poor Judkins so to have to keep dinner hot."
As she spoke her grey lips trembled like a child's.

They were silent.—O, I must think of something to talk about, Nan
10 was saying over and over again in her mind. She was staring at the
little Corot that hung beside the mantel. A poplar overhanging water,
greywhite like milkweed silk.

"Do you remember, Auntie, when I was a little girl what esctasies I
used to go into over that little picture? When you used to tell me
about abroad, I used to think of everything as pale green and silver
grey, like that picture."

"A funny, impatient little girl you were," said Aunt M. softly. "Poor
Maria used to worry so about your tantrums, but I used to reassure
her by saying it was merely temperament and that you'd be a great
20 artist some day. . . . If she had only been spared to us to hear you
play. . . ."

The door bell rang.

"There they are," said Nan with relief.

"And they are not late after all. Punctual to the minute . . . O, my
dear Cousin Jane, how glad I am to see you. And James you've grown,
I declare. . . . Helen, you'll kiss your old cousin, won't you, dear?"

Cousin Jane Turnstable was a tall woman with silvery hair caught up
smoothly under a broad hat. Her eyebrows were black, and her face
had all over the same unwrinkled, milky texture as her cheeks. The
30 boy and girl were both blonde and very thin. They all stood in a group
in the center of the buff and blue carpet of the parlor, and the voices of
the Turnstables chimed softly together like well-attuned bells against
Nan's deep voice and the quavering voice of her aunt.

"Nancibel, you won't mind showing Cousin Jane and Cousin Helen
where they can take their things off, will you, dear?" said Aunt M. At
the same moment Mary Ann came through the sliding doors that led
to the dining room and announced solemnly: "Dinner's on the table,
mum."

"This is nice," said Aunt M. when they were all seated round the
40 table, where amid a glitter of silverware the creases stood up stiffly in
the heavily starched linen cloth: "Quite like old times." And as Nan
let the brown croutons slide off the spoon into the tomato bisque, a
heartbreaking lassitude came over her—I'm twenty-eight and every

seventh day of my life I must have done this. Twenty-eight by fifty-two, what does that make? But some one was speaking to her. "And how did you enjoy September at Squirrel Island?" Cousin Jane Turnstable was asking in her musical voice.

After dinner with the thickness of over-rich icecream still in their mouths, they went into the parlor for coffee.

"I suppose I shall never go abroad again," Aunt M. was saying. "My traveling days are over. But if I did, it would be to take for one last time that drive from Sorrento to Amalfi when the lemon trees are in bloom. . . . I'm afraid it is a little blasphemous to say it, but I can't imagine heaven more beautiful. You surely have taken that drive, Nancibel."

"I've never been south of Florence, Auntie." With bitter poignance she sat remembering the smell of lemontrees. She was moving the spoon round her small cup of coffee with a slow movement of long fingers. She thought of Fitzie eating banana split and telling about the girl who'd run off with an Italian smelling of garlic like a young Greek god. Poor Fitzie, who had none of that in her life, always making up romances for other people.

"I seem to remember," Aunt M. went on, "having heard Phillips Brooks say that no one could really feel the beauty of such sights and remain an unbeliever."

"Ah, yes, so true," said Cousin Jane Turnstable.

"O dear," said James, his voice breaking.

Nan looked up at him suddenly. His face was crimson. He had spilt half a cup of coffee over his neatlypressed grey trousers. Nan took the cup out of his hand and set it on the mantel while he sheepishly fumbled for the spoon on the floor.

"No harm done," she said. "Come upstairs; it'll wash right out. I'll give you a cloth to rub it with."

"I'm afraid you think I'm dreadfully dumb, Cousin Nancibel. That was the dumbest thing to do," he said in tearful voice going up the stairs.

"Nonsense. I might have done it myself," she answered, laughing. "Anything to break up the monotony of Sunday afternoon! . . . Right in here, James. You sit on the bathtub and hold it tight. I'll rub it with a little soap. Here's a cloth."

The boy did as he was told.

"Why, that'll come right out. You'll never notice it," said Nan briskly rubbing the cloth held against his thin thigh.

"You don't like Sunday either." His eyes looked up into hers with a sudden flash.

She wrinkled up her nose and he laughed.

From the wet, woolly cloth came up a rough little smell like from Wenny's homespun. As she thought of Wenny, she felt herself flushing hotly. The boy looked up at her hard for a second and then the flush suffused his fair skin until he was red in his ears and in the roots of his flaxen hair.

"That'll do," said Nan gruffly. "No one will notice it now." She walked hurriedly to the stairs and down.

"You'll play for us a bit, Nancibel?" said her Aunt when she was back in the parlor.

10   "All right. You'll accompany won't you?"

She brushed past James without looking at him as she went into the hall to fetch her violin. She was furious at herself for having blushed. As she leaned over to unstrap the violin case, the blood pounded in her temples and filled her eyes so that she could scarcely see. The blood in her ears was the sound of the grindorgan playing "The Wearing of the Green" after tea yesterday, when Wenny's cheek had been beside her cheek and they had looked at the throbbing star in the west. She tossed her head back and stood for a moment, her teeth firm together, the violin in one hand and bow in the other.—And the

20   girl who played the violin in the Fadettes had run off with an Italian who smelt of garlic like a young Greek god. O, Fitzie's a romantic fool.

"How well you are looking today," said Aunt M. from the pianostool. "Shall it be Bach, Nancibel?"

*   *   *

A yellow mist had come in off the harbor during the evening so that walking home after the concert the streets were dim and unfamiliar and each arclight had a ruddy halo. Nan walked beside Fanshaw, whose greenish raincoat made him look taller and thinner even than usual. Ahead of them they could hear Wenny and Betty Thomas laughing together.

30   "What do you think of Betty?" Nan was saying in a low voice.

"She's your latest discovery, isn't she? . . . A trifle . . . er . . . unconscious I should say. No harm in her . . . I wish she hadn't such a burr in her voice."

"O, you are chilly."

"I didn't mean to be so pompous. She seems to like music. So rare in a musician."

Nan laughed.

"You seem to be feeling very superior this evening, Fanshaw. What have you done to be so cocky?"

40   "Little enough, God knows . . . Nan, I wish we could get Wenny

settled somehow. I'm worried about him. He ought to get to work at
something more definite."

"But he's so enormously alive, Fanshaw. How can one worry about
him? O, if I had half his vitality, sensitiveness . . ."

"So much of that is sheer nerves . . . in a man. In you it's different.
There's something rock bottom about women that men haven't at all.
We are lichen. If we are too alive we burn up and shrivel. . . . I
wonder if he isn't a little too alive."

"Nonsense."

"Do you know you do us a lot of good, Nan?"

"If you think, young man, that I'm going to be anybody's rock of
ages, you are mistaken, I can tell you that."

The others were waiting for them at a corner where a drugstore sent
planes of white and greenish light slanting to the mud-filmed pavement.

"This is my street, people," said Betty Thomas.

"But we'll take you to your door. Remember the holdups," said
Wenny with a laugh.

"It'ld be so dreadfully exciting to be held up."

"It's on my way home anyway, Betty." Nan took the girl's arm and
pulled her with her across the street. The two men followed them up a
street of apartment houses where patches of lighted windows made a
yellow blur in the fog above their heads. Before the word Swarthcote
they stopped.

"Good night all," said Betty Thomas. "Thank you, deary, for the
lovely supper and everything."

The door closed behind her. With Nan in the middle, the three of
them walked on.

"How cozy it is this way in the fog," she said.

"It makes me feel wonderfully sentimental," Wenny said slowly.
"Wagner makes me feel sentimental anyway, but Wagner plus fog . . .
like sitting on the curbstone and letting great warm tears roll down
one's cheeks till the gutter simply gurgled with them."

"I say," said Fanshaw.

"Not a bit of it," broke in Nan. "I feel jolly, like roasting apples in
front of an open fire. We're so secure all three of us together this way
and the world drifting by, dinner at Aunt M.'s and tomato bisque and
croutons . . . and love and hate and all that outside drifting by like
fog."

"Harmless you mean, Nan. I shouldn't say so. . . . Do you think it's
harmless, Wenny?"

"Maybe for some people, Fanshaw."

"No, I don't mean that. O, you are so lackadaisical, Fanshaw," Nan

said bitterly. "I mean something more active. . . . The three of us
conquering, shutting the fog and the misery out, all that helpless
against us. But I'm talking like a book."

"You are a little, Nan," said Wenny very gently.

Nan felt what she wanted to say slipping out of her mind, ungrasp-
able. The three of them walked on in silence, arm in arm, with Nan in
the middle. Beginnings of sentences flared and sputtered out in her
mind like damp fireworks. Slowly the yellow fog, the cold, enormous
fog that had somehow a rhythm of slow, vague swells out at sea sifted
in upon her, blurred the focus of herself that had been for a moment
intensely sharp. She so wanted to say something that would make that
moment permanent, that would pin down forever the sudden harmony of the three of them so that she could always possess it, no
matter what happened after. Epigram, that was the word. There had
been Greeks who had cut the flame of an instant deep on stone in
broad letters for centuries to read.

"I wish we could walk like this always."

Her throat was dry. At the sound of her thin voice, all her thoughts
scuttled into the dark like cockroaches in a kitchen cupboard. Her
mind smoothed to vacancy.

"How do you mean?" asked Wenny.

"Well, here we are," said Fanshaw in a singsong tone.

"The Swansea," in gold Gothic letters shaded with black, stared at
her from a wide glass door. Beyond white steps another glass door,
unmarked. Nan remembered how she used to feel when she was a
child and people were getting ready to go into dinner and bedtime
came. She turned her back on the sourly familiar letters. Opposite, a
few twigs of trees leaned into the warm tent of light from a streetlamp
out of dark immensity of fog. The light slanting out through the glass
door gave a gleam on Fanshaw's glasses that hid his eyes. She pressed
ever so slightly his long, limp hand and Wenny's hard hand. Wenny's
face was flushed from the rawness of the fog, and there was a glint in
his eyes that made her catch her breath joyously. She wanted to say
something. They turned away, raised their hands vaguely and walked
off. Fanshaw had leaned over and said something to Wenny that had
made him laugh. The door closed behind her. She had a glimpse of
the letters "The Swansea" inside out. She took her key out of her
purse and unlocked the inner door. She hated Fanshaw, his glasses
that hid his eyes, his long, limp hands. They had gone off carelessly,
laughing. And Wenny, too, with the grime round his collar and his
shambling walk like an Italian laborer's. She pushed open the sliding
door of the elevator that had a familiar everyday smell of dust and

machine oil. The door slid to behind her. She put her finger on the
button marked 4.—It was the girl in the Fadettes who had gone off
with a brown man, garlicky, with bright teeth like the Greeks' were
who made epigrams. Nan closed her eyes as the elevator started to
rise. She was very tired.

III

J . FANSHAW MACDOUGAN'S left shoe pinched the upper part of his foot, and a damp chill from the fog-moistened pavement seeped through the thin soles as he walked with long strides beside Wenny. These things gave a vaguely peevish whine to the flow of thoughts through his head.—If only I had the money, he was thinking, I would have ten pairs of shoes and a valet to wear them until they were comfortable. The form of an advertisement in a paper started into his head: Wanted—a valet, must wear No. 9 shoes, best references required; and himself in a dressing gown of pale-colored silk looking over the applicants from a great, tapestried easychair.—O, how one could live if one had the money, and the people who had it never seemed to know how to use it, except Mrs. Jack Gardner in her Italian palace.

"I was thinking what I'd do if I had a million dollars, Wenny."

Wenny turned, his eyes snapping, and laughed. The glimpse of his face laughing tilted up into the full, white glare of an arclight lingered in Fanshaw's eyes and faded, the way a stranger's face out of a crowd would sometimes linger and fade.—Nan's face, too, the profile as she turned to put her key in the lock of the glass door, was still sharp in his mind, behind it a memory of the smell extraordinarily warm, honied, artificial of the flowers among the pictures in Mrs. Gardner's gallery in the Italian palace. Strange that Nan should have worn a hat like that this evening. Unbecoming, made her look like a schoolteacher. The New England in her coming out. Such a wonderful person had no right to look that way. That night at the fancy dress dance at the Logans she had looked her best, her face oval, Sienese, and the hair tight back from her forehead under a jewelled net, like a girl by a Lombard painter. There had been such distinction in the modelling of her forehead and cheekbones and her slender neck among all those panting, pigeonbreasted women. How rarely people were themselves. Out of the corner of an eye, he glanced at Wenny walking beside him with short steps, doggedly, his face towards the ground.—A trio we are, Nan and Wenny and I, a few friends my only comfort in this great, snarling waste of a country. We don't fit here. We are like people floating down a stream in a barge out of a Canaletto carnival, gilt and dull vermilion, beautiful, lean-faced people of the Renaissance lost in a marsh, in a stagnant canal overhung by black walls and towering steel girders. One could make a poem or an essay out of that idea, some people could; Wenny, if he weren't such a lazy little brute. Why couldn't I?

"Didn't you think Nan looked tired tonight?" asked Wenny suddenly.

Fanshaw was loath to break into the rhythm of his thoughts.

"I did," said Wenny again.

"Why should she be tired? She hasn't worked very hard this week." 10

Wenny said nothing. The street was muffled by the fog all about them. In Fanshaw's mind were phrases from Lamb, vague thoughts of fogs over London. They came out on the springy boards of the bridge that seemed to sway ever so little under their feet. The fog above the river was denser and colder. Their steps were loud on the slats of the sidewalk. Halfway over they passed a man and a girl, bodies cleaving together so that they made a single silhouette. Fanshaw caught Wenny's backward glance after them.—Rather unhealthy, the interest in those things, he thought. Further along they heard a regular heavy tread coming towards them, a policeman. 20

"He'll break their clinch," said Wenny, giggling. Fanshaw was annoyed.—Vulgar, he thought, why notice such things? Other ages perhaps had put beauty, romance in them: Paolo and Francesca floating cloudy through limbo.

"These last few days I have been often thinking of that passage, Pico della Mirandola riding into Florence in the time of lilies. Then it would have been less futile to be alive."

"How do you know, Fanshaw?"

"You have no nostalgia of the past, have you, Wenny? It's that things were so much cleaner, fresher. Everything wasn't so muddled and 30 sordid then."

"Can't things always have been muddled and sordid? I think they were."

"Those people on the bridge and you giggling at them. I can't understand it, it's so low."

"Then, by God, you can't understand anything." Wenny's voice broke; he was angry and walked faster. Fanshaw thought of a phrase out of *The Book of Tea;* a man without tea was a man without poise, refinement. Wenny had no tea. How amusing his rages were. They went along without speaking. In the bright circle of each arclight, he 40 glanced at Wenny's sullen face, the prominent lips, the strangely soft-textured cheeks, the slightness of the waist under the shirt that bagged at the belt revealed by the flapping, unbuttoned coat, the

clenched, swinging hands. There were puddles in the road. It was dark between arclights, a few glows from windows loomed distant among weighty shadows. Shadowy forms seemed to move slouchingly just out of sight. Fanshaw felt he was walking unawares through all manner of lives, complications of events. Thought of holdups brought a vague fear into his mind.—Footpads. There ought to be more lights. If it weren't for these wretched Irish politicians who ran things . . . When they crossed the railway tracks, there were little red and green lights in the fog, the wail of an engine far away. A bell began to ring,
10 and the old man dozing in a little shack with a red and a green flag propped against his knees jumped to his feet. Like Rembrandt the shadows, thought Fanshaw. The bar came down behind them. Lights flashed on the track, and they could hear down towards Cambridgeport the chug of a locomotive and the slow bumping of the wheels of freightcars over a crossing.

"Let's stop and watch it go past," said Wenny.

"No, my feet are wet."

They walked on.

"I think I'll try an' get a job on a section gang on the railway this
20 summer, Fanshaw."

"A fine Italian laborer you'd make, Wenny; why you would never get up early enough, and think of the food and the bunkhouses, fearful!"

"I think I'd like it for a while."

Through chinks in the great bulk of the Armory, light and a racket of voices trickled out into the fog like sand out of a cart.

"I guess it's a dance," said Wenny.

The day that Ficino finished his great work—translating Plato was it?—Pico della Mirandola rode into Florence and the lilies were in
30 bloom, Fanshaw was thinking, and wondering whether he would have enough money to go abroad comfortably next summer.—If I could only leave Mother.

"For cris' sake lemme walk between yez a sec," came a breathless voice from behind them.

Fanshaw hastened his stride. His muscles were tense. A holdup.

"Walk slow like. Lemme walk between yez for cris'sake."

Fanshaw looked desperately up the long straight street towards the glare of Central Square. Not a policeman, of course. The man walked panting between them with red sweating face stuck forward. Fanshaw
40 dropped back a step and came up on the outside of Wenny.

"What's the trouble?" Wenny was saying.

"Hell to pay . . . Fight in the Armory, see? I don't know what it was about. . . . I was lookin' at two fellows fightin', an' a guy, a big, tall

guy, comes up to me an' says, 'Well, what about it?' Then he called me
a sonofabitch. . . . I guess he was a Catholic, one of them South
Boston guys. I hit 'im in the jaw, see? An' then I saw the bulls comin'
an' I beat it. You don't care if I walk between yez, just to the corner?"

"Of course not," said Wenny.

At the first corner, the man left them.

"I'll run along to home and Mother now," he said.

"Wasn't that rich," cried Wenny laughing. "Say, suppose we go
back to see what's happening."

"The policemen would probably arrest us as accessories. You don't   10
believe that man's story, do you? Probably a burglar making off."

"You are an old sourbelly this evening. What's the matter?" Wenny
hopped and skipped along beside him roaring with laughter.

"I am rather depressed. Music depresses me."

They had reached the long, brightly-lighted oblong of Central
Square where the fog was thinned by the shine of the plateglass
windows of cheap furniture stores and the twisted glint of tinware in
the window of Woolworth's. Young men loafed on the edge of the
sidewalk, and stumpy girls chattered in the doorways of candy shops.

"Where were you born, Fanshaw? I can't seem to remember."   20

"Why?"

"I was thinking up where people I knew were born. Nan was born
in Boston, Beacon Hill. . . . Central Square would be a comical place
to be born."

"You knew perfectly well I was born in Omaha. You just want the
satisfaction of hearing me say it."

Scraps of talk kept impinging upon them as they threaded through
the groups on the sidewalk, giggles of young girls, kidding intonations
of men.

"I only lived there until I was twelve," Fanshaw was saying. In his   30
ears rang the phrase: An' I gave her one swell time. "Then my father
died and Mother moved East. She'd always wanted to live in Boston.
The day we were settled in our little house in Brookline, she brought
me in on the car to see the Abbey paintings. She was bound I'd take
to the arts."

"By the way, how is your mother now?"

"About the same, Wenny. Poor lamb, I'm afraid she never will get
much better. She's so patient about it."

They were out of the square, walking past dwelling houses set back
from the road. A smell of leaves and autumnal earth came to them. In   40
Fanshaw's mind was the picture of a grey head against a pillow, heavy,
despairing wrinkles from the nose to the ends of the mouth, where
was a wry, peevish twitch of pain; his mother shapeless in a lilac

dressing gown propped up in the easy chair in the library amid a faint, stale smell of cologne and medicines.

"I wonder if it will always be like this, this meaningless round of things. It would have been if I hadn't met you, Wenny."

"D'you mean I'm a horrible example to keep you on the straight paths of virtue?" said Wenny harshly. He shook off Fanshaw's hand that was on his arm and thrust his hands deep into his pockets.

"When I'm with you, I feel as if there were something I could do about life. Remember the passage about 'to burn with a hard, gemlike flame'?"

Wenny grunted.

"We must get something graceful and beautiful into it if we die in the attempt. I haven't the energy. . . . I'm going to talk about myself, you can't stop me, Wenny. . . . Mother has a curio cabinet. You know it, in the corner of the drawing room with the shepherd à la Watteau painted on the panel. Out in Nebraska when I was little I used to spend hours looking at the things: a filigree gondola from Venice, the Sistine Madonna in mosaic, carved wooden goats from somewhere in Switzerland, the Nuremberg goose boy . . . you know all those desperate little mid-Victorian knick-knacks put in the cabinet so that they won't have to be dusted. I think my mind is like that. It opens. You can put things in and they stay there, but nothing moves. That's why I am so appropriate to the groves of academe. . . . You're dynamic."

"A damn bundle of frustrations, that's all I am, Fanshaw, if you only knew. Funny how we each think the other has the inside dope on things. . . . My father had it about God or thinks he had. He is sure of himself anyway. Only man I ever knew who was."

"But you are sure of yourself."

"The hell I am . . . Let's have a drink. I am fearfully thirsty."

"What you wanting, a soda?"

Wenny laughed. They went into a candy store that was thick with the smell of fresh-cooked chocolate. A boy with tow hair and a pimply face was washing glasses. Fanshaw found himself staring with a faint internal shudder at the red knuckles as his fingers moved round swiftly in glass after glass under the faucet. They drank orangeade in silence; Wenny paid the girl behind the cash register, who showed two gold teeth in a smile as they went out. Fanshaw was already thinking with eager anticipation of his room with its orange-shaded lamp: the cozy, bookish smell of it, the backs of his books in their case of well-dusted mahogany and the discreet sheen of the gold letters of titles in the lamplight, the sepia Primavera over the mantel, the neatness of his bedroom, the linen sheets on his bed, the clean aloofness of fresh pajamas.

"I often wonder why I go out in the evenings at all."

"Why not?"

"Things seem to me so ugly now, all this rasping and grinding. It used not to be so when I was in college, but now it makes me feel so unpleasantly futile. When I'm in my room with everything about me as I have grouped it, I feel futile too, but pleasantly futile, artistically futile."

"Fanshaw, that's all utter rot."

"That's no argument, Wenny, to call a thing rot."

"But it's rot just the same."   10

They walked along silent again.—How hopeless to make oneself understood. Through the sting of bitterness Fanshaw remembered the first time he had seen Wenny. He had sat beside him in a classroom in front of the yellow varnished desk of the instructor. There was the dry smell of chalk and outside lilacs swayed against a blue sky full of little rosy clouds; the hideous lassitude of words in an even voice that smelt of chalk and blackboards, and beside him a thin, brownfaced boy with moist, brown eyes intent on everything, on the chalky words of the instructor, on the lilacs outside, on the swallows that flashed against the sky. And now they walked back side by side   20
towards Cambridge as they had walked hundreds of other nights at about this hour, and his arm touched Wenny's arm occasionally as it swung. Was it four years, five years, they had known each other? Hopeless all these futile walks, this constant juggling of words. Wenny's stride was even with his stride now; occasionally the backs of their hands touched as they swung. For all they could tell each other, they might be on different continents. Fanshaw felt frozen in ferocious loneliness. And now there was Nan. The thought that he might love her, that he might be losing himself to her, sent a trembling through him that he tried to brush aside.   30

"Strange how we are all settling down," he said. All the while he was thinking of love, his boyish idea of love elegant over teacups, suppertables on terraces at Capri, a handing of old-fashioned bouquets with a rose in the center, red rose of passion, romaunt of the rose.

"I haven't settled down," said Wenny, savagely. "I wish I had."

In a smoker once Fanshaw had overheard a story about a rose. The recollection brought a curious little feeling of sickness, stale cigar smoke and smutty eyes in a leer, flabby jowls laughing.

"I mean all our group at college," he heard himself saying.   40

"What else can they do, they've none of them the guts to do anything or be anything. . . . Nan hasn't settled down."

"I was going to say. She has just started on the rampage."

"That's because she is a woman. They go on developing. Men don't."

They were walking up Mt. Auburn Street. A group of boys passed them, striding jauntily, chattering in high voices. Fanshaw caught the eager tilt of heads, the smooth contours of faces in the green lamplight. There was a catch in his voice.

"How like a ghost it makes you feel," he said.

"Do you mean you wish you were back there again?"

"After all, youth is the only thing."

"If there is anything in my life I bitterly resent, it is that. The time I wasted in college. . . . Sentimentality about youth is the cheapest of all sentimentalities."

"Won't you come in a minute? Here we are."

Wenny shook his head.

They stood irresolute a moment on the doorstep.

"Do come up and tell me what you mean. You so rarely commit yourself to an arguable statement like that. . . . I'm open to conviction of almost anything."

"I must go along home," said Wenny. He turned, raising an arm, and walked fast down the street.

The stairs creaked under the carpet as Fanshaw climbed slowly, two steps at a time, to his room. He turned the key and went in. Objects were illuminated by a swath of light from the arclight at the corner that cut through the curtains and made a bright oblong on the ceiling. On the broad desk beside the window, papers gleamed white and an inkbottle gave a glint of jet. Fanshaw pulled down the shades of the two windows and clicked on the reading lamp on the desk. Examination books in blue covers made a neat pile on one corner. On another were bundles of folded papers held tight by elastics. In the center were many pencils and pens of different colors in a shallow copper tray. Fanshaw felt the peevish despair slipping off him. He went into the alcove where the bed was, took off his shoes and coat slowly, thinking of nothing, his eyes following the twisting figures on the chintz window curtains. Then he walked across the floor to the bookcase, his feet at ease in slippers, and pulled aside the blue silk curtain that kept the dust off his books. For a long time he contemplated the colored oblongs of their backs, the gilt and black and red type of titles, deciding what he should read.

*   *   *

The air was raw. Clouds, ruddy from the glare of arclights, sagged like awnings over the streets. The three of them were walking briskly down an oozy, black alley near the market.

"Where are you taking us, Wenny?" said Nan. She rested a greygloved hand on Fanshaw's arm for a moment as she stepped over a pile of fruitskins on the curb.

"You said you wanted a walk before dinner"; Wenny sauntered ahead, talking over his shoulder.

"We are getting it. I didn't know there were so many streets in Boston, did you, Nan?" Fanshaw spoke with a little sniggering laugh. The ooze of grimy, unfamiliar lives out of these dark houses oppressed him.—Unhealthy it must be down here. Typhoid, consumption, ty-phus, diphtheria. He felt himself putting his feet down gently as he walked as if he feared that at a loud step the pulpy darkness would burst suddenly into oaths and shouts, dirty hands clutching at his coat and whisky-steaming faces thrust into his.

"Now you know where you are," said Wenny.

They had come out into the shine and scuttle of Hanover Street, where men and women, dark, bulky shadows in overcoats and mufflers and bits of fur, flitted constantly past the broad show-windows bright with intricate glints on shoes and hardware and sourish colors in clothing stores and gleaming cascades of cheap jewelry over black velvet under the three ominous gold balls of pawnbrokers.

"Gee, I'm glad it's Saturday night!"

"Why, Wenny?" Fanshaw stood on the curb beside Nan, blinking a little, dazzled by the noise and hustle.

"Because it's Saturday night, you old owl. . . . This way."

"You aren't going to take us into more dark alleys and get us black-jacked for your entertainment, are you, Wenny?"

"I'm going to give you the best bottle of white wine you ever had in your life. Here we are."

"VENICE" read Fanshaw on the window.—Stood in Venice by the Bridge of Sighs, a prison and a palace on each hand. Byron; rather a rotter he must have been, or perhaps passionate, implusive, hot, like Wenny. The verdict of history.

They were sitting at a round table in the window. The waiter, a grey, eggshaped man with sagging pockets under his eyes and a sagging vest too large for him, was bending over the table. The others were ordering. How ravishing Nan was tonight in a black dress with great spots of burnt orange embroidery; her eyes under the small black hat trimmed with the same color were full of little green sparks.

"I swear, Nan," Wenny was saying, "you are the only woman in this blooming town who knows how to dress."

"Where did you get that dress, anyway? I have never seen it before," chimed in Fanshaw. He had a vague feeling of pique at not having said it first. Nan and Wenny seemed to get along so well this evening. He felt out of place down here in the slums. The food would probably be horrid.

"This is delightful, Wenny," Nan was saying. "What I want to know is why have you never brought us here before?"

The lint from the napkin came off on Fanshaw's blue serge suit.— What a mess. Mechanically he started wiping off the knife and fork when the waiter set them down before him.

"Like in Europe," he said aloud. "You must forgive me, Wenny, but
10   I am suspicious of this famous restaurant of yours."

"And look there, a fiasco, just like in Italy," cried Nan. "Why this is wonderful."

"Genuine Orvieto, Miss," said the waiter solemnly.

"And look at the gondola. . . . Fanshaw, do get over being cross and look at the gondola at the foot of the stairs, with a lantern in it too."

"That's for the orchestra. They'll be here in a minute, a ladies' three-piece band as I heard a man call them one night. One of them's awfully good-looking."

Fanshaw looked about the room. At another table a man and a
20   woman were eating intently. They had sallow, puffy faces and looked into each other's eyes as they stuffed their mouths with spaghetti;— depraved looking, thought Fanshaw. Probably Byron had been like that, a puffyfaced man, signs of dissipation. If it hadn't been for drink and women . . . Why couldn't people be beautiful about life?

"Here they come," cried Nan and Wenny at the same moment.

Three women in white were behind the gondola prow tuning up their instruments. All at once with a nervous rush, they started strumming away at "O Sole Mio," with piano, cello and violin.

In the back of Fanshaw's mind were pictures of how he would have
30   lived if he had had as much money as Lord Byron; a palazzo in Venice exquisitely hung with faded silk brocades, bedrooms with old rose and dull gold upholstery, and everything according to period, no jarring note, a villa on Fiesole hill, smothered in flowers, with, in the distance, the russet roofs of Florence and the great dome.

"Nan, do you see the girl who's playing the violin?" whispered Wenny. "That's the girl I meant. She's lovely, isn't she? She's a little like you."

"Wenny, you are seeing things through the Orvieto, but she is beautiful."
40   "It's her lips and chin that are rather like yours."

"Musician's lips," said Fanshaw a little pompously. "Do you like those little snippets of veal, Nan? I don't. Too much garlic. We'll taste it for a week."

"Why, it's fine," cried Wenny uproariously. "It'll put hair on your chest."

"I wonder," Nan was speaking slowly, "I wonder if that could be the girl Fitzie was telling me about. I rather think Fitzie said she looked like that."

"Who?"

"The violinist . . . Must be a month ago, I met Fitzie one day all excited about something. Poor Fitzie does take life so hard. She told me a long cock-and-bull story that ended by impressing me a great deal about a girl in the Fadettes. . . ."   10

At the mention of the Fadettes, Wenny laughed himself red in the face.

"Children should be seen and not heard, Wenny," went on Nan in an even, amused voice. "About a girl in the Fadettes who eloped with an Italian boy and how his wife went round to the theater dragging a lot of squalling children and made a fearful scene. Fitzie couldn't understand how anyone could wreck their chances of a career like that. It would be wonderful if this were the girl."

"What would you have done?" asked Wenny eagerly, leaning over the table.   20

"If I had been the girl? How can I know? I wonder sometimes if just the wanting so hard to succeed wouldn't make you throw the whole thing away in one mad moment. It's hard to explain."

"Sure, I know what you mean. No, but about the Italian?"

"What a silly question, Wenny," said Fanshaw.

"Perhaps not so silly. Who can tell?" muttered Nan turning towards Wenny.

They were silent a moment. The orchestra was playing "The Soldiers' Chorus." The waiter brought coffee.

"And another bottle," said Wenny jauntily.   30

Fanshaw frowned. They had had enough to drink. What a child Wenny was, anyway. With unexpected tenderness he pictured himself putting him to bed drunk, unlacing his shoes, pulling off his trousers. A sudden desire came to him to draw a hand over Wenny's crisp, short hair.

"There is something strangely, fantastically dismal about that gondola with its red light as an end to romance. I wonder where those stairs go."

Nan nodded her head.

"That's what I meant. I wonder if she is the girl. . . . No, Wenny,   40
I'm glad you brought us here, even if we shall taste garlic for a week."

"At least there is the satisfaction of having busted loose," said Wenny eagerly, "for the girl, I mean."

"I never can understand the amazing way people put themselves out to be miserable." Fanshaw found himself suddenly welling with bitter irritation.

"But, by God!" cried Wenny. "You have to put yourself out to live at all; every damn moment of your life you have to put yourself out not to fossilize. Most people are mere wax figures in a show window. Have you seen a dredger ever, a lot of buckets in a row on a chain going up an inclined plane? That's what people are, tied in a row on the great dredger of society. . . . I want to be a bucket standing on my own bottom, alone. . . . Why are you laughing, Nan?"

"You are so eager about it, Wenny, dear."

"What in hell would you be eager about if not that?"

"Why be too eager about anything?" put in Fanshaw in his most languid voice.

"O, you make me tired, Fanshaw."

Fanshaw flushed.—The little rat, he thought, I'd like to smack him for being so silly. If he could get all that energy into something worthwhile. That's the difference between us and people like Pico della Mirandola or Petrarch. They could get all that energy into thought, art for the liberation of the world. We fritter it in silly complications. What a clever idea; if he could only make Wenny understand that.

"That's where my music comes in," Nan was saying, her voice grown suddenly tense as Wenny's. "By living it, by making myself great in it, I can bust loose of this fearful round of existence. What a wonderful phrase that is, the wheel of karma! I understand why women throw themselves head over heels at the most puny man. They have got to escape, if only for a moment, from the humdrum, all the little, silly objects, pots and pans and spools of thread that make up our lives. I've got to get that in my music. Nothing else matters."

Fanshaw was thinking for some reason of Dürer's portrait of himself at the age of twenty-eight. Such grace and dignity. There was a man who had never needed to break loose. They must have been less tied to the wheel in those days.

"But you always have to pay the piper, Nan," Wenny said. "It's no use trying to escape that. It's fearfully dangerous to live. I should say music was less safe than love."

"Not if you use your reason, Wenny," said Fanshaw.

"Who ever had any reason to use? It's an illusion, the result of thinking things over after they've happened."

Nan left the table. Fanshaw found himself glaring indignantly at Wenny.

"Gee, isn't Nan beautiful to look at tonight?"

"O, she is!" said Fanshaw, smiling with forced frankness. He felt a tumult like frightened pigeons in a box inside him. Heavens, suppose he was in love with Nan!

Nan came down the redcarpeted stairs beside the piano, pulling on her gloves. She stood a moment talking to the girls in the orchestra.

Fanshaw leaned across the table.

"Wenny, don't you think you had better not drink any more?"

"What the hell business is it of yours? Haven't had half enough to drink."

Nan came back to the table, a little sociable smile still playing about the corners of her mouth.

"Well, shall we go?" she said briskly.

"Look! Look outside!" cried Wenny; "it's beginning to snow."

In the black space above the muslin curtain that screened the window, they could see big flakes gently, breathlessly tumbling.

"Thank you, sir; come again, sir," said the waiter as he let the tip slide into one of the pockets of his sagging vest.

They were out in the snowhushed streets, the snow brushing their cheeks with occasional feathery gentleness like tips of wings of very cold birds.

"Did you ask her?" said Wenny.

"No. I shall next time. She's awfully nice." Nan was buttoning the fur round her neck.

"Do you want to taxi?" asked Fanshaw, who had thin shoes on.

"Ridiculous, let's walk. I love this, anyway. Don't you, Wenny?"

The black pavement shivered in squirms and lozenges of yellow and red and green light under the feet of people scuttling home out of the wet. All the sharpness of lights and colors and sounds was padded and blotched by the slow flutter of snowflakes swirling down out of the ruddy darkness overhead to vanish in the uneven glitter of the wet streets. Fanshaw took Nan's arm and made her walk fast, up towards the electric star that revolved slowly in front of a movie on Scollay Square, leaving Wenny to saunter behind them. They had passed the outdoor market where a few women with taut lantern jaws still hovered over the nearly empty pushcarts of the vegetable sellers and where brownfaced Italians still barked their apples and peppers and artichokes, when Wenny caught up to them with: "Say, wait a minute."

They stopped outside of a nickelodeon that belched cigarette smoke and calcium light. Overhead, painted in blue letters pricked with red, was the sign: "Pretty Girls Upstairs."

"Ever been up there, Nan?"

Nan shook her head.

"Let's go for a minute; the most grotesque thing you ever saw."

"Absurd. We'll do no such thing," snorted Fanshaw.

Loafers and office boys on their Saturday night bat and drunken sailors and little, over-painted hardfaced girls of the street who had come into the entrance to get out of the snow looked at them curiously as they disputed.

"I think it would be fun, Fanshaw. Come on, be a sport," said Nan.

"It'll smell fearfully," said Fanshaw under his breath.

"All right, just for a minute."

Wenny paid the admission, and they tramped up a creaking stair littered with cigarette butts and marked with dark blotches where people had spat and through a swinging door into a black tobacco-reeking place with seats. At the end of a smoky tunnel in front of a curtain the color of arsenic and gangrene, five women badly stuffed into pink tights like worn dolls twitched their legs in time to the accentless jangle of a piano. The light streamed out from them among eager red faces, moist lips, derbies, felt hats, caps shoved back on heads. At every pause in the music, men whistled and shouted at the girls. Now and then a girl dropped out of the wiggling, tired dance and jerked herself off the stage or a new one joined in the invariable twitching step. Fanshaw felt the fetor of hostile bodies all about him. Standing in the back behind some sailors, holding Nan's arm firmly in his, he kept whispering in her ear: "Nan, let's get out of this." The man in front of them turned, and Fanshaw caught the bulge of his eyes as he stared at Nan.

"Come on, I'm going," he said aloud.

"Don't you go with that stiff, girlie. You stay along with me," said the man, leaning drunkenly towards her. He had a yellow, lean face with a hooked scar on one cheek.

"I'm going," said Nan suddenly in a cold, hard voice. "You can stay if you like, Wenny."

The door swung behind them. They brushed past some boys clattering up the stairs with shouts of laughter. Once on the pavement, Fanshaw breathed deep of the snowy air.

"We'll take the car at Scollay Square," he said in a reassuring businesslike tone. In him a voice kept saying, "That dirty little kid, that dirty little kid," and, exultantly, "Nan can't like him after this."

Nan said nothing but walked beside him with cold, precise steps. At the entrance to the subway, Wenny came up to them and said: "All right. Good night," in a sudden, curt tone, and went off, walking fast down Hanover Street again.

The Huntington Avenue car filled up gradually with people. As it growled through the tunnel past Park and Boylston, the row of faces opposite joggled as meaningless as turnips jounced in a cart. And again Fanshaw throught of Albrecht Dürer's self-portrait with the yellow curls and the dandified black and white flounced shirt and the calm, self-possessed mouth.—If I could be like that, he was thinking, and not like these, and there's that suit I meant to have pressed today. I'll take it round after my nine o'clock class; and the weekly tests and Mrs. Gerald's dinner invitation to answer. He half closed his eyes.— That wine makes me drowsy.

* * *

"I've so wanted, so prayed, dear, that you might have a beautiful, lovely career," Fanshaw's mother was saying in a weak voice, her head swaying from side to side ever so little against the pillow.

Fanshaw nodded and drew up his chair beside hers. Outside the window, some barberries were very red against the snow in the thin twilight of the winter afternoon. Snow scene by Brueghel.

"And really, dear, it must be admitted," went on Mrs. Macdougan with a little smile, "that you have done very well in the five years since you left college. You have made yourself beloved and respected, dear, in the walk of life you have chosen. . . . Don't shake your head, you know it is true. Why, Mrs. Appleby was telling me only yesterday how highly Mr. Appleby thought of your work under him. O, I was proud of you! And I shall be prouder yet, I know it, if I live long enough. . . . Yes, I shall. O, dear boy, when I was raising you, and I had such trouble raising you, you were sickly, you know, dear, like I am now. . . . I used to think how you'd be big and strong and a comfort to me when I was old, just like you are. If God hadn't seen fit to try me with this affliction, how happy we would be together."

"But, Mother, you are going to get well, you know. This summer, maybe, we'll be able to go abroad."

"Nice of you to say it, dearest. . . . Do you think you could make me a cup of tea? I'd so like a cup of tea. These afternoons are so long."

"But, Mother, you know you're not supposed to have tea."

All the little wrinkles about her eyes and the corners of her mouth deepened. She patted her grey pompadour, that had slipped a little to one side of her head, with a querulous hand.

"I didn't have any yesterday," she whined. "I'm so thirsty, Fanshaw."

"All right, I'll get Susan to make some."

When he came back from the kitchen, she said, her grey eyes wide, staring with excitement:

"I was thinking, Fanshaw, supposing you married and some dreadful woman won you away from your poor mother; what should I do? You're so sweet to me; you take such care of me."

Fanshaw turned red to the roots of his sandy hair.

"Not much danger of that," he said stiffly. "We'll have a nice cup of tea in a minute, very weak, so that we shan't get too nervous, shan't we dear?"

"I know it's so, Fanshaw. Some girl has got a hold on you. Don't trust her, dear, don't trust her. Women are so wicked. She's after your social position or thinks you make a good salary. . . . O, I'd die, I'd die if someone got you away from me." Mrs. Macdougan was sitting bolt upright in the chair, beating on her knees with little puffy hands. A wisp of grey hair had fallen down over her forehead, revealing a bit of the black rat under the pompadour. "They are such scheming crea-
10   tures, so deceitful and wicked, and I so want you to have a beautiful career and be a comfort to me."

"O, now please, dear! O, now, please dear!" Fanshaw was saying, clenching and unclenching his hands, staring into the crowded twilight of the library behind his mother's head.

Susan, tall, with genial horse teeth, came in with a tray of tea-things.

"O, your hair's acomin' down, mum. Can't I fix it for you, mum?"

"Do, Susan, please," said Mrs. Macdougan in a faint voice, drooping against the pillow.
20   Fanshaw brought up a small table and poured out a cup of tea. His lips were compressed and trembling. When Susan had gone, he said in a quiet, expressionless voice:

"Now, Mother, you are getting yourself worked up over nothing. I assure you there is nothing whatever between me and any girl."

"You always were a truthful boy, but no matter, no matter. . . . There's not enough sugar in this tea, dear. O, why don't people ever give me things the way I like them?"

Fanshaw dropped another lump in her cup. She began to drink the tea in little sips. The wrinkles in her face relaxed. Fanshaw was
30   looking out of the window at the snow, rosy with sunset, and the intense purple shadows behind the barberry bushes. His mind was all drawn hotly into the image of Nan that day at the Logans with a net of pearls over her hair like a girl by a Lombard painter. Against the snow, the fervid rose and purple, how fine she would be, against a snow scene by Brueghel.

"Well, I must leave you, Mother," he said. "I must go over to Cambridge."

"Don't be late this evening, will you?"

"No, dear."

*   *   *

40   The wind was nipping and frosty, with a smell of mudflats on it and salt-eaten piles. Fanshaw, walking up T Wharf between Wenny and

Nan, sniffed with relish the harbor air, looking at the agewarped houses and the masts and tackle of the fishing schooners against the grey sky. He had pulled his buff woolen muffler up until it covered the lobes of his ears and had sunk his hands deep in his overcoat pockets. On the forehead between the eyes, the wind pressed now and then biting as cold iron.

"If I had been a man," Nan was saying, "I should have gone to sea."

"But think of it in this weather. . . . It's delightful to take a stroll and look at the harbor and the shipping and go back to a warm room. But think of being out in it always. Such beastly cold, grimy, monoto- 10 nous work." Fanshaw felt his teeth almost on edge as he spoke. How differently made people must be who could stand that sort of thing.

The wharf was empty. From the stubby stovepipes of the galleys of the close-packed schooners came an occasional rift of blue smoke, a whiff of rank pipes and bunks snatched away in a gust of wind.

"I may go yet, someday," said Wenny.

"But think," Fanshaw shuddered. "Think of handling frozen ropes in a wind like this." He thought of gritty ropes cutting through gloves and flesh, ripping the calloused flesh of men's palms. That story of Jack London's he had read years ago. It must have been that that put it 20 in his head, the look of blood on ice-jagged, tarry ropes.

The harbor was wide, bright silver, tarnished where the wind made catspaws. One tug steamed seaward, cutting into the wind with a rustle of foam about a bluff, grimy bow, dragging long coils of brown smoke. They were standing beside some piles at the end of the wharf.

"I have my chance now," said Wenny. "The bust-up was complete this time."

"How do you mean?" Fanshaw and Nan said in unison.

"My chance to go to sea . . . I've broken off relations . . . with my relations. . . . Bad pun, isn't it?" 30

"You mean you had a row with them?" said Fanshaw. "I can understand that. Poor mother and I nearly came to blows. . . . It's the holiday spirit. Christmas is a dreadful time. Don't you think so, Nan?"

"I like Christmas," said Wenny.

"But, Wenny, you said complete." Nan put a hand on his arm.

"I mean it. I shall never have anything to do with them again. . . . I never have rows."

"But what on earth happened?" Nan's voice was very gentle.

"Absolutely nothing. My father and I had a little chat about life and eternity. How silly, I am getting all worked up talking about it. O, I 40 suppose I'd better tell you to get it off my system. It's not a bit important. I laid on for life, and he laid on for eternity. . . . Naturally, being a clergyman, eternity is his line of goods. We got sore. I'm never going to take anything more from him, either his money or his insolence."

"But how are you going to live?" cried Fanshaw.

"What the hell? I've got as much muscle as the next man."

"But you're so impractical, Wenny."

"It must have been more than that. How did it start?" said Nan, tapping with her patent leather toe at a loose board.

"It started . . ." There was a catch in Wenny's voice. Then gruffly: "He said something unpleasant about a snapshot I had on my desk.
10   It's too ridiculous."

"But you'll have to give up your M.A.," went on Fanshaw.

"Damn good thing, too. I was just hanging round Anthropology in the hope of getting in on an expedition to South America."

—And Wenny owes me a hundred dollars, the thought crept unexpectedly into Fanshaw's mind. Never get it now.

"But Wenny," Nan was pleading, "I think you are probably exaggerating the importance of the whole thing. I don't see that it's necessary to get on your high horse like that."

"You would, Nan, if you knew them. You can't imagine how fearful
20   it is down there. A Congregational minister's house in Washington. The snobbery and the mealymouthedness . . . God, it's stinking. . . . You see, I never really lived with them. My mother's sister brought me up mostly here in Boston. You see, I had three brothers and a sister, and I was the ugly duckling; and my aunt, who was an old maid, took me off their hands. She was a fine woman. She died the year I went to college. She lived on an annuity and left me just enough money to skimp through on till junior year, when my father said he'd help. . . . I have nothing in common with those people down there, and now, because they were giving me money, they
30   decided I must do what they wanted, and they hate me and I hate them. I was a filthy coward to ever take a cent from him, anyway. . . . And so here I am at twenty-three, penniless, ignorant, and full of the genteel paralysis of culture. . . . Silly, isn't it, Nan?"

The rising wind whined through the rigging of the fishing schooners, and the waves slapped noisily against their pitchy bows. Fanshaw's feet were numb and his forehead ached.

"Let's walk along," he said. "I'm frozen. I'd like some hot chocolate, wouldn't you, Nan?"

"But Wenny," Nan was saying, "you ought to stay on a little while to
40   get your breath, as it were. . . . You took your room in Conant for the whole season."

"But how am I going to pay the term bill, I'd like to know?" There was a little tremor in Wenny's voice that made him cut off his words sharp.

They turned and walked down the wharf again, the wind shoving and nudging at them from behind. In the lea of the buildings were a few old men with red faces sitting on boxes smoking pipes.

"Still," said Wenny with a sudden laugh. "I'm glad it happened. It tears off this fearful cotton wadding I've been swaddled in all my life. We'll see what the world is like now, won't we Fanshaw, old duck?" He slapped Fanshaw hard between the shoulders.

"The trouble is, can one live without it?" said Nan.

—Fearfully good-looking the boy is, all excited and flushed like this, Fanshaw thought.

"By God, I intend to!"

"I thought you looked different, Wenny, when you got off the train," Nan said.

"It was fearfully decent of you two to meet me. . . . Makes me feel as if I had somebody, no matter what happened."

"I've often thought," Fanshaw said, "that there was something that cut us three off together, like people in a carnival in Venice, who might drift in their wonderfully carved state gondola down a dark canal . . ."

"And find themselves in the Charles . . . Exactly!" cried Wenny, laughing.

They had left the wharves and were walking through the grey, many-angled buildings of the business section. It was the lunch hour, and the streets were full of clerks and stenographers hustling from their offices to their lunch; from out of the tiled caves of lunchrooms came a smell of bacon and old coffee grounds.

"What sort of work are you going to do? I suppose you'll try a newspaper; everybody does."

"Let's not talk about that now, Fanshaw. Where on earth are you taking us?"

"To Thompson's Spa."

"Why not the Parker House, where we can have something to drink?"

"I'd rather have hot chocolate. I am frozen," said Nan.

They rounded the old State House.

Thompson's Spa was like a bird store, full of shrill women's chatter, bobbing hats, rows of powdered faces eating at narrow counters, smell of chocolate and sandwiches and sarsaparilla.

"Look, there's Betty Thomas! . . . What are you doing here, Betty? Sit here before somebody nabs the place," said Nan.

"O just shopping. Dear, you should see the hats, straws at Filene's. Why, how do you do, Mr. Macdougan, and . . . you! Why, this is a reunion!"

"Are they reasonable?"

"What, the hats? . . . Marvellous values, really."

Betty Thomas's nose was a little red from the cold. She held, balanced between finger and thumb, a salad sandwich that dripped mayonnaise into her plate; the three unoccupied fingers were arched airily in space. There was something about her amiable chatter to Nan, about the amiable, fussy chattiness of the women all about them that rasped on Fanshaw's nerves; the sum of it was shrill and ominous.

"But Wenny, what are you going to do? . . . I'm fearfully worried," he said in a low voice, leaning towards Wenny's ear. Like a haze about them was Nan's and Betty Thomas's chirruping talk:

"My dear, have you heard the latest? Up at the conservatoire . . ."

"Honestly, I don't give a damn, Fanshaw. I'm so sick of this hanging on the outskirts of college. . . ."

"I think your department would get you a scholarship. You must go put it up to them. It's ridiculous to let a thing like this wreck your career."

". . . And Mrs. Ambrose absolutely refused to sing a note. . . ."

"My dear Fanshaw, if you knew how utterly sick and fed up I was with all that . . . No, I'm going to live this time."

". . . And Salinski said . . ."

"But don't be a fool. Look, I'll try to scrape up some cash for the term bill. I think I can do it."

"You mustn't. I don't want it paid. . . . I'm not going to keep on with this farce any longer."

". . . A middle register, like an angel . . . And she told Fitzie that he said . . ."

"You make me tired, Wenny. You must be sensible."

"Don't you see that I'm trying to be, for the first time in my life?"

". . . met a man who said Romoulet wasn't teaching the belcanto at all . . . O, I'm so afraid, dear, of ruining my voice. . . . So many people . . ."

"Well, so long. I'm going to fetch my suitcase," said Wenny shortly. "I'll see you people later." He threaded his way out through groups of women and sallow men waiting for seats.

"I'm afraid your friend doesn't like me," said Betty Thomas pouting.

"He does, I assure you. He's a little distraught today. He's often like that, isn't he, Nan?"

Nan laughed, as she began fitting her gloves on again.

"Poor child. . . . All too often."

"It's no use taking it too seriously," said Fanshaw.

"No, I don't suppose one ought to take Wenny seriously," Nan whispered slowly. "And yet . . ."

"Are we taking the car?" asked Betty Thomas.

"I'll come up as far as your place and then go on over to see Mother. . . . I haven't been there all day," said Fanshaw.—Career, he was thinking. Will Nan or this girl make careers? Career in music, diva, prima donna, like Ethel Barrymore in *Tante*, Adelina Patti; Doris Keane in *Romance*. Suites in hotels full of expensive flowers. For me a career wouldn't be like that. Too absurd, poor dear mother wanting me to have a lovely career. Epicurus would not have approved of a career.

At Symphony Hall they got out of the car.

"Nan, you'll invite me to your first concert in there, won't you?" said Betty Thomas.

"If you'll invite me first." They laughed to hide their eagerness.

They walked up a street of brick and brownstone houses with narrow windows stuffed with fussy curtains on the parlor floors. Occasionally a girl passed them with a folder of music under her arm. From the houses came a perpetual sound of scales taken up and down, up and down by tenors, sopranos, contraltos, tinkled on pianos, scraped on cellos and violins, tootled on flutes. From somewhere came occasionally the muffled bray of an English horn.

"Fearful street, isn't it?" said Fanshaw.

"So Betty and I aren't the only ones. . . ."

"You mean who want to scale Symphony Hall? O, it's a common disease, Nan. . . . Well, I must go back and get the car over to Brookline. If Wenny goes to see you, do try and get him to be sensible."

*　　　*　　　*

Fanshaw had marked the last paper in the test on Florentine sculpture. He got up from his desk yawning.—O Lord! he was thinking, I'll never be able to look Donatello or the Ghiberti doors in the face again. He leaned over, arranged the pencils in their tray, put the papers away in the drawer, and slowly took off his tortoiseshell spectacles.—My eyes are smarting; I mustn't work any more tonight. The case closed on his spectacles with a faint clack.—Poor Wenny, what a rotten shame; but if he would not learn tact, discretion, what on earth was there to do? So idiotically childish. Fanshaw walked with long, leisurely stride into his bathroom, where he hung his dressing gown on the back of the door. He came back with yellowstriped pajamas

under his arm and sat on the edge of the bed to take off his shoes:—
"Fearful how this business upsets me," he muttered aloud. Much too
fond of Wenny, his dark skin, his extraordinary bright eyes. One
ought to have more control over one's emotions, senses. These beastly
shoes aren't comfortable yet, must have them stretched. At grade
school in Omaha, there had been that curlyhaired boy, Bunny Jones.
Walking home from school one day, they took the roundabout way
beyond the railroad yards. Must have been May, for the locusts were
out. Mother never could abide the smell of locusts, insisted they gave
10   her a headache. Bunny had suddenly put an arm round his neck and
kissed him and run off crying in a funny little voice, "Gee, I'm
skeered." Curious the way streaks like that turn up in one. Pico della
Mirandola wouldn't have been afraid of such an impulse if it had come
to him. There were so many scandalmongers about this place. How
fearful anything like that would be. He wasn't free like Wenny. He
had his mother to take care of, a lovely career to make. How bitterly
silly the idea was. He folded his trousers over the back of the chair.
And it was really Nan he cared for. Love, he thought; the word
somehow rasped in him. When he had put on his pajamas, he stood in
20   front of the dim mirror a second rubbing his fingers through his short
sandy hair. Wonderful it would be to have yellow curls like Dürer in
his portrait. He turned out the light and got into bed.—O, the
window! He got up, pushed the window up halfway and retreated
hastily before the blast of cold air that stung his flesh under the loose
pajamas.—Comfortable, this bed; better than the one I have at
Mother's place. He closed his eyes and drew the covers up about his
chin. Streets, he thought of, long streets of blind windows, dark, cold
under arclights, and himself and Wenny and Nan walking arm in arm,
hurrying from corner to corner.—Can't seem to find that street, and
30   on to the next corner between endless rows of blind windows con-
verging in a perspective utterly black beyond the cold lividness of
arclights.—Must have lost our way in these streets.

He opened his eyes with a jerk. The room was familiar and quiet
about him, the accustomed bulk of the desk opposite the bed. Out on
Mt. Auburn Street voices, occasional steps. He closed his eyes again
and fell asleep.

IV

W*ENNY* walked alone down a long street of arclights. Every instant, he seemed to walk from end to end the whole street of his life. Back in his childhood, it had been unaccountable and dark, overhung; where was it he had walked down a narrow alley between towering, blind brick walls that trembled with a roar of hidden engines?—The terror of it had been like that. Then breaks of lollipop-colored sunlight, little redroofed houses back among lawns of green baize, set about with toy evergreens, at doors varnished, farmers' wives in Dutch caps, tiny, like through the wrong end of the telescope, shepherding Noah's animals out of the cardboard ark; and the smell of the varnish scaling   10
off toys, grain of wood grimed by the fingers, black gleam of the floor under the bay window. Then streets to go out in alone, runnings to the corner drugstore, vast, glittering, reeking with dangerous smells, to buy aspirin for Auntie. Terror of faces looking out through grated area windows. And now all that's over. I am going to live. The uneven, frozen slush on the pavement crunched underfoot.

And the little, funny store where they had candy canes striped like barberpoles and toy trumpets; tin, shiny through green and red bright paint; and the feel of rough brown paper twisted funnel-shaped, cornucopias, horns of plenty, Auntie said they were. And the   20
smell of schoolrooms and ink on his fingers, and himself walking home fast to get away from Pug Williams, who said he'd smash his dirty mug in. Fire engines and bare, proud arms of firemen loafing in the enginehouse. Muckers, bad smelling in brown-black clothes, who threw snowballs at you and wrote dirty words on the pavement, reckless, who had no aunts to scold them.—And tonight walking fast away from all these memories, because tomorrow I am going to live.

And there had been the time he had first discovered memories, when he had held his life out at arm's length and looked at it. And the streets had been full of girls then, the tilt of heels, ankles, calves   30
swelling under wind-yanked skirts; the hot blush and the sudden trembling heartbeat when his eyes met a girl's eyes; the girls giggling over sodas in corner drugstores. The smell of hot asphalt and oil from a steamroller puffing and clanking in front of the house, the wonderfulness of engines and boats, whistles and the churned harbor water

77

as the liner left the wharf. Ballantyne read with smarting eyes after
bedtime, black faces against blue sea and parrakeets greener than an
emerald chattering shrill, and himself brownly naked in the surf of
lonely beaches. Now for all that. No more dreams, I'm going to live
tomorrow.

The funny, excited anticipation when he first saw the sign in the
subway: Out to Mass. Avenue and the College Yard; then the intonations of arguing voices, hands knocking the ashes out of pipes, card
catalogues in the library, the dazzle of unimagined horizons with
10   phrases of all the philosophers going by like the transparencies in a
political parade. His aunt in a coffin, her grey face as brittle under
glass as the imitation flowers in showcases in Peabody. His father and
mother bustling about through the choking smell of lilies. During the
service he had run away and locked himself in the bathroom and cried
like when he had been in a temper when he was very little.—And
now, here I am, and what am I going to do to live without dreams?
Tomorrow and tomorrow . . . how silly, that's Shakespeare.

He was walking down a straight, deserted street through Cambridgeport. A few trees cut the cold glint of light against windows and
20   scrawled shadows over the uneven snowpiles along the gutters. He
walked fast, staring at the arclights that were violet in the center and
gave off green and orange rays through the thin mist. At a corner in
front of a red A. P. store, a group of boys followed him with their eyes.
Muckers.

"O, Algy! . . . It's late, Algernon," they taunted him in falsetto
voices as he passed. A snowball whizzed past his ear.

"How in hell do they know I'm in college? Must be the smell," he
muttered amusedly. A sudden tingle of curiosity went through him to
know about those boys on the corner. How he'd lain awake at night
30   thinking of muckers when he was a kid, making himself stories of
fights, things with girls, adventures he'd do if he were a mucker, if he
were to run away from Auntie and be a mucker. He thought of himself
scuttling over roofs from the cops, shots twanging hard in the zero-
green night, dancing belly to belly with a painted girl in a cellar.—But
enough of dreams. Tomorrow I'm going to live.

Busy his mind had been all the evening, urging his tired legs on to
its throb, clanking out memories raspingly, the way a press turns out
papers; all at once he knew why. He had to keep from thinking of
Nan.

40   "O, Nan," he said between clenched teeth. For an instant he felt
her acutely walking beside him, leaning on his arm, her cheek against
his cheek. He trembled as he walked. His body was a funnel of
blackness in which his life was sucked away, whirling like water out of

a washbasin. He jerked himself to a stop. He was at a corner in front of a drugstore. At the top of the greenly lit window, his eyes followed the letters of a Coca-Cola sign.—That will be the first act, he was thinking, I shall tell Nan. I can't go now. I'm too tired now. . . . And all at once a great wave of jollity bubbled up through him.—Of course I'll go and tell Nan. To love Nan, to walk arm in arm with her, the ache of desiring all eased, to talk endlessly to her, touching her. . . . Now I'll go home and go to bed. In the morning early I'll go to see her before she's up, arrive carrying the milk and the paper. His heart pounding with anticipation, he started walking fast again down a cross street. He had a feeling of suddenly scrambling onto a mountain top from which he could see endless valleys radiating into sunlight, full of gleam of roads and streams and beckoning woods, and swift shine of rails taut about the bulgings of hills. From now on he would burst through the stagnant film of dreams, his life would be a headlong adventure. Tomorrow Nan and living. They'd go away from Boston, where they were caged by these dead customs, where there were ghosts at every corner, constricting ghosts.

At Massachusetts Avenue the wind was like a razor in his face. The blundering yellow oblong of a car came towards him along the black straight track through the rutted snow. He ran, slipped and with a laugh landed on the step.

"Wait till the car stops," said the conductor mechanically. "Safety first."

Wenny dropped into the seat beside a lean, redfaced man with flappy ears.

"Hullo, Wendell," the man said. "How's your museum work going?"

"It's gone. I'm chucking the whole shooting match."

"Why on earth?"

"I'm going abroad. I don't know what I'm going to do. I am going to do something. This isn't anything."

"But why drop out now? Why not wait for your M.A.? You haven't been . . . er . . . fired, have you?"

Wenny laughed and laughed.

"No. Things have come to a jumping off place, that's all. I want some more satisfactory . . ." Wenny smothered an impulse to boast.

"I see," said the man with a queer look.

"No, you don't . . . Because I don't either. . . . But that's how things are, and to hell with the M.A."

It was good to pull off his heavy coat in his own room once the door had slammed behind him. The warmth made him very drowsy.

"Tomorrow," he said aloud as he tugged at his necktie.—Gee, it's

lucky I had that row with Father. I'd never have waked up for years. When he had his clothes off he stretched himself and yawned.—Old fool, Fanshaw, I wonder why I like him, he was thinking. We'll outlive his old dusty Picos and Mirandolas, anyway. O, and Nan, Nan. The thought of her body in his arms, of her slender body in the bed beside him, made his head swim in a haze of throbbing lights, sharp like chirruping of crickets, sleepy like dryflies. He clicked off the electricity and let himself crumple onto the bed. After a minute he shivered and pulled the covers high about his face.—And think that
10 we're going abroad. Out among islands in a pearly-blue sea, dolphins danced, from the islands great gusts of fragrance came like music on the wind, the plunk of an anchor in blue bay-water, pink and yellow houses jostling on the sandy shore. . . . He lay laughing happily, so that the bedsprings shook.

*   *   *

When he woke up the hands of his piefaced alarm clock were at seven. The sun was barely up. The poplars behind the dormitory cast streaky shadows on the pitted snow where here and there a bit of upturned crust glowed ruby and topaz color. Wenny reached out of the window for an icicle that glittered from the gutter above his head.
20 It was cold against his tongue, tasted the way soot smelt. He threw it at a sparrow perched fluffily on a bush. "Top of the mornin', Mr. Sparrow!" and closed the window. The sparrow was tiny and violet black as he flew into the dazzle of the sun. Wenny dressed hastily, wondering whether he should shave.—I can't take the time; what the hell does it matter, anyway? An old woman was scrubbing the stone steps.—Cold, her hands must be, he thought as he rammed his hands into his overcoat pockets.

The lunchroom was almost empty.

"Scrambled eggs and bacon on toast and a cup of coffee," he said to
30 the towhaired, pink-cheeked youth who was slipping into a white jacket behind the counter. "Fine morning, isn't it?"

"Ain't no fine mornin's at this job. I call a fine mornin' a mornin' I can lay in bed."

Wenny laughed.—It'ld be fun to be a busboy for a while, the grotesque people telling you yarns over coffee. Not here with these damn college snobs though, in a lunchwagon down in the North End. How many existences. Walt Whitman had it in "The Song of Occupations." The toast and bacon crackled under his teeth. He noticed the clock.—Hell's bells, only half past seven. I can't help it, I'll wake her
40 up. She won't care. Nan asleep in her white bedroom, her hair plaited, sitting up in a dressing gown, he leaning over her talking to

her, the smell of her hair in his nostrils. He would come up from behind and put his hands on her breasts and kiss her.

He paid the fat cashier, whose eyes drooped sleepily on either side of a spongy, pendulous nose. Wondered how long his money would last; one day, two days, four days? The icy pavement flew under his feet. Beside the Charles he stopped a moment to watch a rift widening, very black in the ice. Behind him was the throb of the power plant and the soaring brick chimneys.—It would be fine to build chimneys like that. I mustn't dawdle. . . . I'll go crazy if I don't see Nan. Kiss me Nan.

He was flushed and his ears and fingers tingled from the wind and his eyes were jumpy from the dazzle of the snow through the Fenway. "The Swansea," the gilt letters, a little worn, slanted ornately down the glass door. His throat felt tight, all the blood seemed to have ebbed out of him. He wondered if he were going to faint. Miss Taylor, said the visiting card above the bell. The little black button bit into his finger, he pushed it so hard. Again. Again. At last the thing in the lock clicked. He pushed the door open and ran up the stairs. On every landing, papers, milk bottles. Cautiously Nan's door opened under his knock.

"Why, Wenny, you startled me half out of my wits," she said in a yawning voice. "I thought you were a telegram."

"I am."

She opened the door so that he could see half her face between the tumbled pile of her hair and the green dressing gown clutched about her chin.

"Wait a sec. Go into the library. I'll get something on. What on earth is the matter?"

In the library Wenny fell into the Morris chair and buried his face in his hands. He was trembling like a whipped dog. He was falling through zone after zone of misery like in a nightmare.

"Had any breakfast? I'm putting on coffee," came Nan's voice from the kitchenette.

"Fine!" Something unbearably false in his tone made him wince like a lash.

He stared about the room terribly afraid of the moment when Nan would come. Opposite him was the piano's great white complacent grin.

She was in the room, between him and the piano. He was looking up at her, at her oval face that capped the aloof slenderness of her body in green clinging crepe with long sleeves.—O God, to put my hands on her breasts, to touch my lips to the richness of her neck.

"Well, you are an early bird this morning, Wenny."

She stopped beside the window. Behind her head, clouds skidded across a green patch of sky.

"It's cold this morning," he heard his voice say.

"I'm afraid we'll have a thaw before the day is out. . . . O, Wenny, I hate this wretched climate. Why aren't we all millionaires so that we could escape the Boston climate?"

"Why not escape?" The words stuck in his throat.—You damn fool, pull yourself together, a little furious voice was saying in his head.

"Ah, the coffee's boiling over. . . . Wenny, run and fetch the milk and the paper, will you, please?"

He ran eagerly to the front door. The paper had a bitter, diurnal smell that smacked of his father, black and white, stuffy looking like his father in black with his collar round backwards. He dropped the paper again and slammed the door.

"Here's the milk."

The kitchenette was full of velvety, warm coffeesteam.

"Do you mean to say those awful people downstairs have stolen my *Herald* again?"

"I left it there. I want to talk. . . . I've got to talk to you, can't you see?"

"What's the matter?"

Her eyes were in his. He couldn't see her, only her eyes, grey like the sea.

"Well, Wenny, we must have breakfast first. Have you patched it up with your family?" The words were elaborately emotionless, clinking, rounded like the cups and saucers she was putting on the tray. He was out of the trembling husk of his body looking at himself, hating, out of her grey eyes. When she leaned to take the tray, he could see a faint coppery down on her neck under the dressing gown. To kiss her there.

He let himself fall heavily into a chair. She set the tray on the little table by the window.

"One or two? Of course you want two, don't you, Wenny? What fun to breakfast like this, you and me."

Wenny took a gulp of coffee.

"For God's sake don't be so casual. . . . It's hideous." The coffee choked him. He coughed. "Nan, I'm crazy about you."

"Now, Wenny, you haven't come here so bright and early to make love to me," she said with a hurried, nervous laugh.

"Don't, Nan." He yanked at her hand.

"Wenny, you hurt me, you're spilling my coffee. . . . Look, are you drunk?"

"I swear to God I've never been so serious in my life."

"Hold your horses, Wenny boy, we are too old friends to carry on this way. It's too silly. Do talk sensibly."

"I've been holding myself in so long. . . . I can't do it any more. I'm going to live like a human being, do you understand, Nan? From this moment on, you and I are going to live."

As he jumped to his feet, his knee hit the table, bowling over the cream pitcher.

"O, the carpet, Wenny," said Nan in a whining little voice. "Have you no respect for my carpet?"

"Damn the carpet, Nan. I'm crazy about you. I want to kiss you."   10

He fell back into the chair and covered his face with his hands, his fingers writhed in his hair that was curly with sweat. Nan ran out into the kitchenette and was back with a cloth sopping up the white puddle of milk. She rubbed the carpet tensely, as if everything depended on its being unspotted.

"Nan, I'm so sorry to give you all that trouble."

"You are such a little silly."

"O, what can I do? Nan, for God's sake understand that I love you. I must have you love me."

He went towards her blind with his arms out. She put her hands   20
roughly on his shoulders and shook him the way an angry school teacher shakes a child. Her voice was full of shrill hatred.

"Be quiet, I tell you. You shall be quiet."

"You mean you don't love me."

"Of course not, you little fool . . . Please go away; it's my time to practice. I don't love anyone that way."

Her eyes were dilated and burning. The kimono had fallen from one shoulder and showed the beginning of the curve of a breast. Her long fingers dug into the flesh of his shoulders. His back was against the door.   30

"O, this is fearful, Nan."

The hat in his hand, red gleam of varnish on the door closing behind him. Then stairs again, numbered doors, milk bottles, newspapers. He brushed against the elevator man, whose eyes rolled white in a black face, and through the glass door where climbed the letters of "The Swansea" in reverse, and out into the grey street. As he crossed, a truck nearly hit him. A man with a grease smudge on an unshaven cheek under a shiny visored cap leaned out snarling: "Wanter git kilt, ye sonofabitch?"

Want to git kilt. . . Want to git kilt. . . Wenny picked his way very   40
carefully across a snowpile and sat hunched on a bench under a skinny tree.—Anything to forget Nan, her ringing voice saying: Of course not, you little fool, the warm curve of her breast, the down in the

hollow of her back under the green crepe. He beat against his forehead with his fists. O, he'd go mad if he didn't stop thinking of her. Anything to stop thinking of her. Death to stop thinking of her, death a motortruck hurtling down the frozen street and a voice shrieking: Wanter git kilt, ye sonofabitch, and hard blackness, eternal. To crawl into bed and draw the covers up to your chin and sleep. That's what it would be like to git kilt. No more agony of hands to touch, lips to kiss, so downy and warm it would be, asleep in a bed of blackness.

The back of the bench was hard against the nape of his neck. He
10 was shivering. He got to his feet. The sky had become overcast with dovecolored mackerel clouds that cast a violet gloom over the apartment houses and the etched trees and the rutted yellow slush of the street. Wenny tugged at his watchfob. The familiar round face, slender Roman numbers. God, only half past nine? How many hours ahead. He walked on numbly.

*   *   *

"Some cold, ain't it?" came a voice beside him. "Ain't no time for keepin' the benches warm." Wenny turned his head. Beside him on the bench was a fellow without an overcoat, of about his own age, with a compact, snubnosed face, lips blue and a little trembling from the
20 cold. It was afternoon; he was sitting on the Common.

"Of course it's cold," said Wenny testily, looking straight before him through the trees at the dark shapes of people and automobiles passing in front of the shopwindows, gay and glinting along Tremont Street. Like that his thoughts passed and repassed, miserable silhouettes against the shine and color of his memories. It hurt him to leave the mood of processional sadness he had slipped into at the end of dumb hours of walking. After a long silence, the man at the other end of the bench continued in the same confidential tone.

"Ain't no time for keeping the benches warm, I can tell you. . . .
30 Out of a job, are you?"

Wenny nodded.

"Up against it?"

Wenny got to his feet.

"I guess I'll walk along," he said.

"Mind if I walk with you?" said the young man, jumping up and thrashing his arms about. "Bad onct you let yesself git cold this weather. You don't never git warm agin. Got a flop for the night?"

Wenny nodded. They started walking down the path.

"I ain't yet. I'll git one though. It's too turrible cold out."
40 "Are you flat?"

"Like a buckwheat cake."

"I mean, haven't you any money?"

"Money!" Wenny's companion stopped in his tracks shaking with laughter. "Jumpin' jeeze, that's funny. That sure strikes me funny. Why, I ain't had a piece of change the size of your little finger for so damn long. . . ."

"How do you make out?"

"O, I make out fine, 'xceptin' when my luck goes back on me like today."

"Been in Boston long?"

"Nope. Tumbled in here 'bout three days ago from Albany. Too cold up there. I ain't got the hang of it yet. Bum town, I'd say. Though you can't tell about a town till you learn it."

A rolled up newspaper lay on the path before them. The young man without an overcoat made a grab for it, shooting a skinny chapped forearm out of the frayed sleeve of his coat.

"Useful things, newspapers," he said as they walked on. Then he turned and looked at Wenny fixedly a minute. "Lost your job? . . . You ain't bummed much, have you? Lost your job?"

"I've hardly been out of Boston."

They were rounding the dry basin of a pond that was piled with muddy snow from the paths.

"Et today?"

"Of course. . . . Look, I've still got a couple of dollars. Suppose you come and have a drink with me. Say, what's your name?"

"The guys called me Whitey down where I come from. And say, if you want to set me up to something, for Gawd's sake make it a hamburger steak. Honest, I ain't et a thing since I been in Boston city."

"Gosh, come along. I'll take you to Jake's."

"Hell, it don't hurt you not to eat onct you git used to it. I kin go days without eatin' an' never notice it."

"Gee, I'm hungry too. I forgot to eat any lunch."

In the German restaurant there was a thick smell of beer and fat wurst and sawdust. Whitey took off his cap, exposing a closely cropped towhead, and sat stiffly on the shiny, reddish wooden bench. Wenny ordered beer and hamburger and potatoes of a fat-faced waiter, who looked from one to the other out of suspicious pig eyes.

"Gee, you're treatin' me white. I guess you're a millionaire on the loose."

"I wish I was," said Wenny, laughing. "No, I just had a fight with my father."

"Like me when I left home."

"How long have you been bumming round like this?"

"'Bout a year an' a half."

"Where do you come from?"

"Perkinville, a little jerkwater town back in South Dakota."

"Good beer, isn't it?"

"I'll tell the world it is. . . . So you had a fallin' out with the old man, did ye too?"

"I sure did."

"Did he trun a flatiron after you?"

"No," said Wenny laughing, his mouth full of potato.

10   "Mine did. A red hot one too."

"How did it happen?"

"O, I dunno. Things was pretty rough round our shack anyway. I used to run away for a week at a time an' stay with some guys I knew, an' the old man kep' sayin' how's I ought to be workin' to support the family an' all that. He wasn't workin', but he always wanted us kids to work. . . . An' I come home one night feelin' top notch with a couple of drinks in me. We'd all been down the line, an' I was tellin' myself how I was goin' to lay off that stuff an' hold down a job. An' just as I gits to the house I hears em hollerin' blue murder. . . . Ma took in

20   washin' an' used to do the ironin' in the evenin's. . . . Well, I looked through the kitchen winder and, jeeze, there was Ma and the old man chasin' her around the kitchen with the ironin' board n' beatin' at her with it, an' there was a tub full o' clothes to soak by the stove, and Ma just picked up that tub an' dumped it on the old man's head, sayin': 'Take that, ye dirty beast,' an' ran out of the house. Jeeze, I was mad at him. . . . An' I runs in and tells him to quit beatin' up Ma, and he had the clothes all hangin' round his neck and the water pourin' off his head; but he was roarin' drunk though. Jeeze it'd a been funny if I hadn't been so scared. I always was scared of the old man. An' he

30   stood up with his eyes all red lookin' at me scoldin' an' cursin' at him. 'Curse at yer father, will yer, you yellow-bellied bastard?' he says. An' then he picks up two flatirons, red hot on the stove, an' comes after me. . . . Honest to Gawd, I couldn't move, I was so scared, like when you're scared in your sleep. All I could do—jeeze, I remember it clear as anything—was yell: 'They're red hot, they're red hot.' One of 'em went through the winder with an awful noise, an' I ran out of the house and used my legs till I fell down cryin' on the side of the road a mile out o' town. . . . I jumped a freight an' went to Milwaukee, an' I ain't been back since. I'm goin' though in about a year an' plant myself

40   among the weeds. This is no life for a white man."

"What about girls?"

"O, they don't bother me. I get it now and then. But I don't miss it."

"It bothers me."

"What I like is goin' round to new towns, hoppin' freights an' all that. Jeeze, I been some places in the last year. I've worked in Akron, an' Cleveland, an' Chicago, an' Atlanta, Georgia. If I'd had the sense to stay down south, I wouldn't be freezin' to death at this minute. . . . An' Tallahassee, an' Key West. I passed up a chance to go to Havana. 'Count the lingo. An' Galveston, an' South Bend, an' Topeka, an' Pittsburgh, that's where they pick you up an' put you on the stone crushers. An' Duluth, an' Cairo, an' Albany, an' New Orleans. Ought to see them high yallers down there if you're stuck on girls. I didn't get to the coast, but I was in New York and Philly. . . ."

"Have some more beer?"

"No. . . . Jeeze, I'm talkin' too much, I guess."

"Hell no, I like to hear you."

"Well, I'll beat it this time. Got to meet a friend o' mine on the Common. . . . See you some time."

He pulled his cap over his eyes, put up his collar and slouched out the door. Wenny sat sipping his beer. He wished Whitey had not gone. His mind was fearfully empty and dark.—Why couldn't I do that, bum from town to town? That's the worst that can happen to me anyway, and that sounds fun. That way, I can forget her and all this life. Start afresh as if I had just been born. He got to his feet firmly, put his two dollars down beside the check and walked out into the street. A sudden, wild elation had seized him. He hadn't a cent in the world. What should he do now, reborn without a cent?

It was already dark. The wind made his cheeks tingle. Of course he knew what to do. He'd pawn his watch. Down the street a little way, three gold balls glinted above a show window in the full glare of an arclight.

*   *   *

His forehead and eyes in the carmine ring of a Ward 8 becoming oval as he tipped it to his mouth, half a slice of orange bobbing in the midst of it, the lemony claret taste in his mouth and excitement shooting in hot and cold shivers through his blood. Opposite a girl's face, cheeks firm under powder, giving way suddenly in loose, purplish skin under the eyes, hair fuzzy and yellow. Beyond, through blue arabesques of tobacco smoke, tops of instruments from the orchestra playing "Goodby, Girls, I'm Through," a chromo of George Washington in a gold frame hung with a festoon of red, frilled paper. In his mind muddled the towns Whitey had told him about, Akron and Cleveland and Chicago and Atlanta, Georgia, and Tallahassee and Key West, and Fanshaw's delicately intoned voice saying: "Like beautiful leanfaced people of the Renaissance lost in their vermilion barge"

. . . Ellen wasn't leanfaced; plump cheeks, plump breasts. He was living now. Now he'd forget how his father looked with his collar round backwards, he'd forget Nan with Ellen, realer than old fool Fanshaw's vermilion barge.

"You're one of these college boys, aren't you, dear?"

Her tired fingers, overwhite, played nervously with a cigarette box on the table.

"Why?"

"'Cause you keep askin' me my life history. I'm not a fiction maga-
10 zine. Tellin' stories isn't in my line, see?"

"I'm sort of interested in people's life histories today, Ellen. I'm just beginning mine."

"I knew I was robbin' the cradle," she said, and laughed, showing to the gums a set of teeth like the teeth in a dentist's showcase. "But I didn't know it was that bad."

Wenny felt himself blushing. He took another long drink of the Ward 8. Leanfaced people of the Renaissance with falcons on their wrists, quoting Greek in bed with their great-limbed, rosy lemans, riding days over parched hills to find the yellow, half-obliterated
20 parchment that once spelled out would resolve the festering chaos of the world into radiant Elysian order. Whitey loafing on street corners in New Orleans watching the high yallers drive by in barouches. By God, I must live all that.

"Ever been abroad, Ellen?"

"The Fall River boat's about the biggest liner I ever took."

"Waiter, two more Ward 8s."

"Make mine a ginger ale highball, kiddo."

—Silly, this blather of the Renaissance, ham actors mouthing "To be or not to be". . . Like Whitey, that was better. But first I'll have to
30 be so girls don't bother me. Shall I go home with her? I wish she was better looking. Down the line . . . He wouldn't care how she looked. . . . I get it now and then, but I don't miss it. And Nan; is Nan just girls bothering me?

"You're blue this evenin', kiddo, ain't they treatin' you right? Tell it to mommer."

Wenny jerked his chair round and put an arm about her waist. Her head sank on his shoulder.—Smell of her hair, what was the perfume she used? Rouge too, sweetish, fatty smell of rouge from her lips. She beads her eyes. His hand touched her breast limp under her bodice.
40 Firm Nan's breasts would have been. This morning how he had wanted to put his hands on Nan's firm breasts and kiss her.—Don't think of it. When I am sated I will forget Nan, everything. He kissed her lips. Her eyes were bored, flameless between their beaded lashes.

"Look out, kiddo, don't get too close. This is a respectable joint. I doan wanter get in wrong here."

Wenny seemed to stand apart from this body of his touching the girl's body, to look at it critically through the tobacco smoke as if from the bleary eyes of the chromo of Washington. And when he is sated, his voice seemed to say, when his flesh has grown very cold, he'll be like Whitey, going round to new towns, walking down roads, hopping freights: Tallahassee and South Bend and Havana and Paris and Helsingfors and Khiva and Budapest and Khorassan . . . riding over more parched hills than the leanfaced people of the Renaissance had ridden over, in search of words, of old gods' names more powerful than any they ever dreamed of. Under the table, his hand was on her thigh. His heart was pounding.

"What do you think about when you're blue, Ellen?"

"Me? I don't think when I'm blue. I drink."

At the next table a man with three chins, whose bald head swayed from side to side, was trying to stroke with a puffy ringed hand the arm of the redhaired girl opposite him. A waiter hovered over them threateningly. The room was swinging round in smooth spirals to the sound of "The Blue Danube."

Wenny's heart was pounding. His hands were cold.—Afraid, are you? a voice sneered in his head. To live you can be afraid of nothing. The Greeks were not afraid. The leanfaced men were not afraid. By god they were. Men flagellated themselves round the altar of Apollo on Delos. They recanted on their deathbeds and stuck their tongues out eagerly for the wafer. And can David Wendell, silly little Wenny, son of a minister with his collar on backwards, can I conquer fear? I must. Her flesh was hot under his hands.

"Let's go, Ellen. Where do you live?"

"Ain't so far from here. I'll show you. I got a swell room."

The wind blew cold down streets of blank windows. At the corner she slipped on a frozen puddle.

"Oupsidaisy!" He caught her with a laugh.

"Jeeze, I wrenched my ankle. . . ." She drew the breath in sharply through her teeth. "Hell of a note . . . Say, kiddo, got plenty of jack?"

"I've got enough."

"I'll treat you nice, honest I will. I like you, real pash. Make it twenty, will you? A buck don't go far nowadays. Make it twenty, kiddo."

"I don't think I can give you as much as that. I'm broke."

Nan this morning in her green kimono shaking him, her long fingers digging into his shoulders.—O, I must forget her.

"Not often you can get a girl like me, deary. I'm mighty careful. . . ."

"Don't worry, I'll give you all I've got."

They passed a Chinaman in a fur coat standing under an arclight.

—Nan, I hate you. Nan, I'll kill you out of my mind. Tomorrow, when I've killed you utterly, I'll begin to live.

They stopped at a red brick house with a sign "Furnished Rooms" in the window. The key was in the door, clicked; the door opened. Dim gaslight in the hall.

—Whitey had said: "O, they don't bother me. Down the line. I get it now and then, but I don't miss it." I'll be like that tomorrow.

The carpet on the stairs had big roses on green; it was frayed and torn. The stairs creaked. The house smelt mustily of rotting wallpaper, of ratnests.

"Here we are, deary. . . . Ain't bad, is it? Wait a sec, I'll light up."

—Nan, you are beaten, dead. "Must not" is dead. Wenny's legs were trembling. His tongue moved about in his mouth like a thirsty dog's. He dropped into a chair by the door.—Nan, God, how I love you, Nan.

"Tired are you, deary? D'you know you look powerful like a guy I had a crush on wonct. Near croaked of it, honest. . . You see, for all I could do he wouldn't give it to me. . . . Kerist, I'm glad that's over. Worse than a spell of sickness. . ."

—To be free of this sickness of desire. I must break down my fear. Of what, of what? The social evil, prostitutions of the Canaanites, venereal disease, what every young man should know, convention, duty, God. What rot.

"You get into bed, deary. . . . I must fix my hair. Sheets are nice and clean, see. I always have clean sheets on my bed. . . . Maybe you'll come to see me often now. Safer, I'm tellin' ye to go to one girl steady. You know what you're gettin' then. . . . Pretty, ain't it, this shimmy? Got it at Filene's in the bargain basement . . ."

He was standing against the door, crumpling his felt hat in his hands. He tried to speak; no words came.

She was naked, sitting on the edge of the bed under the gasjet, eyes wide and mocking; her breasts hung free as she leaned towards him. In his head was a ghastly sniggering. He was out the door.

She grabbed him by the wrist from behind.

"No, you don't. I've had them kind before . . . Just want to peek an' run. Gimme somethin' or I'll raise the roof, you low-down sonofabitch of a cheapskate you."

"Here, take that; it's all I've got."

He piled crumpled greenbacks in her hands. A half-dollar fell to the floor. She stooped, naked, groping for it.

He rushed down the stairs, slammed the door, out into the icy glare of the arclight in the street. Coward, the word was like a pack of hounds screaming about his ears, yelping, tearing.—This is what you've done to me, Nan. Tomorrow was colonnades of stage scenery tumbling about his ears. Through it he was fainting with desire for the woman's body naked on the bed under the gasjet and Nan's eyes, sea-grey, drowning him, the smell of her hair. He leaned against a lamppost and stared with stinging eyes down the empty darkness of the street.

V

ON FANSHAW'S desk was a large white envelope and within that envelope another envelope which contained engraved cards faced with tissuepaper. Fanshaw pulled off the tissuepaper and ran the nail of his little finger lightly across the lettering:

Mr. and Mrs. Heaton W. Harrenden
Announce the Marriage of their Daughter
Alice
to Mr. Chamberlain C. Mason
at Twelve o'clock, Noon,
February Fifteenth, Nineteen Hundred and Twelve
at Harrenden Manor, Durham, Massachusetts.

Then there was a little card:

For the accommodation of guests a special train will leave the North Station, Boston, at eleven-fifteen, returning from Durham at five-thirty.

And another little card:

Mr. and Mrs. Heaton W. Harrenden request the pleasure of your company at the wedding breakfast at two o'clock, February fifteenth, nineteen hundred and twelve, at Harrenden Manor.

A letter from Cham had been tucked in:

Dear Fanshaw: You've got to come. Mrs. Harrenden says she wants an old-fashioned wedding, but Allie and I are going to try to pep it up a bit.
Yours, Cham

Let's see, Fanshaw was thinking, what ought one to wear at a noon wedding? Noon. The time Cham and I took those two chorus girls canoeing at Norumbega Park, the mudsmell of the river . . . And now Cham's marrying an heiress. Harrenden's Snowflake Meal. Like telegraph poles from the train, the years slip by, so fast and nothing to catch hold of. Ought I to get a cutaway? He sharpened a pencil neatly into the scrapbasket and sat a long time wondering. Buckingham's should it be, or would Filene's be cheaper?

*   *   *

Through the coal smoke that gripped his throat, Fanshaw caught a whiff of roses. A girl in a mink coat with a large bunch of pink roses at her waist had just brushed past him. She must be going to the wedding, too, he thought, and started walking in the direction she had gone, following with his eyes the signs that announced the trains: Portland Express, North Shore Local. . . .

"Hello, Macdougan, where the hell are you going?"

"I'm going to a wedding. What are you doing here this time of day,   10 Henley?"

"I'm off to a wedding too." Henley had a booming voice; he was a tall, dark man with a moustache, thickwaisted.

"Cham Mason's wedding?"

"Sure. . . . I didn't know that dignified people like you went in for weddings."

"I don't often, Henley. . . . But I roomed with Cham Mason when we were freshmen."

"Frankly, Macdougan, I find weddings of great anthropological interest. . . . Savage survivals."   20

They were in a crowd of very dressed people passing through a gate in the end platform, all about them fur coats, flowers, fuzzy hats, bright shoes. "O, how do you do, Mrs. Glendinning!" "Yes, dreadfully cold." "Why, everybody anyone ever knew in the world is here!" "No, those are the Pittsburgh people." "Imagine having a special train." "Yes, those are the Harrison-Smiths, my dear."

"Say, Macdougan, suppose we get in the smoker, where we can chat quietly," whispered Henley, fitting his derby back on his head. "This is too much of a good thing. . . . There's something so prurient about women at an affair like this."   30

"After all a wedding . . . Go ahead."

"Why they are parlor cars. . . . Here we are. . . . A wedding is the only piece of straight sex-ceremonial left to us."

"How's that?"

"The ring, my dear fellow, the ring . . . What could be more of a symbol than a ring? Why, among the aborigines of the Caribbean . . ."

"Why, look who's here! . . . Why, this is a class reunion, boys." A red, round face, topped by straight black hair slicked across a bald forehead, was poked in the door. "You remember me, don't you, Henley?"

"Sure I do, Randall. I haven't seen you since our last class day. How are you? . . . As I was saying, Macdougan, among the aborigines of the Caribbean . . ."

"I think I'll join you fellers if you don't mind. Gee, it's great, isn't it, that old Cham is gettin' hitched?"

"That depends . . ."

"Not if you know the bride." Randall hitched up his blue serge trousers and let himself sink down broadly on to the leather seat. "Ah . . . A lovely, sweet girl."

"Yes, I know her," said Fanshaw frostily. He turned and looked out at the empty windows of the train on the next track. Through them he could see more windows, people sitting in a parlor car. There came a toot from the engine, and the empty windows and the windows with people in them began to glide past. The seat rumbled; the train was moving; smoke cut out the view, cleared to reveal bridges and black water over which gulls veered screaming. Five gulls on the edge of a cake of ice.

A leather case of cigars was poked under his nose. "Thanks, I never smoke cigars." Fanshaw kept his face turned to the window, letting Henley talk to this Randall man.

"Yes," he was saying with a heavy laugh, "I been to some mighty funny weddings."

"I never miss one when I can help it."

"There was a wedding down in Philadelphia I once went to where the groom passed out before the ceremony. That was a funny wedding."

"What was the matter?"

"Dry martinis, that's all. We had to put him under the showerbath to bring him around enough to stagger up the aisle. . . . He got mixed up and tried to lead one of the bridesmaids up to the altar. It was a barrel of monkeys, that wedding was. . . ."

Fanshaw was looking out at the bare trees and the rows of grey suburban houses. The smoke from the engine unrolled dense and white across the landscape against a leaden sky. Above the grinding rumble of wheels, he could hear the two men talking beside him.

"I saw a man drop down stone dead at the altar once."

"You don't say?"

"Dreadful thing . . . Heart failure it was that did it. The bride had just said about love, honor, and obey, when the fellow began to stagger around. When they picked him up, he was dead. A good chap too, important in the Elks and secretary of the Pittsburgh Chamber of

Commerce. It was a great shock to everyone. Marrying the girl he was going to marry had been thought the crowning success of his career."

"Funny time of year to have a country wedding, isn't it?"

Fanshaw turned laughing from the window.

"Most eccentric . . . Why, everything's full of hoarfrost."

When the train reached Durham station, the sun was shining palely. The cars exuded furs and orchids and derby hats and canes from either end. Outside the station, several limousines and taxicabs were lined up waiting for the guests, and in front of them, pacing up and down the platform with the stationmaster, was a tall, sallow man in a silk hat and a frock coat, of which the straight line was broken in front by a sudden little potbelly that looked like a football tucked in under his vest.

"That's Mr. Harrenden," said Henley. "Let's walk up to the house to avoid the rush. . . . Gosh, look at that feather. I bet she's one of the Pittsburghers."

"In full warpaint too," said Fanshaw, tittering.

"How do you do, Mr. Harrenden?"

"Howdy, boys . . . Glad to see you. Step right into one of those cars, or perhaps you'd rather walk. Leave more room for the lovely ladies. . . . See you up at the house. . . . Why, how do you do, Mrs. Harrison-Smith?"

"Come on, Macdougan," said Henley. Fanshaw followed him through the station. They walked briskly through the main street of the town, past a row of new, concrete stores, and out along a macadam road that crunched frostily underfoot. Now and then, a limousine full of guests passed them.

"It's only half a mile and we have plenty of time."

"Do you know Miss Harrenden, Henley?"

"Very well . . . Why, I almost wanted to marry her myself at one time. She's a very lively young person."

Fanshaw glanced at him furtively out of the corners of his eyes. Henley had flushed red.

"Cold, the wind, isn't it?" Fanshaw said after a pause and turned up the velvet collar of his coat with a gloved hand.

"Extraordinary study a wedding is from the point of view of psychoanalysis."

"How do you mean?"

"Everybody gets a certain vicarious satisfaction out of it, don't you think so?"

"You mean the culmination of a romance? That sort of thing? . . ."

"I mean out of the two nice young things going off to bed together. . . . The rest of it is just sublimation."

"I don't think that's altogether true. . . . I think they romance much more about how they are going to buy furniture and found a home and have new visiting cards printed."

"Sublimation, all of it. Look how excited all those overdressed women are."

"Just because they are going to a party and meeting their friends and trying to look their best . . . I don't agree with the Freudian emphasis on the lowest in our natures. I don't think it's a good thing. . . . Anyway, civilized people don't let themselves think about those subjects."

"That's what I'm saying. . . . But what they think is just a veneer. Underneath our conscious thoughts and taboos, we are oversexed and anthropophagous savages."

They were walking up a drive bordered by barberry bushes of which the berries stood out scarlet over the greybrown lawn. They scraped the soles of their shoes against the scraper beside the door on the semicircular Colonial porch and found themselves being divested of their hats and overcoats by a maid, who gave them numbered checks in return. Then clearing their throats slightly, smoothing the tails of their cutaways with one hand, they advanced up the hall to where in a black and silver dress with a tinsel Egyptian shawl over her shoulders stood Mrs. Harrenden smiling and pyramidal.

"Dick Henley, I haven't seen you for years. We must find time to have a chat. . . . How do you do, Mr. . . . Mr. . . ."

"Macdougan."

"Of course . . . You'll find the young people right upstairs in the library. . . . I suppose you still are classed among the young people, Dick. All seem mere children, to me at any rate. . . . You will help me to make an old-fashioned jolly wedding of it, won't you? It's not a social affair at all. No one is invited but a few indispensable, intimate friends. So vulgar, these great society weddings . . . So much nicer to have only a few intimate friends . . ."

With a silky swish, Mrs. Harrenden stalked towards the door, which was encumbered by a new car full of guests.

At the top of the brown-carpeted stairs, they ran suddenly into Cham Mason, who was crawling on his hands and knees across the upper hall.

"Hello, Cham."

"Why, if it isn't Fanshaw . . . Look, for crissake, help me. . . . Susie Beveridge has broken her string of pearls. We're looking for them because with all these strange people . . . How do you do, Henley? I hadn't seen you." He got to his feet unsteadily and rubbed his hand across his closecropped, yellow hair. "Gosh, I'm tight as a tick. . . . Come into the library and have a cocktail. . . . I got to have a lil' sip to sober me."

"I thought you were looking for the wedding ring," said Henley.

"Right after a lil' sip to sober up we must look for pearls again. Two of 'em rolled into the hall."

They followed Cham into the library, a great wainscoted room dense with the sweetness of the yellow mimosa that stood in pots in the fireplace. A group of girls and young men lounged round a brass smoking table on which was a shaker and an array of cocktail glasses shining in the grey light that poured in through a broad window. In a Morris chair sat a fatfaced girl, her eyes brimmed with tears, holding a lot of various-sized pearls in her cupped hands.

"Count them again, Susie. . . . Maybe you've got them all," somebody said.

"Have a lil' cocktail with us, and then we'll all look, an' we won't stop looking till we find every last one of 'em."

"But it's time, Cham," whined the girl in the Morris chair.

"Well, where's Allie? I'm ready. . . . Here's looking at you, Fanshaw."

"Brush off your knees, they're all over dust. . . . I hear the orchestra tuning up. Come along, everybody."

"For God's sake, don't anybody get me started laughing," said Cham, straightening himself up and goosestepping stiffly towards the door.

"Come on, Cham, they are waiting," said in a voice staccato with excitement a little greyhaired, greyfaced man in a frock coat too long for him, who appeared in the door.

"All right, Dad, I'm coming. . . . But where's Allie? I refuse to be married without Allie."

Fanshaw drank down his cocktail and followed. Behind him he heard a voice still whining, "I don't know where to put my pearls." He pulled the door to and started down the stairs beside a black toque with a cockade like a Westpointer's in it.

"My," the girl was saying, "you should have seen the rehearsal of the ceremony this morning. It was a scream. Everybody got the giggles so we couldn't go on."

"Sh-sh," went someone. Everything was quiet but for the rustle of dresses, an occasional cough or a sound of creaky tiptoeing. They were packed into a long drawing room, down the middle of which an aisle had been made by a row of little orange trees in pots. Fanshaw flattened himself against the wall beside a picture that he was in constant fear of knocking down. The string orchestra grouped about the piano in the far corner behind the palms struck up. Everybody craned their necks.

"That's the overture," whispered someone.

"What, deary?" came in broken, elderly tones.

"The overture, Mother, . . . Beethoven."

"Ah, Beethoven."

"Sh-sh."

10   The overture stopped. In the silence, feverish whispering was heard in the hall and a man's voice loud and angry: "And for heaven's sake don't forget which pocket it's in."

"Sh-sh."

The orchestra was playing Mendelssohn's "Wedding March." Fanshaw could see the heads of people moving two by two up the aisle to the end of the room where the minister stood with a purple stole round his neck. The bride and groom were hidden by an orange tree, but he could see the backs of the bridesmaids in peachcolored silk and a shimmer of orange tulle on their hats, and the light shining on Mr. Harrenden's bald head. A sneeze across the room was stifled in a 20   handkerchief. There was some coughing in the wedding party, and the minister began to read the service in a chanting, nasal tone. Fanshaw was breathing deep of a heavy, lemonsweet smell. . . . Must be orange blossoms.

*   *   *

The table stretched long and white in both directions, bordered by faces, black coats, bright-colored hats. The shine of silver and plates and champagne glasses was blurred by cake crumbs, rind of fruit, nutshells, napkins.

—Gracious, have I had too much to drink? The thought streaked across the shimmer of Fanshaw's brain and the sound of voices and the 30   smell of food. He was half turned round in his chair, talking rapidly and smoothly, in spite of the fact that his tongue felt bigger than usual, to the girl next to him, who wore a pink dress and kept laughing and laughing.

"Cultivated people in this generation," he was saying, "are like foreigners who suddenly find themselves in a country whose language they do not know, whose institutions they do not understand, like people in one of those great state barges the Venetians had, that Canaletto drew so well. . . ."

"Isn't this wedding a scream?" said the girl in pink, laughing and 40   laughing. "I've never been to such a nice wedding as this, and this is my fourth already this winter. . . . If a winter wedding's like this, what would a spring wedding be like? . . . Aren't they just too lovely together? I think Chamberlain's awfully goodlooking, don't you?"

They were standing up, moving into another room, bright dresses and black coats jamming the doorway. Fanshaw found himself sitting alone in a deep armchair smoking a cigar. What he needed was some coffee, he was saying to himself. After an old-fashioned jolly wedding he needed coffee. He got to his feet and walked with care and deliberation to the table where the coffee service was.—My, things are happening fast. Careful, I must be careful. There was no one in the room but a short, pudgy man in a grey suit who was drinking a whiskey and soda, shaking the glass meditatively between every sip.

"Where have they all gone?" asked Fanshaw querulously.

"Getting out the Stutz, I guess."

"How's that?" Fanshaw gulped some coffee.

"Didn't you know that the young couple were going on their honeymoon in the big, red Stutz Harrenden gave them? An elegantly matched pair."

"Cham and I roomed together, freshman year in college," Fanshaw found himself saying.

"Ah, college! That's the place to make connections."

They stood looking at each other, nodding their heads knowingly, Fanshaw with his coffee cup, the pudgy man with his highball glass, when the sound of a racing motor attracted their attention. It was followed by a shout from the front of the house. Fanshaw went to the window and pulled back the curtain. The guests, cheering and laughing, filled the colonial porch and surrounded a shaking roadster in the drive. Fanshaw caught a glimpse of Alice Harrenden's pale face under a little brown hat and veil as she climbed into the car. Her eyes were swollen and her lips tight as if she were going to cry. Cham waved a buff cap and opened the cutout. Rice hailed on the car. An old sneaker hit Cham in the head. He honked the horn, bent over the wheel and the car shot around the bend of the driveway. People looked at each other constrainedly and began going back into the house.

—Somewhere quiet till this passes off, Fanshaw was thinking. He made his way back through the house and out into the garden.—Why, I'm staggering down the path. Mucky underfoot from the thaw. Bench to sit on. Dry bench. He leaned back and stared up at the streaming, greypurple clouds that brightened to yellow in spots where a little sun broke through.—Oughtn't to have drunk so much champagne. After all, if no one noticed . . . Jolly thing an old-fashioned, jolly wedding. My wedding. The Macdougan wedding. If it could be Nan. But Wenny . . . No, no. Someone I've not met yet. Perhaps she'd have red hair, auburn hair, a Titian blonde. Aretino had to flee Venice when he was accused of sodomy. He had eight beautiful mistresses in a great palace on the Grand Canal. And I've never had a woman. Wedding parties, fellows phoning easy girls, through all that, lonely as a cloud. Horrible coward, I guess. That night walking with Wenny along the road to Blue Hill, couple of girls wanting to be picked up, their eyes under the arclight clicking into ours. Hullo, kiddo. Hello, cutie. But Wenny, that sort of thing just isn't done. Danger of exposure, too, scandal, disease. And the street through Somerville, dark under the May-rustling trees, pink blobs of arclights and the shuddering, green fringes of foliage about them and the hips, the wabbly hips of stumpy girls. When walking, when welldressed people walked, thinking of the Renaissance, of distant splendid things, all this surged about them out of the long streets of night. Festering web of desire, grimy, probing hands, groping eyes, toughs and hard girls circling like dogs before a fight. Wrestling, sweaty bodies, hands palping, feeling, feeling up . . . O, I don't want to think of all that. Oldfashioned, jolly wedding. Pull yourself together.

Fanshaw sat a long while with his head buried in his hands, his elbows on his knees, staring at the gravel between his feet. After a while he got up, cold and stiff. The dazzle of the champagne had passed off. The orchestra in the house was playing a foxtrot.—Probably caught a cold sitting out here like an idiot. He walked meditatively towards the conservatory, scraped his feet off on the mat and stepped in. The warm, sugary air was soothing after the rawness of outdoors. He stood a long while looking at the little sprouts that had formed at the tips of the fronds of a big Australian fern. The door at the end of the conservatory opened, letting in a burst of ragtime from the drawing room, voices, sliding of feet on a hardwood floor. All of a sudden, he wanted to go away, to be walking by himself down the road to the station. He went out into the garden again for fear someone should see him and speak to him. He'd slip away without saying goodby. Such a crowd, no one could possibly notice. Groping in his pocket for his coatcheck, he went round the house towards the front door. In an embrasure beside a fieldstone chimney was a trellised bench, on the bench a hat of orange tulle, beside the hat a fluffy, peachcolored dress, a flushed face thrown back, a long lock of undone hair curling spikily over a shoulder, and stooped about her, half holding her up, a young man in a black suit. Her eyes were closed, his face crushed into hers. One hand gripped the young man hard like a claw by the elbow. Fanshaw stood a moment, breathless, staring at them. Then he walked off fast with the blood throbbing in his ears.

On the way to the station, he kept thinking:—And the years slip by like telegraph poles past you in the train, and people marry and spoon on benches, and I'm always alone, moral, refined, restrained. If I were only made like Wenny, I'd enjoy life. Disgusting, though, out in the open like that, where anybody could see, worse than factory hands at Norumbega.

One must try to be beautiful about life.

VI

DROPS fell shining from the trees about him into the trodden, yellow slush of the path at his feet. In the air, shuddering with the foretaste of spring of the thaw, were constant rainbow glints of water. Wenny's knees and shoulders ached. His feet were swollen from frostbites. The bristles on his chin rasped against the upturned collar of his coat.—Well, it would be spring soon, he was saying to himself, and this spring . . . Fanshaw's grey raincoat and long, meditative stride and his rubbers flashed past among the Saturday afternoon crowd. Without thinking, Wenny ran after him.

10 "Hello, Fanshaw."

"O, Wenny," Fanshaw thrust out both hands; "I've been almost worried sick about you. Where have you been? My dear boy, you look a wreck."

"I don't see why."

"Here it is, four days you've vanished from the face of the earth."

"I haven't been anywhere else that I know of."

"Nan's been fearfully uneasy."

"That's funny."

"That's quite all right. She told me all about it. I told her it was just

20 nerves, that morning. She thought it was, too. You must take better care of yourself. But Wenny, where have you been?" Fanshaw's voice was full of hasty reassurance.

"Looking for a job."

"You poor child! Look, I've got to go to the Touraine. We can wash up and go up to Nan's. She said she'd be in at teatime."

"No, I'd rather not."

"You must come, Wenny. O, when will you grow up? Let's walk along, we're obstructing traffic."

"First, you must lend me fifty cents," said Wenny with a dry, little

30 laugh. "I'm most split with hunger."

"Can't you wait till we get out to Nan's? She'll have tea for us."

"No, I can't, Fanshaw, you old fool. I haven't eaten since yesterday morning, or maybe it was the day before that."

"Good God! There's Dupont's opposite. Let's go up there, a horrid place, but you won't mind eating something there, will you? But Wenny, why didn't you tell me you were all out of money?"

As they climbed the stairs, a smell of food and baking powder filled Wenny's nostrils. He inhaled it eagerly. In the restaurant it was very stuffy; a couple of waitresses in starched aprons were sitting at tables. A grimy man in his shirtsleeves carried in a tray of freshwashed glasses in through a green baize door. As Wenny pulled off his overcoat he thought: I'm going to faint. Letting the coat drop to the floor, he grabbed the table and lowered himself into a chair. The expression of consternation on Fanshaw's face as he picked up the coat made Wenny   10 laugh so that his eyes filled with tears.

"Well, what will you have? Don't eat too much, it might make you sick."

"O, Fanshaw, you're such an old woman."

The waitress, a rawboned woman with dead cod's eyes, hung over the table threateningly.

"Bring me some boiled eggs and tea and toast, right away, please." Something in Wenny exulted strangely under the hostile glare of the waitress as she looked at his muddy shoes and unshaven chin.

"Three minutes?"   20

"Yes, and quickly, please."

The waitress rustled starchily away.

"How funny, Fanshaw, I'd been thinking of boiled eggs for hours and I never thought about their being three minutes."

"But where have you been, you poor child? . . . I've been to Cham Mason's wedding."

"Heaps of wonderful places. . . . I've been finding my place in society."

"Where?"

"On the benches in the Common."   30

"But why didn't you go to the Alumni Employment Bureau? They'd have found you a job."

"I didn't want that kind of a job."

The smell of the bread the waitress set before him was over-poweringly sweet. His fingers trembled so, he spilt half the egg on the side of the glass in breaking it. He ate hurriedly without tasting anything.

"Bring me two more eggs, please. . . . Lord, but tea is wonderful stuff." The warm savor of tea filled his head. All of a sudden, he felt very talkative. "I tried to ship as a seaman. You stand in a large room   40 full of pipesmoke, and a man chalks up the names of ships on a blackboard. . . . The finest names of ships: there's been the *Arethusa* and the *Adolphus Q. Bangs* and the *Heart's Desire* and the *Mus-kokacola* or something like that. . . . But I always seemed to get down to the office too late, or I didn't have five dollars to give the mate or something. Didn't have much luck with busboy either. It's amazing, Fanshaw, how many people are just crazy to wash dishes."

Wenny laughed and choked over a gulp of tea.

"Don't eat so fast," said Fanshaw sharply.

"Why not?"

"You'll choke, that's why."

10   "God, I wish I would. . . . Have you ever . . . felt so's you didn't care if you choked or not? That's me . . . D'you know I met a fine kid named Whitey. He could go without eating three days an' never notice it. I could never do that. I don't guess there's much of anything I could do."

Fanshaw was looking at his watch.

"Really, we should be going. . . . I've got to go out to dinner; Wenny, I wish there were something I could do to help."

"You can pay for my eggs, you old put you."

Fanshaw paid the check; then he said rather solemnly:

20   "Look, you must let me lend you some money."

"All right, give me five bucks."

At the door, Wenny waited a moment for Fanshaw to come from the washroom. His head was singing dizzily. It's all up now, he was saying to himself. He thought of his room and his bed; delicious it will be to stretch out between the clean, smooth sheets and sleep.

Going up Huntington Avenue on the car, he felt a haze of contentment stealing over him. All about, people nodded to the joggle, hatchetfaced women and flabby-jowled men. Fanshaw's talk and his own answers droned beyond a great, drowsy curtain in which the

30   phrase "Par delicatesse, j'ai perdu la vie," wove in and out endlessly. Outside, autos slushed through streets running with the thaw. Fanshaw was saying something about the deceitful warmth of the day, springlike.

In front of them, four seats ahead, in a blue hat with cherries on it, was Ellen. Wenny clenched his teeth; why should his damn pulse speed up so? She turned and stared at him with a comical little expression about her mouth. He drew his eyes away quickly, felt himself hideously flushing.—You skunk, afraid to recognize her because she's a whore, are you? Don't want Fanshaw to know, do you?

40   clicked a crisp, angry voice in his head. Her lips were pale today, without the sweetish, fatty smell of the rouge on her lips that night. And only four nights ago; how long. He didn't dare look at her again.

The car stopped.

"Come on, Wenny," came Fanshaw's voice briskly.

They were splashing along towards the purple lacework of twigs of the Fenway trees. Fanshaw was talking unconcernedly about a Caravaggio the museum had bought that had turned out to be spurious. And there were the worn, gold letters "The Swansea" sliding down the glass door and the oil smell of the elevator.—O, I must go away from here. Then Nan's oval face, a green flash of her eyes in his, her voice strangely caressing. Brainstorm, the comfortable word. Teacups clinking and the steam of the teapot and dusk very misty over the Fenway.

Why hadn't he gone away with Ellen, spoken to her, kissed her in front of Fanshaw? If she'd fallen in love with him, it would have been up to the ears, the whole hog; those women were like that.

"You just missed Fitzie," Nan was saying. She had just poured herself out a cup of tea into which she shook meditatively a few drops of cream from the empty pitcher. "O, she's such a scream. . . . I don't know what I'd do without her. Now I know all the gossip and about the Summer Street murder case and everything. . . . And do you remember the girl in the Fadettes we thought was the violinist at the Venice? Well, that wasn't the girl at all. Fitzie told me all about her. . . . It seems she came back to try to get her job again, and Mrs. Thing, who runs it, said of course it would be impossible. I don't see what her morals have to do with her playing, do you? And the poor girl's going to have a baby. . . . Fitzie was so funny about it, said she thought it was terrible things like that should happen so soon. . . . O, what would I do without Fitzie?"

"But the fellow she went off with must be a scoundrel," said Fanshaw. "Poor woman!"

"She ought to have thought twice before she did it, that's all. It's not his fault particularly."

"And dry-rotted scraping out *Light Cavalry* for the Fadettes . . ." Wenny caught himself. No, he wasn't going to say anything. Nan looked him full in the face for an instant. Her eyes were dark, dilated; he thought she was going to burst into tears.

"Such droll things have been going on at the conservatoire." Nan, her face flushing, threw herself into a stream of small talk. "Poor Isolda Jones is madly in love with Salinski and had hysterics during her violin lesson, and there's a dreadful scandal about the last Symphony concert. It seems that . . ." She stopped talking. No one spoke. They could hear the brisk snapping of the steam pipes under the window. Fanshaw moved his spoon uneasily about in his saucer. "Wenny, have some more to eat," she said sharply and got to her feet and went to the window.

10

20

30

40

Wenny sat without moving, staring at her back, dark and slender against the dusk.

"You must be dreadfully exhausted, Wenny," said Fanshaw in a low voice.

"The evening star's red tonight," said Nan from the window. "Is it on account of the mist, or is it Mars, I wonder?"

"We could look it up in the almanac," said Fanshaw vaguely.

Wenny stood for a moment in the window beside Nan. His blood throbbed with other remembered stars, blooming green in the ame-
thyst sky above the Fenway, gulped suddenly by the stupid cubes of the further apartment houses. The green of them somehow shone in the lamps down brick streets where he and Nan had gone arm in arm in a forgotten dream of walking with her through a port town and seeing at the end of the street masts and tackle and bellying sails and white steam puffs from the sirens of steamers, and going together out to sea some sunset time.—She's in love with me. If I had the cour-age . . .

"Well, I must be off to the Hargroves' for dinner," said Fanshaw in a cheerful voice. "O, it is a relief to know you are all right, Wenny. We
were worried sick about you."

"I'm tired. I must go home," said Wenny firmly and turned away from Nan.

He went away without looking at her again.

*   *   *

My dear son:

It has pleased me more than I can say to hear of your sensible and manly course in taking a job. I am sure that earning your own living you will find inspiring and helpful, and that you will come to regret your past cal-lousness and restlessness. Indeed, this great trial may be a disguised blessing. We all have to learn by experience. I myself went through
moments in my youth inexpressibly painful for me to recall, bitter mo-ments of profligacy and despair, and that I came through them with my soul alive was only by the merciful Help of the All-knowing and All-forgiving Creator in Whom I have never lost faith, nay, not for one instant.

You, my dear boy, I trust and pray, will follow the same course. I cannot but think that had I not let my poor sister Elizabeth take you from us, from your real Christian home, your battle might have been less hard.

Your mother joins me in love and in the earnest hope that you will come back to us.

Your loving father,

JONAS E. WENDELL

Wenny folded the letter and put it back in his pocket. This was the third time he had read it. He gulped the rest of his coffee and left the lunchroom full of hurried breakfasters. Outside, the east wind stung his face, made his eyes water.

—Then it was March. Now it's April. Last time I told myself I'd kill myself if I stuck it another month. In September that was and in February, and now it's April. The music of the spheres makes the months revolve. . . . Think, you fool, think. Bitter moments of profligacy and despair. That's me all right, except he got the profligacy and I get the despair. Go whoring and repent and yours is the kingdom of God. A fine system all right, but he repented so damn hard he spoiled my fun. Like being a eunuch, funny that, a generation of eunuchs. Your sensible and manly course in taking a job, wasting breath coaching Mr. Dolan's dubs, accounted quite a genius at it, too. Inspiring and helpful. God! Poor Auntie's education. That's what it's done to me; and next winter teaching, helping to inoculate other poor devils with the same dry rot.

He was walking out along Massachusetts Avenue broad and dusty between the little jigsawed houses of Somerville. It was a bitter, slategrey day of razorcold wind. In the irritation of his mood, he took joy in the dust smarting in his eyes and the ache of the cold in his forehead. Gradually, his thoughts faded under the regular beat of his steps. It was Sunday, and church bells had begun to ring.—Gee, I must go home or I'll be getting blue again, he said to himself; the biddy'll have done the room. He walked back towards Cambridge without thinking of anything, shivering, his hands deep in his pockets. When he had slammed the door behind him, he threw himself on the bed, with cheeks that throbbed from the wind, and lay a long while staring at the ceiling.

He yanked at his watch. Ten-thirty. Now he's waiting while they sing the first hymn, fiddling with his prayerbook, wondering if he's forgotten any of the main headings of the sermon. And I'm just like him. Less energy, that's all. A chip of the old block. Listen to them settling back flabbily into their pews in the mustard yellow and mudpurple and niggerpink light from the imitation stained glass windows. Now they're on their feet again, better than trained seals. His voice so suave, so booming—my voice will be like that—Let us pray.

Wenny sat up on the edge of the bed.—God damn my father; I will live him down if it kills me.

He started turning over the pages of the books on his table, seeking escape in their familiar, chattering type, in the accustomedness of their smell, from the eating acid of his thoughts. Outside a church bell still spilt an occasional ragged zinc splinter of sound into the sterile wind.

*   *   *

Outside of Herb Roscoe's door, Wenny was struck by the usual, faint smell of oiled leather and pipesmoke. A tall man in a grey, flannel shirt, with face and neck and forearms lean and very tanned, opened the door slowly to his knock.

"How's the armory?" said Wenny.

"Pretty good. How's yourself?" said Roscoe in a bass, drawling 10 voice. "Sit down." As he spoke, he swept a pile of books off one of the arms of the Morris chair. Then he stood in the fireplace, where a pair of high, leather moccasins were to soak in a pan of oil, polishing a rifle while he talked. "Gee, you should have seen the scores we made at rifle practice yesterday. Not a soul could hit a barn door. I think we'll have the rottenest damn team. . . . I hate this place."

"So do I," said Wenny, lying back in the chair with his eyes half closed.

"Why don't you get out of it? I'm goin' the very minute I get my degree like a flash o' greased lightnin'."

20   "Haven't got the energy."

"Hell, man, it don't take much energy to buy a railroad ticket."

"Doesn't it?"

"How's your soft job?"

"I'm going to chuck it soon. I think I'll go to Mexico with you, Herb."

"All right, come along. Better learn to shoot though."

"I've had another letter from my father."

"How's he now?"

"Tickled to death."

30   "Well, that's good. I'm glad to hear it. You know you oughn't to be so highbrow about your father. I imagine he's a good scout." Roscoe put the rifle up on the rack over the mantel and began to fill a pipe, slowly and methodically, "D'you know, I think all this father and son agitation is foolishness, Wendell. You are like your father, we all are, so why fuss about it? Nobody's forcin' you to live with him. But I wouldn't stay on round here. It isn't healthy for you, seeing how you feel about it. I wouldn't stay a minute except for the library."

Roscoe walked back and forth in front of the fireplace as he talked with the soft, lithe steps of a man accustomed to stalk noiselessly 40 through woods.

"Say, Herb, will you lend me that little .22 revolver of yours for a day or two?"

"What do you want with it? You aren't going to shoot up the dean of the Graduate School with it, are you?"

"No, no," said Wenny, laughing a little shrilly. "It's curious . . . I'd like to carry a gun for a day or two. . . . In the first place, I've never done it, and the thought of death in my back pocket makes me a little nervous, and I'd like to try my nerve out, and then I just might need it. . . . I'll tell you why. . . . . I'm going in for low life a little. Heavy slumming . . . I'll tell you about it in a day or two, honestly I will, when things get under way a little. There's a woman in the case and everything and a bum and a Chinaman." 10

"Gee, I wish you'll let me in on it. I'm just pining away for excitement in this dull hole."

"Honestly, I'll tell you all about it in a day or two, but I'm such a damn coward I want to test my nerve out alone first. Don't be uneasy if I don't turn up for a day or two. I'll be all right."

Roscoe handed him a little, blue steel revolver and a handful of cartridges.

"Don't get pinched for concealed weapons." 20

"Never fear," said Wenny, jumping tensely to his feet.

"Do be careful, Wendell; it's always the man scared of a gun who shoots himself or the innocent bystanders instead of bagging his game. Get me?"

"O, I'll be careful. Anyway, there won't be any shooting. Just a precaution, like rubbers. But I must be off. I have an engagement. Thanks a lot."

Wenny, going out the door, caught a contracted look of anxiety on Roscoe's tanned face as, puffing at his pipe, he strode back and forth in front of the fireplace. Wenny went down the dark, brick corridor 30 towards his own room, the gun in his back pocket pressing hard and cold on his thigh.

*   *   *

Wenny walked along muddy paths in the Fenway. Patches of snow among the shrubberies were crumbling fast in the tingle of spring that flushed the misty afternoon. The twigs of forsythias showed intensest yellow against the sopping grey of the turf. In the gravel paths there was a tiny, lisping sound of water as the frost came out of the ground. The rustle of it in the ruddy light was maddening like the rustle of silk.—This womanish hysteria, he was saying to himself; to escape it tense and collected the way the earth slithers out from between the 40 tight fists of winter. A man and a woman, frowsy and middle-aged, sat on a bench, a hat with mauve pansies beside a dust-grained derby; as Wenny passed, the woman was tapping restlessly on the gravel with a narrow, pointed toe. The thought came to him:—Perhaps Nan and I will be like that, afraid to look in each other's eyes because we didn't dare when we were young, and talk about if we'd done this and if we'd done that. . . . What a rotten thing to think about the first day of spring.

10   In his back pocket, a hard shape pressed against the fleshy part of his thigh; from its focus, his whole being was stiffening to hardness.

He turned and with a sudden spring in his step crossed the street from the park, passed the livid, tomblike oblong of the Dental Clinic, and pulled open the glass door of "The Swansea." A grindorgan was playing at the curb. The glass door slammed behind him, cutting off the "Marseillaise" on an upward note. He ran up the stairs and stood still a moment in front of the reddish-stained door.

Through a bitter film of constraint, he saw Nan in a pearlgrey dress pulling open the door for him.

"I never saw that one before."

20   "This dress? Do you like it?"

Down the hall came the aviary sound of people at tea.

"They'll be gone in a minute; don't look so worried." Nan looked in his face with a little, mocking smile that faded out tremulously as she spoke. "Do wait, Wenny, I want to talk to you."

He followed the swish of her dress down the corridor. Richly, the curve of her neck caught a glow of creamy rose from the pearlcolored silk.

"Have a cup of tea," she said in her hostess voice after introducing him to a large woman with beaded, tragedy eyes and a lean, whiny-

30 voiced man who stood beside the teatable. Balancing a cup, Wenny settled himself against the wall beside the mantel, tried to think of nothing.

" . . . Dreadful, isn't it, how Boston is being transformed?"

"No, really, you wouldn't know it any more."

"We'd got used to the Irish, but now walking across the Common you don't see a soul who's not a Jew or an Italian."

"But don't you think they bring us anything?" Nan's voice, indifferent, from the teatable.

"What can they bring but fleas? The scum of south Europe . . ."

40   " . . . O, Nancibel, you do have the most delightful teas."

"Why, Jane, I often wonder why on earth I do it. Doesn't it seem the height of absurdity to collect a lot of mixed people, a regular zoo, in a room and pour a little tea down their throats and tell them: 'Now, have a good time?'"

"But one must have some sort of society. . . . And you know perfectly well you are just fishing, Nancibel. Why, the cleverest people in Boston come to your teas, and as for celebrities!"

"Mr. Preston, won't you let me give you a little more tea? Yours looks cold and horrid. . . ."

" . . . No, I wouldn't call *The Way of All Flesh* a great novel."

"But, really, I'd like to know what is great then."

"A great satire but not a great novel . . . It's too embittered, not   10
Olympian and balanced enough to be truly great."

"But as a philosopher . . ."

"Ah, as a philosopher . . ."

Through rigid, glassy layers, Wenny watched the nodding of heads, lifting of teacups, setting down of plates, brushing of fingertips. Occasionally, he saw himself going through wooden gestures of politeness, heard himself speak. At last they had all gone; he was alone with Nan in the room that smelt of tea and scalded lemon and cake. Outside the windows, the ruddy mist was purpling to twilight.

"O, Wenny, why on earth do I do it?"   20

"I guess because you like it, Nan."

"Probably you're right." She laughed happily. "I'd never thought of that before. . . . No, I hate it, and all those people. Imagine what Fitzie told me today. She said you always turned up as a sign that tea was over and it was time to wait not on the order of her going but go at once. . . . Isn't she a fool? Then she added that it was rumored round Jordan that my engagement to Fanshaw would be announced any day. . . . O, Wenny, people are a scream!"

"I probably do look rather grouchy when I come here and find a lot of those young hens cackling about your technique and that wretched   30
old cadenza hound. . . ."

"It's pretty ridiculous, Wenny, that two people who know each other as well as we do can't talk. . . ." Nan interrupted suddenly, speaking slowly, choosing her words: "Can't talk about our . . . can't explain ourselves. O, I wonder if we'll ever know each other."

"Perhaps the fact that we need to explain ourselves . . ."

"You mean it proves that we can't ever?"

Wenny nodded.

"Or perhaps it's just cowardice," he went on after a long pause, feeling all his life throb sickeningly within the cold bars of his ribs.   40
"Almost everything is that."

"Why can't we be sensible?"

"It's not sensible, it's alive I'd want to be. . . . But this is repeating," he said harshly with trembling lips, straightening himself up. It was as if a rind had burst in him, letting out warm, sweetish floods; as if he were crying beside a grave where she had lain dead for years and lifetimes, his memory full of an ivory body he had loved.

They were silent, not looking at each other.

There was a knock at the door. Nan drew her breath in sharply and went to open. Wenny heard Fanshaw's voice in the hall.

"O, I'm so glad to find you. I thought it'ld be just my luck to miss you both and spend a dull evening all alone. I have had the most detestable day."

"Let's walk in town to supper," said Nan in a hurried, throaty tone.

Walking down a broad street towards town, they had the dome of the Christian Science Church ahead of them, swelled with purple against a tremendous, scarletflaring sky across which grimy clouds of pistachio green scudded on gusts of rising wind. Sharp flaws of cold were clotting the mist and chilling all reminiscence of thaw and spring out of the air. Footsteps rang shrill and fast on the pavements and were lost in the clang of streetcars and whir of motors grinding slowly in the heavy traffic on Massachusetts Avenue. Overhead, above the bright shine of shop windows through which faces drifted steadily, outline drifting into outline, like snowflakes past an arclight, the sky was a churning of dark green clouds fast blotting the clear, fiery afterglow. Wenny could hear himself talking to Fanshaw as they walked, but all the while he was intent on the people he passed; smooth, velvety-warm masks of young men and girls, wooden masks of men bleached by offices, crumpled masks of old women; under them all seemed to tremble something jellylike and eager, something half caught sight of in their eyes that had thrilled to the warm afternoon, that this sudden, cold searching through the dusty, concrete grooves of the city congealed to shuddering crystals of terror. He wanted to climb on a hydrant and talk, to draw people in circle after circle about him and explain all the joy and agony he felt in words so simple that they would tear off their masks and tell their lives, too; it would be his face, his eyes, his mouth molding words all about him when the masks were off. The picture sharpened painfully in his mind.

"Look at all that yellow broom in the window," Fanshaw was saying. As they passed a flowershop, they caught a momentary sweet gust of hothouses. "That's the real plantagenet, I think, that the Black Prince wore on his helmet. Strange to think of it this cold night in a Boston flowershop."

"Say it with flowers," Nan put in laughing.

"Exactly," said Fanshaw. "Yet why should there be that horrid rasp in the advertising phrase and the unction in 'langage des fleurs'? Do things seem beautiful only when they are unaccustomed?"

"Perhaps it's that not being customary and diurnal puts them in the proper light . . . so that we can really see them," said Nan.

"I think it's just that we like to kid ourselves along. This may be a moment as important in the history of Boston as the time of lilies, when Pico della Mirandola first rode into Florence, as you and Mr. Pater are so fond of telling us, Fanshaw," broke in Wenny. "But we don't know anything about it. We'd probably have gone grumbling and growling into town for dinner if we'd lived in Florence then, just as we do here, and complained what a dull town it was."

"But can't you imagine people of another caliber altogether from us?"

"Perhaps I can, Nan . . . but what I mean is it's our fault, not the fault of the century."

"What's our fault, Wenny?" asked Fanshaw smiling indulgently.

"That we are so damn rotten."

"But we're not. What we've lost in color and picturesqueness, we've made up in . . ."

"In sheepishness and cowardice, I'll grant you that."

"Now, Wenny."

Wenny saw himself in bitter distortion, standing on a hydrant confessing idiocies in phrases out of his father's letters to crowds who wore his face as a mask on their own and bleated approval like sheep, baa, baa, at every pause. It all dissolved into an obscene muddle of leering faces.—If I could only stop thinking.

They were cutting diagonally across the Common under a hurrying sky lit by a last, mustard-green flare from the west. The electric signs along Tremont Street bit icily through the lacy pattern of the stirring twigs of trees. The wind was getting steadier and colder, occasionally shot with a fine lash of snow.

"No, but we couldn't live without the ideal that somewhere at some time people had found life a sweeter, stronger draught than we find it," Fanshaw was saying, "that the flatness of our lives hasn't been the rule. . . . I don't think the fault's with us at all, Wenny. I think we're great people. . . . It's just this fearful environment we have to live down, the narrowness of our families, our bringing up, the moral code and all that. The people of the Renaissance were great because they lived in a great period. . . ."

"Well, we haven't had much chance yet; give us time, Wenny," said Nan.

"Time means nothing. You can't make "Narcissus" into the "Prelude" from *Tristan* by working on it. The germ would be here."

"But we are learning, Wenny. Taught by our ideal of the past, of the Greeks and the people of the Renaissance, we are learning to surround ourselves with beautiful things, to live less ugly, money-grabbing lives."

"Culture, you mean. God, I'd rather rot in Childs' dairy lunches. Culture's mummifying the corpse with scented preservatives. Better let it honestly putrefy, I say."

"And while we argue about how we ought to live, things muddle
10 along," said Nan.

"And the months go by. . . . Look at me, I'm twenty-three years old and I've done nothing ever, never anything of any sort," cried Wenny savagely.

"But you're not even hatched yet, Wenny. Give yourself time. . . . When you've got your M.A."

"Won't be any different ten years from now. I know it won't. You know it won't."

Nobody answered. Wenny walked along at Nan's side, his fists clenching and unclenching nervously. They had reached the Park
20 Street corner of the Common. The steeple of the church stood up lithe and slender out of the muddle of arclights into the tumultuous sky, where the frayed edges of clouds trailed along ruddy from the reflection of streets. In the lee of the subway stations, sailors loafed with the broad collars of their jackets turned up, watching the wind tussle with the skirts of a couple of girls, who strutted back and forth with jerky, impatient steps. A trail of Salvation Army lasses hobbled by following a fat, redcheeked man with a cornet. Through the narrow, crowded street toward Scollay Square, the wind was less searching. There was warmth in rubbing shoulders, meeting eyes. In
30 the floods of light in front of the moving picture houses, dapper young men in overcoats belted at the waist waited for girls they had made dates with. A fat man threw away his cigarette and advanced towards a blonde girl who had just crossed the street; with one hand he was straightening his necktie. The smile on his puffy, razorscraped face kindled in her straight lips. Up a side street, a man in a red sweater was preaching about something in a voice like a sea lion's. In the middle of the square, a policeman had hold of a holloweyed little man whiskered like a bottlecleaner whom he was shaking by the shoulder and roaring at. Wenny jumped back to avoid a truck lumbering up
40 noisily out of Cornhill.—Why didn't I let it run over me? Then the shop windows of Hanover Street, full of price signs, were sliding past. Wenny felt vague interest in the streets and people he was walking among, the sort of disconnected interest he had felt when a child in

the tableaux in the Old Mill at Revere, gliding along through expressionless dark, occasionally peering out at incidents, random gestures and faces.—A year ago, he was thinking, I would have imagined
every man, woman, and child I met part of some absurd, romantic
vortex I was just on the point of being sucked into myself. I know
better now. Do I?

"Funny, the thought," he said aloud, "that I pass people on the
street and say to myself what wonderful lives they must be living, and
they look at me out of their own emptiness and say the same
thing. . . . We're going to the Venice, aren't we?"   10

"Mind, no garlic," put in Fanshaw.

"We'll even let you have the eternal broiled lamb chop without
hooting."

A flurry of snow, fine as sand, drove down the street.

"What do you think of this for the Boston climate?" said Nan. "A
blizzard in April."

"Here we are!"

The restaurant was nearly empty. They shook the snow off their
overcoats and settled themselves at the round table in the window.

"What's so nice about this place, in spite of the garlic and the stains   20
on the cloth and everything," Fanshaw was saying, "is that it gives us a
breathing space from Boston, a quiet eminence where we can sit
undisturbed and look about us. . . . O, Wenny, do pull up your
necktie."

"Now, Fanshaw, you shan't heckle Wenny," said Nan, laughing.

The orchestra had struck up "Funiculì, funiculà" with great vigor.
Wenny was looking at the girl who played the violin. Something in the
tilt of the chin was painfully like Nan, only all the features were
heavier, the lips coarser and less intense; many men had kissed them
perhaps.—To kiss Nan's lips. No, I mustn't think of all that.I will drive   30
it out of me, down into me. Tonight it's calm; cold I must be, to weigh
everything. In spite of him, the tune filled his mind with streets full of
carnival, scampering, heavybreasted women pelting him with roses.

"The ladies' three-piece band is doing itself proud tonight," he
shouted boisterously.

—Like this always, these dreams. I must put an end to them. It's on
account of these dream women I've not made Nan love me; everything has slipped by. What's the good of dreams? It's hard actuality I
want, will have. These exotic moonings, so calfish . . .

Yama, yama, blarc of brass bands, striped flags waving against   40
picture postcard scenery, brown oarsmen with flashing teeth and
rings in their ears, pulling the boat throbbing, swift, across the purple
bay; and Nan; both of us lolling on red cushions. Bay of Naples and

musical comedy moonlight and a phonograph in a flat in a smell of baby carriages and cabbage, grinding out love songs. "Funiculì, funiculà." O, the mockery of it.

"Gee, what a horrible tune, though."

"Hackneyed, I should say, Wenny, but it's rather jolly, and when they play it on those boats on the Grand Canal, it's almost thrilling. . . ."

"To Cook's tourists and little schoolma'ams from Grand Rapids."

"Isn't it a little like sour grapes that we should be so scornful of
10   them?" put in Nan gently.

"I'm not scornful of them. I am them. . . . We are just like them. Can't you see what I mean, Nan? I can see that they are ridiculous and pitiful. How much more ridiculous and pitiful we must be."

"But from that point of view everything must be . . . well, just ashes; everybody ridiculous and pitiful," said Nan slowly, with a flash in her eyes. "I'm willing to admit that in a sense, I suppose, yet certain things are dreadfully important to me—my friends, my music, my career, my sense of fitness. I don't see that those things are ridiculous. . . . Of course, one can make oneself sound clever by
20   making fun of anything, but that doesn't change it anyway."

The hot light in her eyes, flushing her cheeks, her parted lips, were a stab of pain for him.

"O, I can't say what I mean," muttered Wenny.

"Do you know what you mean?" said Fanshaw.

"Perhaps not."

"And you forget what you're so fond of talking about, Wenny."

"What?"

"The gorgeousness of matter. That's your pet phrase."

—Taste of veal with tomato and peppers, savor of frizzled olive oil,
30   little seeds mashed between the front teeth into a prickly, faint aroma, and wine, the cool curve of the glass against my lips, the tang of it like rainy sunsets. I could sit here imagining it and never drink, imagining Nan's lips. . . . He picked up the glass and drank off the goldcolored wine at a gulp so that it choked him. He coughed and spluttered into his napkin.

"I follow you there, if you include the idea of material pleasures being purged of their grossness, by reason, fitness, as Nan says. So made the raw material of beauty," Fanshaw was saying. Wenny coughed and spluttered into his napkin.
40   "Drink a litte water," Fanshaw added.

"More Orvieto, you mean," said Wenny hoarsely. "By the way, is Orvieto in Tuscany?"

"No, in Umbria, I think; that's where the great Signorelli frescoes of

the Last Judgment are, that strange, dry, hideously violent piece of
macabre."

"Gee, I'd like to see them."

"You will, some day."

"If I don't see the actual subject first . . . No, Burton Holmes is as
far as I'll ever get towards Umbria."

"Why lots of people work their way over."

"You haven't seen me do it yet, have you? That's what I was saying.
The world is full of people doing every conceivable sort of thing. The
streets are full of them. You can see the things in their eyes."

"Well, why not you?" said Nan breathlessly.

"Before I came to college, I spent my time dreaming, and now I
spend it gabbling about my dreams that have died and begun to stink.
Why, the only genuine thing I ever did in my life was get drunk, and I
haven't done that often."

Wenny drank down his wine again. His hair was wet. His heart
pounded with exultation in the look of wincing pain on Nan's face.

"Suppose we start home," Nan said. "I have a little headache
tonight."

Out in the streets, the snowflakes danced dazzlingly, ruddy and
green, and shivered gold through flawed crystals of light from windows and arclights. Faces bloomed and faded in a jumbled luminous
mist, white as plaster casts, red as raw steak, yellow and warted like
summer squashes, smooth and expressionless like cantaloupes. Occasionally, a door yawned black and real in the spinning flicker of the
snow and the lights, or a wall seemed to bulge to splitting with its
denseness. In the shelter of the subway entrance, they stood hesitat-
ing a moment.

"Why don't you both come out to my place?" said Nan in a pleading
voice. "We'll make some chocolate or something."

"No, I want to think," answered Wenny.

"But you can think there all you want. . . . And it's such a miserable night."

"I'm going to Brookline to Mother's, anyway; I'll go as far as your
door," said Fanshaw.

"You can amuse yourselves picking my character to pieces all the
way out," said Wenny boisterously.

They none of them laughed.

"Well, then, good night."

Wenny watched them go down the steps, Nan in her long buff coat,
Fanshaw with his wet hat pulled over his eyes. Nan half turned and
waved with a little thwarted gesture of the hand. For a second she
paused, then with the slightest shrug of the shoulders followed Fan-

shaw's tall figure out of sight past the change booth. Wenny took two
steps to follow, but the impulse died sickeningly like a spoiled sky-
rocket falling. He thought he was going to cry, and turned about and
walked recklessly into the blinding, bright dance of the snow.

*   *   *

The wind had dropped. Great, sloppy flakes were spinning slowly
down between the houses, filling the tents of light cast by the street
lamps. Wenny had been walking fast with long, irregular steps
muffled by the crunching carpet of the snow. His feet and legs were
wet and very cold. At a corner he stopped and leaned a moment
10   against a wall. The shadows in the windows of the house opposite
were blackly concrete and the walls heavy-built out of reddish
darkness. People were ghosts with faces of unnatural bright pink that
flitted past him through the leisurely chaos of the snow. In their eyes,
at the edges of hats, from the ledges of shop windows, glittered little
globules of moist brightness. From gutters came a continual drip of
melted snow.—Now, what bar haven't I been to? he kept asking
himself, as he stood listening to the little hiss of the snow and the
slushy padding of footsteps.—I'd forgotten Frank Locke's; and he
walked on with lurching strides.
20   After the velvety blur of the snow, the bar room assailed him with
needles and facets of glitter on brass and crystal that shivered in the
mirrors into sharp, angular grottoes. He shook the snow off his coat
and let himself fall heavily into a chair. The hard shape in his back
pocket rapped against his hip. His spine went cold at the touch of it.
"A martini cocktail, please," he said to the thin, large-eyed man
with a scrawny neck who came for his order.
The little mirrors in the ceiling and the glinty knobs and bottle ends
of the partitions all radiated endlessly in dusty looking glasses on the
walls, so that Wenny felt himself drunkenly spinning through air
30   heavy with beersmells and whisky and old tobacco smoke in the
middle of a crazy merrygoround. The men at tables round him were
tiny and gesticulating. The cocktail stung his mouth, sent writhing,
gold haze all through him. The glass was the center of a vortex into
which were sucked the cutting edges of light, flickering cones of green
and red brightness, the voices and the throbbing rubber faces of the
men in the bar. In his mind Fanshaw's voice and his father's voice
droning like antiphonal choirs:—Leanfaced people of the Renaissance
carried away helpless in their vermilion barge through snarling streets
shaken with the roar of engines: Stand therefore having your loins girt
40   about with the breastplate of righteousness . . . Of course, that's what
it reminds me of here, looking through the colored globes in the

drugstore window where I used to go to get aspirin for Auntie. Par delicatesse, par delicatesse . . .

"Waiter, another cocktail, please."

—This cocktail, smooth, smooth, hot tropic beaches, and the lean-faced men in their great barge deepchanting, sliding through lagoons of islands of the South Seas (first love, first South Sea island, the great things of life); brown girls girdled with red hybiscus pulling nets full of writhing silver through parrotgreen water. . . . God! I must pull myself together. I must think, not dream. . . . In the beginning was the word. . . . Think! and Noah begat three sons, Shem, Ham, and Japheth. . . . Poor little me, with holes in my stockings, sitting in my bedroom that had the cracked looking glass learning Genesis for Dad: The earth also was corrupt before God, the earth was filled with violence. . . . And God looked upon the earth and behold it was corrupt . . . corrupt . . . I must think, not dream putrid dreams. Dreams, the corruption of misery, soggy, thwarted. If I had a clean, sharp knife to cut away dreams. Herb's little gun will do as well. Par delicatesse j'ai perdu la vie.

"Hey, another martini, please."

He had no sense of being drunk any more. Things were still, icehard, iceclear all about him.—The little, neatly painted world of his childhood had been like that, breaks of lollipop-colored sunlight, little redroofed houses back among lawns of green baize, set about with toy evergreens, at doors varnished, farmers' wives in Dutch caps shepherding Noah's animals out of a cardboard ark, all cute and tiny, like through the wrong end of a telescope; and the smell of the enamel scaling off toys, the grain of wood grimed by the fingers, the dark gleam on the floor under the bay window.

"Another martini, please."

He drank it slowly in little sips, watching himself in the looking glass beside him. His hair was very curly with sweat, his dark eyebrows jauntily arched, his lips moist and red. He drank and the man in the looking glass drank. He stared into the black wells of the dilated pupils. Panic terror swooped on him all of a sudden; this face was not his face. The face was thinner, the upper lip tight over the teeth, the hair smooth and steel grey, the jowls pinkish, close shaved, constricted by a collar round backwards.—My father's face, and Dad's voice: David, my boy, taking a job has pleased me more than I can say, sensible and manly course . . . I am sure that earning your living you will find inspiring and helpful and regret callousness and restlessnesss. . . . I, myself, had bitter moments in my youth inexpressionably painful for me to recall of profligacy and despair. . . . A thin shrieking, interrupting in his head:—My God, I'm going mad, mad,

mad. The pulpit voice boomed louder:—It was like this, David, I was
not content with my lot and told myself in my boyish pride that life
was short and the world wide, and wanted to run away to sea. I was
one of those filthy dreamers mentioned in the Gospels who defile the
flesh, despise dominion and speak evil of dignities. And I fell so low
that, inexpressibly painful to recall, I took up in a low dive with a
scarlet woman and arranged with her that she should give herself to
me for five dollars, and I followed her to her room and she divested
herself of her clothes, and I stood before her trembling with lust, and
all at once a sword cleaving me, a light searing me, I felt my flesh
corrupt before God, and I felt the mercy of God in a great white light
about me, and I rushed out sobbing and called upon God. And that is
how, dearly beloved brethren, I was called to the ministry. . . . Let us
pray. . . .

Rustle of Sunday dresses, a couple of coughs from the back, Wenny
in short pants kneeling trembling in the full, booming blast of his
father's prayer, watching the patches of pink and purple and mustard-
yellow light cast on the pew ahead by the sun shining through the
colored glass of the windows, then caught away in a dream of red
Indians running through a birch wood, and roused by the long,
droning inflections: Do good and communicate and forget not, for
with such sacrifice God is well pleased. Women's voices shrilling high:

How firm a foundation ye say-aints of the Lord . . .

and the sound of money clinking in plates.

Everything was spinning again, and he was saying over and over:—I
must pull myself together, pull myself together, for that face is my
face and my father's voice is my voice.

"All right, mister, closing time." There was a heavy hand on his
shoulder.

He reeled out into the street, his hand over his face to wipe away
the memory of the dilated pupils of his eyes in the looking glass. The
air was cold and harsh in his nostrils, against his temples. He walked
slowly through streets neatly carpeted with snow that made tiny
whirlwinds at corners in the clear gusts of wind. His thoughts clicked
with mechanical precision.—I'm sober now; I've got to decide. Up
towards Beacon Hill. Something always goes mad in me when I go to
Frank Locke's. Mustn't go again. Again! How silly, as if there were
going to be any agains. Now in me my father'll be dead. Par delicatesse j'ai perdu la vie. Mustn't hurry. Pleasant to stroll about a town
the last night before going away; bought your ticket and everything.
Where? Want ad: Respectable house offers agreeably furnished room,

suitable for suicide . . . How fine to be cool like this. This is the secret at last. Never been happier in my life. Or am I just hideously drunk?

Slippery down this hill. The bridge the subway goes over, that's it. He felt for his watch. Gone, of course, pawned a thousand years ago to sleep with Ellen of Troy.

It was very quiet over the river. The snow lay straight on the ledges of the bridge. The lights of the esplanade flickered like stars through the clear, bleak night and cast little, tremulous sparks over the lacquered surface of the water.

The wind had blown all tracks out of the snow. Wenny cleared off the rail behind one of the turrets and sat looking at the water.

—Perhaps lovers have met here. No, the cops'ld be after them. No place for love in the city of Boston; place for death though.

He pulled the little revolver out of his back pocket and held it at arm's length.

—I have nerve for this, why not for the rest; for shipping on a windjammer, for walking with Nan down streets unaccountable and dark between blind, brick walls that tremble with the roar of engines, for her seagrey eyes in my eyes, her lips, the sweetish, fatty smell of Ellen's lips. Maybe death's all that, sinking into the body of a dark woman, with proud, cold thighs, hair black, black. I wonder if it shoots.

The trigger was well oiled. The shot rang out over the water. The rebound jerked his hand up.

—Shoot? Sure it does. Quick, now, there'll be somebody coming. Spread out your bed for me, Nan Ellen death.

He climbed to his feet on the parapet and pressed the muzzle of the gun under his chin. Warm it was. Black terror shrieked through him. He was breathing hard. With cold, firm hands, he made sure the barrel pointed straight through his throat to his brain. He pulled the trigger.

His body pitched from the parapet of the bridge, struck the snow-covered slant of the pier, and slid into the river.

VII

*F*ANSHAW opened his eyes, stretched himself in bed, and was aware, hazily, of luminous, grey sheets of rain outside the window. He reached for his watch and his glasses.—Seven-forty-three, that means ten minutes more of delicious languor. He took off his glasses again and lay staring at the ceiling, happily thinking of nothing. The steam-pipes were popping and cracking, and there was a dribble of water from the bathroom.—Ought to have them fix that faucet. His mind was groping to remember what the nine o'clock section meeting would be about. Fra Angelico, Lorenzo Monaco, Gozzoli, names of
10 Italian painters streamed through his head.—But we're through with them; must be about the Dutch, or some Fleming. Why cudgel his brains?—This was April: April, May, June, then the treadmill stopped. Freedom. Imagine living always free like a Chinese sage in a hut of rice matting beside a waterfall; to retire to an exquisite pavilion ornamented with red and black lacquer, living on rice and tea and trout from the stream. The mist steaming up out of the valleys and the constant shimmer of moisture on the green, delicate leaves of ferns. And Wenny for an attendant to carry the begging bowl, or Wenny, brown from the sun, gleaming with sweat as he worked the rice fields
20 with a piece of scarlet cloth about his loins. Days eternal with quiet to elaborate thoughts of such subtlety that . . . How delicious to lie here and let his mind ramble.—And Nan. Only five thousand a year would do amply for a villa in Italy somewhere, perhaps on the shore near Sorrento. The old dream of love; roses handed over supper tables at Capri, on a terrace with low music . . . Sweet and low, sweet and low, wind of the western sea . . . and the moon rising out of the dark sea. No, Capri would be too crowded, full of noisy, fast people. A grey, old house somewhere with a courtyard. Mr. and Mrs. J. Fanshaw Mac-dougan, at home. Nan, the way she had looked that night at the fancy
30 dress party at the Logans, her hair caught back from her forehead under a jewelled net, playing the violin in a long, raftered hall a little musty with the smell of the old incense-drenched tapestries, and through the windows, in great, cool gusts, the scent of jasmine from the garden. Little trips to hilltowns to look at frescoes, caffe con latte in station restaurants, jokes about Karl Baedeker, a cab rattling pleas-

antly over the cobblestones, driven by a brown youth with a flower
behind his ear . . . Then he remembered bitterly his mother's
wrinkled cheeks against the pillow and the peevish lines at the ends of
her mouth.—Poor lamb.

He jumped up with a jerk and looked at his watch.—Lord, a
quarter past eight. I shan't have time to shave. He ran, shivering a
little, to shut the window. What beastly weather to be having in April.

The coffee at the cafeteria had a sour taste that morning, hastily
swallowed amid a rattle of dishes on tin trays and shrill talk. Fanshaw
was peevishly telling himself this was the last year he'd lead this dog's   10
life, getting up out of bed this way every morning to hear a lot of
young nincompoops make themselves ridiculous about the history of
painting. If only it weren't for Mother, all the things he would be able
to do! Travel, literature, research. Crossing the yard, he began to feel
better. His unbuckled arctics clinked cheerfully as he walked. The
groups of boys in brown hats at the doors of the lecture halls, the
tattoo of springy footsteps on the boardwalks, the ringing voices and
the softmolded cheeks flushed by the rain spun a net about him,
warm and full of freshness, that gave him a sense of being within
protecting walls and proceeding nonchalantly toward some aim. What   20
else could he do that would give him such pleasant surroundings and
freedom for part of the year? And this youth always welling up about
him. He sat down at the yellow-varnished desk in the semicircular
lecture hall that smelt of chalk and turpentine that drifted in from the
Museum to push off his arctics, and then strolled about, chatting with
students and giving an occasional glance at his watch. Of course, he
might try being agent for some dealer, he was thinking as he talked.
There was money to be made that way. Awfully low, of course. Still,
for a year in Italy, to talk endlessly with good friends like Wenny and
Nan at supper tables in the moonlight in a smell of roses. The class   30
was under way, would soon be over. That story overheard in a smoker
about a rose. How disgusting, nauseating; one couldn't keep things
like that out of one's head. "Rubens," he was saying, "No, I don't see
why we should waste much time on Rubens, Mr. Jones; more acreage
than intensity in Rubens, and all of it smeared with raspberry jam."
The class laughed.

After the lecture hall had emptied, Fanshaw stood a moment
behind the desk thoughtfully plucking at the elastic round a bundle of
papers. Let's see, he'd have time to go over to Wenny's for a moment
before starting to sort those photographs. Pulling on his arctics again,   40
he walked down the road towards Conant. The snow was being
gnawed away under the beat of the warm rain. Now there'd be some
spring. It was time he and Wenny and Nan were going to Nahant

again. He climbed the stairs and knocked at the room door. The door was unlatched and swung open. The bed had not been slept in. There were no papers on the desk. Fanshaw felt a sudden catch of excitement in his throat.—Could he be out with some woman? Wenny, with drunken eyes and flushed cheeks, in the arms of a fat, painted blonde. Horrible. He was too fine for that sort of thing. Poor kid. On the mantelpiece was a little snapshot of Nan propped against some volumes of *The Golden Bough*. Fanshaw barely glanced at it and flushed as if he had caught himself intruding into some inner privacy.—Poor
10   Wenny, he probably is crazy about her.

Fanshaw scribbled a note on a piece of yellow paper and left it on the desk:

> Wenny, you little debauchee, where are you hiding yourself? Come over at tea time.
>
> F.

In the hall outside he found Herb Roscoe shaking the water off an oilskin slicker.

"How do you do? Have you seen Wendell about anywhere recently?"

20   "No, I haven't seen him in the last couple of days. . . . I don't quite know what he's up to these days; looks like to me he was in love or somethin', he's been actin' so queer." Herb Roscoe laughed and gave the slicker a final shake.

Fanshaw's face stiffened.

"O, I don't think it's that," he said coldly, nodded, and went down the steps.

While he was crossing the little triangle of grass in front of the seated statue of John Harvard, Fanshaw stopped a moment to sniff the moist air that for the first time that season smelt of earth and gardens.
30   The rain had stopped, and there were breaks of blue in the brightening sky. A grimyfaced boy ran by calling an extra. Fanshaw was turning away, so as not to see the great blocks of print, when his eye caught the headline:

BAFFLING HARVARD MURDER MYSTERY
Body of Harvard Graduate Student . . .

Fanshaw grabbed the boy's shoulder.
"That paper."
"A nickel cause it's an extra."
I must go home. He folded the paper almost stealthily and strode
40   across the yard, neither looking to the right nor to the left.—Get

home before anyone speaks to me. How hideous if anyone should speak to me. Professor Walpole, grey beard and narrow, steelrimmed glasses, was coming down the boardwalk; he stopped and smiled benignantly at Fanshaw:

"You've heard the news, haven't you, Mr. Macdougan?"

"What news?" asked Fanshaw, his hands quaking, his tongue dry in his mouth.

"Why, we are going to have a Velázquez for two months. . . ."

"How wonderful! . . . Pardon me, won't you? I've got a pressing engagement."

Fanshaw had shoved the paper into the pocket of his raincoat. He darted across Massachusetts Avenue in front of a trolley car. At last he was on Holyoke Street.—O, it was raining again. The drops danced in the puddle in front of his door. Green door, yellow house, here he was. He walked slowly up the stairs, locked and bolted his door on the inside. There he unfolded the paper carefully and began to read:

Body of Harvard Graduate Student Found Floating in Charles. David Wendell, Washington, D. C., Boy, Shot Through Head. Was He Murdered on the East Cambridge Bridge?

Police Completely Baffled.

At eight-twenty this morning . . .

For a moment, Fanshaw could not read the bleary print. The bitter smell of the newspaper filled his nostrils.—Of course it's a mistake, a beastly mistake, he said aloud.

At eight-twenty this morning, Patrolman John H. Higgs of the seventh precinct observed an object that he took to be an old coat floating among cakes of ice near the Esplanade below the East Cambridge Bridge. Upon investigating, however, he decided that it must be the body of a drowned man and summoned assistance. When the body was recoverd, it was identified through a seaman's union card and receipted bill from the Bursar of Harvard University as that of . . .

Fanshaw let the paper fall to the ground. He was sitting, breathing deeply, on the edge of the bed. He took off his coat and overshoes. Seaman's union card.—So Wenny really was trying to go to sea? Wenny tugging at a frozen rope, his curly hair clotted and briny, the rope tearing the skin off his hands. Fanshaw picked up the paper again feverishly.

. . . According to the medical examiner at the morgue, where the body was immediately placed, death was not caused by drowning. The young man, Dr. Swanson alleged, had been shot through the jaw by a pistol of small calibre held close to the neck. The bullet had penetrated to the brain and death had resulted instantaneously. The hypothesis has been advanced that the student might have been waylaid and robbed at some time during the phenomenally violent blizzard that swept this city last night and afterwards murdered and the body thrown into the Charles River Basin, perhaps from the East Cambridge Bridge. . . .

—How horrible! Of course it's true, something had to happen to Wenny; he was too reckless, too beautifully alive.

10   He crumpled the paper up.—I must get Nan. We must go to see at the morgue to make sure. O, these filthy newspapers. He dropped the paper in the grate and set a match to it. The flame roared a moment in the chimney; then the black ash collapsed into flakes.

There was a knock at the door. Fanshaw stood a moment with his fists clenched.—I suppose I must see who it is. He drew the bolt and stepped back, very pale, with compressed lips. "Come in," he said. A short, youngish man with fat cheeks that showed a trace of black beard opened the door and came towards him holding out a hand effusively.

"Mr. Macdougan, I believe."

20   "My name is Macdougan."

"I have information that you could give me details of the life of that unfortunate young man; you see, I'm a reporter from the *American*. My name is Rogers. I'm on special articles mostly." He looked up at Fanshaw sideways with a smile.

"Thank you . . . I know . . . er . . . nothing except what I just read in your paper. . . . I'm afraid I can't talk to you now. . . ." Fanshaw was desperately trying to think:—These beasts'll try to get up a scandal. There's nothing they'll stick at. Nan and I must keep out of it. . . . If I were to lose my instructorship. . . .

30   "You see, it is this way, Mr. Macdougan . . . Won't you take a cigarette?" The reporter settled himself in a chair, lit a cigarette, pulled his trousers up at the knees, and continued in his oily, whee-dling voice: "You see, Mr. Macdougan, my paper, as you know, is at present out to clean up the police department of this city, which is disgracefully inefficient. We are going to fight them with every means in our power. Publicity and publicity and more publicity for every instance of neglect and corruption we can unearth. We intend to make the streets of Boston safe for the most delicate girl at any hour of the day or night. . . . That is why we are so interested in procuring all the
40   details of a case like this accident that overwhelmed your unfortunate young friend. I'm sure you want to help us in this."

"But I don't know anything. I last saw David Wendell at dinner last night in Boston. I am not in the least certain that it's he who was murdered."

"What time last night?"

"O, I suppose at around ten. . . . We'd been dining on Hanover Street. . . . But I can't talk about this now."

"I am sure you will appreciate my position, Mr. Macdougan; it's only in the interest of justice, with that poor young man's interest at heart, that I intrude this way on your grief at the loss of a dear friend. . . . Did you dine alone with him?"

"No. . . . But look here, I must go."

"You wouldn't mind giving me the name of the other party? He and you were probably the last to ever see him alive. He might be able to help us."

"I'm afraid I can't give you the name."

"The third party was a lady, then?"

Fanshaw blushed red. He stared hard in the man's wheedling eyes.

"I must get in touch with the police to find out what really happened. . . . Please excuse me."

Fanshaw pulled on his overshoes and took his coat from the bed.

"Have you thought of any motive anyone could have for wanting to kill young Wendell, Mr. Macdougan?"

"None, of course not."

"Do you think it could have been suicide?"

Fanshaw felt the beads of sweat trickling down his cheek. He motioned the reporter out the door and slammed it behind them.

"I don't know. . . . It might have been anything."

He started down the stairs.

"If you are going to the morgue now, I should be very glad to go with you, Mr. Macdougan," said the reporter, following him with the same confident smile. "Perhaps you don't know where it is."

"Thank you, no!"

Fanshaw tore up the street towards the college office.—The reporter stared after him blandly from the doorstep.

—Publicity, thought Fanshaw as he walked desperately fast, pitiless publicity. And his mind seethed with faces of people in streetcars, in restaurants and soda fountains and bars, their eyes bulging with delight, people in subways and under streetlamps reading of Wenny's death in paragraphs of smeary print. The headlines seemed reflected in their ghoulish eyes as they read gluttonously every detail of the bullet searing the warm flesh, the warm flesh quenched in the water of the Basin, the body that he and Nan had loved, talked to, walked with, floating like an old coat among the melting icecakes at eight-twenty this morning. Youth had been killed. In offices and stores and front parlors and lonely hall bedrooms, sallow-jowled faces sucked the blood through the nasty-smelling print of the extras. The streets swarmed and seethed with faces drinking Wenny's blood.

He walked hastily into the college office, past a row of scared freshmen waiting a reprimand, and asked for the dean of the Graduate School. He felt calmer in the quiet dinginess, among the low voices of the office. All the blood and clamor and hideousness of the streets was shut outside.

10   "Yes, come right in, Mr. Macdougan."

*   *   *

The steam from the spout of the big, blue teapot rose between Fanshaw and the sunlight of the window. He sat staring at its slow spiral, his cup forgotten in his hand. Beside the mantelpiece Nan, her brows contracted and a flush on her face, was reading a piece of the Sunday newspaper. In the blue, velvet armchair, Miss Fitzhugh sat hunched up, occasionally giving her red eyes a little dab with a handkerchief.

"O, dear," Miss Fitzhugh was quavering faintly, "I haven't been so upset since I broke off my engagement and sent Billy back his ring."

20   "Please don't break down again, Fitzie, dear," said Nan savagely, letting the paper drop out of her hands. "My sense of humor is somewhat worn to a frazzle. . . . My God, what swine people are!"

"But after all, dear, it's not as if we really believed he was dead. The word has no meaning to me now. . . . Why, I feel so happy in his presence, more than when he was alive; don't you?"

"It's these papers that infuriate me, being dragged out naked this way by these beasts, these bloodsuckers, for everybody to gloat over. . . . God, I never want to go out of doors again."

"But after all, dear, it's such a marvelous romance. . . ."

30   "O, Fitzie, will you please shut up?"

Miss Fitzhugh got slowly to her feet and put her untasted teacup down on the table.

"I'll go away now and come back for a minute after supper to see if you want anything."

"O, you are a dear, Fitzie." Nan followed her out into the hall.

Fanshaw sat stiffly in his chair looking out of the window at the sunny, cloud-flecked sky. In his hands he was folding and unfolding the newspaper Nan had dropped. Headlines in the ornamental print of the magazine section danced and writhed and squirmed mockingly

40   through his head:—Was it love lured young David Wendell to his doom? Known to frequent low companions . . . inveterate slummer

. . . Despair over money matters or jilting by Back Bay girl led him first to try to ship as a sailor and at last to that final orgy in a foreign restaurant on Hanover Street . . . Victim of infatuation for some beautiful flower of the slums . . . I must get this out of my head or go mad. Fanshaw started walking back and forth in front of the window, clasping and unclasping his hands behind his back.

Nan came back into the room, her face calmer, a little smile hovering at the edges of her lips.

"I'd have just lain down on the floor and shrieked if Fitzie had stayed any longer."

"She has the holy stupidity of an early Christian saint," said Fanshaw. "But let's have some hot tea, Lord knows we'll need it."

"There's fresh hot water on the gas."

"I'll get it."

In the kitchenette, he stood still a moment with the teakettle in his hand.—The smell of the morgue, the old, wax-faced man in uniform who led the way down a grey passage, and Nan's heart beating madly against his arm when they came to the slab where the body lay diminished and pitiful under a sheet . . . Fanshaw tried to rid his mind of the memory. The steam from the kettle was scalding his hand. As he was leaning over to pour some hot water into the pot, Nan looked up into his face from the armchair and said:

"Do you feel this fearful ache, as if your head would burst with it all?"

Fanshaw nodded quietly, poured himself some fresh tea, and went to sit by the window. Wenny's face, when the sheet was pulled off, bruised and mashed, the strange, smiling look of the blue, full lips, and his shoulders rigid and calm like very old carved ivory.

"What have the people in the Fine Arts Department had to say about all these beastly insinuations?"

"They've been extremely decent, as far as I know; of course the university doesn't like one's getting in the papers."

"Poor little Wenny, even dead he gets us into scrapes."

"Doesn't it make you hate people?"

"I can't walk along the street without shuddering, Fanshaw. . . . I'd always thought of all the faces drifting by along the pavement, joggling opposite you in trolley cars, as vaguely friendly and lovable; I wanted to be part of them, to dive into the crowd like into a sea. . . ."

"That was Wenny's idea."

"But now I know what swine they are. If they had a drop of human kindness, these hideous articles in the papers wouldn't be allowed."

The headlines were filing in procession again through Fanshaw's mind:—Drink and infatuation for a woman lead minister's son to his death . . . Following the will-of-the-wisp of pleasure through the tortuous mazes of Boston's tenderloin shatters young graduate's career . . . Lovely Back Bay girl Conservatoire student figures in East Cambridge Bridge suicide. Mystery of missing revolver . . .

"O, if I could get it out of my head and forget it."

"How's your mother, Fanshaw?"

"I really don't know, Nan. . . . No better and no worse."

The bell rang. Nan raised herself slowly from the chair and went to the door. "Why, Betty Thomas!" Fanshaw heard her exclaim.

10   In spite of himself, Fanshaw had unrolled the newspaper. On the heavily ornamented magazine page was a picture of a young man in a dress suit brandishing a revolver in the middle of a spotchy snowstorm. See next Sunday's Magazine Section for What Drove David Wendell, Good Looking, Successful, Beloved by Parents and Friends, to Blow out His Brains that Night of Wind and Blizzard on the East Cambridge Bridge.

"Put that paper away," said Betty Thomas in her ringing voice. She wore a grey skirt and a burnt-orange sweater that molded to the ample curve of her bosom. "I'm going to make Nancibel play some

20   Bach or something with me. . . . You people are getting morbid, sitting around with these dirty, yellow sheets all day."

"You're right, Betty," said Nan. "Will you have some tea?"

Betty Thomas shook her head, smiling.

"D'you mind if I open the window, though? The air's splendid outside, cold and smells of spring."

Nan had brought out her violin.

"Let's play . . . I haven't practiced for three days."

Fanshaw sat by the window, shivering a little in the cold air. The sound of the violin being tuned rasped on his ears. Then they started

30   playing a solemn, circular tune that made him think of a minuet, and today made him twitch all over with impatience. He got to his feet and tiptoed out. The two girls' absorption in the music annoyed him. He walked down the stairs and strolled across the Fenway, where a few nursemaids were wheeling babies about in the late afternoon sun.

He crossed a bridge over a railroad track. The sound of a train whistle in the distance sent a pang through him of helpless nostalgia for travel and railway carriages and the smoke of stations and the unfamiliar smell of hotel rooms.—He got so little of all he had longed

40   for before he died, Fanshaw was thinking; and what I long for, how little of it shall I get! He felt tears welling up within him.

At the corner where he waited for the Brookline car, some work men were repairing the track. Under baggy, blue shirts, the muscles of arms and shoulders moved tautly. A smell of sweat and rank pipe came from them. Wenny would have wanted to be one of them, redfaced, spitting men with skillful, ugly hands. The men who had dug the grave had been like that, men digging everywhere were like that; strange how through all the tense idiocy of the funeral, and Wenny's father and mother very solemn and professional, and the father's little speech to the effect that he believed, as he believed in God Almighty, that his son had not died a suicide but had been done to death by some low companion or other, he had felt that the only people there Wenny would have liked were the two hickory-faced men with spades who filled in the grave, their thick backs bending   10 and straightening as they shoveled in the reddish dirt. Fanshaw suddenly pressed his lips hard together as he remembered the undertaker's man unscrewing the silver handles from the coffin before it was lowered into the grave, and Wenny's father in black broadcloth eloquently reading the burial service, and the rattle of the first shovelful of dirt and stones on the coffin.

The car stopped in front of him with a shriek of brakes.

Fanshaw sat stiffly in the rattling streetcar that smelt of cheap perfume and overcoats and breathed-out air, staring unseeing out of the window.   20

"O, Muriel, isn't that suicide case dreadful?"

A girl's voice from the seat ahead roused him. Two blonde girls in tam-o-shanters were bending over a newspaper.

"That boy never killed himself, I'm certain," said the other girl.

"Do you think he was murdered?"

"Yes, deary, I do, by the husband of the woman he had wronged . . ."

"But, Muriel, he didn't wrong anybody. . . . He killed himself for grief because a Back Bay beauty spurned his love."

"Lot o' piffle, that stuff . . . I wouldn't kill myself for any man."   30

"O, but Muriel, you might. Think, if he was a duke or something in disguise and dreadfully handsome, with curly hair and a strong, silent face."

"Like fun I would."

"O, but Muriel, don't you think it would be just wonderful to have something like that happen . . . a suicide or something? Of course, it'ld be just terrible, but . . ."

A smell of chewed peppermints filtered gradually back to Fanshaw. The streetcar had speeded up noisily, so that he could no longer hear what they were saying.   40

*   *   *

"I wonder, Nan, if death doesn't make one feel how very acutely one is alive, the thought of one's own death, or the death of someone beloved," Fanshaw said, turning suddenly to Nan, seeking out her eyes. It had been on his tongue all day, but somehow he had not been able to say it till now. He was tingling hot with the excitement of saying it.

"Or do you mean that we feel in ourselves the dead person alive?" Nan's eyes flashed green in his.

"No, no, Wenny wouldn't have meant that."

They sat on Fanshaw's overcoat, their backs against a boulder. Behind them were patches of sprouting emerald grass in the clefts of
10 rocks and rows of shingled cottages, shutters still fast for the winter. At their feet the surf hissed and rattled on the pebbly beach. The sea was slate-grey with an occasional whitecap. From the deep indigo line of the horizon, cumulous clouds steamed up heavy and flushed with spring, with a hint of rain in their broad, shadowy bases. In the back of his mind, Fanshaw was remembering the scalloped wavelets and the blown hair and the curves like grey rose petals of Botticelli's waveborn Venus.—What was the Latin that went with it: Cras amet qui numquam amavit . . .? No, how ridiculous.

"What did you think of his father, Fanshaw?"
20 "O, impossible, completely impossible."

"I wonder . . ."

They were silent a long time, looking out to sea. Fanshaw leaned back with halfclosed eyes, conscious of Nan beside him, felt vague, rosy contours, slender and leaping like the figures on a black-figure vase, dancing within him. He was very happy.

"Nan, I wish I could paint."

"Who's stopping you?"

"I suppose that sort of thing is pretty futile nowadays. . . . It would have been fine, though, to have been born in a time . . ."
30 "Wouldn't Wenny have been angry hearing you say that?"

They turned towards each other and laughed.

"Wenny could have done anything. . . . Think that all his life should be gone, like a glass of wine poured on the ground."

"Such a biblical metaphor." Nan laughed deep in her throat. "Maybe you and I are the ground, Fanshaw, who can tell?"

"Tares and thistles probably . . . Don't you wish we were the lilies of the field?"

"That makes me think of the Reverend Jonas. . . . I wonder if all of poor old Wenny's troubles didn't come from that. Wasn't it a case of
40 . . . what's the quotation about the fathers have eaten sour grapes and the children's teeth are set on edge?"

"Don't you think it's a little vulgar to know the Bible so well?"

They both laughed. Down the coast, the sun had burst through the clouds. The spreading rays brightened on the sea to great patches of heaving silver. Far out the sails of a schooner shone out suddenly like mother of pearl.

"O, isn't it superb here this afternoon, Nan? And think that I didn't want to come."

"I like it. . . . Suppose we stayed forever?"

"After all the hideousness of this spring?"

"Let's not talk about it. . . . I won't remember it. What's today?"

"I think it's the twentieth."

"Well, for me it's May first. I won't be cheated of my spring. I'm just   10
going to begin it all over again. And practice! Fanshaw, if you only
knew how I was going to practice!"

"Look down the coast now. . . . With the dark clouds and the rays
from the sun and the sailboat and everything, isn't it exactly like one
of those funny old English engravings? Seascapes they used to call
them. Even to the musty color."

Nan's arm was against his arm. She had taken off her tailored jacket,
and her round arm, faintly brownish against his grey tweed, was bare
from above the elbow. She wore a sort of tunic of dull red silk with a
little black embroidery on it that left a deep V at her neck and fell   20
suavely over her slight breasts as she leaned back against the rock. A
dizzying flush went through him as his eyes followed the shadowed
curve of her neck to the sharp chin and up the oval contour of her
cheeks. Her lips were faintly puckered, her eyes, green and grey,
very solemn, looking into his. His heart was thumping like mad in his
chest. He gulped and looked away over the sea that was green and
grey like her eyes. A quick, inexplicable chill went down his spine. It
was a moment before he could speak:

"Nan . . ." He paused, his tongue dry, "Nan, don't you think we
need our tea?"   30

"Yes, come along," she said and jumped to her feet.

"I was getting a little chilly." Fanshaw bent to pick up a pebble to
hide his flushed face. He threw the pebble as far as he could out
across the surf, caught up his overcoat and followed Nan. She had
already started across the rocks. They walked round the edge of the
harbor towards the town. Under the grey sky, slightly marbled with
sunlight, the shingled, sharp-roofed houses scattered unevenly among
lanes and low picket fences, looked out hostilely through the small
panes of their windows at the sprouting tulips and hyacinths in their
dooryards.   40

"Are we going to the redheaded woman's?" said Fanshaw after a
while.

"Where else can we go?"

"Nowhere, I suppose, but she does give one such small cups." His voice faltered as he spoke. What a waste of breath were all these trivialities when he ought to be telling Nan . . . If he could only catch the proper note, mock-serious, flippant, as one would have made love to a marquise with powdered hair in a garden by Lenôtre. And Wenny had loved Nan. Fanshaw was trying to imagine some sulfurous, boiling passion. He saw Wenny, brown and flushed, sweaty and dusty like a runner after a race, break through all this stage scenery of New England houses and trees and sea, tearing it apart
10 with hard, knobbed fingers, the way he'd pulled down the window curtains in the room on Mount Auburn Street one night when he was drunk. Wenny's face, dead, purple splotched under the sheet on the marble slab at the morgue.—And Nan and I going on, springtime and autumn, breakfast and luncheon and dinner.

They had reached the teahouse. A coldframe under the window was full of violets. They settled themselves at a little table, breathing deep of the fugitive scent of the violets.

—After all, Fanshaw was thinking, does it bring any more to kick against the pricks? A certain position in the world . . . He could hear
20 his mother's tremulous voice:—Your beautiful, lovely career. Perhaps it's best for Wenny that he died. Wenny, grown old, sodden, drunken, losing his fire and his good looks; Verlaine's last absinthe-haunted days; Lord Byron, a puffy-faced Don Juan; the verdict of history. Circumspectly, with infinite grace, they went about life in the eighteenth century, never headlong, half-cocked. Nan and I can be like that.

"Delicious, isn't it, to smell this mixture of tea and violets?" he said.

"I was thinking," said Nan, "how wonderful if he were only here.
30 Isn't it silly?"

"I was thinking of him, too," said Fanshaw.

—And Wenny loved Nan. Yet was it any more unbearable for him than just now when I looked in her eyes and a light like the light bursting out from the center in that Greco nativity shot all through me? Never to have held a woman in your arms and kissed her. Pent-up aching rivers . . . Called for madder music and for stronger wine.

The redhaired woman leaned over to put a plate of toasted muffins on the table. Her round breasts hung heavy against the thin muslin of her blouse. There was a faint, rancid smell from her armpits.
40 —She doesn't wear corsets; sloppy, that modern style. Here comes the bride, here comes the bride . . . Make a formal declaration. A marriage license engraved with cupids and hearts. Wobbling from side to side . . . Sukie Smith and I walking round the block singing

that one Fourth, smell of lindens, and people laughing at us and asking if we meant it, until Mother stopped us. Here comes the groom, straight as a broom!

"What a comfort tea is, Nan. I feel my tongue getting loose again. I wish we could talk about ourselves a little."

"I hate it above anything, but let's. . . . Do you know, Fanshaw, I think sometimes that the more people see of each other the less they get to know? You can tell a stranger anything, but a friend . . ."

"It's awfully hard to say anything about what I really feel. . . . If we only had the eighteenth-century code of badinage."   10

"On ne badine pas avec l'amour."

Fanshaw felt something like terror thrill him. He was tapping with a teaspoon on the table. Nan looked straight at him with narrowed eyes.

"That's what I meant, Nan, I . . ."

"But why not, after all? . . . Why not play with love to keep it from playing with us?" cried Nan wildly. The radiance of her eyes hurt like a too bright light.

"O, Nan, what are we going to do about ourselves, you and I?"

"Fanshaw, whatever happens, remember that my music is terribly   20 important to me."

"But there is something more important to us than anything."

Nan put her hand out to him suddenly across the table. He pressed it gently with long, white fingers. He felt his careful restraint tottering. When he was very small once, he had tried to balance himself on the fence of the back yard, above a rosebush in flower, and the drone of the bees and the fragrance of the dull, carmine flowers had made him dizzy, and he had lost his balance and tottered and swung his arms wildly. Then he had fallen and lain crying on the path among the fallen petals, his face all scratched and bloody from the thorns. He   30 patted her hand gently. Neither of them spoke.

"Dear Nan," he began when the silence had got to swirling fearfully about his head.

"There are the Turnstables," said Nan sharply. "They are coming in here."

They got to their feet. Mrs. Turnstable, in a long motor coat, came up to them, followed by her blonde son and daughter.

"Why, Nancibel, how delightful to run upon you here! And how do you do, Mr. Macdougan? Why, this is luck. . . . Isn't it delicious here today? Our first real spring day."   40

"Hello, Cousin Nancibel."

Chairs scraped. Another table was pushed up. Under cover of the clinking of more teacups being brought and Mrs. Turnstable's musical

voice talking about what a dreadful spring it had been, Fanshaw sat
silent, feeling his frenzy of excitement ebb deliciously. This was saner.
Control. Control.

"O, Mr. Macdougan, have you seen *Prunella*? Such a beautiful play;
I'm sure you'd like it. I've been twice, and I am taking the children
tomorrow. So romantic and dainty . . ."

"It's a Pierrot play, isn't it?"

"Yes, I was wondering if the veritable commedia dell'arte can't have
been something like that."

10   "Why, very probably."

While he talked, Fanshaw was furtively watching James Turnstable's thin pink and white face. The boy was eating toast and staring
at Nan with worshipping blue eyes. At length, when she turned to
him and said, "More tea, Jamesie?" he grew red to the ears and
stammered, "Please, Cousin Nancibel."—An attractive kid, Fanshaw
was thinking. O, the cycle of it.

"There'll be lots of room. . . . We'll all go back to Boston together
in my car," Mrs. Turnstable was saying. "Don't you love Marblehead,
Mr. Macdougan?"

                    *   *   *

20   Fanshaw's mother sat by the library window looking out into the
garden that was full of the fiery chalices of Darwin tulips.

"Once I'm well, Fanshaw, we must rebuild the garden. There aren't
any peonies. I've always wanted some of those beautiful yellow
peonies in the garden. You must get me some next time you see them
in a flower shop."

"I will, indeed, Mother," said Fanshaw from the easy chair where
he was reading.

"What are you reading, dear?"

"Just a thing about Umbrian painters."

30   "Come here and tell me about it. . . . You never tell me anything
about your work anymore."

Fanshaw moved to the window ledge beside her chair and stared
out into the garden.

"Mother," he said, without looking in her face, "what would you say
if I were to marry some day?"

"But then we couldn't go abroad this summer, could we, dear?"

"I'm afraid we aren't going to be able to do that anyway."

"Why?"

"Because I'm afraid you won't be quite strong enough, dear."

40   "How ridiculous, Fanshaw. Of course I'll be well in a couple of

months. How long is it now since Dr. Nickerson said I'd be well in a couple of months?"

"It's nearly a year, Mother dear. Of course he didn't say that definitely. . . ."

"You wait and see how quickly I'll get well. . . . But, Fanshaw, I don't believe in a boy marrying too young."

"I'm nearly thirty, Mother; that's old enough surely."

"Your dear father was thirty-five when he married me. And, Fanshaw, there are so many things we'll want to do together when I get well. And if that girl loves you as she ought, she'll wait for you years, if   10 need be. . . . And the expense of the wedding and all that . . . O, I think it's an extravagant idea."

"I'll think about it, Mother."

"O, darling, I've got such a headache."

"Here comes Susan with your medicine, dear. That'll make you feel better."

Susan stood over her, showing her long teeth in a smile.

"Here's your tablet, mum, and I'm bringin' ye a cup of malted milk right away."

"Thank you, Susan," said Mrs. Macdougan with a wan frown. "And   20 be sure to make it sweet enough. It was just horrid yesterday." Susan's eyes met Fanshaw's. She smiled tolerantly as she smoothed the grey hair back from the old woman's forehead.

*   *   *

There was a Hellenic purity about the sunlight along the river that afternoon, Fanshaw was telling himself, something that made one think of Praxiteles and running grounds at Olympia. The stadium in the distance across the meadows and the white bodies of the rowers in the shells stretching and contracting to the bark of the coxswains stood out like the reliefs on a temple against the azure and silver sheen of the sky and the river. From some birches by the river, the   30 notes of a song sparrow tumbled glittering. On the wind came an indefinable mushroom-scent of spring. Fanshaw's mind was full of suave visions of the future that evolved rosily like slow, highpiled clouds. He would get a scholarship from the department on which they might live in Italy for a year. Extra money might be made appraising and attributing things for some art dealer. There would be Spain and Greece and North Africa. Magazine articles might appear about pictures and places. They could get a villa somewhere with lemon trees near the sea, breakfast in the morning leaning over the balustrade watching the bronzelimbed fishermen draw their boats up   40

on the beach below; long strolls in the moonlight through overgrown
gardens of myrtle and cypress, and Nan, dressed as she had been that
night at the Logans (she would always dress that way—like a Renaissance princess), in his arms, silken and shuddering.

Fanshaw felt himself flush as he walked with slow strides along the
turf by the river.

—And Wenny had loved Nan. Perhaps it was through his death
they had been brought together. The ways of destiny, *La Forza del
Destino*, by Verdi. Perhaps they could afford an apartment in one of
these places by the river. "The Strathcona." Fun it would be, decorat-
ing it. And Wenny had loved her. That's how I felt towards him, I
suppose. No harm, now that he's dead. This afternoon, the Attic
gleam of rowers in the sun, swallows circling in a blue sky glittering as
with mica; if I could paint, I would do him against such a background,
hair curling crisp about his eager, narrow forehead, eyes laughing, lips
winesmudged and full, brownly naked, like the Bacchus in that
picture by Velázquez, defying the world.

Fanshaw was twirling some pink clover blossoms between his fingers, occasionally sniffing at them. The sense of Wenny's presence
became suddenly intense to him, as if he could feel the hard muscle of
Wenny's shoulder against his arm, as when they had walked together.
He closed his eyes for dizziness.

He opened his eyes and looked about him. Round a bend in the
river, at the end of a silvery blue reach, was a bridge and, beyond, the
fantastic pile of the abattoir with its tall, bottle-shaped chimney. A
rough smell of singed hides came down the wind. Fanshaw turned
into a path up the hill towards a shrubbery behind which showed the
crowded obelisks and crosses of the cemetery, crossed a wooden bar
and found himself wandering among neatly laid-off grass plots and
gravestones with the dust of the stone cutting still on them. He passed
a mock orange in bloom and remembered how he used to breathe
deep the fragrance from the bush at the corner of his mother's lawn in
Omaha until he almost swooned from it.—That fancy that Wenny had
once had that all the tombstones ought to be effaced and cemeteries
turned into amusement parks with dancehalls and rollercoasters and
toodling calliopes. There was a smell of lilacs . . . When lilacs last in
the dooryard bloomed. Perhaps that was what had made Wenny say
that the smell of lilacs made him think of death. Then he was staring at
the newest stone:

DAVID WENDELL: AET. 23

—The Rev. Wendell, as Nan called him, had thought the Latin was
appropriate to a scholar. On the reddish mound new grass, fine as
hair, was sprouting. How little any of it had to do with Wenny. On the

next grave, a stalk of frail, paper-white Madonna lilies trembled in the wind. It was in the time of lilies Pico della Mirandola had come to Florence and in the time of lilies he died, having failed in his great work of reconciling Christ and Apollo. Wenny would have been like that. O, if more people had only known him, if he had lived where there was an atmosphere of accomplishment instead of futility, his name might have rung like Pico's to the last syllable of recorded time.

"How do you do, sir?" came a wheezy voice from behind Fanshaw's back; he turned and found an old man with a pert, wizened face in blue cap and uniform standing beside him.

"A friend o' the party buried there, ain't you?" went on the old man.

"Why, yes, I am."

"I thought I'd recognized ye from the funeral," said the old man, brightening up. "I guess you'll be a-noticin' that they's been tramplin' an' settin' on it."

"How frightful! No, I hadn't noticed it. But who would do such a thing?"

"O, they don't mean no harm by it. You see, there ain't lights here."

"You don't mean they are body snatchers?"

"Lord, no. . . . It's just young folks. You see, the watchman just can't make his rounds fast enough to keep 'em from grassin'. . . . 'Ticularly in the spring. It'ld fair surprise ye to see the mashin' and the spoonin' that goes on in the most high-class cemeteries. Yessiree, it'ld fair surprise ye."

"But how do they get in?"

"How did you get in? Ain't no fence at this end."

"You mean they come and make love in the cemetery?"

The old man looked up sideways at Fanshaw and gave a wrinkled wink.

"There's nothin' they don't do, I'm tellin' ye. Worse than the canoes in Norumbega Park for barefaced grassin'. Listen to what happened last night. You know that there tower atop o' the hill? Well, we always lock it up tight, but last night the watchman forgot to, and when the patrolman made his round at 'bout midnight, he heard 'em agigglin' and carryin' on up in the tower and found the door was open, an' he went up with his lantern. . . . And they wasn't a bit ashamed or mortified when he found 'em. . . . They just laughed, the fellers and the girls, when he ran 'em out of there. . . . I don't know what young folks are comin' to in this day an' age. . . . And they wasn't furriners neither."

"How extraordinary," said Fanshaw as he walked away. He looked at his watch.—Three o'clock; Nan would have finished practicing. He

walked fast for fear the old man would catch up and talk to him
again.—Nasty old face, he had. And yet Nan and I, and Wenny,
whom we loved, dead. Everywhere love springing like hair-fine grass
to obliterate the new graves. O, the pitiful cycle of it. But life would
be so unsatisfactory without Nan. Mother's voice, her wrinkled face,
yellow and limp against the pillow, under the pompadour that was
always a little crooked and showed the black, coarse hair of the rat:
And later, Fanshaw, dearest, when you've made yourself a lovely,
beautiful career, you'll probably marry some sweet, homey girl and
10   settle down and be a comfort to me. Probably Mother was right.
There comes a time when you can't go on living alone any longer. Of
course a quiet retreat with books, one would always have to have. And
with Nan's passionate interest in her music, there would not be any
difficulty in that. And then to let oneself go. At last someone with
whom I can let myself go.

He was waiting outside the pompous, wrought iron gates of the
cemetery for a streetcar. He climbed on a half-empty car and watched
the people straggle in as it drew near to the subway entrance. There
were old women with spiteful lips and peevish, shifty eyes, flashy
20   young men in checked caps, lanternjawed girls, sallow, seedy fathers
of families. Once, after a long argument, he had asked Wenny: But
what do you want? and Wenny had looked round the car with eager
eyes and said: Not to be myself, I guess, to be anybody, any one of
those people but myself. In the subway Fanshaw looked, furtively, so
that they should not notice him, from face to face, noting the tired
skin round their eyes, the dissatisfied lips.—Comes from drudgery in
offices and factories, he was telling himself, always regimented, under
orders, and then, in the evening the sudden little spurt of human
brilliance, shopgirls and little clerks and ditchdiggers walking merrily
30   through twilight streets. Tremont before theater time, or at six o'clock
with the dome of the State House glowing through dusky trees. Then
the night; mystery of doorways, gangs of boys loafing sullenly under
arclights at corners, grassing in the cemetery, furtive loves over
newlydug graves, always afraid of the policeman striding slowly down
his beat; electric signs and burlesque shows, "Pretty Girls Upstairs,"
lumpy women, stuffed in pink tights, twitching lewdly at the end of a
smoke-rancid hall. . . . We can do better than that, Nan and I, escape
all this grinding ugliness, make ourselves a garden walled against it
all, shutting out all this garish lockstep travesty of civilization. . . .
40   Land where it is always afternoon. Afternoons reading on the balcony
of a palace in Venice, vague splendors, relics from the Doges,
Aretino, Titian, and Nan with her hair brushed back from her forehead, in a brocaded dress like a Florentine princess on a cassone.

Park Street. Fanshaw got to his feet and shuffled in a jostling stream of people out the car.

*   *   *

Nan had been playing "Jardins sous la pluie." Fanshaw sat looking out of the window into the glassy twilight, in which a few stars already shimmered like bubbles ready to burst. The music and the incredible fresh green of the leaves in the darkening Fenway had brought on a mood of queer sensibility, so that he felt very happy and almost on the verge of tears. He got to his feet and walked over to the piano, where he stood awkwardly, watching Nan's long fingers flash across the keys. Then he took her gently by the shoulders and said:

"Come and look at the twilight. . . . It's unbearably poignant, this violence of spring."

They stood side by side in the window, looking out at the darkening trees.

"Nan, it'll be rather fun, won't it, setting up a ménage? And think how delightfully absurd the wedding will be and all that."

"Yes, I think it'll be fun. Will your mother hate me dreadfully?"

"Poor mother, she's like a child. She'll get used to you and be fearfully attached to you in no time."

"We must keep our liberty and our work, Fanshaw, whatever we do."

Fanshaw was startled by the tenseness in her voice. There was a hollow look about her cheeks he had never noticed before.

"Do you know," Nan was saying, "I'm rather frightened about my music tonight. I mean the divine fire, the power to let oneself go, to rule imperiously an instrument and an audience. . . . But I'm dreadfully determined. You won't go back on me, will you?"

"What a funny question."

"But why are we talking in this stilted way, already under the shadow of the holy institution? . . . We've known each other long enough to get married without a quiver, I should say."

"Perhaps it is that we've put on so many brakes in our time that it's a little difficult to take them off now we want to," drawled Fanshaw with a wan smile.

Nan laughed excitedly. Fanshaw had put an arm around her shoulder. He felt her body stiffening against his.

"Fanshaw," she said in a changed voice, "do you see that star?"

"L'étoile du berger."

Above the dark roof of the apartment house across the park, a star hovered green and trembling like jelly. They watched it in silence. Nan turned her face up quickly towards Fanshaw's in sudden, passionate hunger. He folded her in his arms and kissed her lips lightly. With her head against his chest and her body rigid in his arms, he stared out across her tumbled hair as the star sank flickering out of sight. He was trembling. He was full of swift shudders of foreboding. He bent his head to kiss her hair.

She tore herself away from him and threw herself sobbing into the armchair.

"Fanshaw, I can't . . . I can't do it. It's all false," she was crying in a thin, choked voice.

Fanshaw was standing stiffly in front of her. He felt desperately cold and tired.

"Nan, this is horrible. . . . Pull yourself together."

She turned to him a twisted face wet with tears.

"No, go away for the present. . . . Leave me alone."

She slipped to the floor and lay with her head on the blue velvet seat of the chair, her sandy hair undone, her body shaken with sobs.

In a curious maze of pain, Fanshaw walked down the apartment-house steps. Through spring-reeking streets, full of laughs and flower scents and flushed cheeks and kidding voices of boys and girls arm in arm, he walked with long, sedate steps home.

VIII

THERE was a dark scattering of people through the beehive-shaped, yellowshot emptiness of the Boston Theater. On the stage, in white dresses against red draperies, the ladies' orchestra played the overture to *Light Cavalry*, violin bows sawing in unison, cheeks puffed out at trumpets, drumsticks dancing. In front stood the conductress in a neat tailored suit, waving her arms discreetly. Nan sat on the aisle with her little black hat topping some packages on the seat beside her, watching the flitting of the conductress's white gloves, thinking bitterly of suffragettes setting bombs under Asquith in London, while the shiny, glib marchtime of the music made her remember Balaklava   10 and her spine going cold as she read: "Into the valley of death charged the six hundred" at Aunt M.'s years ago. How was it things she read never thrilled her now like that? Rights for women ought to excite her as much as that silly, antiquated poem. The music had stopped; two women in front of her were talking about the cretonnes at Jordan Marsh's. Let's see, had she bought the lace for the V, the ruching Miss Spence wanted, that blue crepe de chine, the buttons? She'd make sure on her list anyway after she'd picked up Fitzie. Fine, it would be, if Miss Spence could finish that dress in time for Aunt M.'s tomorrow night. All those old people put her on her mettle; they'd think the   20 brightness of it daring, bleared eyes watching her as she stood straight in tight royal blue, a gleam of red caught into her hair out of the violin. She had to affirm her separateness from poor dear Aunt M. and her friends. The orchestra was playing selections from *The Tales of Hoffmann*, which set Nan remembering being in Paris with Gertrude Fagan, the smell of tea and pastry through the foggy tang of the air on the rue Cambon, shopping, jumping in and out of cabs with silky things in tissue paper packages, hotel François Choiseuil and the two of them giggling together in the evening beside a pink shade over sole with wine sauce.—If it had been Wenny in Gertrude's   30 place . . . ; the thought set her blood seething. But I have you, my love: the words fluttered in her throat. She moistened her dry lips with her tongue. The music had stopped.

Nan looked about her restlessly. On the stage, she could see Fitzie among the violins, next to a tall, redhaired girl. That was where the

other girl, Mabel something, used to stand last fall, the girl who ran
away with the flushfaced boy Fitzie told about, with bright teeth, the
Italian who looked like a young Greek god, like Wenny perhaps. And
he was dead. In all these months, she should have got used to his
being dead, but still when she thought of him, she had to tell herself
quickly he was dead, to escape the horrible pain of thinking of him,
wishing him alive. Or did that all mean there was no death, that he
was utterly surrendered to her? Fitzie'ld say that, poor, lonely Fitzie.
Dull program it was this afternoon; a dismal ending for all that work
10   and hysterical eagerness up at the conservatory, a lady cellist in the
Fadettes.

Nan began to listen to the music again. They were playing the
march from *The Twilight of the Gods*, over-solemnly. The conductress
brought down her baton for the last time. People got to their feet. The
lights went on. Nan was adjusting her hat, held two hatpins in her
mouth. Had she got all her packages? She walked out slowly into the
crimson, sunset light of Washington Street, and round through a cold
swirl of dustladen wind to the stage door. The women of the orchestra
were coming out: short women in highcollared shirtwaists, a tall girl
20   with high cheekbones and yellow hair, two stout women with glasses,
both rippling with the same laughter, the harpist, a consumptive-
looking girl with face white, drooping like a snowdrop, and blue rings
under her eyes; then Fitzie walking with jerky little steps,
pigeonbreasted.

"O, Nancibel, how sweet of you to wait. . . . I'd just decided you
wouldn't."

"Why should you think that?"

"O, I don't know. I guess I must think sometimes that you're a little
upstage, dear; simply horrid of me, and I don't mean it a bit. Maybe
30   it's that anybody who didn't know you would feel that you were a
little, just the weenciest bit."

"I don't think I am, Fitzie."

They were drifting up the street in a compact stream of people like
on a moving platform. Nan looked from face to face that passed her in
a chilly flutter of expectation. She knew that before long she would
see a man she would think was Wenny. What was this tremor that
went through the procession of faces at sunset time, browned them,
put blood in their lips, sparkle in their eyes, so that suddenly, as if
dolls should come to life, she would feel that she was going to meet
40   Wenny? Dreading the pain of it, she tried to forget herself in Fitzie's
shrill gossip of how the harpist had sauced the conductress and would
have been fired except that she was such a good player, and she'd only

had to apologize, and everybody had been in a dreadful temper, and they'd played the *Götterdämmerung* piece much too slowly. So they reached Park Street.

"Fitzie, suppose we have tea at my place. D'you mind? I want to get there before Miss Spence goes away."

"It'll be charming, and is the dress finished, the blue satin? You will let me see it, won't you? I so love looking at lovely dresses, the way I liked fairy tales when I was little. Even if I can't have them. . . ."

"There's nothing very fabulous about this one."

"O, you're so lucky, Nancibel, to be able to afford lovely dresses."   10

Nan thought of the dresses of the women in the Fadettes, angular, with the restlessness of bargain counters, fussily trimmed.—It's not the money, she told herself, it's knowing what to wear.

"Is Mr. Macdougan back from Europe yet?" asked Fitzie with downcast eyes once they had settled themselves in the streetcar.

"Yes, he's back," said Nan dryly. The car ground rattling round a corner in the tunnel and climbed out into the shattered dusk of the street. Nan had a glimpse of lights among the trees of the Public Garden. She narrowed her eyes to see the people along the pavements moving dark against the filmy brightness of shopwindows.   20

"Nancibel," said Fitzie after a pause, "I was so sorry about that . . . when it happened."

"When what happened?"

"You know what I mean, dear. . . . Like Billy and me, you know."

"How absurd. I was never engaged to Fanshaw. Can't you people understand that a man and a woman can be friends? All this sentimental tommyrot makes me furious."

"It isn't that, dear. You shouldn't say such things, Nancibel. Love is so beautiful."

Nan did not answer. She was thinking of Wenny bursting into her   30
room that spring morning, how the flame of him had frozen her into a helpless clicking automaton, and when he had gone she had watched him from the window rush across the street and all the rigid life had gone out of her so that she lay with her head on the windowledge and looked at the empty, snowpiled street . . . agony, not beauty, that was, agony.

"Art Museum," called out the conductor. They alighted and walked slowly along past the pompous, marble oblong of the dental clinic.

"O, Nancibel, I'd forgotten to tell you," cried Fitzie, suddenly turning excitedly to Nan, "I've seen Mabel Worthington."   40

"The girl from the Fadettes, your friend who eloped?"

"Yes, and just imagine it, she's terribly successful."

"What, at eloping?"

"Why, I don't just know about that. She's living at the Vendome, just think of that. I think she's managing concert tours, and she's married and everything. Several of the girls have been to see her."

"So she married the boy she eloped with? The Italian you said was so good looking."

"No, she didn't. . . . That's what's so queer. She's Mrs. Van Tropp-fer, and her husband's a Dutchman."

Nan burst out laughing.

10   "How shriekingly funny."

"The Swansea": the gilt letters slanted down the glass door. They were in the elevator that had a familiar oilheavy smell. Nan was still laughing. Under her laughter, she was pleased to be getting back to her apartment. All afternoon she had looked forward to seeing how far her dress would be along.

"O, how do you do, Miss Taylor? I was just going," came Miss Spence's voice from the bedroom. "Now I can try fitting . . . It was such a lovely afternoon, too lovely for words for those who can afford to go out in it. . . . O, how do you do, Miss Fitzhugh? You'll be able to

20   tell us what you think of the dress. . . . If you don't mind, we can fit it right now, because I mustn't be home late this evening, and the cars are so crowded." Miss Spence was a little woman who talked continually, her mouth bristling with pins, in an even, whiny voice; her hands were all the time darting about in front of her like lizards.

"What a beautiful blue," Fitzie was saying. "O, my dear, what a treat to see it fitted."

"Too lovely for words," echoed Miss Spence.

"It must have cost an enormous lot."

"Nonsense. . . . Fitzie, d'you mind putting some water to boil in

30   the kitchenette? . . . When do you think you can have it ready, Miss Spence?"

"O, dear, now let me think; would day after tomorrow do?"

"But I want to wear it to dinner tomorrow. My aunt is giving one of her musical evenings."

"O, how lovely that must be. O, I must try." Miss Spence's stubby hands fluttered up and down the satiny front of the dress. "How about length?"

"Stunning, stunning!" cried Fitzie, who had come back from the kitchenette. "A wonderful concert gown it would make."

40   "Do you think so?" said Nan and felt a warm glow suffuse her whole being, so that she could not help throwing back her head a little and straightening her shoulders.

"Too lovely for words," whined Miss Spence through the pins in her mouth, standing back against the wall to look.

*   *   *

"I seem to remember having heard Phillips Brooks say once," Aunt M. was saying, "that a meal without fellowship was almost an enormity. It's so true. As one grows older, Nancibel, one has to eat so many lonely, tasteless meals."

Nan looked at her aunt across the round primly set table, where the four candles under their silver shades cast creamy light on the starched cloth and gave forks and spoons and plates blue, uncertain shadows.

"But I find it rather pleasant to have a meal alone now and then. . . . It gives me a chance to collect my thoughts."

Aunt M. was lifting a cup of cocoa to her lips, carefully, like a child; she smiled wryly and said with a glint from the candles in her eyes:

"Because you can have company whenever you want. Nobody wants very much to have supper with an old woman like me."

"Why, Aunt M., you know I love to talk to you this way. The only reason I don't come oftener is that I'm so busy nowadays." Nan's fingers on her lap were tapping nervously against her knee.

"Of course, of course, dear, I understand. With your music and everything. I used to be very busy, too, and even now I'm not idle, am I?"

"I should say not."

"And then, watching your career, Nancibel, dear, I live over my own life. Think of it, dear, when I was young in those years after the rebellion. . . . Mary Ann, Miss Taylor will take her coffee in the other room."

"Yessum."

Aunt M. got to her feet, brushing a few crumbs off her silk dress and went through the portieres into the parlor. Nan glanced at herself in the mirror over the mantel as she followed.—How pale I look tonight, she thought.

"When I was young, in those years after the rebellion, Boston was a very busy place. And we were all so sanguine for the future. But now, even if I were strong enough, I would go out very little. It all seems so strange and ugly to me. And where is it going, this hideous chase after money?"

"I find a sort of splendor in it," said Nan brutally. They sat side by side on the curve-backed sofa, Nan with a small coffee cup in one hand.

"I'm happier indoors. But even here there's no real peace. The traffic on Beacon Street is so distressing."

"Marblehead would be a nice place to live."

"O, no, you wouldn't have me leave this house, would you, Nancibel, dear? This is my home. Do you remember in Mr. Emerson's poem . . .

> Why seek Italy,
> Who cannot circumnavigate the sea
> Of thoughts and things at home?

10   I feel that way about this house. Why, since I lived in my mother's house, I haven't lived anywhere else. How well I remember the first excitement of having a home of my own."

"When was that, Aunt M.?"

"I have never told you, have I? It was after I decided I would never marry." Aunt M. paused. Mary Ann rustled in to take the tray of coffee things.

"Anything else tonight, mum?"

"No, I won't need anything more. Good night, Mary Ann."

"Good night, mum."

20   "Nan, it's a long time since you brought Mr. Macdougan in to see me."

"He's very busy this year. He's giving a course of his own."

"A very clever young man, Nancibel . . . But I was telling you about the events that led up to my taking this house. It was something very near to me, which I have told to very few."

Aunt M. turned towards Nan and let her voice drop to a shaky whisper. Her eyes seemed strangely large and young and tremulous, staring out of the yellow, wrinkled face.

"I had engaged myself when very young—we were more pre-
30   cocious in those days—to a youth of good family and connections. You've even met him, but I shall not tell you who he is. We decided to wait several years before marrying, and in the meantime there was not a dance or party in Boston suitable to a young girl where I was not to be found merry with the merriest."

—People in crinolines bowing low and dancing to waltzes by Auber; our generation is different from that. We count more. Music welling out from the broken molds of old customs. We are really breaking away, seeking something genuine; true culture. Aunt M. wouldn't believe if I tried to explain.

40   "One night at a ball on Louisville Square at the Hillis's I was much struck by the appearance of a young man. I'd never seen any one so

handsome before, and to this day I have never seen the like of him. . . . Nancibel, I'm getting old. A year ago, even, I don't think I would have been able to tell you all this without my heart fluttering. . . . You are a dear girl to listen so attentively to your poor old aunt's reminiscences. Don't let me forget to go up to bed the minute the clock strikes ten."

They were sitting side by side on the curve-backed sofa. The old woman had snuggled close to Nan like a child listening to a ghost story. Nan's glance roamed nervously about the room. For a long while, she stared at her Aunt's hand that lay pudgy and freckled, with   10 swollen knuckles, in her slender, white hand.

"He was an Englishman named Verrey, though his skin was so dark everyone thought him an Italian. He paid court to me more charmingly than you can imagine. Every day of my life, he sent me a great bunch of Malmaison roses. Without telling anyone, I broke off my engagement. Mother was dreadfully uneasy about me, and all the family hated young Verrey because he looked so foreign. I was nearly ill about him. O, Nancibel, you can't imagine how wonderful he was, so dashing and chivalrous. And so it kept up. I stopped going out and used to spend all day in my room thinking of him. My father forbade   20 him the house, so that the only way I had of communicating with him was that a certain time each day I used to come to the window and he would walk slowly up and down the street in front of the house. I thought I'd cry my eyes out, he looked so sad and dejected. Then, to make a long story short, he came to see me one day when I was alone in the house. He was so perturbed he could hardly speak. He said I must run away with him instantly or he'd go mad with love of me. He tried to kiss me. It was terrible. I ordered him out of the house and I never saw him again. But I was fearfully ill. Several days after, I went to bed with brain fever. For weeks they despaired of saving me."   30

Nan was pressing her aunt's hand hard.

"And then?"

"Nothing. When I got well, nothing seemed to matter much. Convalescence has that effect. From that day to this, I've never been able to abide the smell of roses. But, my dear, I must go up to bed. I feel badly all day if I don't get my proper sleep. . . . Forgive my boring you with these old women's stories. We were very silly when I was a girl. How out of date I must seem to a generation brought up on Ibsen's plays."

"Yes, our ideas are a little different nowadays," said Nan.   40

Outside, the streetlights sparkled diamond hard in a clear wind. Nan walked fast, her thoughts desperately tumultuous. The keen October air and the clatter of her heels on the empty pavement of

Beacon Street were a relief after the senile stuffiness of her aunt's parlor.—And I'll be like that, spending my life explaining why I didn't dare live. No! No! Poor Aunt M. had nothing to fall back on. I have my music, my career, my sense of humor; it's not as if I were helpless before things like Fitzie. And she remembered how she'd stood at the piano the other night in that closefitting dress of royal blue satin and felt their eyes on her, and felt light coming into the bleary eyes of old people as she played to them.

10   She had reached Massachusetts Avenue, where the pavements were full of people coming out of the moving-picture theaters, standing in knots on the corner waiting for streetcars. For a moment she was caught up, elated, in the stream of windfreshened faces, bodies uncramping deliciously after the stiff seats of theaters. Her eyes ran thrillingly over faces that streamed past her, like her fingers over pianokeys. She walked fast, with exhilaration, until at a corner where she turned up past a drugstore, the curve of a cheek under a boy's mashed-down felt hat, full lips laughing, and a brown hand, ditchdigger's hand, swung suddenly into light, made her stop still trembling. Dizzy blackness welled up through her. She stood panting on the
20   corner. Whites of eyes, heads jerked towards her, puzzled looks as people passed. She walked back and forth in front of the drugstore. A hallucination, of course. But could she have seen him? Before she knew it, she had called out: "Wenny!" People were looking at her. She walked hurriedly up the dark street, breathless, running away from them. She spun in the grip of a horrible nausea.

                    *   *   *

"Why, Confucius looks sleeker than ever, Nan," said Fanshaw, and ran the tips of his fingers round the big, blue teapot. They sat in the open window, looking out at the misty, russet trees of the Fenway, with the teatable between them.
30   "He never goes hungry, or rather thirsty."
"Imagine this weather for the end of October. . . . St. Martin's summer."
"That's a nice name for it."
"Nicer than ours. Indian summer always makes me think of Hiawatha."
A sound of pounding and spades cutting gravel came up from the street below. Nan watched the blue backs of four laborers bend and straighten, bend and straighten as they worked in a hole in the street. A man in a black felt hat with a corncob pipe stuck in his beet face
40   stood over them.

"Curious for them to be tearing up the street at this time of the year," said Fanshaw, languidly.

"Our watermain burst. There wasn't a drop of water in the house this morning."

"How awkward."

Nan did not hear him. One of the laborers had looked up. For a moment his eyes were black, shining into hers.—O, but he can't really see me from down there. The face was lean, brown between curly, black hair and an unshaven chin. With an eager child's smile, he raised a hand. As the hand fell, she had a glimpse of a dark chest scooped into taut muscles towards the belly under his open blue shirt. He was again a blue back bending and straightening with the three other backs. Crazy fires danced through her.

"Yes, I had to go round to Gertrude Fagan's to wash." There was a dead veil between her and Fanshaw.

"And how is the fiery Gertrude?"

"Very well."

"The last time I met that lady on the street she cut me dead. . . . I suppose she's too taken up with the world beyond to notice us terrestrial beings."

"Nonsense, Fanshaw, Gertrude's an awfully nice person. . . . You must have done something she didn't like. She's very easily offended."

"Do the spooks continue to flourish?"

"You mean her automatic writing. Well, what of it? You shouldn't scoff at things you don't understand."

"That's better than being awed by them, Nan."

"Anything more I can do for you, miss?"

It was the Irish girl who came to clean. She stood in the shadow by the door with her hands at her sides; pretty, smiling lips.

"No, nothing tonight, Marion. I'm sorry I kept you so late today."

"That's all right. Good night, miss."

Nan smiled warmly at her through the dusk of the room. At the end of the hall, the door shut sharply.

"More tea, Fanshaw?"

"No, thanks."

While she poured a few drops of tea into her cup, she glanced out the window again.—Italians they were, probably, smelling of pipes and sweaty shirts and garlic. There's Marion. If I were Marion Reily instead of Nancibel Taylor . . . to stroll along twilit streets with backward looks through the lashes; that boy'd rub the clay off his hands and follow me; kidding talk on park benches, fumbling, work-rough hands, ditchdigger's hands, hardmuscled arms crushing, moist, hot lips bearing down, panting. The cold voice of Aunt M. when she was a little girl too excited at the circus: "Careful, Nancibel. Careful, Nancibel."

"But Fanshaw," she was saying, straining to keep the tumult out of her voice, "suppose there were a life after death."

Fanshaw did not answer for a moment. She saw his eyes, dusky grey, troubled. The straight line of his lips tightened.—All this is me, small talk over teacups and polished hardwood floors and Fanshaw's
10   drawling Harvardese. Marion's neat, dark figure had gone off down the street with quick, jerky steps. Nan looked back into the darkening room.

"Is there any reason to believe," Fanshaw was saying in a tone that arrested all her attention suddenly, "that people in the next life would be any less futile than people in this life? It's horrible to want to do away with death."

"How can you feel that way? It's all such fun," she said, bois- terously. So Fanshaw, too . . . She felt he was changing the subject.

"Coming back on the *Baltic*, Nan . . . you should have seen Edgar.
20   He blossomed into a regular society butterfly and actually forced me to play bridge with some dreadful girls named Van Ryn he dug up somewhere."

"New Yorkers?"

"Yes."

"Was the famous Mrs. Harry Van Ryn along?"

"Was she? You should have seen how she dressed! Might have thought it was the *Lusitania*. Her daughters were quieter than she was, and rather more intelligent, I must allow them that."

They were silent a while. Rosy afterglow flowed like water through
30   the window.

"Where did you go besides Siena?"

"O, to Arezzo, Urbino, and then to Assissi and San Gimingiano."

"You wretch, stole a march on me. . . . And there I was up at Squirrel Island with Aunt M., bored to the ears. Never mind, I'll have my revenge some day."

—Fitzie's Italian, who smelt of garlic and looked like a young Greek god, dark face and a boy's full wistful smile. The gods were ever young, and Mabel Worthington eloped with youth and married an elderly Dutchman for his money and lived at the Vendome.
40   Fanshaw was on his feet.

"Must you run away so soon?"

He nodded. Her cheerful, social voice rang bitterly in her ears as she stood in the middle of the empty room. She was full of dull, surprised pain, like a disappointed child.—So that's dead, she heard herself say. Am I growing old? Is everything going to die like that? Twenty-nine isn't old.

She switched on the light and took her violin.—I can get in an hour's practice before getting ready to go to the Smithers. . . . O, I can't play. I'm too wretchedly nervous this afternoon. Perhaps Gertrude'll be in. She went to the phone in the hall to call the number. As she waited with the receiver against her ear, something made her remember Fitzie saying in her shrill excited whisper: And Salinski says you played as if you had a soul.—Let's see, when was   10 that? Think I've been in this apartment nearly four years, four years scraping on the fiddle. Gertrude doesn't answer. Tomorrow morning I must get hold of Fitzie. She promised to take me to see that girl. Quite exciting her career has been: the Fadettes and then that disreputable episode with the Italian. How much she must know about life! Probably decided she couldn't play or she wouldn't have gone into the agency business. Wonderful to cut loose the way she has. Fitzie says she comes from quite a good family out in Waltham.

Nan had put the teacups on the tray with the pot and was carrying them out into the kitchenette.—O, that wretched girl forgot the   20 garbage. She took up the little zinc pail and put it on the dumbwaiter. I'll ask John to empty it as a special favor. While she stood pulling on the rope, gingerly, so as not to dirty her hands, she heard loud laughter from one of the kitchens below.—Wish I'd noticed more about the people living in this house; there must be some queer fish. She felt herself smiling.—How shocked Aunt M. was when I told her where I'd taken an apartment. She washed the teacups and the pot and left them to dry in the rack beside the sink. When she opened the tin box to put the cake in, there came to her a familiar smell of stale bread and crackers. Must make toast of that bread for breakfast   30 tomorrow. She dropped the lid sharply.—Why do I go on doing these little things day after day? Always meals. The indigestion of the little. A woman's life may always be that. O, I must know about other people's lives. Mabel Worthington, is her life just pots and pans and combs and nailfiles and doilies? She went into her bedroom.—Only half-past six by the little porcelain clock on the mantel, a whole hour before I need be at the Smithers. She lifted the shade and peered down into the blue darkness of the street. The workmen had gone. Under the lamppost, she could see the patched place they had left. She let herself sink into a chair and remained a long while looking out   40 the window with the shade between her and her room. Occasionally, a man or woman walked past from the direction of Huntington Avenue.—On their way home to dinner. Endless family tables, and other tables, kept women pouring out champagne for fashionably dressed men, the fast set. Women throwing back their heads and laughing through the smoke of their cigarettes. Perhaps that's how Mabel Worthington would be, with high-piled hair bleached with peroxide and a whisky voice. If I were like that, dining tonight with Wenny among cocktails and offcolor stories. The Back Bay siren. Lovely Back Bay girl figures in East Cambridge Bridge suicide. She shuddered and threw open the window. Fog was coming in, blurring the streetlights.—He always loved the fog. Perhaps once more out of the streaming faces and the clicking feet, his funny, shambling walk, his hands, ditchdigger's hands, the hair curling crisply about his forehead, the way it curled on foggy nights . . . As the fog thickened, the people passing under the window became shadowy and the sound of their steps dull and muffled.

Behind her in the room, the clock struck seven silvery, discreet little strokes. Nan jumped guiltily to her feet. She must dress. As she arranged her hair, she wondered if she should take her violin. They'd be sure to ask her to play, but perhaps they would think better of her if she said she had forgotten it.

*   *   *

"Perhaps it's suede you wanted, miss," said the thin, blonde saleslady, narrowing her eyes as she leaned towards Nan across the counter.

"The material doesn't matter a bit. It's a certain color I'm looking for, can't you understand?" said Nan peevishly. She held herself in and said again, firmly, in her natural voice: "A warm pearl grey."

Nan was very tired. The late afternoon bustle of the department store and the atmosphere of perfumes and women's furs and breathedout air and the close smell of fabrics were almost unbearable. She had been shopping all afternoon so that her legs ached and she had a faint pain between her eyes. While the woman went off for a new box of gloves, Nan stared dully at the holly-wreathed sign above the counter: "Do Your Christmas Shopping Early." Her eyes followed the wearisome curlicues of the gothic capitals.

"Here you are, miss," said the saleslady, with a desperate attempt at sprightliness in her voice.

"That's it," said Nan. She found herself looking in the white face of the saleslady, itself a little like wrinkled kid. "Busy time this must be for you."

"Busy! No time to breathe."

"I don't see how you do it."

"Don't think about it. Only way. Never think about things," said the saleslady, breathlessly writing out the slip.

Nan found herself drifting down the aisle of the store, a package added to those under her arm and stuffed into her bag, among fat, jostling women and angular women with disapproving lips and small, tired women with saggy eyes; she glanced in the waxen face under slimy hair of a floorwalker, tried ineffectually to approach the notions counter, and at last found herself looking at the clock beside the elevator. Half-past four, time to meet Fitzie at the tearoom. The elevator smelt of oil, heavy, like castor oil.—Was it her mother's voice, or some governess's out of her childhood: Now, Nancibel, if you can't be more ladylike you'll have to take some castor oil. How tired she was this afternoon. Silly to come shopping in the afternoon so near the Christmas season.

> Christmas comes but once a year.
> Let us laugh and have good cheer,
> La la dee dee, la la dee dee.

Beyond nodding cherries in a grey woman's hat, the face of the elevator man, black face with an ivory grin, and his suave, negro voice announcing: "Mezzanine floor: Ladies' and misses' garments and imported lingerie, ladies' and misses' hats and footwear. Way back, please. . . . Second floor: Men's and boys' clothes, ready and custom made, sporting goods; Men's and boys' haberdashery and footwear. Let the lady out, please. . . . Third floor: House furnishings, rugs, verandah furniture and imported goods" . . . At the top floor, Nan stumbled out of the elevator and had to sit down on the bench in front of it, she was so tired. She counted over the little packages on her lap.—That's right, I haven't lost anything.

"Nan, it's all fixed."

Fitzie, in a red hat with a feather, popped out of the soggy mass of women in the elevator, crisp and bristling with excitement. She sat down beside Nan on the bench.

"My dear, you look a sight; you must be dreadfully tired. Never mind, some tea'll freshen you up famously. . . . But it's all fixed about our tour."

"You mean the orchestra?"

"Of course, Nancibel. We open next Monday in Montreal."

"It'll be dreadfully cold up there, I should think."

"But think, dearest, how wonderful! I've never traveled in my life before. We'll go all the way out to the Coast, San Francisco and all that."

"Fitzie, before you go we mustn't forget to call on Mabel Worthington. I'm very curious to meet her."

"O, we will, but let's get a table before they are all snapped up. I'm
perishing."

The waitress had pretty brown eyes.—She can't be more than
eighteen, thought Nan, as they sat down. Eleven years younger than I
am. What happens in eleven years? Nothing. Everything. A mere kid
Wenny would have been eleven years ago, inky-fingered, curlypated
schoolboy.

10   "And how's your aunt?" Fitzie was asking.

"I'm rather worried about her. . . . Poor Aunt M. hasn't been a bit
well this last month. I've been trying to get her to go south."

"I should think Florida'ld be just the thing."

"She's afraid she'd be lonely."

"Why don't you go with her?"

"But my music, Fitzie! I can't afford to lose a whole winter at this
stage of the game, and Salinski's promised me some extra hours."

"O, I see."

Nan frowned.

20   "You don't mean you think I ought to give up everything and go, do
you?"

"Of course not, but the conflict between one's love for one's family
and one's wanting a career is sometimes dreadful, positively dreadful. . . . Of course, it's none of my business, and I shan't say anything
one way or the other."

"But what tommyrot . . . You know perfectly well how I feel about
my career."

"Of course, dear, of course," said Fitzie, nibbling at a piece of toast.
"You'll be interested in what Mabel has to say about that. She's made
30   more of a career than any of the girls in our time at the conservatory."

"I don't mean quite that by career," said Nan, laughing.

"Of course not, you are much too wellbred, dearest. . . . But could
you go tomorrow?"

"Not tomorrow . . . But how about Saturday?"

Nan gulped down a cup of weak, milky tea with relief. The chatter
at the tables round about and the smothered selection from *The
Arcadians* out of the victrola in the corner of the tearoom sucked all
the remaining energy out of her so that she sat limp, staring at her
friend's new red hat.—Utterly ridiculous, like a redbird, she was
40   thinking.

"Why not tomorrow?" insisted Fitzie. "I shall be dreadfully busy
Saturday. It'll be my last useful day. We leave Sunday night. Isn't it
too wonderful! Think of the places I'll see and the people I'll meet and
everything. . . . Of course, it'll be exhausting too."

"I almost wish I were going with you."

"But you can't have engagements all day tomorrow, Nancibel."

"I'm going to stay in the house tomorrow."

"O, you poor dear!" Fitzie leaned over and patted Nan's hand. "That's quite all right. Of course, I understand. Of course, we'll go Saturday."

Nan winced. She felt a sudden rage against all this womanish chatter and chirping talk. The smell of women, perfume, furs, dry goods was choking her.—I must get out of here.

"Walk with me to the Touraine, Fitzie. I'm going home in a taxi."

"You extravagant thing. But I simply can't. I've got so much to do . . . preparations for departure."

"And that Worthington girl?" asked Nan in a carefully offhand voice as they were going down in the packed elevator.

"O, I'll call her up and make a date. She's always in at teatime. Shall I phone you, dear?"

"Yes, do." Fitzie's short, pigeonbreasted figure was caught into the stream of women down the main aisle of the store, over which the arcs hovered like lilac-white balloons. A last glimpse of the red hat.—O, I should have spoken of it; she'll be offended. But such a sight . . . The revolving doors swung Nan out onto the pavement, where the air was cold and hard. The signs down Washington Street brandished metallic facets of light. The crowd streamed endlessly dark against the motionless glow of the wide windows of stores. From automobiles moving in compact, opposed streams came the rasp of racing motors and a smell of scorched gasoline. Nan made her way slowly through a barbed, painful tunnel of light and noise and cold. At length with a little sigh, she sank back into the springy seat of the taxi and let the packages slip out of her hands. There was a musty smell about it that brought up childish dreams of elegance.—That picture eternally repeated in the movies of the elegantly gloved heroine stepping into her limousine. To arrive that way, stately, at the side doors of concert halls, to be handed out by sleekhaired men in frockcoats, to stand a moment waiting in a long, tightfitting dress of royal blue, her violin in one hand, a smell of roses about her, and from everywhere the terrible dizzy murmur of the waiting audience. Had Mabel Worthington attained all that already? Why, she can't even play, all she's done has been to flaunt her sex. She must be a veritable harlot. I must see her to find out.

They were turning the corner out of Massachusetts Avenue. Nan tapped suddenly on the window.

"I want to stop at that fruit store. . . . That's right."

"All right, miss," said the driver, smiling. He was a pertlooking young man with a red face and a horseshoe scarf pin.

—Why am I so timid? I have personality as much as the next girl, she was thinking as warmed by the young man's smile she wandered about the fruit store trying to decide what to buy. At last she lit on some pears. While the Greek, a sallow man with a long nose and close-cropped hair, was putting them in a bag, she spied some Japanese persimmons in a box. "O, I must have some of those for the color."

"They are mighty good . . . sweet as honey," said the Greek.

"At last!" she muttered, closing her eyes with a little sigh when,
10 having paid off the taxi, she stood in the elevator of "The Swansea." As she let the packages slide from her arms into the armchair in the living room, she felt a crushing sense of loneliness. She poured the orangered persimmons into a blue bowl on the teatable.—How beautiful they are. If I only had someone to show them to. She threw herself into a bustle of preparations for supper. She lit two burners in the kitchenette.—Toast and boiled eggs, and then I'll go to bed with a book. The usualness of the smell of the gas-burners and boiling water and toast oppressed her. Was she going to spend all her life puttering about that miserable kitchenette? If I were at Aunt M.'s in the little
20 room I had when I was a child, it would be cozy to be made a fuss over and have breakfast brought up to me in bed by Mary Ann in the morning.

After supper she remembered she hadn't looked at the letters she had brought up from the mailbox.—One from Salinski. What on earth?

Dear Miss Taylor:
    It is with infinite regret that I must announce to you that on account of great and pressing business I shall be forced to omit your next three lessons, making our following engagement for January 26. . . .

30 —I know what that means. He's losing interest in me. He can't treat me like that. I'll phone him. He has no right not to explain what he means. She went to the phone and jerked off the receiver. Then she put it back weakly and burst into tears.—O, I'm all distraught this evening. How horribly silly. I'll go to bed and read. With streaming eyes she began to undress.

Once in bed, in her white bedroom, with the reading light over her shoulder and the rest of the room in cozy shadow and the persimmons in their blue bowl on a chair within reach, she began to feel calmer. She lay a long while staring at the ceiling with Locke's *Beloved*
40 *Vagabond* unopened in her hand.—Is it just that I'm feeling low this evening, or is everything crumbling, breaking down to let in the

floods of platitude the way the noise of pianolas seeps in through apartment-house walls?

The persimmons glowed like lacquer.—Sweet as honey, the Greek had said they were. Vermilion, the color, was more than red or orange. Was it Wenny or Fanshaw used to talk about how the three of them were like people out of another age lost in a grey swamp of dullness in their vermilion barge? Another age. If she'd lived in another age. The grandeur that was Rome. Decline and fall. What careers women had then. Dread career of adultery and crime. Messalina. Was it on the Pincian her gardens had been? Somewhere in Baedeker. Carried in a litter through howling streets, swinging above the torches and the black, dripping backs of slaves, with an arm about the neck of a young, curlyhaired lover, long, ringed fingers clasped about the hard muscle of his shoulder, into the walled gardens, winy with the smell of overripe fruits, sweet as honey. Great gates closing on streets full of crowds that shrieked challenging, mocking, Messalina. In the hush of the garden on the Pincian, she and Wenny in each other's arms, with their lips touching, sweet as honey. Nan felt hot shudders go through her, her cheeks were fire. She pressed her dry eyes against the white, cool linen of the pillow and lay on her face rocking to and fro. Then she jumped out of bed and began to walk about her narrow bedroom. She must go out. The streets were thronged with men, lovers.

From the apartment below came the sound of a piano and a man's nasal voice singing:

> I know a spot where the sun is like gold
> And the cherry blooms burst with snow.

Nan threw open the window and looked out into the empty street. Two cats, arched, scuttling shadows, were circling about the lamppost. The night was suddenly ripped with their caterwauling. Shivering with cold and disgust, Nan sat a long time in the chair by the window, her palms pressed against her hot, tearless eyes. Down the street she heard from time to time the love-wail of a cat.

*   *   *

A bellboy's brown back, shiny with buttons, preceded them down the dark, red-carpeted hall. In spite of Nan's casual stroll beside Fitzie, who walked with her face pushed forward eagerly and a smile ready on her lips, she felt uneasy.—I merely want to see what she's like, she said to herself, constricting her flutter of excitement as she constricted her wrists, buttoning her tight kid gloves. Merely to observe. The boy knocked on a brown door at the end of the hall. Nan could feel her heart pumping.

"Come!" The voice was deep, throaty under velvet. The room opened bright, wide, with looped salmon colored curtains; brisk air smelling of flowers, freesias there by the window.

The woman walked towards them, holding out a hand.

"Hello, Fitzie. Why, how splendid . . . I always wanted to meet you, Miss Taylor. . . . You see, I admired you from afar, up at Jordan." Her hand was firm and cool. She had brown eyes, a skin flushed with
10   olive, hair like ebony, and at the waist of a simply-cut, tuniclike black dress two small red chrysanthemums. "Do sit down. O, it is good of you to have come."

As she sat down, she spread out one arm along the top of the brocaded sofa. Above a long brown neck, Pre-Raphaelite neck, poised a little pointed chin. Nan felt herself sitting opposite stiffly with pursed lips; she let herself sink back in her chair.

"O, Fitzie, I've heard about the tour. Isn't it great? I almost wish I were going along. Think of the squalling and squabbling there'll be; won't it be grand? It was funny enough going out to Worcester that
20   time, but the grand continental tour of the embattled Fadettes'll be an unholy shriek."

There was a knock at the door. A waiter came in, half hidden under a teatray balanced over one shoulder.

"Would either of you prefer a cocktail or a glass of port or something?"

"O, no, tea will be just delicious," said Fitzie, shaking hastily the red feather of her hat.

"Nothing could be better than tea, Mrs. Van Troppfer," said Nan quietly.
30   "Did you know, Fitzie, I've given up the violin? After all this time, isn't it ridiculous?" The brown eyes were looking in Nan's, wide, amused. "Yes, I'm afraid I'm a rolling stone, and certainly I shan't gather moss. Think how they'd be horrified up at the conservatory. . . . I'm going to try to sing again. You see, I always had wanted to sing and only took up the violin because I could get quicker money by it. Then I had mother to support."

"Really, I never knew that," said Fitzie, suspending a spoonful of pastry halfway to her mouth.

"O, families are a perpetual problem, aren't they?" said the Worth-
40   ington girl, laughing.

Nan ate a cream cornucopia delicately, between sips of tea. The crisp pastry and the faint cheese flavor in the white cream made her think of Paris, station restaurants abroad, and fogs and concerts.

"We are going abroad again in a week or two, and I'm going to work

like a Trojan . . . try to strike while the iron's hot. You see, my
husband and Hammerstein claim that I have a good stage presence
and ought to take a whack at the Opera Comique. That's what the
Fadettes did for me! I keep telling them that I'm too long-necked to
be a singer . . . but I guess I'll take a try at it. Maybe I'll have luck."

"Your husband must have great connections," said Fitzie in a
humble tone.

"That won't do any good unless I manage to learn to sing, will it?"
She turned laughing to Nan, "Do have a little more tea, I'm afraid I'm
boring you with all my chatter. . . . I hear you are studying with   10
Salinski, Miss Taylor. How do you find him? He knows the instrument
all right, but it's difficult to hold him down, he's getting so social these
days."

"Still, if he's really interested in your work," Nan heard herself say.

"O, that's another thing. . . . He never was interested in me, I
know that."

There was a knock at the door. "Come!" called the Worthington
girl. The bellboy came in with a telegram on a plate.

"All right, bring it here; thanks."

It was a creamfaced boy with a snub nose. Nan watched a tense,   20
adoring look come into his eyes as he put the plate within the
Worthington girl's reach.—That's how she does it. The boy left the
room hurriedly, flushing as if her smile stung. With languid fingers,
she crumpled the telegram.

"You must excuse me," she said. "Isn't it wretched being in a hotel
this way? They never give you any peace. . . . Did you ever study
music in Paris, Miss Taylor?"

"No, only in Boston."

"I was wondering if they were as stupid over there about it as they
are here. Isn't it hopeless?" She laughed happily, cuddling into the   30
corner of the sofa and taking little bites out of a cream cornucopia.
"Still, we'll see what turns up."

"Who are you studying with?"

"O, that's the great question. . . . It's really more difficult than
getting married. I have to look them over, and they have to look me
over."

Nan began to put on her gloves.

"Must you go?"

"I'm afraid so."

"Then so must I," said Fitzie hastily. "It's been just lovely to see   40
you, Mabel dear."

"I was hoping Van Troppfer would get in before you left. . . . He'll
be disappointed not seeing you."

The Worthington girl went with them to the door. As they turned the corner of the red-carpeted hall, Nan had a glimpse of her smiling at them from the half-open door, tall and dark against a streak of light.

They walked down the stairs and out on the street in silence. Then Fitzie turned suddenly to Nan and said:

"Isn't she just wonderful? . . . Now you must tell me what you think of her. O, she's the girl who'll have a career."

"I suppose her vulgarity was to be expected. She wears her clothes beautifully, doesn't she?"

"Well, she always did do that. Everybody admitted her to be the best-dressed girl in the orchestra."

"I wonder where she learned it?"

"I believe she came of a good family in reduced circumstances; that's all there is about it."

"Well, Fitzie, I'm going home. If I don't see you again before you go, here's wishing you all the luck in the world." Nan leant and kissed Fitzie on the cheek.

"You will write, won't you, deary? I'll let you know the addresses."

"Of course, I will."

Nan walked fast down a cross street.—What a relief to be alone. Shouldn't have left Fitzie so abruptly, but couldn't stand her chatter a moment longer. Silly to be so upset; what am I so upset about, anyway? My nerves are jumpy as the dickens this winter. In a cold fury of dismay, she walked home through the yellow twilight, her chin pressed into her fur neckpiece as she leaned against the wind that blew razorkeen down the long street that led to the Fenway and made her ears sting and her forehead ache. Muffled by closed windows, shattered by the gusty wind, there came to her from the houses on either hand wail and tinkle of music students doing their scales on piano and violin, growls of cellos, trilling of dramatic sopranos.— Street of scales; they expect to climb into life up their scales like up ladders. She remembered savagely she hadn't practiced that day. And that Worthington girl, did she ever practice, did she work and contrive to get on, or was everything as easy to her as the bellboy's frightened blush under her smile? And this husband she had picked up, what could he be like? A short, loud man in a checked suit probably, with a bulging red vest and a brown derby. I'm glad I didn't see him, men like that are too disgusting.

She dug her chin into her fur and battled furiously with the wind.—If it'ld only snow, it wouldn't be so cold. At length the letters spelling out "The Swansea" were dark against the light ahead of her, she was in the elevator; the key was clicking softly in the lock of her door. The homelike smell was soothing to her nostrils. Thank heavens, I left the heat on. Before taking off her hat and gloves, she stood a moment in the window, her hands over the steampipes. The sky, beyond the hardetched tangle of branches of the Fenway and the purple cubes of the further apartment houses, was a wide, empty yellow, chilling to green overhead. Nan felt its bitter emptiness like a rasp on a half-healed wound. With wincing lips she pulled down the shade and turned her back on the window.

That night, she dreamed that she sat in the great yellowshot beehive of the Boston Theater and that Fanshaw sat on one side of her and Wenny on the other, both in evening dress, and she was a little girl in spotted calico with her hair in pigtails, and on the stage was the orchestra of the Fadettes playing like mad, and in front of them Mabel Worthington with her mouth open and her head thrown back and a sheet of music agitated in front of her, and Nan kept turning to Wenny and to Fanshaw and saying: "I can't hear a word, not a single word." Suddenly Wenny had slipped from her side and was in a taxi with his arms round the Worthington girl, kissing her, kissing her, and Nan was in another taxi driven by a young man with a red face and a diamond horseshoe in his tie, and they were hurtling through red-flaring streets under a black sky, streets lined with faces staring and hands pointing, and to all Nan's crying to them to tell her where he had gone, there was no answer but hissing and stamping and catcalls.

Nan sat up in bed, rubbing her forehead, trying to remember what she had been dreaming. The glow of the streetlight in her window was full of furtive, padded movement. Snow. She stretched her arms out above her head; the iron rods of the bed were cold against her skin. Then all at once she found that she was crying. She pulled herself under the clothes again and rubbed her arms against her body. "Wenny," she said softly aloud and lay staring out at the tender fluttering of snow outside the window.

*　　　*　　　*

Nan closed the front door gently behind them.

"My, I'm glad to get in again," said Gertrude Fagan.

"Why, dear?"

"It's so horrible, a night like this. I hate it all."

"What do you mean? But we'd better go up to my room. We'll wake Aunt M. if we sit down here, and it's so hard to get her to sleep again."

"I don't suppose she's much better, is she?" whispered Gertrude Fagan as they tiptoed up the heavily-carpeted stairs. Nan winced when a board creaked on the second flight.

"No," she was whispering over her shoulder, "though there doesn't seem to be any danger of another stroke just at present. There doesn't seem to be any cure for the aphasia, though Doctor Smythe talks wisely enough about it. . . . Whew, it's hot in here."

Nan went straight to the window and pushed it up hard. A heavy scent of lilacs came in off the Public Garden, where the occasional lights were misted with the green of young leaves. Beyond, the electric signs of Boylston and Tremont Streets sent a great glare up into the milky, spring sky. An automobile whirred past. There were steps on the pavements. She turned back into the room.

Gertrude Fagan sat on the bed with her hat on her knees. The
10   reading lamp she had just switched on threw her eyes into shadow.

"Look, Nancibel, at my shadow on the wall," she said harshly. "Wouldn't think I had a hooked beak like that, would you?"

"How absurd, Gertrude! Look, this is the room I used to have when I was a little girl. . . . I'll put you up next door."

"But, really, I ought to go home."

"No, you'll be perfectly comfortable here. You know you don't like going home alone at night."

"Not a night like this," said Gertrude Fagan, shuddering.

"But it's the finest night we've had this spring."
20   "I hate it; it makes me feel unclean, as if I hadn't washed all day. And there's a sense of unclean things prowling about one. . . . It shatters my nerves a night like this."

"I wonder if I don't feel that way too, really," Nan said in a low, dead voice. "Look, Gertrude, are you too tired to work the board again tonight?"

"You mean you want to try again?"

Nan nodded.

"Of course I could keep it up for a little while," said Gertrude Fagan, getting eagerly to her feet. "You're sure your aunt won't mind
30   if I spend the night? Seeing me appear mysteriously at the breakfast table might surprise her."

"Poor Aunt M., she's gone beyond surprise, Gertrude; she probably won't recognize you. It's almost as if she were dead."

"Horrible! She was such a brilliant person. . . . I always felt there was a strange magnetism about her, something I couldn't explain, like about you. Probably all your family had it. . . . What a nice room this is, the antithesis of those horrible paths across the Common. . . . O, didn't you feel it, Nancibel, in the theater and shoving our way through the crowd home, a horrible lack of spirituality in all the
40   faces?"

"Rather that they have strange secrets I can never know." Nan was leaning over the chiffonier, fumbling in a drawer. "Here's the Ouija board." She turned into the swath of light, holding out before her a yellow, varnished board with a semicircle of letters on it.

"He taught you to think that. His was an earthspirit. Now he is purified."

"Please, Gertrude, . . . You never knew him," Nan snapped out. Her fingers were taut about the edge of the Ouija board.

"Why, I met him several times."

"I mean really knew him."

"Why are you angry at me, Nancibel?"

Without answering, Nan began taking the books off the small table where the reading light stood. She drew up two chairs and put a small, three-legged wooden pointer on the board. Then she went to the window again and looked down into the welter of broken lights and green-spun shadows of the Public Garden. That night of premature spring the three of them had walked into town under a sky of coppery flame and all the streets had fallen into a rollicking procession behind them, and they had seemed gay and strong enough to trample the whole world, was this all it led to, these choking lilacs that smelt of death? Or was it all mirage, false? Behind her she could feel Gertrude Fagan moving restlessly about the room. Nan half-closed her eyes and breathed deep of the fetor of blossoms and gasoline and lurking bodies; then came back to the table, her face still and pale. Gertrude Fagan already sat with the tips of her fingers on the wooden pointer, her eyes black, fixed on the black of the window.

"Think of David Wendell, Nancibel," she said in a shaky voice.

Nan put her fingers on the other end of the pointer and closed her eyes. Above the pounding of her heart, she could hear the slow rasp of the other girl's breathing. So they waited.

IX

"WELL, it was a great war while it lasted." Major Baldwin sat swinging his brightly-polished puttees from the edge of Fanshaw's desk. "What are you going to do when you go home?" He turned towards Fanshaw a steaklike face from which emanated a distinct steam of cocktails.

Fanshaw looked up from the photographs of Red Cross activities he was sorting, let his eye roam across the golden and rusty roofs that stretched away under the window past domes and more domes to-wards St. Peter's and Janiculum, glanced at the blue, reflected light
10 on Major Baldwin's puttees, at his elegant whipcord breeches and his Sam Browne belt, red and shiny as his puttees, until at last he found himself looking into his blue, watery eyes.

"I suppose . . . I guess there's nothing to it but to go back to teaching the young idea how to appreciate art."

"Why don't ye stay in relief work? . . . There'll be jobs for years." Major Baldwin kicked his heels against the desk and threw back his head and laughed and laughed.

"Colonel Hopkins is in there," said Fanshaw, jerking his head back towards the mahogany doors behind his desk.
20 "I don't give a hoot in hell about Hopkins. . . . Listen here, I've got some dope, see? . . ." He leaned over and whispered noisily in Fanshaw's ear. "Old Hopkins is going to get his. . . . They're starting an investigation of the organization from the ground up. A Congres-sional investigation . . . Goin' to be hell to pay. Let's get out and have a lil' drink."

Fanshaw looked at his watch.

"I can't go for half an hour yet. . . . I'm not supposed to leave my desk till five."

"Hell, up in my office we don't keep any hours at all."
30 "You aren't so near to centers of operation."

"You mean to that old fool?" Major Baldwin pointed with a stout forefinger at the mahogany doors. "The investigation'll fix him. . . How soon are you packing up for home?"

"Probably in a couple of weeks . . . I'm afraid I'll have to finish up this album of "Child Relief, 1918–1919," first. . . . I'm bored to death with this work, aren't you?"

Major Baldwin got to his feet and went to the window. He stood a long while looking out, twirling his cane in one hand. Fanshaw continued sorting photographs of ragged Italian children.

"Gosh, I don't see it," said Major Baldwin suddenly.

"See what?" Fanshaw was poring over a group of a Red Cross captain and a nurse with soup ladles in their hands surrounded by ragged Neapolitan guttersnipes.

"Going home after this."

Fanshaw pushed his chair back silently and got up from the desk. They both leaned out of the window and hung over the city that seemed to sway in the great waves of honeycolored sunlight, like jetsam in a harbor swell. They could smell gardens and scorched olive oil, and a drowsy afternoon murmur came up to them, punctuated occasionally by the screech of a tram round a corner or a shout or a distant church bell.

"That's true. . . . There have been many enjoyable . . ."

"I tell you, Macdougan, it was a great war. . . . Gosh, look at that girl in the garden there. . . . No, just coming out from under the arbor. Look at that throat. . . . Isn't she a pippin?"

Fanshaw laughed.

"You're incorrigible, Baldwin."

"That's why I don't want to go home. . . . I'm afraid that if I go home they'll correct me."

"I don't know. . . . They say things are very gay in the States. . . . Flappers and all that."

"What's this about flappers?" came a cracked voice behind them. The voice broke into a wheezy laugh. "So this is how the publicity department does its work, is it?"

"Just about," said Fanshaw, turning round to face a small, greyfaced man with shaggy eyebrows. "Are you shutting up shop, Petrie?"

"Yes, it's four minutes after five. . . . Look, does either of you men want to sail home from Palermo on the *Canada* next week?"

"Heavens, no, I'm staying on till they drive me away," shouted the major.

"I'd like to go," Fanshaw said quietly. "I've been away two years. It's time I went to see what the university has to say about my job."

"Beginning to think of the girl I left behind me, are you?" asked the greyfaced man creakily.

"Ha, ha! That's it." Fanshaw laughed loud and lifted his hand as if to slap his thigh. He found himself looking with constraint at his lifted hand and put it stiffly into his pocket.

*   *   *

Le Capitaine Eustache de la Potinière had a red scar on his left cheek that stretched from the lower rim of his monocle to the tip of his distended nostril. As he sat beside Fanshaw in the joggling cab, the medals clinked together on the breast of his tight-waisted khaki uniform.

"The people on the street are looking at us as we drive by," he was saying. "They are telling each other: There go two of the bravest of our allies. . . . The Italians like that sort of thing: medals and people riding by in cabs. . . . Captain Macdougan, never forget that there is
10   a brotherhood among the Latin peoples." Thereupon he sat up stiffly in the cab, blonde moustaches bristling, and clicked his hand up to a salute. An Italian officer in a long, blue cloak saluted ferociously from the curb. Fanshaw found himself also stiffening to salute. . . . Funny feeling, the victorious allies riding about in cabs, saluting one another to a clink of medals. America had done all that, won the war, and he had done his bit himself; after all, relief work . . .

"Excuse me if I stop at this chemist's a moment," said the French captain. "There is something I must get before they close." And he poked the driver in the back with his cane, crying out: "Arretez ici, cré
20   nom d'un chien!"

While le Capitaine Eustache de la Potinière was in the shop, Fanshaw lolled in the cab and stared down the grey Palermo street, where the dust gave a shimmering outline to the patches of sun and shadow. Now and then he straightened up and answered the salute of some Italian soldier. His puttees were too tight and cut into his legs above the ankle. Never mind, this was the last day. Tomorrow, sailing for home, a civilian, no more uniform, no more inspecting colonels to talk to. Strange and different it will be coming back from the war. The thought was elating. And Nan Taylor, what will have become of her? A
30   year since he'd heard of her.—Poor Nan must be getting quite an old maid by this time, and, as for me, if it hadn't been for the war, this curious life in Italy, relief work . . .

Le Capitaine Eustache de la Potinière was coming out of the shop, red and spluttering.

"Did you get what you wanted?" asked Fanshaw.

"These dirty Sicilians don't seem to understand. We'll try another place. Alley oop! Continuez! . . . We'll dine in the grand manner, won't we? . . . Imagine, this is my first day of Europe after a year of Africa. If I had not chanced to meet you, Captain Macdougan, I
40   should have bored myself to death."

"Then you weren't on the front for the victory?"

"I was in the battle that made the victory. The war was won in the first battle of the Marne. . . . That's where I almost lost my leg and picked up a medaille militaire. . . . Ah, there's another chemist. . . . Arretez donc. Bon. . . . Perhaps you could help me explain."

They got out of the cab and went into the shop.

"What I want is tincture of yohimbine . . . a very useful product . . . a slight aid, that's what it is."

The clerk was a small, yellow man with a bald head, who wore a stained pongee jacket. He looked up through slanting eyeglasses at the French captain, who stood over him twirling the end of his moustache.

"Avez-vous de la teinture de yohimbine, monsieur?"

"Non comprendo, signore."

"Won't you explain to him what I want? . . . It's a little help, a slight aid." Le Capitaine Eustache de la Potinière waved a tightly-gloved hand under the druggist's nose.

—Is this man crazy? Fanshaw was thinking. Why am I riding round in a cab with this man?

"Cré nom d'un chien, por l'amore!" shouted the French captain. "Teinture de yohimbine."

Fanshaw felt himself turn red.

"I don't imagine they have it," he said hastily and walked out of the shop. He had barely got into the cab when the French captain followed.

"Ce sale pays," he was muttering. As he climbed into the cab, his usual bland smile crept back over his face. "Now we can dine," he said. "It takes more than a slight contrariety to ruffle old campaigners, eh, Captain Macdougan?"

"All right, let's have dinner," Fanshaw assented weakly.

—How on earth did I get in with this ridiculous Frenchman? he was bitterly asking himself. Last day in Italy, too, that I had intended to be so pleasant. Intended to go up to Monreale to see the mosaics and the view.

"I cannot tell you, Captain Macdougan," his companion was saying, "how pleasant it is to spend an evening, after all those weary years of the war, frontier posts and that sort of thing, with a man of your culture and refinement, may I even say sophistication. . . . I said to myself when I met you this morning in the Red Cross office: There is a man of parts, an unusual person. . . . With me, there are no half measures, I am a man of action. . . . So I immediately invited you to dinner. I am sure neither of us will regret it."

"Indeed, not for my part . . ." stammered Fanshaw. They had driven up in front of a small empty restaurant. The hollow-eyed waiter at the door agitated his napkin in welcome.

Fanshaw and le Capitaine Eustache de la Potinière sat in a cavern-

ous stage box at the opera, Fanshaw with his chin on his hand leaning across the plush rail and the Frenchman sitting straight upright in his chair with his bemedalled chest expanded, nodding his head solemnly in time to the music. On one side was a mottled horseshoe of faces, on the other the dustily lighted stage across which moved processions of monks, tenors in knee breeches, baritones with false beards; below them out of the glint of brasses and the shiny curves of violins and the gleaming bald heads of musicians, the orchestra boomed and crashed. Verdi's long, emphatic tunes throatily sung
10   brought up to Fanshaw's mind his boyish dreams out of Walter Scott and Bulwer, of hazardous enterprises and maidens' love hardily won. He felt as if he wanted to cry.—How silly and dusty this all is, he kept saying to himself. And here I am after the war a Red Cross captain, and everything has happened that can happen, and Wenny's dead years ago, dead as this old opera, and Nan's an old maid, and here I am sitting next to this crazy Frenchman with his medals and his stories of native women. . . . Right after the opera I'll leave him and go back to the hotel, get a good night's rest, and run up to Monreale before the boat goes; twelve that is; plenty of time. A long, lyric duet
20   had reached its inevitable finale. The horseshoe was full of clapping hands, nodding heads. The French captain got to his feet and clapped, leaning out from the box. Wants to have them see his medals, said a voice savagely in Fanshaw's head.

In the intermission, they sat drinking Marsala in the bar.

"I didn't tell you," le Capitaine Eustache de la Potinière was saying, "how I happened to be present at the battle of the Marne. It is a very funny story."

—I'll say I have a headache and go home; I can't stand any more of this wretched man, Fanshaw was thinking.

30   "How did that happen?" he asked.

"It's very funny. . . . You know, the little Moroccan ladies are charming. I had one at that time as a . . . governess, to keep me out of mischief. I was sent from Casablanca to Marseilles on a little mission, so I got the idea of taking my little lady along and got a week's leave to go up to show her Paris. My wife was safely in Aix-les-Bains with her parents, and there we were, my Moorish governess and I, enjoying la ville lumière, when suddenly, boom, the war breaks out!" He took a sip of his glass and swept the faces of the people round the bar with his superior stare.

40   Too repulsive, the mentality of a man like that. It's not the immorality, it's the ugliness of that sort of thing that disgusts. When he finishes this story, I'll go home. Fanshaw cleared his throat.

"Of course I knew war was coming, but I hadn't counted on its being so soon. . . . The first thing that happened was my wife wired to Paris that she'd meet me in Marseilles. All officers on leave were ordered back to their posts immediately. I was fond of my wife and I wanted to see her, but I knew I could never smuggle the little Moorish lady through Marseilles without her smelling a rat. What was I to do? I was in the devil of a pickle. I hung on in Paris a day trying to decide, and the next day packed off my little governess all alone. Poor little thing, she didn't know a word of French. Then I went to the minister of war and got myself transferred to the French front and had my wife come up to Paris to see me off, and before I knew it I was right in the middle of the battle of the Marne. Comical, isn't it?"

Fanshaw laughed stiffly. The bell was ringing for the last act.

The two tenors and the two baritones had gone into a monastery. The soprano had become a hermit and lived in a cave. The contralto was disguised in a domino. The chorus promenaded with imitation torches through an arcade in the back of the bluelighted stage. Everything was monkish and ominous in the music. The two tenors threw their hoods off their heads and drew swords from under their cloaks and brandished them over the footlights and sang a duet. The baritones stepped stealthily out from behind the wings, and the duet was a quartet. The soprano threw herself, shrieking, between the swords of the tenors. The contralto, dressed as an abbess in purple robes, came out through a door in the back. It was a sextet. The tune, shrieked on tight vocal chords, filled to the roof the horseshoe-shaped theater. Fanshaw half turned his head. The French captain was whispering with a stocky, sallowfaced young man, who held his hat in his hand and leaned forward respectfully out of the back of the box. But things had happened on the stage. The tenors lay dying, the soprano had thrown herself to the ground, the contralto elevated a large cross with her portly arms, and the back of the stage was filling with the chorus of monks and their torches.

"Très bien, très bien!" cried le Capitaine Eustache de la Potinière as the curtain came down, and clapped with gloved hands. "No, after you!" Then, as he followed Fanshaw down the steps into the lobby of the theater, he said: "It would be a good thing if more French and American officers were seen together at these affairs. It would improve our relations with Italy. . . . They are impressionable people. In Italy one must be seen."

The sallowfaced young man was waiting for them outside the theater. "Vous suivez moi," he said in nasal French.

"But where are you going? I'm afraid I must go back to my hotel."

"But surely you'll cast just a glance at them. . . . It won't take long. They are said to be very handsome."

"Why, who?" Fanshaw was suddenly very agitated.—Think, if after all these years . . . Of course, an interesting thing to see for once; sociological study. "What do you mean? I don't understand," he said.

His companion burst out laughing.

"The little ladies of Palermo, of course . . . Come along, everything's arranged."

"All right." Of course, just a glimpse, to see what a place like that was like. Nobody could know, he'd never see this Frenchman again.

They followed the sallowfaced man up a steep, dark street. Fanshaw
10 looked up at the sky that was bubbling with stars. The streak of bright sky overhead narrowed as the cornices of the houses drew together. The street was empty. Once a cat brushed past his legs. At last they stood panting on the broad stepping-stone in front of a door. The guide's three knocks resounded hollowly.

"Such calm," whispered le Capitaine Eustache de la Potinière in Fanshaw's ear, slipping a hand under his arm. "At such moments I admit that I am rather agitated, always. I congratulate you on your calm."

The guide knocked again. Somewhere up the street a rooster
20 crowed.

"It must be midnight," said the French captain.

The door swung softly. A fatfaced woman stood in the hallway holding a taper above her head, and stared at them searchingly through narrowed eyes. She and the guide talked in low, hurried Sicilian.

"Vous suivez moi," said the sallowfaced man.

They walked after him up a winding, stone stair, the woman following with the taper. They came out on a landing, went through a passageway, and found themselves in a brightly lighted room with
30 pink wallpaper and gold-framed mirrors.

"Ah!" said the French captain, pulling off his gloves. They sat down at a marble-topped table with carved ebony legs. The fatfaced woman who had opened the door hung over them, grinning. "Let's drink a little something. . . . Une bouteille de Marsala," he said and rubbed his hands. "I like the quiet, gentlemanly way you Americans do these things. Very distinguished."

The woman opened a cupboard and produced a bottle and glasses on a silver tray. She poured out four glasses.

"A desso," she said, and her grin reached nearly to her ears.
40 Two girls in evening dress swished in operatically through the door. One wore pink and the other blue. The girl who sat down beside Fanshaw had a small mouth and large, tired brown eyes.

"Lei," she said with enthusiasm, "parla Italiano?"

"Si, un poco," stammered Fanshaw, blushing.

"Ah, if you speak Italian, mon capitaine," said the French captain, "would you mind explaining to this little lady of mine what I told you about the Yohimbé tree? . . . It's very important."

"I don't remember," said Fanshaw in a crisp, angry voice, and turned again to the girl in pink beside him.

*   *   *

A bar of light burned his eyes. Through musty darkness from beyond the foot of the bed, a bar of light came whitely at him. Gradually, other streaks arranged themselves at right angles to the light. It was the sun through a shutter beyond the foot of the bed. He had no pajamas on. His chest suddenly contracted with sickening agitation. There was a sound of breathing beside him. Very cautiously, he slipped from between the sheets and groped about the room. His clothes were on a chair. He pulled them on anyhow and put his hand on the knob of the door. The gentle breathing from the bed was regular, like a child's. Softly, he turned the knob and opened the door. The shriek of the hinges was a knife in his ribs. He hurried through the parlor with its pink wallpaper and gold-framed mirrors that smelt of stale cigarette smoke and lipsticks. The door onto the stairs was open. He slunk down the winding staircase, straightening his necktie as he went. Then he found himself in an enclosed court. In the upper wall that glowed with dazzling sunlight were windows with balconies full of potted geraniums, red and pink, stirring like flame in the sun. The pavings of the court had just been washed, and a cool, wet stone smell came from them. Which way now? Two geese waddled past him, letting a little querulous quacking noise dribble from their bloodorange bills. Under an archway, an old woman sat shelling peas into a saucepan. She looked up at him and said something he did not catch as he darted past her and out the street door. He walked slowly down the sloping street. In the doorways were brightly dressed children with dirty mouths and stringy, uncombed hair. The street was full of dust and flies; shouts and shrieked talk and sounds of braying donkeys and rattling carts swarmed about his ears. In front of the theater, he hailed a cab that carried him with a quick jingle of harness through sunny, humming streets to his hotel. There he went to his room and ordered a bath.

It was ten o'clock. He dressed again, carefully, in clean clothes, breakfasted off coffee and rolls and honey, paid his bill, and had himself driven to the boat.

Once on board in his ample, white stateroom with his baggage about him, a terrible lassitude came over him. He sat in his bunk

staring up at the blue round of the porthole, through which came a
sound of derricks and a smell of pitch and a sunseared wind off the
harbor.

The day he and Nan had sat together on the beach at Marblehead
and listened to the waves hiss and rattle among the pebbles and
thought how all the strength of Wenny, now that he was dead, might
perhaps . . .—Poor Nan, if I'd had the nerve . . .

He looked at his watch. Half past. At the same moment, the ship's
whistle started booming loud and throbbing. The noise tailed off into
10   a harsh wail.

> Tarred and feathered and drawn in a cart
> By the women of Marblehead.

—Wenny used to sing that. Poor kid, he'd had nerve enough. The
time he and Wenny had walked at night down a street in Somerville
where the rare arclights were pinkish blobs among the shuddering
green fringes of elms and Wenny had wanted to pick up a girl. Stumpy
girls with heavy jowls strolling in couples, swaying from the hips. It
was mostly the ugliness. . . . Yohimbine.

Tina had been pretty in her pink dress.

20   And now I'm going back. Venetian Art and Culture in the Eighteenth Century. The afterglow of the Renaissance. In a vermilion
barge, lost . . . in the Charles, Wenny had said.

And Nan had understood; she had never been surprised at Wenny's
killing himself. Perhaps they'd had secrets, things in common, the
two of them, that he had never known. The thought stung.

Exit to Massachusetts Avenue and the College Yard, and the museum and tea with professors' wives. Think of going back to that after
this life overseas. If he could love Nan, if he could take her, it would
be different. That was hopeless, dead as Wenny, dead as grand opera.

30   "Gosh, I don't see it. . . . Going home after this," Baldwin had
said, and they had leaned out together over the gold and rusty roofs
and the domes and obelisks swaying in the great waves of honeycolored sunlight, and smelt gardens and scorched olive oil, and
seen a girl with a brown throat come out of an arbor beneath them.

Suppose he didn't go. . . . There was time to get off the boat. One
crazy thing in a lifetime.

He got to his feet, his heart dancing.—I won't go.

A bell started ringing far away on another deck.—That means
there's five minutes. There's time. I can get another Red Cross job. I
40   can travel. I can have women.

He picked up a suitcase and opened the varnished door. The

companionway was full of people, officers, Red Cross men, buzz and
chatter of farewells. Fanshaw slammed the door of his stateroom and
pushed his suitcase back under his bunk.

—Don't be a fool.

He threw himself on his back on his bunk and put his hand over his
eyes. Once they got out of sight of land, he'd get a good nap. Now he
must go up on deck and take a last look at Palermo. A fine sight: the
town piling up to Monreale, and the gardens, and behind them the
cloudy, dark hills of Sicily.

—I've been thinking too much. I won't think of anything any more. 10

And I'll go back and go to and fro to lectures with a notebook under
my arm, and now and then in the evening, when I haven't any
engagement, walk into Boston through terrible throbbing streets and
think for a moment I have Nan and Wenny with me, and that we are
young, leansouled people out of the Renaissance, ready to divide life
like a cake with our strong hands.

The whistle soared from a loose rattle of steam into a drumming
reverberation. The engines began to move slowly, thump after thump,
and Fanshaw felt the bunk shake under him as the steamer drew away
from the wharf. 20

Textual Notes

25.1-3   *Et si per talen.* "And if through love / I lose all my youth, / the songs of birds will help me little." From "Mout m'es bon e bel" by Peire Vidal, Provençal poet (fl. 1175–1215). Walter Pater asserts that "The central love-poetry of Provence, the poetry of . . . [among others] Pierre Vidal, is poetry for the few, for the elect and peculiar people of the kingdom of sentiment" (*Walter Pater: Three Major Texts (The Renaissance, Apprecia-tions, and Imaginary Portraits)*, ed. William E. Buckler [New York: New York University, 1986], p. 84).

27.24   Bryce's *American Commonwealth.* James Bryce's *The American Commonwealth*, 2 vols. (New York: Macmillian & Co., 1888), went through numerous editions. Used in high schools and colleges, the abridged edition was a textbook for the study of American government.

27.30   Mount Auburn Street. In her recent biography of Dos Passos, Virginia Spencer Carr notes that "the private dormitories on Mount Auburn Street's 'Gold Coast'" were exclusive private residences for the wealthier students (*Dos Passos: A Life* [New York: Doubleday & Company, 1984], p. 52).

27.31   "Sweet and Low." Popular song (with lyrics adapted from Alfred Lord Tennyson) by Sir Joseph Barnby (1838–96), English composer.

27.34   *Lampoon. The Harvard Lampoon*, satirical magazine founded in 1876.

29.21   Selkirk Glacier. Located in British Columbia, the Selkirk Glaciers were the subject of several books by 1912. The allusion introduces the tone of cold and ice that will dominate the novel.

31.17   Norumbega. A park near Cambridge. Writing in 1903, Edwin M. Bacon describes Norumbega Park as Boston's "favorite pleasure ground" (*Boston: A Guide Book* [Boston: Ginn & Company, 1903], p. 116). He adds that "canoeing is the all-engrossing sport on this part of the river" (p. 116).

32.7-9   "I know a place." Lines from "Four-Leaf Clover" (1898), a poem by Ella Higginson (1862–1940).

34.39-40   "O Waltz Me Around Again Willie." Popular song with words by Will D. Cobb and music by Ren Shields, copyrighted in 1906 by F. A. Mills Co.

35.17   "School Days." Popular song with words by Will D. Cobb, music by Gus Edwards, copyrighted in 1907.

36.7   Comparative Literature I. The Harvard course guide for 1913–14 lists this as a "general survey" of European literature.

36.24-27   "And there on beds of violets blue." From John Milton's "L'Al-legro," 21–24.

36.40-37.2   "Not the angels in heaven above." From Edgar Allan Poe's poem "Annabel Lee," 30–33.

38.8   Chabrier. Alexis Emmanuel Chabrier (1841–94), French composer.

40.37   witch of Endor. The witch consulted by King Saul, 1 Sam. 28:7.

41.22-23   "The Wearing of the Green." Popular patriotic Irish song (author unknown), which dates from approximately 1797.

41.35   "L'étoile du berger." "The Shepherd's Star."

43.10   Buhl cabinet. Furniture with designs of tortoiseshell, silver, brass, and so forth, inlaid in wood.

44.29   *Après-midi d'un Faune*. The Boston Symphony Orchestra performed *Prélude à l'Après-midi d'un Faune* (1892–94) in its twenty-second concert (23 and 24 April) of 1915. In his "Programme Note" on this piece, Philip Hale quotes Gosse's interpretation of Mallarmé's poem, the inspiration for Debussy's score: "A faun—a simple, sensuous, passionate being—wakens in the forest at daybreak and tries to recall his experience of the previous afternoon. Was he the fortunate recipient of an actual visit from nymphs, white and golden goddesses, divinely tender and indulgent? Or is the memory he seems to retain nothing but the shadow of a vision, no more substantial than the 'arid rain' of notes from his own flute?" (p. 1314). The awakening eroticism seems to be the point of Dos Passos's allusion.

48.34-35   "O My Darling Clementine." Popular song, words and music by Percy Montrose, copyrighted in 1884.

49.1   "The Slave's Dream." Lines from "The Slave's Dream," by Henry Wadsworth Longfellow (1807–82), are quoted at 49.5-6.

49.31   Nahant. According to Bacon, Nahant is "the oldest of eastern summer resorts" (*Boston*, p. 159).

50.11   Corot. Jean Baptiste Camille Corot (1796–1875), French landscape painter.

51.3   Squirrel Island. In her biography of the writer, Virginia Spencer Carr notes that as a boy Dos Passos vacationed with his father and mother at Squirrel Island, Maine, for a few days (*Dos Passos*, p. 32).

51.20-21   Phillips Brooks, noted Boston Episcopal bishop and orator (1835–93).

53.31   Wagner. Richard Wagner (1813–83), German composer.

56.12   Mrs. Jack Gardner. Mrs. Isabella Gardner built Fenway Court. As Robert Shackleton notes, "It was a romantic plan romantically carried out. Mrs. Gardner brought across the ocean actual parts and fragments of old Italian buildings, that the basis should be actually Italian, and here she built her Venetian palace, and filled it with rare and costly examples of old time European art" (*The Book of Boston* [Philadelphia: Penn Publishing, 1916], p. 203).

56.35   Canaletto carnival. Giovanni Antonio Canal (1697–1768), (known as Canaletto), completed many canal and river scenes. Perhaps Dos Passos is alluding to *The Bucintoro Returning to the Molo on Ascension Day*, a painting that depicts one of Venice's most important festivals, the "Wedding of the Sea" and that includes several richly gilded boats. As Adrian Eeles notes, "the origin of the ceremony goes back, by tradition, to the Doge

Pietro Orsoleo's naval victory over Dalmatia in about the year 998, apparently on Ascension Day. Every Ascension Day thereafter the Doge was rowed out to the Lido to confront the sea, an act symbolising Venice's naval supremacy" (*Canaletto* [London: Paul Hamlyn, 1967], p. 33).

57.12   Lamb. Charles Lamb (1775–1834), English essayist.

57.23   Paolo and Francesca. Dos Passos alludes to canto 5 of Dante's *Inferno*. The souls of Paolo and Francesca (who in life had an illicit love affair) are punished in hell (not limbo) by having to wheel in endless flight—an apt symbol for their inability to control their passions.

57.25-26   "Pico della Mirandola riding into Florence in the time of lilies." Walter Pater's comment in his essay "Pico della Mirandola" clarifies this allusion: "Camilla Rucellai, one of those prophetic women whom the preaching of Savonarola had raised up in Florence, declare[d], seeing him for the first time, that he would depart in the time of lilies—prematurely, that is, like the field-flowers which are withered by the scorching sun almost as soon as they are sprung up" (*Pater*, p. 100).

57.38   *The Book of Tea*. A book written by Kakuzo Okakura (1906; reprint, New York: Fox, Duffield and Company, 1912). In his literary diary for 15 June 1915, Dos Passos notes that he read this book and found it "charming" ("Literary Diary, 7 Dec. 1914–20 Nov. 1916," University of Virginia [accession #5950AC, Box 3]). The "phrase" that Fanshaw remembers is not to be found in *The Book of Tea*, but the sentiment is everywhere in its pages. Several quotations from this work may shed some light on Dos Passos's novel. Okakura notes that "we shall not blame ourselves for making so much of the tea-cup. Mankind has done worse. In the worship of Bacchus, we have sacrificed too freely" (*The Book of Tea*, ed. Everett F. Bleiler [New York: Dover Publications, 1964], p. 2). Thus we may read *Streets of Night* as built on polar opposites: tea drinking (identified most closely with Nan and Fanshaw) and wine drinking (associated most closely with Wenny). In particular, tea suggests a finely tuned aestheticism. (We might remember Dos Passos's comment years later in "Camera Eye 25": "grow cold with culture like a cup of tea forgotten" [*The U.S.A. Trilogy: The 42nd Parallel, Nineteen Nineteen, and the Big Money* (New York: Modern Library, 1938), *The 42nd Parallel*, p. 302].) Okakura notes that "we stigmatise the untamed aesthete who, regardless of the mundane tragedy, runs riot in the springtide of emancipated emotions, as one 'with too much tea' in him" (p. 2). However, the issue needs some caution, for the prescription of tea taking, as described by Okakura, is associated with the very values that Wenny believes in when he praises the "gorgeousness of matter" (*Streets of Night*, p. 116 above). Okakura notes that teaism is closely related to Zen, which recognized "the mundane as of equal importance with the spiritual" (p. 28). Furthermore, "the whole ideal of Teaism is a result of this Zen conception of greatness in the smallest incidents of life" (p. 29). It might be useful, then, to note Dos Passos's implied distinction between Fanshaw's religion of aestheticism and Wenny's devotion to aesthetics. The former separates beauty from the sordid to appreciate it in isolation; the latter finds beauty even in the mundane.

58.11   Rembrandt. Rembrandt van Rijn, Dutch painter (1606–69).

58.28   Ficino . . . Plato. Pater notes that Pico della Mirandola came to Florence on "the very day . . . on which Ficino had finished his famous translation of Plato into Latin" (*Pater*, p. 96).

59.33   Brookline. According to Bacon, Brookline "is the richest suburb of Boston and in many respects the most attractive, with numerous beautiful estates and tasteful 'villas' and charming drives" (*Boston*, p. 109).

59.34   Abbey paintings. In the Boston Public Library, the "decorations of the Delivery Room . . . are by Edwin A. Abbey, and illustrate the legend of the Holy Grail" (Bacon, *Boston*, p. 82).

60.9-10   " 'to burn with a hard gemlike flame.' " In his conclusion to *The Renaissance*, Walter Pater writes, "To burn always with this hard, gem-like flame, to maintain this ecstasy, is success in life. In a sense it might even be said that our failure is to form habits: . . . it is only the roughness of the eye that makes any two persons, things, situations, seem alike" (*Pater*, p. 219).

60.15   Watteau. Jean Antoine Watteau (1684–1721), French painter. Pater describes Watteau's style as "something of lightness and coquetry" (*Pater*, p. 245).

60.18   Sistine Madonna in mosaic. The *Sistine Madonna* (1513) by Raphael. Dos Passos is alluding to a copy of this famous painting made in mosaic.

60.18   carved wooden goats. Switzerland is noted for its folk art. For examples of rural and primitive art, including carved animals, see Daniel Baud-Bovy, *Peasant Art in Switzerland*, trans. Arthur Palliser (London: The Studio, 1924), plates 407 and 409.

60.19   Nuremberg goose boy. The statue *Man with Geese* (1530) in Nuremberg.

60.41   Primavera. Painting (ca. 1478) by Sandro Botticelli (1445–1510), Italian painter.

61.33   Capri. Island near the Bay of Naples.

61.34-35   romaunt of the rose. *Roman de la Rose* (ca. 1230), medieval French poem by Guillaume de Lorris, an allegory about love.

63.15   Hanover Street. In the North Boston/Waterfront area.

63.31   Byron. George Gordon, Lord Byron (1788–1824), English poet.

64.11   "look there, a fiasco." A "fiasco" is a wine bottle that is rounded on the bottom and has a woven raffia basket for a stand.

65.28-29   "The Soldiers' Chorus." "Gloire immortelle de nos aïeux," from act 4, scene 3 of *Faust*, an opera by Charles Gounod (1818–93), French composer.

66.19   Petrarch. Francesco Petrarca (1304–74), Italian poet.

66.25   wheel of karma. For a brief discussion of this term, see David L. Vanderwerken, "Dos Passos' *Streets of Night:* A Reconsideration," *Markham Review*, 4 (October 1974), 64.

66.30   Dürer's portrait. The *Self-Portrait* of 1500, which is signed "Albrecht Dürer of Nuremberg . . . age twenty-eight." According to James Snyder, this portrait "blatantly reveals his self-esteem as one especially gifted, the artist as Christ" (*Northern Renaissance Art: Painting, Sculpture, the Graphic Arts from 1350 to 1575* [New York: Harry N. Abrams, 1985], p. 325).

69.12   Snow scene by Brueghel. This seems to be a generic allusion rather than a specific one—evoking the mood of such paintings as *Hunters in the Snow* (1565). As James Snyder points out, "Brueghel is one of the first landscapists to concern himself with presenting accurate climatic conditions beyond the most obvious snow covering or sprouting branch. Weather is the outward display of the moods of this primary life" (*Northern Renaissance Art*, p. 503).

70.33   Lombard. Lombardy is in Northern Italy.

70.41   T Wharf. The wharf that once stood on the Boston waterfront at the foot of South Market Street, between Commerical Wharf and Long Wharf.

71.20   Jack London (1876–1916), American writer of adventure stories, such as *The Call of the Wild*.

73.33   Thompson's Spa. According to C. R. Athearn, writing in 1926, Thompson's Spa is a "famous Boston institution . . . at 237 Washington Street—a place which is tremendous in size but always crowded at noon" (*Boston in Seven Days* [New York: Robert M. McBride & Co., 1926], p. 32).

73.34   Parker House. Hotel at School and Tremont Streets.

74.1   Filenes. Famous Boston department store.

75.9   Ethel Barrymore in *Tante*. *Tante*, a play by A. D. Sedgwick and C. H. Chambers, opened on Broadway at the Empire Theater on 28 October 1913, with Ethel Barrymore (1879–1959), playing the role of Madame Okraska.

75.9   Adelina Patti. Adela Juana Maria Patti (1843–1919), Italian operatic soprano.

75.10   Doris Keane in *Romance*. Doris Keane (1881–1945) played the character of Margherita Cavallini in Edward Sheldon's three-act play *Romance*, which opened at Broadway's Maxine Elliott Theater on 10 February 1913.

75.12   Epicurus. Greek philosopher, 342?–270 B.C.

75.14   Symphony Hall. At the intersection of Massachusetts and Huntington Avenues, Symphony Hall was the home of the Boston Symphony Orchestra.

75.33   Donatello. Donato di Niccolo di Betto Bardi (1386?–1466), Italian sculptor.

75.33   Ghiberti doors. Lorenzo Ghiberti (1378–1455) sculpted two sets of doors for the Florentine Baptistery. E. O. Stanley's guide to Boston (1888) notes that "among the many interesting objects in the upper hall [of the Boston Museum of Fine Arts] is a cast of the second Ghiberti bronze gate of the baptistery in Florence" (*Boston and its Suburbs: A Guide Book* [Boston: Stanley & Usher, 1888], p. 6).

77.24   Muckers. In "Camera Eye 7," Dos Passos contrasts the upperclass "Rover Boys" with the lower-class "muckers," who "put stones in their snowballs write dirty words up on walls do dirty things up alleys their folks work in the mills" (*U.S.A.: The 42nd Parallel*, p. 81).

78.1   Ballantyne. Robert Michael Ballantyne (1825–94), English author of juvenile adventure stories, such as *The Coral Island*.

78.12   "the imitation flowers in showcases in Peabody." A guide to Harvard describes the Ware Collection of glass flowers in the University Museum. "The exquisite models are made exclusively for this University by two European artists, father and son, named Blaschka. . . . The collection now comprises illustrations of more than three hundred species, together with their analytical details, magnified in such a manner as to display all structural features in a perfect manner" (Frank Bolles, *Harvard University: A Brief Statement of What Harvard University Is, How It May Be Entered and How Its Degrees May Be Obtained*, 3d ed. [Cambridge: Harvard University, n.d.], p. 92.

78.17   "Tomorrow and tomorrow." Shakespeare, *Macbeth*, 5.5.19.

80.36   North End. Once the home of the Boston aristocracy, the North End by the early part of the twentieth century had become the "foreign part" of the city, housing "Russians, Armenians, Israelites, Norwegians, Poles, Italians" (Bacon, *Boston*, p. 54).

80.37–38   "The Song of Occupations." Poem by Walt Whitman.

85.29   Jake's. German restaurant, Jake Worth's, on Stuart Street.

87.29   Ward 8. A mixed drink.

87.36   "Goodby, Girls, I'm Through." Popular song, music by Ivan Caryll, lyrics by John Golden, published by Chappell & Co., 1914.

88.28–29   "To be or not to be." Shakespeare, *Hamlet*, 3.1.55.

89.20   "The Blue Danube." "An der Schönen blauen Donau," a waltz by Johann Strauss (1825–99), Austrian composer.

89.25   Delos. A Greek island, the site of an oracle of Apollo.

90.23   "prostitutions of the Canaanites." In the Old Testament, the Canaanites were proverbially associated with prostitution. See, for example, Ezek. 16:29.

94.4–5   "aborigines of the Caribbean." Perhaps an allusion to Edward Westermarck: "Among the Caribs, the bridegroom received his bride from the hand of the Piache, or medicine-man, and certainly not as a virgin" (*The History of Human Marriage* [London: Macmillan and Co., 1903], p. 76). Chapters 4–6, 23, and 24 of Westermarck's book were required reading on the course syllabus published in 1910 for "Anthropology I" at Harvard. Dos Passos took this course in the 1915–16 school year.

98.13   Mendelssohn's "Wedding March." Incidental music to Shakespeare's *Midsummer Night's Dream*, by Felix Mendelssohn (1809–47), German composer.

100.1   Titian. Tiziano Vecellio (ca. 1477–1576), Italian painter.

100.1   Aretino. Pietro Aretino (1492–1556), Italian satirist. In his diary in 1918, Dos Passos writes that he "[f]inished a nasty little life of Pietro Aretino—written by some prudish French flubdub of a professorial prig. Aretino seems to have been a truly wonderful sort of a person—blackmailer of the first order, satirist with a blunt fury." Dos Passos goes on to complain about the "prurient" and repressive critics, who are unnecessarily bothered by "the shocking life of the cynic, the voluptuary" (*The Fourteenth Chronicle: Letters and Diaries of John Dos Passos*, ed. Townsend Ludington [Boston: Gambit, 1973], p. 178).

100.6   Blue Hill. Blue Hill Reservation is eleven miles due south of Cambridge, the site of the Blue Hill Observatory, which was owned by Harvard University.

102.24   Touraine. Hotel on Tremont and Boylston streets.

104.30   "Par delicatesse j'ai perdu la vie." "Through fastidiousness I lost my life." Townsend Ludington records Dos Passos's quoting of Paul Verlaine in 1917: "De trop de delicatesse / J'ai perdu la vie" (*Dos Passos*, p. 132).

105.4   Caravaggio. Michelangelo Merisi da Caravaggio (ca. 1565–1609?), Italian painter.

105.31   *Light Cavalry. Die leichte Kavallerie* (1866), operetta by Franz von Suppé (1819–95), Austrian composer.

105.38–39   "a dreadful scandal about the last symphony concert." This allusion is meant to show Nan's propensity for "idle gossip," but perhaps in composing the novel Dos Passos was thinking back to an event that occurred in 1917, when the most "dreadful" scandal in the symphony's history occurred. Dr. Karl Muck, the conductor of the Boston Symphony and an Austrian by birth, was caught up in the rising tide of anti-German sentiment that was being produced by America's entry into World War I. On the eve of a concert, an editorial in the Providence Rhode Island *Journal* demanded that Dr. Muck play the "Star Spangled Banner" as part of the performance the next night. Dr. Muck was apparently unaware of this request to show his allegiance to America—and a furor subsequently developed. Eventually, Dr. Muck was arrested by the United States government as a subversive alien, though the case was never tried. The story is told by M. A. DeWolfe Howe (*The Boston Symphony Orchestra: 1881–1931* [New York: Da Capo Press, 1978], pp. 130–36).

110.15   "Marseillaise." The French national anthem, written in 1792, words and music by Claude Joseph Rouget de Lisle.

111.8   *The Way of All Flesh*. Title of the novel (1903) by Samuel Butler (1835–1902), English writer.

111.27   Jordan. Jordan Hall, the auditorium built in 1904 for the New England Conservatory of Music.

112.40   plantagenet. A sprig of broom, symbol of the House of Angevin.

112.40   Black Prince. Edward (1330–76), Prince of Wales and Duke of Cornwall, son of Edward III.

113.43–114.1   "You can't make 'Narcissus' into the 'Prelude' from *Tristan*." This statement is equivalent to "You can't make a silk purse out of a sow's ear." "Narcissus" was a popular but not very profound piano piece by Ethelbert Nevin (1862–1901). *Tristan und Isolde* (1865) is by Richard Wagner. The following sentence is probably corrupt. Dos Passos undoubtedly meant, "The germ wouldn't be there."

115.1   Old Mill at Revere. Revere was the Coney Island of Massachusetts. According to Joseph E. Garland, who has documented its history in the early part of this century, "the sensation of the [1902] season was a water ride inside an enormous wood and tarpaper structure called The Old Mill that went up in roaring flames after only two seasons; the customers escaped simply by pushing out through the tarpaper walls" (*Boston's Gold Coast: The North Shore, 1890–1929* [Boston: Little, Brown, and Company, 1981], p. 17).

William F. Mangels notes that an amusement water ride, which was to become known as the "Old Mill," was created in London in 1891 by Arthur Pickard, who called his ride the "Canals of Venice." Pickard's invention was improved on in America by George W. Schofield, who "added dark tunnels with weird scenery calculated to startle the riders in the boats as they slowly drifted by" (*The Outdoor Amusement Industry: From Earliest Times to the Present* [New York: Vantage Press, 1952], pp. 121–22).

In his compilation of historical tidbits from the *Revere Journal*, Peter E. McCauley II finds an entry for 24 May 1902, which notes that "The 'Old Mill' on the Boulevard will be opened on Memorial Day. Here will be found the River of Mysteries, which appeals to one's spirit of adventure. From the moment one steps inside the boat, your attention is attracted and held by the wonderful sights along the shore." McCauley also notes an advertisement for the Old Mill in the 27 June 1903 issue: "The most popular amusement ride on the beach. A ride up the mysterious river. A trip to Spain and the Hades. Under the sea, under the earth. Down south to fairyland. See the lions and tigers." A story on 13 August 1904 reports that the ride burned to the ground. (*"Revere Beach Chips": Historical Background from the Revere Journal* [Revere, Mass., 1979], pp. 54, 59).

115.26   "Funiculì, funiculà." Popular song (1880) by Luigi Denza (1846–1922).

116.8   Cook's tourists. Thomas Cook (1808–92), an Englishman, founded his famous travel agency in 1841.

116.43–117.1   "Signorelli frescoes of the Last Judgment." A series of frescoes painted from 1499 to 1504 by Luca Signorelli (ca. 1445–1523) in Orvieto Cathedral, Italy.

117.5   Burton Holmes. In Boston, the Burton Holmes Travelogues were given at the Tremont Temple. They consisted of lectures with motion pictures and illustrations. Each year the lectures focused on a group of related geographic areas. For example, the lectures in January and February 1915 were on England, Scotland, Ireland, German Austria, and Allied powers. In 1916, the lectures were on various regions of the United States, such as the South and California.

117.6   Umbria. A region in Central Italy.

118.18   Frank Locke's. Restaurant in Winter Place, "a little blind alley that runs out of Winter Street" (Athearn, *Boston*, p. 43).

120.4   filthy dreamers. "Likewise also these filthy dreamers defile the flesh, despise dominion, and speak evil of dignities," Jude 8.

120.23   "How firm a foundation ye say-aints of the Lord." "How firm a foundation, ye saints of the Lord, / Is laid for your faith in His excellent word," composer unknown (Samuel J. Rogal, *Guide to the Hymns and Tunes of American Methodism* [Westport, Conn.: Greenwood Press, 1986], p. 113).

122.9 Fra Angelico, Lorenzo Monaco, Gozzoli. Fra Angelico (Giovanni da Fiesole, 1387–1455), Lorenzo Monaco (fl. 1388–1422), Benozzo Gozzoli (ca. 1421–97), Italian painters.

122.24 Sorrento. Town in Southern Italy, on the Bay of Naples.

122.35 Karl Baedeker. Karl Baedeker (1801–59), publisher of travel guides.

123.33 Rubens. Peter Paul Rubens (1577–1640), Flemish painter.

124.8 *The Golden Bough.* Sir James Frazer's *The Golden Bough: A Study in Comparative Religion*, first published in 1890. Frazer's work is mentioned in the course outline for "Anthropology I" at Harvard.

125.8 Velázquez. Diego Rodríguez de Silva y Velázquez (1599–1660), Spanish painter.

132.16–17 Botticelli's waveborn Venus. *Birth of Venus* (1482), by Botticelli.

132.17–18 "Cras amet qui numquam amavit." "Let he who never loved love tomorrow."

132.40 "the fathers have eaten sour grapes." Jer. 31:29.

134.5 Lenôtre. André Lenôtre, French landscape architect and gardener (1613–1700), creator of the gardens at Versailles.

134.22 Verlaine. Paul Verlaine (1844–96), French poet.

134.34 Greco. El Greco, Domenikos Theotocopoulos (1541–1614), born in Crete, painted in Spain and Italy.

134.35–36 "Pent-up aching rivers." "From Pent-up Aching Rivers," a poem by Walt Whitman.

134.36 "Called for madder music." "I cried for madder music and for stronger wine," from Ernest Dowson's "Non Sum Qualis Eram Bonae sub Regno Cynarae" (1896).

135.11 "On ne badine pas avec l'amour." "Love is not to be trifled with." The title of a play (1834) by Alfred de Musset (1810–57), French poet and dramatist. Dos Passos calls de Musset "the darndest ass in literature" (*Fourteenth Chronicle*, p. 113) but at the same time defends him. In 1919, Dos Passos saw *On ne Badine pas avec l'Amour* and described it as "one of the loveliest things I've ever seen on the stage . . . written in a superb futuristic casual style" (*Fourteenth Chronicle*, p. 244).

136.4 *Prunella. Prunella: Or, Love in a Dutch Garden*, by Harley Granville-Barker and Laurence Houseman. When the play opened in London in 1904, Granville-Barker played the role of Pierrot. The play had its Broadway premiere at the Little Theater on 27 October 1913.

136.7 Pierrot. Pierrot is "a typical character in French pantomime, thievish and greedy, artless and without moral sense; dressed in loose white garments, with his face whitened" (Paul Harvey and J. E. Heseltine, eds., *The Oxford Companion to French Literature* [Oxford: Clarendon Press, 1959], p. 557).

137.26 Praxiteles. Athenian sculptor, fourth century B.C.

138.8–9 *La Forza del Destino*, opera (1862) by Giuseppe Verdi (1813–1901), Italian composer.

138.16–17 "Bacchus . . . Velázquez." *Los Borrachos* (1629), by Veláz-quez.

138.36–37 "When lilacs last in the dooryard bloomed." Title of poem by Walt Whitman (1819–92).

138.42–43 "new grass fine as hair." An allusion to Walt Whitman's "Song of Myself," sec. 6, 1.110: "And now it seems to me the beautiful uncut hair of graves."

140.43 Cassone. Large Renaissance chest often holding a bride's dowry. A painting of a biblical or mythological scene, appropriate to marriage, often decorated the chest.

141.3 "Jardins sous la pluie." A piano piece from *Estampes* (1903) by Claude Achille Debussy (1862–1918), the French composer. In the type-script and in the first edition, Dos Passos had Nan playing Pelléas. *Pelléas et Mélisande* (1902), an opera in five acts, also by Debussy, presents a love triangle of Mélisande and two brothers, Pelléas and Golaud. Townsend Ludington reports that in 1919 Dos Passos saw this opera on numerous occasions (*John Dos Passos: A Twentieth Century Odyssey* [New York: E. P. Dutton, 1980], pp. 180–81).

143.9 "suffragettes setting bombs under Asquith." Herbert Henry As-quith (1852–1928) was Britain's Prime Minister from 1908 to 1916. His opposition to and difficulties with the militant suffragettes are summarized by Roy Jenkins (*Asquith: Portrait of a Man and an Era* [New York: Chilmark Press, 1964], pp. 246–48).

143.10 Balaklava. The Battle of Balaklava was fought in the Crimean War on 25 October 1854.

143.11 "Into the valley of death." A line from Alfred Lord Tennyson's poem "The Charge of the Light Brigade," which immortalized the Battle of Balaklava.

143.15–16 Jordan Marsh's. One of Boston's noted department stores.

143.24–25 *The Tales of Hoffmann. Les contes d'Hoffmann,* opera in prologue, three acts, and epilogue by Jacques Offenbach (1819–80), French composer.

144.13 *The Twilight of the Gods.* The *Götterdämmerung,* part 4 of *Der Ring des Nibelungen* (1876) by Richard Wagner.

146.2 Vendome. Boston hotel at 270 Commonwealth Avenue.

148.5–6 "Mr. Emerson's poem." "The Day's Ration," by Ralph Waldo Emerson (1803–82).

> Why seek Italy,
> Who cannot circumnavigate the sea
> of thoughts and things at home, but still adjourn
> The nearest matters for a thousand days?

148.36 Auber. Daniel François Esprit Auber (1782–1871), French com-poser.

149.39 Ibsen. Henrik Ibsen (1828–1906), Norwegian playwright. In a letter, Dos Passos compliments one of Ibsen's plays because "it deals with flesh and blood instead of with the sugar coated sentimentalities of the higher things according to Ella Wheeler Wilcox or the Lady's *Home Companion"* (*Fourteenth Chronicle*, p. 120).

150.31–32   St. Martin's summer. When Indian summer occurs in November, it is referred to as St. Martin's summer, after St. Martin's Day, 11 November.

150.35   Hiawatha. "The Song of Hiawatha" (1855), poem by Henry Wadsworth Longfellow.

152.31–32   "Siena . . . Arezzo, Urbino, Assissi, San Gimingiano." A grouping of towns in central Italy.

155.15–17   "Christmas comes but once a year." Unidentified lyric. Because this allusion is in the context of a childhood memory, perhaps these lines are a corruption of the familiar Mother Goose rhyme: "Christmas comes but one a year, / And when it comes it brings good cheer."

156.36–37   *The Arcadians. The Arcadians*, a musical play in three acts, lyrics by Arthur Wimperis, music by Lionel Monckton and Howard Talbot, published by the Chappell & Co., copyright 1909. "Arcady," one of the songs goes, is "where love is lord."

158.39–40   Locke's *Beloved Vagabond*. William John Locke's *The Beloved Vagabond* (1900).

159.9–10   Messalina. Valeria Messalina, died A.D. 48. Third wife of Claudius I. She was noted for her lust.

160.14   Pre-Raphaelite. A group of English poets and painters in the middle of the nineteenth century who attempted to recapture the spirit of art before Raphael. A characteristic of the figures in the paintings by the Pre-Raphaelites is the extended neck.

166.9   Janiculum. In Rome, the Janiculum is a ridge near the Tiber River.

168.19–20   "Arretez ici, cré nom d'un chien!" "Stop here, damn it!"

168.37   "Continuez." "Go on."

169.1   "The first battle of the Marne." Decisive battle of World War I fought near the Marne River in France (5–10 September 1914).

169.3   "Arretez donc. Bon." "Well, stop! Good."

169.11   "Avez-vous de la teinture de yohimbine, monsieur?" "Do you have any tincture of yohimbine, sir?"

169.12   "Non comprendo, signore." "I don't understand, sir."

169.18–19   "Cré nom d'un chien, por l'amore! . . . Teinture de yohimbine." "Damn it, for the sake of love! Tincture of yohimbine." According to P. V. Taberner, "Yohimbine is an alkaloid obtained from the bark of the West African *yohimbéhé* tree. . . . It has featured as an aphrodisiac in African and West Indian medicine for centuries, and it also appears in some modern pharmacopoeiae under the name of aphrodine or corynine" (*Aphrodisiacs: The Science and the Myth* [Philadelphia: University of Pennyslvania Press, 1985], p. 217). Note that the captain has just returned from Africa.

169.24   "Ce sale pays." "This damn country."

169.31   Monreale. A town near Palermo famous for its Norman cathedral.

170.10–11   Walter Scott and Bulwer. Walter Scott (1771–1832), Scottish novelist, and Edward George Earle Lytton Bulwer-Lytton (1803–73), English novelist.

171.32 "Très bien, très bien!" "Excellent, Excellent!"
171.40 "Vous suivez moi." "Follow me."
172.26 "Vous suivez moi." See 171.40.
172.39 "A desso" [*sic*]. Adesso. "There, now."
172.43 "Lei parla Italiano." "Do you speak Italian?"
173.1 "Si, un poco." "Yes, a little."
174.11–12 "Tarred and feathered . . . Marblehead." From "Skipper Ireson's Ride," a poem by John Greenleaf Whittier (1807–92).

Appendix: Selected Diary Entries on *Streets of Night*

Excerpts from John Dos Passos's manuscript notebook, labeled
Book of Verses, 1914–17
John Dos Passos Collection (# 5950-AC, Box 3)
Alderman Library
University of Virginia

[Pp. 27–28. Appears immediately before the entry dated 26 March 1916]

Le Grand Roman

———————————————

Atmosphere of streets at night.
Supper tables & garish restaurants
Youth in the city.

1. Friendship—the strong
unsympathetic character, the
weak boy who adores him. Man
of white hot burning idealism,
of huge power & desire for self
expression—The scene in the
run-away.

2. Love—a woman—The
strong man has wild   passions   love
affair, absolutely subdues
character of girl to him.
Hideous jealousy on the part
of the boy. Life to him turns to
dust and ashes.

3. The hero strides on—he
progresses—his mores cannot   they
are too wrapped up in the old man. Might
even become evangelist or

something of that sort—He
grows older—the others are
weak & miserable & destroyed
but they keep their youth.
At last he utterly breaks
with them. They drift
away into the sea of faces
that you pass in the streets
at night

———————————————

*   *   *

*[Pp. 70–72 written between entries dated 3 August 1916 and 2
September 1916]*

People at Louise's tea—

~~Reynard Low~~   Cedric Rowley—poet
~~Rowley Bates~~   William Bartlett

                                        business man-
                                             ager
                                             of [?]

                    May Barclay—society column
                                             person
                    Tyler Bates   ~~Letetia~~
                        intro of Ced. R.—of good
                    family—lovely boyish face—
                    characterless—at present—
                    & looking for a job—good
                    voice—gets job in Bank
                    later—(Louise Dale)

                                *   *   *

Louise
        Conversation   amatory
with Cedric—she accuses
him of minor poet passion etc.

———————————————

        Letter of Louise to Annabel
fully explaining her ideas—
before returning to N.Y. to fall
before Tyler Bates

———————————————

Dinner talk with Cedric

*   *   *

"It rained forty days & it rained
                              forty nights
And it did not stop till Christmas
And the old man who survived the flood
Was longleged Bates of the isthmus"
      May Barclay sings it to Louise
hearing she is to marry Tyler Bates

Louise thinks of it on her
marriage night

*   *   *

*[Pp. 89–90 written between entries dated 2 September 1916 and 23
November 1916]*

Louise—Tyler Bates finds her
cleaning shoes in her room
very angry

I

1. Opera
2. Tea
3. Talk & dinner with Ced
4. At Annabel's meets T.B.
5. Passionate adventure with Ced.
      Tells him a thing or two
6. Work—streets interlude
7. goes to Mount A.
8. Letter from there to Ann.
9. The return—full of scorn
and gumption . . . feeding
the tiger—new design
10. May Barclay Ames is
singing Bates song.
11. Views N York uptown hill
                              at night
—starts some essays—
12. TB finds her with
                  shoes
13. She is walking with long
haired person eating a banana meets TB

14. Why?—angry.
15. TB gets raise in Bank
16. She marries him for his looks
17. The Wedding Night

II

Living at Hotel Marie
Antoinette—taken by Mr.
Mrs. John Schyler—president of
bank—
  Society—Domestic affairs
  Regular American life
  Awakening—finds old
essay—
  Talk with husband
  Optimism
Children—comfort—
  Agrees To Go down town
Sees old lodgings
  sits in park & tries to think
  bursts in[to] tears
  Walking along
'Ain't it hell lady?' little
boy she meets shouts out
  Invited to the John Schylers
at Bar Harbor.

              *   *   *

[Pp. 156–157, written between entries dated 18 February 1917 and 8 May 1917]

The Streets at Night Novel

x—tenderly fond of children—
child—pale—tenuous vision of
the world—[Irish?] spun of moon
and auburn and lavender grey

    He is the principle described
character—his suicide ends the first part.

    I shall try to do through
him and Helene (?) two things—1.
Express the streets at night

[?] [?] of vague restlessness

and unformulated desire—the
stri[v?]ing of the heaped and
sweating humans of the city
one does not know whither—
    Ced the character of the
superior person—the man
who wants nothing and gets
everything   who has the
Olympian attitude to the
world—mingled with a
rather base streak of caution.

---

describe people's hands.

Travel Diary of John Dos Passos in Spain and France
John Dos Passos Collection (#5950-AC, Box 3)
Alderman Library
University of Virginia

August 5th, [1917]

    The great war novel is
forming·gradually in my mind.
I have almost a feeling that the
Streets at Night will get
encorporated—will be part I

    Let's, for the splendour of God,
have an outline!
1. Streets of Night

---

x & y friendship
    Miss Z
    The New Egoist
From two points of view first
Serious Cantibridgean atmosphere
    Europe motif—calling or
    recalling—
    Death of X
    Damnation of Y . . .—Alma
How about it—now

Part II The war—
The philosophy of scorn
de trop de delicatesse
J'ai perdu la vie

Substantive Changes to the First American Edition

Dos Passos's Autograph Corrections to the Harvard and Virginia Typescripts

The following do not include changes in incidentals, such as spelling and punctuation.

28.24   *delete* faint *after* a (Harvard MS)
28.26   *delete* a *after* with (Harvard MS)
29.18   *change* on *to* down (Harvard MS)
30.28–29   *add* The bellboy was looking at him. What's he thinking? Fanshaw was wondering as *after* whisper. (Harvard MS)
30.37   *delete* her *after* showed (Harvard MS)
30.38   *change* sweet *to* white (Harvard MS)
31.33   *add* where brown shiny rings spread from it *after* river (Harvard MS)
34.2   *change* neck *to* shirt (Harvard MS)
36.22   *delete* smell of *after* under the (Harvard MS)
37.9–10   *After* past. *move* Gosh, only thirty-five minutes for those two questions! *to beginning of paragraph* (Harvard MS)
38.2–3   *change* doing *to* buttoning (Virginia MS)
38.14   *add* yellow *after* at the (Virginia MS)
38.17   *add* too *after* looking (Harvard and Virginia MSS)
38.24   *add* and let her mouth drop *after* eyes (Virginia MS)
38.34   *change* with a shrill little giggle *to* and let out a shrill giggle (Virginia MS)
39.7   *change* Nancibel *to* Nan (Virginia MS)
39.18   *change* Nancibel *to* Nan (Virginia MS)
39.28   *change* Nancibel *to* Nan (Virginia MS)
39.31   *change* Nancibel *to* Nan (Virginia MS)
40.1   *delete* Chinese *after* blue (Harvard and Virginia MSS)
40.14   *change* he *to* she (Harvard and Virginia MSS)
40.15   *add* tray of *after* put the (Virginia MS)
41.20   *change* limply *to* limp (Harvard MS)
42.14   *add* It's time, *before* Wenny (Harvard MS)
43.8   *change* moment *to* while (Virginia MS)

43.28   *delete* delicious *after* in a (Virginia MS)

43.29   *change* rasping by outside grated *to* rasped by outside, grating (Virginia MS)

43.29   *delete* then *after* and (Virginia MS)

43.31   *change* of the *to* of some (Virginia MS)

44.2   *delete* Then *after* slippers. (Virginia MS)

45.25–26   *change* and asthmatic old men sat on the benches with their chins on silverhandled canes beside little old grey women in porkpie hats *to* in front of a bench where sat an old man with his chin on a silverhandled cane beside a grey woman in a porkpie hat (Virginia MS); *the Harvard MS adds* tiny *after* beside a

45.29   *change* Nan *to* Nancibel (Virginia MS)

45.30   *delete* neatly gloved *after* her (Harvard MS)

46.6   *delete* in its *after* figure (Virginia MS)

46.6–7   *add* in grey *after* tailored (Virginia MS); *add* Their glances were like sticky cobwebs in the woods. *after* tweed. (Harvard MS)

47.43   *change* of Fitzie opening her eyes wide, rapt, and saying *to* of how Fitzie her eyes wide rapt, had said, (Virginia MS)

48.5   *add* in a bay window *after* then, (Virginia MS)

49.9   *change* she *to* herself (Virginia MS)

49.30   *change* deary *to* dear (Virginia MS)

50.8   *add* As she spoke her grey lips trembled like a child's. *after* hot." (Virginia MS)

50.18   *change* Elizabeth *to* Maria (Harvard MS)

52.2   *add* As she thought of Wenny *after* homespun. (Virginia MS)

52.3   *change* fixedly *to* hard (Virginia MS)

52.4   *change* until it reddened his ears and the roots *to* until he was red in the ears and in the roots (Harvard and Virginia MSS)

52.8   *delete* won't you *after* a bit (Harvard MS)

53.2   *add* more *after* something (Virginia MS)

53.14   *delete* gleaming *after* to the (Virginia MS)

53.18   *add* with a laugh *after* Wenny (Harvard MS); *Virginia MS adds* laughingly

53.23   *delete* on a glass door *after* Swarthcote (Virginia MS)

53.32   *change* flow down *to* roll down (Harvard MS)

53.33   *change* my cheeks *to* one's cheeks (Virginia MS)

54.4   *change* laughing *to* very gently (Harvard MS)

56.16   *change* turned up *to* tilted up (Virginia MS)

56.21–22   *add* in the Italian palace *after* gallery (Virginia MS)

57.30–31   *change* Everything was so muddled and sordid then. *to* Everything wasn't so muddled and sordid then. (Harvard MS); *Virginia MS reads* Everything is so muddled and sordid now.

58.3   *change* Shadows *to* Shadowy forms (Harvard MS)

58.6   *add* Footpads. *after* mind. (Virginia MS)

58.11   *add* jumped to his feet *after* knees (Harvard MS)

58.12   *delete* jumped up *after* Fanshaw (Harvard MS)

58.13   *change* flashed down *to* flashed on (Virginia MS)

58.17   *delete* "I'm afraid of catching cold." (Virginia MS)

58.28   *add* translating *after* work— (Virginia MS)

58.42   *change* doan *to* don't (Virginia MS)

59.28–29   *add* giggles of young girls, kidding intonations of men *after* sidewalk (Virginia MS)

60.12   *change* intense *to* beautiful (Harvard and Virginia MSS)

60.15   *change* a shepherd *to* the shepherd (Harvard MS)

60.18   *add* somewhere in *after* from (Harvard MS)

60.26   *change* My father had it about God or thought he did *to* My father had it about God or thinks he had. (Virginia MS)

60.26   *change* was sure *to* is sure (Virginia MS)

60.27   *add* Only man I ever knew who was. *after* anyway. (Harvard MS)

60.31   *change* the candy *to* a candy (Virginia MS)

60.35   *change* glass under glass *to* glass after glass (Virginia MS)

60.35   *delete* glasses of *after* drank (Harvard MS)

60.40   *delete* their *after* letters of (Harvard MS)

60.41   *delete* of the *after* sepia (Harvard and Virginia MSS)

61.18   *add* on *after* everything, (Virginia MS)

61.19   *add* on *after* instructor, (Virginia MS)

61.19   *add* on *after* outside, (Virginia MS)

61.27   *delete* and rigid *after* frozen (Virginia MS)

61.29–30   *change* her disturbed him so that he tried to brush it aside. *to* her sent a trembling through him that he tried to brush aside. (Virginia MS)

62.5   *change* smoothness of the contours *to* smooth contours (Harvard MS)

62.5   *change* greenish *to* green (Harvard and Virginia MSS)

62.16   *delete* by your hatred of youth *after* mean (Harvard MS)

62.23   *delete* greenwhite *after* by a (Harvard MS)

62.37   *delete* reading *after* backs, (Virginia MS)

62.40   *change* They *to* The three of them (Harvard MS); *the Virginia MS changes* They were *to* The three were

63.15   *change* burst suddenly *to* come (Virginia MS)

64.11   *change* And just looked there a fiasco *to* And look there; a fiasco (Virginia MS)

64.36–37   *add* She's a little like you. *after* she? (Virginia MS)

65.16   *change* brats *to* children (Virginia MS)

65.26–27   *add* muttered Nan turning towards Wenny. *after* tell? (Virginia MS)

65.43   *add* "for the girl, I mean." *after* eagerly (Virginia MS)

66.31   *add* Such grace and dignity. *after* twenty-eight. (Virginia MS)

66.32   *change* bust *to* break (Virginia MS)

66.34   *change* was saying *to* said (Harvard MS)

67.3   *change* gondola *to* piano (Harvard and Virginia MSS)

68.4   *delete* broad *after* into the (Harvard and Virginia MSS)

68.11   *add* black *after* into a (Virginia MS)

68.43   *change* jounced over cobbles in a pushcart *to* jounced in a car (Virginia MS); *the Harvard MS deletes* over cobbles

70.34–35   *add* against a snow scene by Brueghel *after* be (Harvard and Virginia MSS)

70.38   *add* will you? *after* evening, (Virginia MS)

71.5   *change* In the *to* On the (Harvard MS)

71.6   *change* like biting cold iron *to* biting as cold iron (Virginia MS)

71.15   *change* of bacon and pipes and stuffy bunks *to* of rank pipes and bunks (Virginia MS)

71.21   *change* sight *to* look (Virginia MS)

71.23   *delete* white *after* with a (Virginia MS)

71.40   *change* I'm getting *to* I am getting (Virginia MS)

72.12   *change* round the Anthropology department in *to* round Anthropology in (Virginia MS)

73.38   *change* an aviary *to* a bird store (Harvard MS)

75.21–22   *add* up and down, up and down by *after* taken (Harvard and Virginia MSS)

76.4–5   *add* These beastly shoes aren't comfortable yet, must have them stretched. *after* senses. (Virginia MS)

76.16   *add* a *after* of, (Harvard and Virginia MSS)

77.1   *delete* memories throbbing to the rhythm of his swift nervous steps. *after* arclights (Virginia MS)

77.7   *delete* set *after* houses (Harvard and Virginia MSS)

77.26–27   *change* tonight I walk fast to get away *to* tonight walking fast away (Virginia MS); *the Harvard MS changes only* I walk *to* walking

78.2   *delete* chattering *after* and (Harvard MS)

78.3   *add* chattering shrill *after* emerald (Harvard MS)

78.11–12   *change* face brittle under glass like *to* face as brittle under glass as (Harvard MS); *Virginia MS changes only* glass like *to* glass as.

78.13   *add* through the choking smell of lilies *after* about (Harvard MS)

78.32   *change* Aunt Susan *to* Auntie (Harvard MS)

79.14   *change* bulging hills *to* bulgings of hills (Harvard MS)

79.16   *delete* real *after* Nan and (Harvard MS)

79.17   *add* these *after* by (Harvard MS)

79.34   *add* . . . er . . . *after* been (Harvard and Virginia MSS)

80.13   *delete* each other *after* jostling (Harvard MS)

80.32   *change* mornings *to* mornin's (Harvard and Virginia MSS)

83.29   *change* shoulder *to* shoulders (Harvard and Virginia MSS)

83.36   *add* The *after* letters of (Harvard MS)

83.40   *change* Sure I want to git kilt, sure I want to git kilt. *to* Want to git kilt . . . Want to git kilt . . . (Virginia MS)

84.18   *add* with *after* age, (Harvard MS)

84.19   *delete* with *after* face, (Harvard MS)

84.21   *change* testily. He was staring straight *to* testily, looking straight (Harvard MS)

85.20   *change* of one of the ponds *to* of a pond (Harvard and Virginia MSS)

86.25   *delete* And *after* house. (Harvard and Virginia MSS)

86.28   *change* neck *to* head (Harvard MS)

86.31   *add* will yer, *after* father, (Harvard MS); *the Virginia MS places* will ye? *after* bastard

86.31   *change* said *to* says; *change* picked *to* picks (Harvard and Virginia MSS)

86.32   *change* came *to* comes (Harvard and Virginia MSS)

86.40   *change* ain't *to* is (Virginia MS)

87.6   *MS reads* No passport. *The Harvard MS changes this to* Scared o' the lingo.; *the Virginia MS changes* No passport. *to* Scared of the war-talk.

87.29   *At this point in both the Harvard and the Virginia MSS Dos Passos has deleted the following:*

> The orchestra at the Dreyfus was playing Goodby Girls, I'm Through above a din of plates and glasses and shrill women's laughter. On the wall was a chromo of George Washington

88.31   *add* Down the line . . . *after* looking. (Virginia MS)

88.36   *change* round *to* about (Virginia MS)

88.43   *change* unfired *to* flameless (Harvard MS); *the Virginia MS changes* unfired *to* unkindled.

89.10–11   *add* had ridden over *after* Renaissance (Harvard MS)

89.20   *delete* from the orchestra *after* Danube (Harvard and Virginia MSS)

89.28   *change* hand *to* hands (Harvard and Virginia MSS)

90.8   *add* Down the line. *after* me. (Virginia MS)

90.14   *delete* too *after* dead (Harvard MS)

90.30   *change* chimmy *to* shimmy (Harvard and Virginia MSS)

90.36   *add* from behind *after* wrist (Virginia MS)

91.5   *add* and *after* gasjet (Virginia MS)

92.28–93.2   *add* He sharpened a pencil neatly into the scrapbasket and sat a long time wondering. Buckingham's should it be, or would Filene's be cheaper? *after* cutaway? (Harvard MS)

93.32   *add* A wedding *after* are. . . . . (Harvard MS)

97.9   *change* stood *to* lounged (Harvard MS)

97.10   *change* a great array *to* an array (Harvard MS)

98.22-23   *The Harvard MS offers an alternate ending to this section:*

> Fanshaw stood with his hands clasped behind his back breathing in a lemonsweet fragrance that weighed down the close air of the room. Of course, that's the orangeblossoms.

98.24   *The Harvard MS offers an alternate reading of the opening paragraph:*

> Fanshaw felt himself smiling as he looked up and down the long white table at the faces flushed above the alternate bright and stiff black of men and women's dresses.

99.9   *change* were *to* are (Harvard MS)

99.26   *change* surged round *to* surrounded (Harvard MS)

100.19   *add* a long while *after* sat (Harvard MS)

101.6   *The Harvard MS provides an alternate final sentence to this chapter:*

And his disgust became stiffened and burnished like an armor about him.

102.15   *change* three *to* four (Harvard MS)

102.21-22   *add* Fanshaw's voice was full of hasty reassurance. *after* been?" (Virginia MS)

103.3   *change* stair *to* stairs (Harvard and Virginia MSS)

103.7-8   *change* As Wenny pulled off his overcoat he thought he was going to faint. *to* As he pulled off his overcoat Wenny thought: I'm going to faint. (Virginia MS); *the Harvard MS changes* he thought *to* Wenny thought

103.10   *change* him *to* Wenny (Virginia MS)

103.30   *add* in the Common *after* benches (Virginia MS)

103.36   *add* in *after* glass (Virginia MS)

104.7   *change* in a strange hoarse voice *to* sharply (Virginia MS)

104.11   *add* That's me . . . *after* not? (Virginia MS)

104.26   *add* Huntington Avenue *after* up (Virginia MS)

104.35   *change* would *to* should (Harvard MS)

104.40   *change* snarled an *to* clicked a crisp (Virginia MS)

104.40-41   *change* today. He remembered the sweetish *to* today, without the sweetish (Virginia MS)

105.7   *add* a green flash of her eyes in his, *after* face, (Virginia MS)

105.28   *change* "A man like that ought to be shot." *to* "Poor woman!" (Virginia MS)

105.32   *change* talk *to* say anything (Virginia MS)

105.36   *add* small *after* stream of (Virginia MS)

105.40-41   *add* They could hear the brisk snapping of the steam pipes under the window. *after* spoke. (Virginia MS)

106.15-16   *change* going off together alone some sunset *to* going together out to sea some sunset time.— (Virginia MS)

106.18-19   *change* cheerfully *to* in a cheerful voice (Virginia MS)

107.12   *change* chances with the scarlet woman *to* fun (Harvard MS); *the Virginia MS changes* the scarlet woman *to* whoring

107.14   *change* Lelan's *to* Dolan's (Harvard and Virginia MSS)

107.19   *change* through *to* between (Virginia MS)

107.28   *change* bed, his cheeks throbbing from the wind, *to* bed, with cheeks that throbbed from the wind, (Virginia MS)

107.29   *change* looking blankly *to* staring (Virginia MS)

107.30   *change* looked *to* yanked (Virginia MS)

107.34-35   *change* yellow, mudpurple, niggerpink *to* yellow and mudpurple and niggerpink (Virginia MS)

108.1-3   *add* Outside a church bell still split an occasional ragged zinc splinter of sound into the sterile wind. *after* thoughts. (Virginia MS)

108.9   *change* deep *to* bass (Virginia MS)

108.10   *add* one of *after* off (Harvard MS)

108.15   *delete* God *after* team . . . (Harvard and Virginia MSS)

108.19   *add* greased *after* o' (Virginia MS)

108.30   *change* "Well, that's damn good. I'm damn glad *to* "Well, that's good. I'm glad (Virginia MS)

108.31   *change* a damn good *to* a good (Harvard MS)

108.37   *change* I wouldn't stay myself, except *to* I wouldn't stay a minute, except (Harvard MS)

108.39   *change* trying to walk *to* accustomed to stalk (Harvard MS)

109.33   *change* Wenny walked among the muddy paths *to* Wenny walked along muddy paths (Harvard and Virginia MSS); *the Virginia MS changes* of the *to* in the; *the Harvard MS changes* of the *to* on the

109.36   *add* the *after* grey of (Virginia MS)

110.1-2   *add* sat on a bench *after* middle-aged (Virginia MS)

110.42   *change* indifferent *to* mixed (Virginia MS)

111.37   *add* ever *after* we can't (Virginia MS)

111.40   *change* feeling everything within the cold bars of his ribs throb sickeningly. *to* feeling all his life throb sickeningly within the cold bars of his ribs. (Virginia MS)

112.12   *change* voice *to* tone (Virginia MS)

112.15-16   *change* grimy green clouds scudded *to* grimy clouds of pistachio green scudded (Virginia MS)

112.19-20   *change* slowly when they came out on *to* slowly in the heavy traffic on (Virginia MS)

112.31-32   *change* He felt a sudden maudlin desire to *to* He wanted to (Virginia MS)

112.36   *change* brightened *to* sharpened (Virginia MS)

113.12   *change* like *to* as (Virginia MS)

113.24   *add* in phrases out of his father's letters *after* idiocies (Virginia MS)

113.25   *add* approval *after* bleated (Harvard MS)

114.20   *delete* where *after* Common (Virginia MS)

114.29   *add* There was warmth in rubbing shoulders, meeting eyes. *after* searching. (Virginia MS)

115.15-16   *add* A blizzard in April." *after* Nan. (Virginia MS)

115.33   *change* rhythmically with red flowers *to* with roses (Harvard MS)

115.39   *add* These exotic moonings, so calfish . . . *after* have. (Virginia MS)

115.40   *change* red *to* striped (Harvard MS); *the Virginia MS deletes* red

115.42   *change* and roses behind their ears *to* and rings in their ears (Virginia MS)

115.42-43   *add* pulling the boat throbbing swift across the purple bay; *after* ears, (Virginia MS)

116.2-3   *add* "Funiculì, funiculà." *after* songs. (Harvard and Virginia MSS)

116.4   *add* , though. *after* tune (Virginia MS)

117.21   *change* flaws and cones and crystals *to* flawed crystals (Virginia MS)

117.22   *change* faded through *to* faded in (Virginia MS)

117.31   *add* , answered Wenny *after* think (Virginia MS)

118.11   *change* seemed *to* were blackly (Virginia MS)

118.11   *change* walls built heavily out *to* walls heavy-built out (Virginia MS)

118.12   *delete* grey *after* People were (Virginia MS)

118.29   *change* so *to* till (Harvard MS); *the Virginia MS changes* so *to* so that

118.41   *add* colored *after* through the (Virginia MS)

119.1-2   *add* Par delicatesse, par delicatesse . . . *after* Auntie. (Harvard MS); *the Virginia MS adds only* Par delicatesse . . .

119.10   *add* Think! *after* word. . . . (Virginia MS)

119.17-18   *add* J'ai perdu la vie. *after* well. (Harvard MS); *the Virginia MS adds* Par delicatesse j'ai perdu la vie. *after* well.

119.33   *change* his dilated *to* the dilated (Virginia MS)

119.34   *change* it *to* this face (Virginia MS)

119.37   *delete* My face *after* backwards. (Virginia MS)

119.41   *add* had *after* myself, (Harvard and Virginia MSS)

119.42   *delete* voice *after* thin (Virginia MS)

120.1   *change* louder in his ears. It *to* louder: It (Virginia MS)

120.24   *add* and the sound of money clinking in plates. *after* Lord . . . (Virginia MS)

120.27   *delete* I am my father *after* voice. (Harvard MS)

120.38-39   *add* Par delicatesse j'ai perdu la vie. *after* dead. (Harvard MS)

122.11   *add* or *after* Dutch (Harvard and Virginia MSS)

122.33   *change* smell *to* scent (Virginia MS)

123.2   *change* thought of *to* remembered bitterly (Virginia MS)

123.14   *add* Travel, literature, research. *after* do! (Virginia MS)

123.25   *change* pushed off his arctics, and strolled about *to* to push off his arctics, and then strolled about (Virginia MS); *the Harvard MS adds* then *after* and

123.41-42   *change* had nearly vanished *to* was being gnawed away (Virginia MS)

125.7   *delete* from horror *after* mouth (Virginia MS)

126.4   *change* young man *to* student (Harvard and Virginia MSS)

126.10   *delete* him *after* see (Virginia MS)

126.31   *change* Rogers *to* The reporter (Virginia MS)

127.30   *add* "Perhaps you don't know where it is." *after* smile. (Virginia MS)

127.32   *change* Fanshaw started tearing down the street *to* Fanshaw tore up the street (Virginia MS); *the Harvard MS changes* down *to* up

127.32   *delete* O, this is hideous, hideous. *after* office. (Virginia MS)

127.34   *add* as he walked desperately fast *after* Fanshaw (Virginia MS)

127.35   *add* faces of *after* with (Virginia MS)

127.36   *add* and soda-fountains *after* restaurants (Virginia MS)

127.41   *change* people *to* he and Nan (Virginia MS)

128.10   *The manuscripts offer two alternate readings to this sentence:*

"Come right this way, Mr. Macdougan," said the officeboy deferentially. (Harvard MS)

—Step right this way please, Mr. Macdougan, said the officeboy deferentially. (Virginia MS)

128.38   *delete* His mind seethed with its phrases. *after* dropped. (Virginia MS)

130.10-11   *change* It was a heavily ornamented magazine page with a picture in the upper left hand corner of a young man *to* On the heavily ornamented magazine page was a picture of a young man (Harvard and Virginia MSS)

130.17   *delete* fresh *after* in her (Virginia MS)

130.19   *change* curves *to* curve (Harvard and Virginia MSS)

130.32   *delete* Something about *after* out. (Virginia MS)

131.13   *delete* in black broadcloth *after* man (Virginia MS)

131.34   *delete* Have a peppermint. *after* would. (Harvard and Virginia MSS)

132.8   *change* rock *to* boulder (Virginia MS)

133.24   *change* were parted. Suddenly he found her eyes, *to* were faintly puckered, her eyes (Virginia MS)

133.29   *The manuscripts offer two alternate readings of this sentence:*

"I feel . . ." he began. The words died on his lips. (Harvard MS)

—Here we are, Nan, he said in a low voice and got to his feet. Parrot voices in his head kept repeating the senseless phrase. (Virginia MS)

133.31   *delete* hoarsely *after* she said (Virginia MS)

134.11   *add* in the room on Mount Auburn Street *after* curtains (Virginia MS)

135.12   *change* chilling his spine *to* thrill him (Virginia MS)

135.22   *change* But life is *to* But there is something (Virginia MS)

135.24   *change* carefully balanced restraint *to* careful restraint (Harvard MS)

135.26   *delete* somehow *after* and, (Virginia MS)

136.14   *change* Jamesy *to* Jamesie (Virginia MS)

137.3   *change* he did not *to* he didn't (Virginia MS)

140.5   *change* her *to* Nan (Virginia MS)

140.26   *add* , the dissatisfied lips *after* eyes (Virginia MS)

141.3   *change* Pelleas *to* Jardins sous la pluie (Virginia MS)

143.6   *delete* in *after* sat (Harvard and Virginia MSS)

143.8   *change* looking at *to* watching the flitting of (Virginia MS)

143.12   *add* at Aunt M.'s years ago *after* hundred (Virginia MS)

143.19   *change* it *to* that dress (Virginia MS)

144.1   *change* year *to* fall (Virginia MS)

144.15   *change* hat with two *to* hat, held two (Virginia MS)

144.22   *change* with white, drooping face and blue *to* with face white drooping like a snowdrop and blue (Virginia MS)

145.36   *add* , agony *after* was (Virginia MS)

146.1   *change* What at? *to* What, at eloping? (Virginia MS); *the Harvard MS reads* What about the baby? *after* What at?

146.2   *add* about that *after* know (Virginia MS)

146.12   *change* heavy oilsmell *to* oilheavy smell (Virginia MS)

146.35   *change* little *to* stubby (Virginia MS)

147.8   *delete* an uncertain *after* cast (Virginia MS)

148.40   *change* at a dance on Beacon Hill I was *to* at a ball on Louisville Square at the Hillis's I was (Virginia MS)

149.8   *delete* and held her hand *after* Nan (Virginia MS)

149.29   *change* awfully *to* fearfully (Virginia MS)

150.2   *change* And I will *to* And I'll (Virginia MS)

150.17-18   *add* and a brown hand, ditchdigger's hand, swung suddenly into light, *after* laughing (Virginia MS)

150.18   *change* suddenly *to* trembling (Virginia MS)

150.37   *change* three *to* four (Virginia MS)

151.11   *change* in *to* into (Virginia MS)

152.16   *change* way *to* away (Virginia MS)

153.30-31   *add* Must make toast of that bread for breakfast tomorrow. *after* crackers. (Virginia MS)

153.32   *add* Always meals. *after* day? (Virginia MS)

154.6-7   *add* Lovely Back Bay girl figures in East Cambridge Bridge suicide. *after* siren. (Virginia MS)

154.18   *change* it would impress them more *to* they would think better of her (Harvard and Virginia MSS)

157.19   *delete* big *after* like (Virginia MS)

157.23-24   *change* motionlessness *to* motionless glow (Virginia MS)

157.27   *add* At length *after* cold. (Virginia MS)

158.34-35   *add* With streaming eyes she began to undress. *after* read. (Virginia MS)

159.22-23   *add* The streets were thronged with men, lovers. *after* out. (Virginia MS)

159.32-33   *The manuscripts offer alternate endings to this section:*

Now and then from far down the street came the long rasping love-snarl of a cat. (Harvard MS)

In her ears dinned the satisfied tenor voice from below:
>   I know a spot where the sun is like gold
>   And the cherry blooms burst with snow
>   And down underneath is the loveliest nook
>   Where the four leaf clovers gro-ow.

(Virginia MS)

159.37   *delete* strangely *after* felt (Harvard and Virginia MSS)

160.3-5   *change* The room was bright, wide, looped salmon colored curtains, brisk air with a smell of flowers, freesias. *to* The room opened bright, wide, with looped salmon-colored curtains; brisk air smelling of flowers, freesias there by the window. (Virginia MS); *the Harvard MS adds only* there by the window *after* freesias

160.15   *add* opposite *after* sitting (Virginia MS)

160.43   *add* abroad *after* restaurants (Virginia MS)

163.24-29   *In the Harvard MS after the word* Snow. *Dos Passos has deleted the following passage:*

From far away came the hoarse snarling wail of a cat. Imagine, on a night like this, she found herself muttering, suppose they think if winter comes can spring be far behind . . . Let's see what's that a quotation from? Wondering she fell asleep.

Then he adds the following:

She stretched her arms out above her head; the iron rods of the bed were cold against her skin. Then all at once she found that she was crying. She pulled herself under the clothes again and rubbed her arms against her body. "Wenny," she said softly aloud and lay staring out at the tender fluttering of snow outside the window.

164.3   *change* Nan went to the window without turning on the light and *to* Nan went straight to the window and (Virginia MS)

164.9   *change* knee *to* knees (Harvard and Virginia MSS)

165.16   *change* had seemed to fall into a procession *to* had fallen into a rollicking procession (Virginia MS); *the Harvard MS adds only* rollicking *after* into a

165.23   *delete* at the table *after* sat (Virginia MS)

165.25   *change* him *to* David Wendell (Virginia MS)

166.10   *add* his *after* breeches and (Harvard MS)

167.39-43   *The Harvard MS gives an alternate ending to this section:*

"Are you sure it isn't a case of the girl I left behind me?" The greyfaced man laughed wheezily.

"Ha ha," laughed Fanshaw. "Perhaps it is," and he raised his hand as to slap his thigh. All at once he found himself staring at his upraised hand and stuck it stiffly into his pocket.

169.44   *delete* The opera was I Lombardi. *before* Fanshaw. (Harvard MS)

170.38   *delete* for a moment *after* bar (Harvard MS)

170.42   *delete* nervously *after* throat (Harvard MS)

170.43   *delete* as usual *after* but (Harvard MS)

171.6   *add* I was in the devil of a pickle. *after* do? (Harvard MS)

172.10-11   *change* The bright streak *to* The streak of bright sky (Harvard MS)

172.22   *change* opened *to* swung (Harvard MS)

174.25   *add* The thought stung. *after* known. (Harvard MS)

174.39-40   *add* I can travel. I can have women. *after* job. (Harvard MS)

175.19-20   *change* felt his bunk shake as the *to* felt the bunk shake under him as the (Harvard MS)

Substantive Variants between the American and the British First Editions

The texts of the American and British first editions differ considerably. The following list includes only substantive differences in wording. Excluded are minor differences in spelling (for example, cliffedge/cliff edge; parlor/parlour), in punctuation (./!), in capitalization (cologne/Cologne), in dialect (O/Ou; blowin'/blowing), in euphemisms for swearing (jeeze/Jesus; crissake/Chris' sake), and in conventions in contractions (you'd/you'ld). The page and line references that proceed each variant are from the current edition. The variants listed below have the text of the first American edition on the left, that of the British edition on the right.

The present edition incorporates the changes that Dos Passos made to the two extant manuscripts, one at the University of Virginia and the other at Harvard (see the list of typescript changes). Because the Harvard typescript was also used to set the type for the first British edition, some of the British variants listed below will be found in the present text.

American	British
27.7 cuff-links. He	cuff-links as he talked. He
27.10–11 under the	under his
27.11 from which	from the front of which
27.24 American Commonwealth	American Constitution
27.27 sunlight seeped	sunlight peeped
27.34 racket. Stoddard, on the	racket. He's an editor of the
27.34 knows all the chorines.	he wouldn't be afraid of chorus girls.
28.1–2 him with set lips, blinking	him, blinking
28.24 a faint smell	a smell
28.26 with a dreary	with dreary
28.35 and tramping	and clattering
28.40 carried a corded	carried an enormous corded
29.7–8 see the moonfaces of two drummers, out of which eyes like oysters stared at him.	see two moon-faced commercial travellers staring at him with eyes like oysters.
29.9 said fifteen of eleven	said quarter to eleven
29.12 the drummers	the commercial travellers
29.12–13 bellboy, of people passing along the street boring	bellboy, boring
29.18 trickling on	trickling down
29.24–25 mouth. Leaving Cham to talk to him, Fanshaw	mouth. Fanshaw

205

American	British
29.25–26 a rocker by the fireplace and hunched up in it sulkily.	a rocker by the fireplace and sat down in it hunched up sulkily.
29.30 this. When the bellboy	this. The bellboy
29.31 clerk, the eight	clerk, making the eight
29.31 coattails flashed	coattails flash
29.32 light. The clerk laughed creakily.	light. They both laughed.
29.39 The soapy flow	There was the soapy flow
30.28–32 whisper. He sat in the rocking chair without moving and stared at the clock. Eleven thirty-six. The bellboy stood in front of the desk, his eyes fixed on vacancy. The bellboy grinned and drew a red hand across his slick black hair.	whisper. The bellboy was looking at him. What's he thinking? Fanshaw was wondering as he sat in the rocking chair without moving and stared at the clock. Eleven thirty-six. Then he noticed that the bellboy was grinning and that he drew a red hand across his slick black hair.
30.34 a giggle	a shrill giggle
30.37 showed her teeth	showed teeth
30.38 of sweet corn	of white corn
31.17–18 A man in a seedy red sweater torn	Two men in seedy red sweaters torn
31.18 was bringing a canoe out	were bringing canoes out
31.19 the river	the brownish river
31.23–24 it. She was protesting in a gruff baby lisp full of titters. "If	it. "If
31.30 hat, palping	hat, pulping
31.33 river, floated in the middle of brown bright rings.	river, where brown, shiny rings spread from it.
32.3 other canoe was	other couple were
32.6 singing off key	singing out of key
32.17 the slight curve	the curve
32.31 in stockings of thin black silk with	in thin silk stockings with
32.35 Hot, I	Hot as hell I
33.3 country, nit!"	country!"
33.10 trees grey in the noon glare. Behind	trees. Behind
33.20 most dollish	most doll-like
33.24–25 "Bring the cushions, Fanshaw," shouted Cham, who was kneeling beside the open picnic basket with a bottle in his hand.	*omitted*
33.26 champagne had made	champagne made

American	British
33.27 his knees	his knee
34.2 his neck	his shirt
34.17 girl scrambled	girl jumped
34.18–19 way and doubling	way, doubling
34.27 deary	dear
34.27–28 path. She lit out after him. "Look	path. "Look
35.16–17 or a man's voice	or somebody's voice
35.40 started slowly	started to walk slowly
36.4 the mashed grass	the Mahal grass
36.7 Literature I.	Literature.
36.12 dress, feeling the whalebone	dress, whalebone
36.15 tree and cried	tree with her dress all fluffed up about her and cried
36.17–18 fluff and the sunshine had lain	fluff. The sun had lain
36.19–20 clasped tight	clasped together
36.22 the smell of mashed	the mashed
37.9–10 Sudden panic seized him. The clock was at twenty-five past. Gosh, only thirty-five minutes for those two questions!	Gosh, only thirty-five minutes for those two questions. Sudden panic seized him. The clock was at twenty-five past.
38.17 good looking.	good-looking too.
38.20–21 out the	out of the
38.34 little titter.	little giggle.
38.35–39.2 asked Fanshaw, who stood tall and blonde in a light grey suit, with his back to the fireplace.	asked a tall, young man in a light grey suit, who stood with his back to the fireplace.
39.16–17 to the teatable	to the table
40.1 blue Chinese teapot	blue teapot
40.13 turn around	turn round
40.14 when he	when she
40.30 "You'd be taken	"you'd taken
40.34 Fanshaw smiled	The fair man smiled
41.4 she said	said she
41.7 long thin hand	long, white hand
41.20 hanging limply	hanging limp
41.22 a grindorgan was	a barrel-organ was
41.33 instant all her life	instant all the life of her
42.13 felt sane	felt safe
42.14 "Wenny	"It's time, Wenny
43.1 think up	think out
43.7–8 reassuring for a moment. Then	reassuring. Then

American	*British*
43.29 drowsy quiet	drowsy quietude
43.39–40 her the way the sticky spiderwebs used to cling	her like the sticky spiderwebs that would cling
44.10 this morning,	this time,
44.21 intensely in her	intensely into her
44.37 of a sugared	of sugared
45.24–26 Garden, where there was still a bit of flame in the leaves of the trees, in front of an asthmatic old man sitting on a bench with his chin on a silverhandled cane beside a little old grey woman	Garden there was still a bit of flame in the leaves of the trees. In front of a bench, where sat an asthmatic old man with his chin on a silver-handled cane beside a tiny grey woman
45.30 felt her neatly gloved fingers	felt her fingers
45.43–46.1 between grass patches	between green patches
46.7 tweed. Fitzie	tweed. Their glances were like sticky cobwebs in the woods. Fitzie
46.12 hair."	hair, skin that looked tanned, it was so brown."
46.15–16 satin of neckties	satin neckties
47.7 calm as	cool as
47.41 clouds. O	clouds through which blue sky shone. O
48.2 into front	into the front
48.8 straight part	straight parting
48.26 "Are they	"O, are they
48.41 all afternoon	all the afternoon
49.2 wallpaper, which Aunt	wallpaper Aunt
49.7 smiled thinking	smiled and caught herself thinking
49.11 from the shaggy world.	from fearful things.
49.26 Practiced every	Practices every
50.17–18 Poor Elizabeth	Poor Maria
50.31 parlor, and the	parlour. The
51.14–15 She was moving the spoon round her small cup of coffee with	She was stirring the coffee in her small cup with
51.18–19 god. Poor Fitzie who had none of that in her life, always making up romances for other people.	god.
52.4 until it reddened his ears and the roots of	until he was red in the ears and in the roots of
52.8 bit, won't you, Nancibel	bit, Nancibel
52.15 the grindorgan	the barrel-organ
52.21 god. O Fitzie's a romantic fool.	god.

American	*British*
52.29 together.	together as they walked briskly along.
53.17 door. Remember the hold-ups," said Wenny.	door, you might be followed by foot-pads," said Wenny with a laugh.
53.29 she said.	said she.
53.32 tears flow down	tears roll down
54.4 Wenny laughing.	Wenny very gently.
54.9 vague swells out	vague smell out
55.3 garlicky, with	garlic-smelling with
57.12 vague thought	vague thoughts
58.2 loomed distant	loomed distantly
58.3 Shadows seemed	Shadowy forms seemed
58.11–12 knees—like Rembrandt the shadows thought Fanshaw—jumped up.	knees jumped to his feet.—Like Rembrandt, the shadows, thought Fanshaw.
58.28–29 work—Plato was it?—Pico	work (Plato was it?) Pico
58.30 was thinking, and wondering whether	was wondering whether
59.35 *deleted after line* 35	Wenny hummed:— You made me what I am to-day, I hope you're satisfied. Fanshaw smiled. "And she ain't no plaster virgin, nei-ther," came a voice from a side-walk loafer. "That's about right," he said.
60.12 and intense	and beautiful
60.13 attempt. I haven't	attempt. . . . haven't
60.15 with a shepherd	with the shepherd
60.18–19 from Switzerland	from somewhere in Switzerland
60.27 anyway."	anyway. Only man I ever knew who was."
60.35 in glass under glass	in glass after glass
60.35 drank glasses of orangeade	drank orangeade
60.40–41 of the gold letters of their titles	of gold letters of titles
60.41 sepia of the Primavera	sepia Primavera
61.17 and besides	and beside
62.5 heads, the smoothness of the contours of	heads, smooth contours of
62.5 the greenish	the green
62.16 mean by your hatred of youth.	mean.
62.23 a greenwhite swath	a swath

American	British
62.37 backs, reading	backs, spelling
62.40 They were	The three of them were
63.7 sniggering laugh	snickering laugh
63.40 Wenny was saying	Wenny said
64.5 brought us	brought me
64.7 What a mess. Mechanically	What a mess, he thought. Mechanically
64.11 And just looked there	And look there
64.35–36 "Nan, do you see the girl who's playing the violin?" whispered Wenny.	"Do you see the girl who's playing the violin?" Wenny was saying in a low voice to Nan.
65.34 over Wenny's crisp	over his crisp
66.2 suddenly welling with	suddenly swelling with
66.34 Wenny was saying.	Wenny said.
67.3 the gondola	the piano
67.25 shivered in	shivered under
67.26 light under	light beneath
67.35 still barked	still hawked
68.4 the broad entrance	the entrance
68.23 the bulge of his	the bulge of lust in his
68.36 and exultantly	and, exultingly
68.36 this.	this. Nan can't like him after this.
68.38 them and said	them, said
68.43 jounced over cobbles in	jounced in
68.44–69.1 with yellow	with the yellow
69.12 Brueghel.	Breughel, something was saying in his head over and over again.
69.26 we'll be able to go abroad."	we'll have enough to go abroad on."
70.34 be.	be against a snow scene by Breughel.
70.41 up T Wharf	up the wharf
71.5 In the	On the
71.5–6 then like biting cold iron.	then, biting cold iron.
71.15 of bacon and pipes and stuffy bunks	of rank pipes and bunks
71.20 been that that put	been that put
72.31 to ever take a	ever to take a
72.37–38 chocolate, would you	chocolate, wouldn't you
73.27 their lunch;	their lunch-rooms;
73.38 like an aviary, full	like a bird store, full
74.16 I'm so sick	I'm sick
74.18–19 go put	go and put
74.33 the belcanto	the canto
74.41 little diswrought	little distraught
75.21 taken with tenors	taken up and down, up and down, by tenors

American	British
American	*British*
75.23 toodled on	tootled on
75.40 where he hung	where hung
76.10 put an arm	put his arm
76.16 of, lovely	of, a lovely
77.2 end the	end of the
77.7 houses set back	house back
77.8 at doors varnished	at varnished doors
77.19–20 funnel-shape	funnel-shaped
77.23 and bare	and the bare
77.26 I walk fast	walking fast
77.29 at arms'	at arm's
78.2 and chattering paraquets	and parakeets
78.3 emerald and	emerald, chattering shrill, and
78.11–12 face brittle under glass like the	face as brittle under glass as the
78.13 about. During	about through the choking smell of lilies, how he had hated them; during
78.29 about those	about these
78.32 from Aunt Susan	from auntie
79.14 bulging hills	bulgings of hills
79.16 and real living.	and—living.
79.17 by dead	by these dead
79.26 with floppy	with flappy
79.34 been fired	been . . . er . . . fired
79.36 No. Things	No. No. Things
79.38 look.	look as if he thought Wenny mad.
80.7–8 the electricity and	the light and
80.10 sea dolphins	sea where dolphins
80.13 jostling each other on	jostling on
80.20 smells	smelt
80.32 mornings	mornin's
81.6 stooped	stopped
81.8 soaring brick	soaring, tall brick
82.29 her neck under	her back under
83.8 whining	whiny
83.10 I want to	I meant to
83.20 her blind with	her blindly with
83.29 shoulder	shoulders
83.36 of Swansea	of "The Swansea"
83.37 a truck	a motor-truck
84.18 age, a	age, with a
84.19 face with lips	face, lips
84.21 testily. He was staring straight	testily, looking straight
84.36 his arm about	his arms about

American	*British*
85.20 basin of one of the ponds that	basin of a pond that
85.25 say, if	say be if
85.26 Gawd's sake	Gawd's same
85.37 suspicious pig eyes.	suspicious big eyes. It was the first time he'd done this sort of thing; he was pleasantly excited.
85.38 you're millionaire	you're a millionaire
86.8 he trun a	he throw a
86.25 house. And, jeeze	house. Jesus
86.28 his neck	his head
86.31 father, you	father, will yer, you
86.31 he said.	he says.
86.32 he picked	he picks
86.32 an' came	and comes
86.33 Honest to Gawd, I	Honest, I
87.6 'Count the lingo.	Scared o' the lingo.
87.17 wished Whitey	wished the boy
87.36 a chromo	a chrome
88.3 Nan with Ellen, realer	Nan in the scarlet woman, realer
88.5 you, dear	you, deary
88.28 Renaissance, ham	Renaissance, sham
88.43 bored, unfired	bored, flameless
89.10 Renaissance rode	Renaissance had ridden
89.20 Danube from the orchestra.	Danube."
89.26 the wafer	the conjuror's wafer
89.27 minister with	minister of the Gospel of putrefaction, with
89.28 his hand.	his hands.
89.43–44 careful . . .	careful. . . . . Sanitary, I'm tellin' ye."
90.14 dead too. Wenny's	dead. Wenny's
90.22 To be	—O to be
90.23 prostitutions	prostitution
90.30 chimmy	shimmy
90.35 sniggering	snickering
91.7–8 and stared with stinging eyes down the empty darkness of the street.	and sobbed.
92.14 five thirty.	four-thirty.
92.26 Snowflake Meal	Snowflake Oatmeal
92.27 years slip by	years are slipping by
92.28 cutaway?	cutaway? He sharpened a pencil neatly into the scrap-basket and sat a long time wondering. Buckingham's should it be, or would Filene's be cheaper?
93.21 of very dressed	of well-dressed

American	British
American	*British*
93.28 whispered Henley	said Henley
93.32 parlor cars	Pullmans
93.32 Is the	A wedding is the
93.39 straight black	straight back
95.7–8 palely. The cars exuded furs and orchids and derby hats and canes from either end. Outside	palely. Outside
95.9 guests, and in	guests; in
95.34 said after a pause and turned up	said, turning up
96.1 think romance	think they romance
96.15 scarlet over the	scarlet against the
96.16 shoes against the	shoes on the
96.26 Of course . . . You'll	Of course. . . . You must forgive me. . . . You'll
96.28 All seems	All seem
96.33 Harrenden stalked towards	Harrenden advanced again towards
96.34 new car full	new limousine full
96.36–37 the upper hall	the lower hall
97.9 men stood	men lounged
97.10 and a great array	and an array
97.27 greyhaired greyfaced man	grey-haired man
97.32 heard a voice	heard the fat-faced girl's voice
97.33 stairs beside a black	stairs, where he found himself next to a girl in a black
97.38 the rustle of	the ruffle of
97.42 a picture	a little picture
98.5 elderly tones.	elderly voice.
98.9 silence feverish	silence came a sound of feverish
98.9–10 whispering was heard in the	whispering from the
98.17–18 silk and a shimmer of orange tulle on their hats, and the light	silk and the light
98.22–23 Fanshaw was breathing deep of a heavy lemonsweet smell. . . . Must be orange blossoms.	Fanshaw stood with his hands clasped behind his back breathing in a lemon-sweet fragrance that weighed down the close air of the room. Of course, that's the orange blossoms.
98.24–27 The table stretched long and white in both directions, bordered by faces, black coats, bright colored hats. The shine of silver and plates and champagne glasses	Fanshaw felt himself smiling as he looked up and down the long white table at the faces flushed above the alternate bright and stiff black of men and women's dresses.

American	British
was blurred by cake crumbs, rind of fruit, nutshells, napkins.	
98.29 of Fanshaw's	of his
99.3–4 room, bright dresses and black coats jamming the doorway. Fanshaw	room. Fanshaw
99.5 What he needed was some	What I need's some
99.6 himself. After an	himself. At an
99.7 he needed coffee.	I need some coffee.
99.8–9 things were	things are
99.9 Careful, he must	Careful, I must
99.26 and surged round a	and surrounded a
99.31 hit Cham	hit him
99.36–37 garden. Why, I'm staggering down the path. Mucky underfoot from the thaw. Bench	garden. The path was mucky underfoot from the thaw. Why, I'm staggering. Bench
100.19 sat with	sat a long while with
100.20–21 After a while he got up, cold	When he got up he was cold
100.22 in the house was	in the drawing-room was
100.24 feet off on	feet on
100.40 gripped the young man hard	gripped him hard
101.5–6 Norumbega. One must try to be beautiful about life.	Norumbega. And his disgust became stiffened and burnished like an armour about him.
102.15 three days	four days
103.6 shirtsleeves carried	shirtsleeves was carrying
103.6–7 glasses in through a green baize door. As Wenny pulled	glasses. As he pulled
103.7–8 he thought	Wenny thought
103.25–26 child? . . . I've been to Cham Mason's wedding."	child?"
103.39 head.	head deliciously.
104.21 five bucks."	five."
104.35 why would	why should
104.36 She turned and stared	She stared
105.33 eyes were dark	eyes dark
106.26 job. I am	job. Indeed, it makes me thankful to God for His visitation upon us of such unpleasant relations as we indulged in when you were last here. I am
106.27–28 your past callousness	your callousness
106.28 be a	be but a
106.35 I not let my	I not sinned in letting my

American	*British*
106.35–36 us, from your real Christian home, your	us, your
106.38 us.	us, chastened perhaps, but strengthened by difficulties and privations.
107.12 my chances	my fun
107.14 Mr. Lelan's	Mr. Dolan's
107.15 God!	Christ!
107.29 while staring	while looking
107.34 back flabbily	back fatly
108.10–11 off the arms	off one of the arms
108.12–13 rifle while	rifle as
108.15 team . . . God, I	team. . . . I
108.31 a damn good	a good
108.37 stay myself	stay a minute
108.39 man trying to walk noiselessly	man accustomed to stalk noiselessly
109.13 wish you'll	wish you'd
109.28 Wenny, going out the door, caught	As Wenny went out of the door he caught
109.33 paths of	paths on
110.2–3 derby; as Wenny	derby, their eyes straight in front of them, sat on a bench. As Wenny
110.13 grindorgan	barrel-organ
110.17 bitter film	bitter tense film
110.21 hall came	hall come
111.6 me give you a	me have a
111.9 great then.	great in them.
111.34 slowly, choosing her words: "Can't	slowly with difficulty; "can't
112.7 drew her	drew the
112.16 on gusts	on the gusts
112.40 That's the real	That's a real
113.25–26 and bleated like sheep, baa, baa, at every pause. It	bleated approval after every word he said. It
113.30–31 stirring twigs	stirring, bare twigs
114.1 be here	be there
114.8 honestly putrefy	honestly purify
114.27 Through the	In the
114.37–38 man whiskered	man whisked
114.39 Wenny jumped	They all three jumped
114.40 hill. Why didn't I let it run over me? Then	hill. Then
115.28 chin was painfully	chin painfully
115.28–29 features were heavier	features heavier
115.33 with flowers	with roses
115.40 bands, red flags	bands, striped flags

American	British
115.43 cushions.	cushions in the leaping stern.
116.2–3 songs. O	songs, "Funiculi, funicula." O
116.21–22 were a stab of pain for him.	were like a stab of pain.
118.29 walls, so that Wenny	walls, till Wenny
118.32 gesticulating.	gesticulating like things seen through the wrong end of a telescope.
119.1 Auntie.	auntie. Par delicatesse, par delicatesse. . . .
119.8 God!	Christ,
119.14 and behold	and beheld
119.17 well.	Well. J'ai perdu la vie.
119.25 all cute.	all cut
119.41 myself, bitter	myself, had bitter
120.4 Gospels	Gospel
120.12 calling upon	called upon
120.21 droning infections	droning inflections
120.21–22 To do good and communicate forget not for with such sacrifice God is well pleased. Women's	Do good and communicate and forget not that with such sacrifice God is well pleased . . . and women's
120.27 voice. I am my father.	voice.
120.33 streets neatly	streets nearly
120.38–39 dead. Mustn't	dead. Par delicatesse, j'ai perdu la vie. Mustn't
121.16 at arms'	at arm's
121.19–20 of engines, for	of the engines behind, for
121.24 rang out over	rang sharp over
122.4 more of delicious	more delicious
122.11 Dutch, some Fleming	Dutch or some Fleming
122.35 restaurants, jokes	restaurants, sprightly jokes
123.25 and strolled	and then strolled
124.27–29 While he was crossing the little triangle of grass in front of the seated statue of John Harvard, Fanshaw stopped a moment to sniff the moist air that for the first time that season smelt of earth and gardens.	Fanshaw stopped a moment to sniff the moist air, that for the first time that season smelt of earth and gardens, crossing the little triangle of grass in front of the seated statue of John Harvard.
125.3 boardwalk; he stopped	boardwalk, stopped
125.6 his hands	his knees
125.16 inside. There he	inside, then he
125.36 Fanshaw picked	He picked
126.3 hypothesis has	hypothesis had

American	British
American	*British*
126.4 the young man	the student
126.12 flame roared	flame reared
126.15–16 He drew the bolt and stepped back, very	He drew back the bolt and drew back a step, very
126.21 I have information that	They told me at the college office that
127.15 The third	O, the third
127.16 Fanshaw blushed red. He stared hard in the man's wheedling eyes.	*deleted*
127.32 tearing down	tearing up
127.35 publicity. And	publicity; filthy, prurient, scandalmongering. And
127.39 ghoulish eyes as	ghoulish leering as
128.1–4 morning. Youth had been killed. In offices and stores and front parlors and lonely hall bedrooms sallow-jowled faces sucked the blood through the nasty smelling print of the extras. The streets swarmed and seethed with faces drinking Wenny's blood.	morning. Their sallow, flabby-jowled faces as they read greedily like vampires. Youth had been killed. They gathered gleefully from their offices and stores and front parlours and lonely bedrooms to drink the hot blood through the nasty smelling print of the extras. The streets swarmed and seethed with faces clamouring to drink his blood.
128.8 streets was	streets seemed
128.10 "Yes, come right in, Mr. Macdougan."	"Come right this way, Mr. Macdougan," said the office boy deferentially.
128.24 I fell	I feel
128.27 bloodsuckers for everybody	·bloodsuckers; that poor boy's corpse dragged through the streets for everybody
128.38 the newspaper	the paper
129.38 to dive	to live
129.39 idea."	idea too."
130.10–11 It was a heavily ornamented magazine page with a picture in the upper left-hand corner of a young	On the heavily-ornamented magazine page was a picture of a young
130.19 ample curves	ample curve
130.31 impatience. He	impatience instead of inducing the usual mood of gentle melancholy. He
130.41 tears welling up within	tears welling sweet and warm within

American	British
131.22　ahead roused	ahead aroused
131.34　would. Have a pepper-mint."	would."
131.38–39　Fanshaw. The streetcar	Fanshaw.—How I hate young girls at that age, he was saying to himself. The street car
132.13　horizon cumulous	horizon tumulous
132.17　went it:	went with it:
133.28-30　speak: "Nan . . ." He paused, his tongue dry, "Nan, don't you think we need our tea?"	speak. "I feel. . . ." he began. The words died on his lips. "Don't you think we need our tea?"
133.35　started across	started up across
134.2　breath were all	breath all
134.4　note, mock-serious	note, serious
134.14　breakfast and luncheon and dinner.	breakfast and dinner and lunch, seeing through.
134.29　if he	if Wenny
135.24　carefully balanced restraint	careful restraint
136.15　stammered, "Please, Cousin Nancibel." An	stammered inaudibly.—An
136.32　Fanshaw moved to the	Fanshaw came and sat on the
138.1-2　overgrown gardens	overgrown garden
138.3　she would	she should
138.8　The ways of	The days of
138.10　The Strathcona.	The "Strathcona," perhaps.
138.35　and rollercoasters	and rollerskaters
138.41　The Rev. Wendell, as	His riverence, as
139.10　uniform standing beside him.	uniform.
139.11　went on	said on
139.37　lantern . . . And	lantern, an' what do you think he found? He found two couples all at it like they was private in some low-down hotel or other. What do you think o' that? And
139.38　mortified . . . They	mortified when he found 'em. They
140.12　books one would always	books I'd always
140.18　entrance. There	entrance, scrutinizing people's faces. There
140.21　argument, he	argument about things, he
140.24　myself. In the subway Fan-shaw	myself. Fanshaw
140.33-34　over newlydug	over new-dug
140.36　stuffed in	stuffed into

American	*British*
141.1-2 Park Street. Fanshaw got to his feet and shuffled in a jostling stream of people out the car.	"Art Museum," shouted the conductor. Fanshaw scrambled hurriedly out of the car.
141.5 bubbles ready	bubbles about
141.29 are we	are you
141.35 arm around	arm round
142.1 her lips lightly	her lightly
143.6 sat in on	sat on
143.16 bought the lace	bought everything she had intended to, the lace
143.24 orchestra was playing	orchestra playing
143.25 Hoffman which set	Hoffmann" set
143.32 the word	the words
144.2 the flushfaced	the dark, flush-faced
144.6-7 him, wishing him alive.	him alive.
144.10 lady celloist	lady cornet player
144.14 feet.	feet, reaching for their hats.
144.19 highcollared shirtwaists	high-collared blouses
144.34 face that	face of the people that
145.15 the streetcar	the street cab
145.16 ground rattling	ground rattlingly
145.18 the trees	the shedding trees
146.1 "What at?"	"What at? What about the baby?"
146.11 "The Swansea": the	"Swansea," the
146.14 All afternoon	All the afternoon
146.15 be along	be ready
146.24 her like lizards.	her, lizard-like.
146.33 it to dinner	it at dinner
147.3-4 Aunt M. was saying	Aunt M. went on
147.7 Nan looked at	Nan was looking at
148.29-30 precocious in those days—	precocious when I was a girl . . .
148.30 and connections.	and all that.
151.3 watermain burst	watermain's burst
151.12-13 the three other	the other
151.14-15 was a dead	was like a dead
151.30 her hand	her hands
151.40 along twilit	along twilight
152.15-16 do way	do away
152.37 boy's full wistful	boy's wistful
153.9 her thrill	her shrill
154.5 a whiskey voice	a coarse voice
154.6 The Back Bay siren.	The newspaper idea of the Back Bay siren.
154.18 perhaps it would impress them more if	perhaps they would think better of her if

American	British
154.24 herself in	herself back
154.29 all afternoon	all the afternoon
155.4-5 fat, jostling women	fat, aggressive women
155.6 the waxen face	the wax-looking face
155.7 a floorwalker	a shopwalker
157.9 of here.	of here. An icy, steel core of disgust was hardening in her.
157.21 swung Nan out	swung her out
157.28 she sank back	she let herself sink back
158.18 life puttering	life pottering
158.40 Vagaband unopened	Vagabond" opened
159.32-33 eyes. Down the street she heard from time to time the love-wail of a cat.	eyes. Now and then, from far down the street, came the long, rasping lovesnarl of a cat.
159.37 felt strangely uneasy	felt uneasy
160.5-6 flowers, freesias. The woman walked	flowers; freesias there by the window. She walked
161.20 a creamfaced	a creamy-faced
162.23 the yellow	the cold, yellow
162.41 the lock	the Yale lock
163.24 Snow.	Snow. She stretched her arms out above her head; the iron rods of the bed were cold against her skin. Then all at once she found that she was crying. She pulled herself under the clothes again, and rubbed her arms against her body. "Wenny," she said, softly, aloud, and lay staring out at the tender fluttering of snow outside the window.
164.9 her knee	her knees
165.9 "Why are you angry at me, Nancibel?"	"Why, you are angry at me, Nancibel."
165.15 spring the	spring when the
165.16 a procession	a rollicking procession
166.11 as his puttees	as the puttees
166.15 in relief work	in Red Cross work
166.34 I'm afraid I'll have to finish	Unless I can finish
167.1-2 I'm bored to death with this work, aren't you?"	Rotten bore."
167.11 from the desk	from his desk
167.22 laughed.	laughed constrainedly.
167.23 Baldwin.	Hopkins.
167.33 Look, does either	Look, do either
167.39-43 "Beginning to think of	"Are you sure it isn't a case of the girl

American

the girl I left behind me, are you?"
asked the greyfaced man creakily.

"Ha, ha! that's it." Fanshaw
laughed loud and lifted his hand as
if to slap his thigh. He found himself looking with constraint at his
lifted hand and put it stiffly into
his pocket.

168.11 blonde moustaches
168.11-12 to a salute
168.13 himself also stiffening
169.5 tincture of yohimbine
169.11 teinture de yohimbine
169.18 por l'amore
169.19 Teinture de yohimbine
169.31-32 see the mosaics and the
view.
169.36 I even say
169.41-42 had driven up in front of
a small empty restaurant.
169.42-43 waiter at the door agitated his napkin in welcome.

170.5 the dustily
170.5-6 moved processions of
monks, tenors in knee-breeches,
baritones
170.7 of the glint of brasses and the
shiny curves
170.11 and maidens'
170.38-39 bar for a moment with
his superior stare.
170.42 throat nervously.
170.43 but, as usual, I
171.6 do?
171.9 Minister of War
172.10-11 the bright streak overhead
172.22 door opened softly.
172.22-23 woman stood in the hallway holding
172.23 head, and
172.32 The fatfaced woman
172.37 The woman
173.4 the Yohimbé tree?
173.17 was a knife

British

I left behind me?" The grey-faced
man laughed wheezily.

"Ha, ha," laughed Fanshaw,
"perhaps it is," and he raised his
hand as if to slap his thigh. All at
once he found himself staring at
his upraised hand, and stuck it
stiffly into his pocket.

blond moustache
to salute
himself stiffening
tincture of araucaria
teinture d'araucaria
per l'amore
Teinture d'araucaria
see the view and the mosaics.

I say even
had arrived at a restaurant.

waiter bowed to them eagerly as
they went through the swinging
doors.

the duskily
moved tenors in knee breeches, processions of monks, baritones

of shine of brasses and glinting
curves
and maiden's
bar with an insolent stare.

throat.
but I
do? I was in the devil of a pickle.
Ministry of War
the streak of bright sky overhead

door swung softly.
woman opened, holding

head with one hand, and
The fat woman
The fat woman
the Iraqis?
was like a knife

American	British
American	*British*
173.18 mirrors that smelt	mirrors. It smelt
173.20 down the winding staircase, straightening	down them, straightening
174.2 and a sunseared	and sun-seared
174.10 harsh wail.	harsh shriek.
174.14 down a street	down some street
174.18 ugliness . . . Yohimbine.	ugliness. . . .
174.25 known.	known. The thought stung.
174.29 different. That was hopeless, dead	different. But that's all dead, dead
174.39 job.	job. I can travel. I can have women.
174.41-175.1 and opened the varnished door. The companionway	and started for the door. He opened the door. The companionway
175.19 felt his bunk shake as	felt the bunk shake under him as

Select Bibliography

The following primary and secondary sources are useful for *Streets of Night*. For a comprehensive list of titles relating to this novel, consult David Sanders's excellent work, *John Dos Passos: A Comprehensive Bibliography* (New York: Garland, 1987).

EDITIONS

Streets of Night. London: Martin Secker, 1923.

———. New York: George H. Doran & Company, 1923.

———. New York: Popular Library, 1962.

———. Typescript. Alderman Library, University of Virginia.

———. Typescript. Houghton Library, Harvard University.

SECONDARY SOURCES

Becker, George J. *John Dos Passos*. New York: Frederick Ungar Publishing Co., 1974. Pp. 31–33.

Brantley, John D. *The Fiction of John Dos Passos*. The Hague: Mouton & Co., 1968. Pp. 38–45.

Clark, Michael. *Dos Passos's Early Fiction, 1912–1938*. Selinsgrove, Pa.: Susquehanna University Press, 1987. Pp. 32–52.

Colley, Iain. *Dos Passos and the Fiction of Despair*. Totowa, N.J.: Rowman and Littlefield, 1978. Pp. 17–26.

Collins, Joseph. *Taking the Literary Pulse*. New York: George H. Doran Company, 1924. Pp. 160–61.

Davis, Robert Gorham. *John Dos Passos*. University of Minnesota Pamphlets on American Writers, No. 20. Minneapolis: University of Minnesota Press, 1962. Pp. 16–17.

"Latest Works of Fiction." Review of *Streets of Night*. *New York Times*, sec. 3 (18 November 1923), 8–9.

Ludington, Townsend. *John Dos Passos: A Twentieth Century Odyssey*. New York: E. P. Dutton, 1980. Pp. 69–70.

"Rambles in Fiction." *The American Mercury* 2 (July 1924): 380–81.

Rosen, Robert C. *John Dos Passos: Politics and the Writer*. Lincoln: University of Nebraska Press, 1981. Pp. 38–41.

Vanderwerken, David L. "Dos Passos' *Streets of Night:* A Reconsideration."
    The Markham Review 4 (October 1974): 61–65.

Wagner, Linda W. *Dos Passos: Artist as American.* Austin: University of
    Texas Press, 1979. Pp. 22–27.

Wrenn, John H. *John Dos Passos.* New York: Twayne Publishers, 1961. Pp.
    116–21.

Index to Introduction and Textual Notes